InitiAl

Steven Thompson

1

He stood over her looking down at his prey. She looked for all the world like a normal person. But he knew differently. She was chosen to be here at that time, in that place. He knew what he had to do next. She would set an example to others. This was the real start of his work. This was the one he had planned for.

She looked up at the man above her. He was stood in front of a bright light. He wasn't familiar to her in any way. She wondered who he was. She couldn't see his face. He spoke not much louder than a whisper so she couldn't make out his voice either. She wanted to know who he was. But that wasn't the biggest or the most pressing thing on her mind. She wanted to know what he has planned for her. She didn't have to wait long.

He moved with clinical speed. Just before she saw his hands move quickly towards her, she heard him say something. Again, she couldn't make it out. A few seconds later she was lying in a small pool of her own blood. He dropped something before walking away. He was glad that he lived alone so he could get cleaned up without interruption or detection. He smiled to himself as he strode towards home. The dark of the night shielded him from any prying eyes that might have been present on the short journey.

2

Augustine Boyle was woken by the vibration from his mobile phone. The nights where he really needed a good sleep he turned off the alarm and left it on vibrate. It was always the case that these were the nights he got a call. Boyle struggled with his sleep.

He hadn't slept well for weeks, or it could have been months or perhaps years. He didn't know what it was that had made this happen. It could have been age. Most of his family suffered with it. His father barely slept beyond the early hours of the morning and drifted off to sleep in the early evening. Augustine missed most of evening television but the invention of TV recorders helped him catch up in the first few hours of the day, so by the time the rest of the country had awoken he had caught them up with their viewing habits. He could then join in on conversation with everyone else at work (when he chatted at work) or with the rest of the family (if he had one). It could have been that. His aunts all suffered with a similar disease. The disease of not being able to sleep. Many people in his profession were night owls. They worked late when the rest of the world had switched off. But he worked early before the rest of the world had even switched on. It made him feel like he had a head start on the people he was trying to catch. Augustine was sure they didn't get up as early as him.

But maybe his sleep was the consequence of those people and their crimes. The things he had seen over the years were enough to keep anyone awake. When he first started his career in the police he was told by the more experienced detectives that you get used to it. The repeat effect of seeing decaying or mutilated bodies was supposed to numb the senses to it. On the first occasion, it would all be too much, even for those with the strongest stomach. The smell was worse than the sight, but the pair of them together turned every stomach the first time. But for Augustine it happened just about every time. He had picked up the technique of using Vaseline to cover the nostrils and prevent most of the smell entering his system. That was the only way he could stop the vomit from travelling in the opposite direction. But the images couldn't be blocked in the same way. There was no method possible of stopping them from entering his brain through the eyes. Augustine was sure that if there was, he would have tried it. The people that he was sent to avenge were a regular theme of his dreams. They would just lie there, as they had when he first encountered them, looking ready for the ground. Have you ever had a friend who was just there? When you look back at the moments of your life, they were present at every one. But they never instigated anything nor were a major player. They were just there. Well these bodies were the same in his dreams. Augustine could see them, they offered nothing in the way of conversation, or even movement but they were always present. Augustine wanted to help, and it was the ones that he had not been able to help that came back to him more frequently. They were the ones that spent the most time with him while he was asleep. There were times when he didn't even want to go off to sleep because he knew what was coming. But when Augustine drifted off, it wasn't long before the stationary bodies were there in front of his eyes, waiting for him to help. He was as helpless in his dreams as he was in real life. He had no answers there either.

But maybe it was his bladder that kept him awake in the early hours. As he had got older and his body had shown signs of age, he was far more aware of his bladder than ever before. Someone he worked with told him that everything was fine until you reached the age of 40, then bits start to drop off. He hadn't realised what she had meant until the age reached him. He went from someone who visited the doctor every five years or so to someone who was there every six months. He didn't want to go, in fact tried to put things off, but there was always something in the pipeline nagging away at his conscience until he had to give in and go back to see the doctor. He felt like a hypochondriac, but it was just the passing of the years. Forty changed a lot of things for Augustine. And his bladder was front and centre of his attention in this matter. Not that he ever went to see a doctor about it. It just worked without care or attention for his entire life without him even being aware that it was present. Then suddenly after 40 it reminded him every morning that it was there, functioning and needed some relief. What else could he do? Maybe it was his bladder that kept him awake.

But in Augustine's mind there was something even more pressing that was keeping him from sleeping beyond the point where his alarm clock changed from showing a '4' at the front of the time to showing a '5' for him. It was linked to the passing of time. He only had so long left on the planet and wanted to leave his mark. As a forty-something with no kids, no marriage (not even a failed one behind him) and no long-term relationship his legacy was looking likely to lie away from passing on his good looks (his own view) his dogged determination (the view of his superiors) and his organisation (definitely the view of others) to someone else. He would have to make his mark through his work unless the unlikely occurred and he met up with a woman that could put up with all his shit, understand that he worked ridiculous hours and still wanted to have children with him after all of this. Augustine didn't hold out much hope. He had a series of short term relationships that fizzled out when the women actually realised what being his partner actually meant. Not that many of these moved along far enough for the other party to consider calling themselves his partner. He hated the word anyway and only used it when he felt he had no choice.

Augustine wanted to leave his mark on the planet. The people he read about at university seemed like the type of people that would be remembered in centuries to come. He studied linguistics at Lancaster University and much of the study had been concentrated in the 40 years before his degree so, unlike history or English literature, there were no luminaries that had been around for centuries. The biggest name in linguistics was more famous for his work outside of the discipline than inside. Noam Chomsky had made his name as a thinker and theologian in the consciousness of the world but his seminal work on linguistics was something that drove the study of the subject forward. Augustine wanted to know that more recent linguists were still being studied and debated hundreds of years after their death, and his death for that matter. That was the way he wanted his work to be viewed in the future. He wasn't quite sure how that would happen but for now he contented himself with working as hard as he could and always putting his name forward for the most difficult assignments. The ones where he ended up without a result in many cases and saw the bodies in his sleep for months after. One day he would solve something that looked unsolvable and maybe his legacy would grow from there. In the meantime, he would look to Chomsky for inspiration.

Augustine Boyle would talk to the others in his team as though he were the great thinker and had all the answers. The problem was that they had worked with him long enough to know that this wasn't true. So, on the short ride to the station that morning he thought about what words he could use to inspire them anew. The early signs were that this was another murder from someone who was careful at the scene. The early forensic work had thrown up nothing at all. Back when he first worked on the force, people were giving up clues left, right and centre. Even with basic detection techniques there were footprints, stray hairs and fibres and fingerprints galore to choose from when piecing the case together. Now it seemed as though every murderer wore gloves, shaved off all their hair and possibly worked naked as well. Augustine blamed it on the proliferation of shows on

TV that gave an insight into the way that detectives solved crime. From Crimewatch to CSI there were ideas there that would get the criminal mind going. Everyone wanted to commit the perfect crime. Just committing any old crime didn't seem in vogue. There were many cases that seemed unsolvable from start to finish. Not that the police force ever let this information be public. As far as the family were concerned, the police were doing everything in their power to solve the murder and bring the perpetrator to justice. In many ways they were, but with little to go on, everything in their power was very little at all. Augustine had been brought right up to date by the officer that was controlling the scene over the phone. There felt like little to go on. As he pulled around the last few corners to the station he slowed a little to compose himself. It was becoming routine to meet together at the station when dealing with a murder. If the body was cold and the event had happened some time before then they were losing little by not going to the scene straight away. If the body was warm then there were reasons to get there as soon as they can and look for clues in the locality. For some reason, many murderers hang around for some time after the crime. They are curious about the police investigation and whether they are bagging up any evidence. But after finding a body that has been there for a while, even only an hour, the latest thinking in police circles that an organised team back at the station was far more beneficial to the investigation than rushing to the location the body had been found in. Plus, it gave the forensics team some time to get their work done without being disturbed. In the day and age of specialist teams and computer analysis, most crimes were solved by crunching the numbers, looking through the evidence and following the most likely outcomes. Augustine wanted to get his team on board with this one. He wanted their full attention so he spent the last few turns of his steering wheel considering what he might say.

"*This one is different, ladies and gentlemen.*"

"*I need your full attention on this case.*"

"*We really have something to work on here.*"

"*Do me proud.*"

But none of these felt right. He had to tell himself that he would find the right words when he was in front of the team. He lived closer than most so he still had some time to think about it when he was sipping his cup of tea in the briefing room. There was something that did make this case different he did need their full attention and, unlike so many other similar cases in the past, they did have something to work on. Maybe this would be the start of his legacy.

Around half an hour later Augustine was sat in front of the rest of his team. There were only five of them on the team now. Augustine blamed cutbacks but it was at least in part that resources were directed to other detectives that took on cases that were easier to solve. As with any part of society that was subject to government funding, the figures dictated a lot in the police. If something brought great returns on the investment then it was well funded. If it didn't then it was seen as unnecessary expenditure and culled. In many ways, he was fortunate that his predilection to pick up the most difficult cases hadn't seen his team cut even further or be out of business altogether. He had known of other detectives in other regions reassigned to different parts of the force if their results were not up to scratch. The fact that Augustine struck lucky, as his superiors saw it, every now and again was probably the sole reason that he was still operating his team. He stood in front of them. He would rather have seen them eye to eye, but protocol dictated that the commanding officer stood and he couldn't very well see the rest of them standing up with him at this time of the morning. Augustine was strange in this way. Sometimes he didn't pay a second's thought to protocol, while other times he stuck to the book like his career depended on it.

"Ladies and gentlemen, we have something really interesting here. It seems as though this might lead on to more murders so we need to solve this one as soon as we can," he announced. He had never felt comfortable addressing a crowd of people in a formal situation. Even just the group of four others that he was used to and worked with day after day gave him butterflies that he had to control. Augustine used some of the lines he had put together in the car. They were like a crutch and he was sure that if he recorded and played back his talks that he would have started them all with the words 'ladies and gentlemen' and also used the word 'interesting' somewhere along the way. He had been on courses designed to help him become a better presenter. They included tips like 'imagine the audience naked' and 'plan out what you want to say on prompt cards' in exchange for his time. But the people he had assembled in front of him here were not the type that anyone, no matter their imagination, would want to think of without any clothes. And he couldn't very well plan a talk on a murder that hadn't even been committed yet. That would put him right at the top of the pile of suspects. He took all of this in his stride and carried on in his normal manner. They knew what to expect and in many ways that was a good thing. If he suddenly turned up with the most polished presenting style in the world then they would be unnerved by it. The last thing that anyone needed was an unnerved team of detectives.

He then played his ace card. He knew that this was the one that would get their attention. All his life he had been told tom keep the ace card and play it as late as possible. His grandfather told him to keep the ace card, or the best domino, in your hand and only use it at the killer point in proceedings. But Augustine always wanted to play it as soon as possible. Once playing cards when he was younger, Augustine had what he thought was a killer card in his hand. He kept hold of it to use at the most pertinent part of the game. The part where it would turn everything in his favour. That point never came and he lost the game of cards with his best card still in his hand. He vowed never to finish anything with his best card still in his hand again. He wanted the opponent to know that he meant business and he wasn't afraid to play his cards when he felt like it, not when the game dictated. In this instance, the ace card would grab the attention of the team and hopefully transform this case into one that they all believed in.

"The killer left a note at the scene. He left a single card with the single letter 'A' on it. We have no idea yet what this means in terms of the crime, but for us it means a case that has interest. It means a case that can take us somewhere. It means a case where we don't feel like we are banging our heads against the wall," explained Augustine. He was talking while looking at his feet, not something that would have helped him pass those courses on presentation. He quickly caught himself and forced his stare away from the floor and towards the people gathered in front of him. They were all sat on the edge of their chairs paying full attention to his every word and every movement. Finally, something had given him the ability to hold the attention of the room for longer than a few seconds. It was a shame that it was a case rather than his style that had engaged the room so, but whatever it was, Augustine would take it. He could also see his boss stood at the back of the room, listening to the way he addressed his troops. She was around the same age as Augustine and had a similar lifestyle to him - no long-term partner, no kids, no husband ex or current. In fact, she had been thrown the accusation that incensed Augustine at times, the one that she had been married to the force, and been as aggressive towards the accuser as Augustine was to his. It was a lazy way for people to think. The two of them were dedicated police officers and had worked their way up to their position sometimes by putting in extra hours but what profession nowadays didn't need that extra sacrifice to get to the top? Augustine used to compare his role to that of the banker who worked back when the markets were in turmoil or the bank faced a crisis that needed extra manpower to deal with. His boss, Marie, used to tell people that she was no different to the accountant that worked ridiculously long hours around the end of the tax year. Either way, they were having the same argument with different people. They were like kindred spirits but the feelings stopped there. There was never going to be anything romantic between the two of them, even if they felt like the last two left on the shelf a lot of the time. Marie was listening as intently as the rest of the team.

"I have spoken to forensics and there is nothing from either the paper or the ink that gives us much to go on. The paper is a mass-produced brand that can be bought in any stationers or supermarket for a few quid a ream. The ink is from a common or garden printer that is the number one seller on Amazon. Do you know how many of these have been sold over the years?" Augustine started breaking down the case, piece by piece. But whatever he said would not have the same impact as the statement about the letter on the piece of paper. Maybe his grandfather was right about not playing your trump card too early.

The next voice he heard was Electra. She spoke softly, "I would estimate about five thousand a year, the way Amazon goes about its business." She was answering his question about the number of printers sold. She never had got used to the way Augustine asked rhetorical questions. Electra, not her real name, was someone that wanted everything in her life compartmentalised and computed. She couldn't leave something unanswered, so whenever Augustine threw in a rhetorical question he would get an honest answer. Electra provided them. It put him off track for a few seconds before he got back to his train of thought.

"It is on Grey Street, on a short ride from here but we need to be wary about how we go about this. Forensics have almost completed their work and that part of the investigation will be over by the time we get there. But I don't want the public alarmed or alerted. Rush hour will be upon us almost as soon as we get there, so people will stop to have a look if we make it obvious there is something going on. It is cordoned off now, so we will take a look, make our individual notes before convening to ask the relevant questions straight after. If we are quick and the weather is OK, then we can do this just around the corner and get out of sight before people start making their way to work. Let's get on the move," Augustine finished his brief instructions to the team. As they got up, each was handed a piece of paper with the basic details derived from the forensic investigation that had already been carried out that morning. It was a confirmation really that they had very little to work with so far. Augustine looked towards Electra and she immediately offered to drive him there. This would give them time to talk. He knew that she had the most innovative brain out of the crew and he wanted her take on what she had heard so far. Although the letter on a piece of paper was something to go on, it wasn't going to solve the case on its own. He needed to think outside the box with this, and Electra was the perfect sounding board for this.

She wasn't given the name Electra when she was born. Her parents preferred the name Alice King. She had graduated from university with a joint degree in law and computing and it was while on her computer course that the name Electra first arose and stuck. The rest of her year were interested in computers on a practical level. They wanted to know how to programme them, what they could do with them and how this fitted into a future role in industry. Not Electra. She wanted to know everything, including the theoretical stuff and the way that computers transferred energy from the socket on the wall to the power to derive the number pi to thousands of decimal places or calculate a prime number with hundreds upon hundreds of digits. Her interest in the electrical side of things came through in the questions she asked her tutors. And the name Electra stuck, because of her fascination with the electrical pulses that converted power of one kind into power of another. From the power made by burning nuclear fusion, to the power to push human comprehension further.

Electra was around five feet three with short blonde hair that she often wore in a wave across her head, like it was a homage to punk rock that had already fizzled out before she was born. She was often mistaken for a lesbian, and approached on more than one occasion, but was definitely straight. She had passed from one man to another since she was old enough to have a relationship but none had ever really worked out. Augustine went through phases in his life where he could find beauty of one kind or another in every single woman he met. Some would be young, some old but he would see something beautiful in their eyes, their smile, their hair or something more like the rest of the men he met - their tits or arse. Electra was different. She would find something negative to focus on in every relationship after it had been going a few months. Just as men felt they were established and settled, she would have worked herself up about an aspect of the man, sometimes incredibly obscure, that she just couldn't get over. Sometimes it was the state of their white underwear after they had worn it for the day, other times it was that they were maybe carrying a little too much weight around the middle. But whatever other people could easily overlook or attempt to rectify (dark pants would have resolved one problem, cutting back on food and exercising the other) but she just couldn't stop obsessing about it and in the end, broke it off with the man. He would usually be devastated as it wasn't something that had ever been mentioned before. She would feel a huge sense of relief that this issue was now done and dusted and she could get on with the rest of her life. That was until a few months later when she had built up another problem with another man and pushed him out of the door. But none of that bothered Augustine. She may have had a hectic and complicated private life at times but it never affected her work. She was always there on time, worked back late voluntarily if needed and was his sounding board when he needed someone to think differently. And that was exactly what he needed at that point. They walked slowly to her car as he finished off his first drink of the day. It was cold by that time but Augustine didn't care. He had never developed the ability to drink tea or coffee when it was hot. Others had usually finished their cup and he was still mulling over whether it was cool enough for the first sip. He looked for a bin inside the last few steps of the station before realising that there was one in the car park. He glugged the last of the cold tea and placed the paper cup in the bin near to Electra's car. She was already inside and added a few revs of the engine to heighten the urgency of the situation to her teammates. Augustine jumped in and the two were away down the road in no time at all. The roads were still incredibly quiet and she drove on the edge at the best of times.

3

Electra looked across at Augustine. He rarely looked nervous, always in control, unless he was sat in the passenger seat of a car. She had known him for well over ten years and he looked no different than when she was first introduced. His curly hair didn't seem to grow and he never spoke about it being cut. With his dimly-lit eyes and never having facial hair to speak of it was as though his head was cryogenically frozen back to a time in his mid-twenties.

Augustine started to ask her questions. He wanted to know what she thought.

"What did you think of all that, Electra?" Augustine knew that there was no point in beating around the bush or trying to be cryptic with her. She only really dealt in absolutes and besides they didn't have long before they would be at the scene. There was no time at all for small talk.

"Well, Gus," she always called him Gus even though nobody else ever did, he didn't mind as long as it was just her. "I am thinking that this is not a one-off. Unless there are other letters that are being uncovered as we speak, this signifies the start of something, or even the middle or the end. Just because we have found this body and this letter first, it doesn't mean that this is the first victim," she told Gus in a way that resembled a parent-child relationship. She spoke to everyone as though they were intellectual inferiors, and because of her large brain and ability to use it to full effect, they usually were. Augustine was one of them. But he didn't care one iota. It was the type of thinking he had come to expect from Electra and quite frankly the kind of thinking he had come to rely on. The rest of the team had their skills, but none could out-think Electra. He sat in silence and let her continue. He feared that an interruption might stop her flow of thought.

"And the killer is trying to tell us something, or tell someone something.

Most murders, and we are assuming this is a murder, aren't we? Most murders are committed in the heat of the moment. We are taught that in primary school, we know that from the movies we see and then we have that drilled into us every day of our working lives as cops. So, most murderers don't take the time to plan to the degree that they leave little or no evidence, although we are seeing far more of this in our investigations day by day. But then if we add on the extra layer that we have a murderer that doesn't want us to know who he is, and I say 'he' because this sounds like a crime of power and that is almost exclusively associated with male murderers, but the same murderer wants us to know something. And he wants to control the timeframe that we know this information. By leaving only a single letter, as far as we are aware at this moment in time, then we can assume that this isn't a hugely long message. By studying any history books relating to crime he will know that most murderers only 'get away' with a few deaths before they are caught. He can't have a four-page essay readied for us," she explained as the car came to a halt. Augustine had been so transfixed by the monologue of his colleague that he had completely lost track of where they were. They were at the scene. There were still most of the signs of darkness present. The street lights hadn't faded, the birds were to begin their chorus and it felt early to everyone. There wasn't any sign of the impending rush hour so they jumped out of the car to go about their work and clean up before prying eyes turned this into a social media phenomenon. People just loved to gossip about something happening in their own back yard. Augustine Boyle had a feeling that they needed to keep a wrap on this for as long as possible to deny the murderer publicity and to get on with the investigation without press scrutiny and the calls from hundreds of people who will claim to know something about the murder.

In the latter stages of an investigation, the publicity is helpful. If the trail starts to run dry then the police often need some help from the public and end up going to Crimewatch to assist with their enquiries. But this was only useful when they had no more leads. If the detectives working the case had pulled on every string they had and ended up with nothing at the end of them, then the public could be of assistance. But the team working the case knew that people would waste their time with calls in this event. Some people meant well, but called in with a name way off the mark, others just made a random call on the off-chance that someone vaguely criminal that they knew night be involved so they could claim the reward while others were just malicious. In their force, this was known as the Dan Miller effect. There was someone who would call in with every crime, every appeal and every Crimewatch re-enactment with the name Dan Miller. It was obviously someone that they didn't like for one reason or another and they took out this hatred by calling in the name Dan Miller for everything. Whether the suspect was a six foot, eight-inch black male or a five foot nothing female with blonde hair, this character would always call in the name Dan Miller. It got to the point where the police had to protect their scant resources and the guy was arrested for wasting their time. He ended up with community service and a suspended sentence and it stopped him calling in that same name time and time again. But in the early day of an investigation, the police worked best on the evidence they had to hand. Calls from the public were taken and investigated, but not sought after actively. This meant that they could generally sift the good leads and allocate the right manpower to them, while gathering the evidence that the scene and crime dictated. Augustine was happy that there had been no calls relating to this so far. It was in a city centre that was usually deserted at that time of the morning in the middle of the week. Great for the criminal, and good for the team that could get to work in their own way, rather than following leads that may send them absolutely nowhere.

The two got out of the car. Augustine jumped up as soon as his feet hit the ground. Something inside him told him that he should be first to the scene. Electra must have had the same feeling because she was quickly alongside him and opened her stride to move ahead without appearing to run and turn this into an all-out race. Augustine was much taller than her and, as a consequence, had a much longer stride so quickly drew back level with her and then matched her step for step so they both arrived at the taped-off area at the very same time. He could have used his authority to hold her back or raced ahead and left her behind but he knew that he needed her on-board with this investigation and he wanted to appease her. They both flashed their ID at the officer stationed at the entrance to the enclosed alleyway and he lifted the tape for them to pass. Augustine looked back in the direction they had just come from as he passed under and saw the rest of the team walking at a fast pace to catch them up. He smiled at them before moving towards the scene with Electra. If only the two of them could solve these case on their own, he thought, we make a good team.

As they walked the last few steps to the body, which was being dimly lit by a portable light, the kind that reminded Augustine of the cinema, it was obvious that the body was not in one piece. Augustine reached for his pocket and applied the Vaseline to his nostrils. Even in the outdoors, he feared the smell of the deceased would be present and he would be overcome by the stench of death. He looked at the body laid out in front of him and wondered how long he would see her in his dreams. It was often the first thought that came over him when he saw a new victim. The sight was so gruesome that he hoped this one wouldn't stay for long at all.

The tall buildings either side of the alley made it feel narrower than it actually was. Augustine hunched his shoulders when he first walked in as though he needed to make room for his frame, but it could easily hold several people walking alongside each other. He looked up at the sky and saw some blue start to mix with the black. The top of the building seemed an eternity away. Augustine wondered if they were being watched. It was as though there were eyes in the sky, beaming down on the work he carried out, judging whether he made the right moves or made a mess of it.

The body was clothed. That was an initial sign that this wasn't a sexual crime. The body was wearing a cheap suit, probably from Primark or George at Asda, the type that young girls buy when they first get a job in an office or a bank - in fact anywhere that they are not provided with a uniform. They buy something cheap and useful before they get their first job and then move on to something more up market when they receive their first pay packet. Amazingly, the head was still wearing a baseball cap. The two parts seemed so incongruous that Augustine at first wondered if they were from the same person. The baseball cap warranted a different outfit on the body; the body in its suit didn't feel like it would have been attached to a head with a hat of any description. The whole team was assembled by now and they all looked just as puzzled as Augustine looked across them for a reaction. He looked back at the body. It was laid on its back with the feet pointed up towards the sky. One arm was laid at an awkward angle, as though it was pointing in a certain direction. It didn't feel as though it hadn't landed there naturally and had been manipulated into that position. But as this was the first beheading victim he had ever seen in his life, he put all preconceptions to one side and decided that this must be the way that people fell and landed when having their head taken from their shoulders by what had clearly been a sharp weapon.

He bent over the body and looked as closely as he could without touching the single piece of paper that contained the letter 'A' that had given this investigation so much intrigue. Augustine had asked the forensic team to replace it on the chest of the victim for maximum effect when his team arrived. He liked the theatre of it. It was approximately four inches by four inches and printed with a regular ink, in a regular script like any regular letter. There was nothing that marked it out as being somehow linked to a murder except for the fact that it was laid precisely in the middle of the chest of a decapitated body. Augustine was expecting it to take on some sinister aspect and turn him cold but when he focused solely on the letter it meant absolutely nothing. He looked at the team and they all nodded then they had seen enough. The full forensic reports would be back waiting for them at the station and they had a little bit of work to do at and around the scene first.

Augustine instructed the team to walk the area for a few minutes before they would convene in the next alleyway to ask questions and discuss what they had found. He asked them all to look around at the surrounding buildings as they walked to see if there were any CCTV cameras that might pick up a glimpse of the killer, or more. Inevitably there were none there. It was as though the killer had thought long and hard about how to work all of this to his advantage. It seemed like they were coming up against someone cold, ruthless and very organised. Augustine wondered how they might be able to crack the hard shell of the way the killer had constructed the crime scene and get to the inside where it was easier to make progress. From bitter experience, he knew that that first strike of that cracked the shell was always the most difficult. But once they got to the softer parts inside, there was always more room to manoeuvre. They had to get inside this case as quickly as they possibly could. He dispatched Electra to be present at the post mortem examination so she could see if there was anything unusual there.

Augustine had always found pathologists excellent at what they did, but it was something they saw every day of their working life. They no longer saw a body of a person in front of them, just a cadaver that needed to be dissected and analysed. Unless you got lucky and found a pathologist that had only been doing the job for a short while, they you would end up with a clinical report that established facts like time of death and method of death, not that there was little doubt with this one. But what he wanted was a cop's view on this. He wanted someone who would pick up the little signs as the pathologist made their incisions, weighed the organs and did all the other parts of their routine. A cop could pick up the look on the pathologist's face as they cut open part of the body and examined what he or she found. Electra was the most eager to face the brutality of the post mortem from his team and also the most likely to analyse the situation for all the small signs that told stories that the black and white pages of a report could never tell.

On one occasion, Augustine had been to watch a post mortem as the ongoing investigation of a murder case. The enlarged liver and the condition it was in was easy to spot for anyone that had been present at more than one post mortem in their life. The look on the face of the pathologist told of a surprise in the way that it had been treated and still wasn't the cause of death. But the fact that the owner of said liver hadn't drunk for many days before the death meant that there was little alcohol in the blood. The report barely mentioned that fact that this was a heavy drinker, a factor that was eventually a large part of the violence associated with their murder and helped Augustine blaze a trail to her killer, from the pub that they both used to frequent. Until that point, there was little to associate the deceased with much anyone else on the planet. After, he had been able to make the right enquiries and link her to the series of events that lead to her untimely death. From that point onwards, Augustine despatched a member of his team to observe all the post mortems for his cases. Electra came back with the best results, time after time.

With Electra on her way to the hospital with the body, and the on-beat police officers tidying up the scene Augustine had to find another way to get back to the station. The commuters were starting to appear in dribs and drabs and soon it would be one of the busiest streets in the city. It was testament to the people he worked with in the police force that nobody would know that they were walking close to the scene of a brutal murder. And hopefully he could keep it off the front pages for a few days too. The national newspapers were leading on a corrupt politician that had been working for several companies with a vested interest in his government department. Rather stupidly, he had failed to declare this to the commission. The deals looked to have been done behind closed doors but as anyone in the public eye can tell you, there is always a pair of eyes on your back. The politician was seen in and out the doors of not one, but two tobacco companies and a pharmaceutical firm based in the United States. He had to that point claimed that the fact he had opposed an increase on tobacco duty and had asked questions in parliament about opening up the pharmaceutical market to companies from overseas was a coincidence. Augustine didn't believe in coincidences anymore, after twenty plus years in the force. The heat on the politician would die down in a few days and the newspapers, especially the tabloids, would love for a new long-running story to take its place. He was determined that his case would not be that story.

As he stopped and looked around at the mostly empty streets that would soon be filled with people on the rush to work, he heard a voice in the background. It was like something that was getting closer and closer to him. "Augustine...Augustine...AUGUSTINE!"

It was Ash. He was offering Augustine a lift back to the station so they could all look at the reports from the forensic team together. Ash was from the United States, but moved over the England when he was only around seven. Augustine often thought that being born in the country that probably invented crimes of this manner would help Ash to look at things in a unique way to the rest of the team. His father had worked for a major American investment bank that decided it might be a good thing to branch out into Europe. Ash's father was given the honour of heading up the company in this respect and Ash and his mother went along so the father had the happy family life that the bank's psychoanalysts insisted was the foundation of great decision making. At seven years old, who was Ash to argue? His mother was a little more able to fight her corner and after enduring three years of her husband coming home from work late and smelling of the cheap perfume she knew his secretary was fond of, she went back home to Alabama and to her parents. The divorce was messy and Ash became a pawn in their battles. But he had established himself in England by that point and his education at a boarding school was proving particularly successful. Ash stayed and his father employed someone to look after the boy when he was home from school. The someone was now his step-mother but Ash has had little to do with his father since he returned to the States and Ash joined the force. He didn't really have the time to go visit, and consoled himself with the occasional phone call to top up the birthday cards that were sent annually in May. It was the least he could do, literally, and Ash just wanted to keep up his side of the bargain until the day his father passed away. After that he was free to be his own man, Ash believed.

Augustine and Ash had always got along. From his early days, Augustine had been interested in American sports. When his school friends were talking about the football in the Monday morning playground, Augustine was talking to anyone that listened about how well the San Francisco 49ers had played the night before or what form Scottie Pippen was in. He soon ran out of people to speak to, as one by one he worked his way around the whole male population of the school without finding a fellow enthusiast. Many of the interests that are considered obscure and worthy of ridicule at school are seen as much more interesting to others when you leave and join the grown-up world. Here you are not restricted to the people you share a classroom or a playground with. You now have the whole world to choose from. When Augustine met Ash, he knew he had a kindred spirit on this front; even the fact that Ash supported the New York Yankees didn't put off the mad Cleveland Indians fan Augustine from talking incessantly about the three US sports that interested him - baseball, basketball and football (or American Football to all those that called the European game by the name football.) They had stuck at it ever since.

"Thanks Ash. That's a great idea. What do you think of all of this? Any ideas yet?" Augustine steered the conversation to the facts immediately.

"I can't get my head around this yet. We are supposed to believe that this happened and we have nothing but the letter 'A'? Is this going to continue right through to 'Z'?" he enquired of his boss. Ash loved to ask questions. It helped him to process what he had seen in his mind.

"We will see the full forensic report when we get back to the station, but for now that is what we are working on. Pretty strange, isn't it?" Augustine fell into the pattern of other people's conversation quite easily. If the other person questioned a lot then he found himself doing it too. It wasn't conscious, but once he had started he would often notice that it was happening. Then he was painfully aware of it, and wondered if the other person had noticed it too. He didn't know whether to continue or desist and ended up becoming embarrassed at the situation he found himself in, unable to devise a quick strategy to get out of it and feel comfortable again.

"Yep. But the letter really intrigues me. I want to find out more. Do you have any theories?" he fired back. Augustine decided that more questions was the order of the day. He ignored the question Ash had asked and said, "It was a clean blow, wasn't it?" It was the best he could do in the circumstances.

"I'm not 100% sure about that. The neck of any human is filled with muscles and thick bone. For something to have cut the head clean off right here in this alley, it would have to be incredibly sharp and thrown with immense force. I don't know that someone can do this in the confined space we have here. Could you?" Ash spoke lazily and sometimes Augustine didn't know whether he was being deliberately obtuse or whether he just didn't grasp English in the same way as he would if he had come home to two British-English speaking parents when he was young, especially the formative years when he first learned to speak. Did he mean could Augustine kill someone? Did he mean could Augustine know about confined spaces and weapons? Did he mean could Augustine throw something with sufficient force? He decided that any answer was a poor one so ignored the question and started towards Ash's car for a lift.

But something told Augustine a walk to work would help. It would certainly give him some time to think about what he had seen before. It was also a slight nod towards the fact that he knew he didn't get enough exercise. A short walk was the only chance he usually got, or usually gave himself, to stay on the right side of obesity and keep up the muscle tension in his legs. A walk it was. Augustine scanned the area again to see if there was anything he had missed before he set off.

"It's alright Ash, I'll walk and see you back at the station in a short while. It's not far and I want to think about the information we have pulled together already this morning," he explained to his colleague and he wandered around the area again.

He hadn't got far when he thought about the railings at the side of the alleyway. They were around seven-foot-high and barbed at the top, so he wasn't seeing them as a means of escape, but he wondered if they had been checked for blood splatters or anything else that would give them a way in to the killer. He started to walk back to the alley and phoned the head of forensics who had been working that morning. Augustine shouldn't have worried. The team were thorough at what they did and the head assured him that the whole alley, including the railings had been swabbed and analysed. There was nothing there to give any clues. Augustine turned back in the direction of the station again and walked purposefully. He felt that all parts of the police were working in tandem here to get the result that he probably needed for his statistics. He knew it would be a long day.

4

Electra watched carefully. She watched as the pathologist got all different tools and instruments out to do his job. She watched as the pathologist took a deep breath and as he prepared to carry out the post mortem on the body. He was painfully thin, not an attractive trait in a man, but one that other women seemed to aspire to, thought Electra. She watched as he moved over to the body. It was clear that he didn't relish the job in any way shape or form. Electra watched people as if it was a study of politics. What she studied was their actions. Most people tried to give off one message to the world about any given situation. But their body language often told a completely different story altogether. Electra did her best to find a place in the room that gave her a view of the victim as well as a good view of the pathologist. She knew from experience that there were going to be signs from both. She recalled that place in the room when she called Augustine from the car as she made her way back to the station. He was walking and the signal between the two of them went from strong to weak. It made parts of the whole conversation difficult to decipher but the overall message was there.

"Gus, I could see that he didn't want me there at that point. He was comfortable with me seeing the whole body that was laid out in front of us but he looked nervous about me looking at his face. It was as though he knew I…." started Electra before a patch that Gus couldn't hear. It didn't sound important so he didn't ask her to repeat.

Electra told the whole story of the post mortem. She told of the way the pathologist studied the brain that was removed from the severed head. His tiny wrists struggled away at the organ like its weight would break them. There were no other signs of injury in the head so he moved on to the rest of the body. She told of the way that he extracted and weighed each of the organs to determine if they were of the right size and condition. In many cases that would be to help determine the cause of death, but Electra felt that he was just going through the motions. He looked for all the world like the role was too much for him. It was like a son who had been passed down the family business while still in his teenage years. His mind and body would be focused on getting drunk and pulling women, but the next morning he would have to get up and make decisions that he didn't really understand. He would grow into it. The cause of death was strikingly obvious. There weren't many people who would survive a wound like that and die of liver damage. She looked at the head and considered if it was the same one that she looked at in the alleyway. The pathologist had already confirmed that it was a single blow and Electra could see that there was little sign of a struggle but something made the head look different to the one she had seen earlier on the ground. Perhaps it was the missing hat. It must have been the missing hat. Where else would they get a head from?

She watched as he carefully took out the heart and weighed it. This was standard practice and Electra picked up nothing from the looks on the pathologist's face or his voice. He carefully took out the organs one by one. He checked them over once and then put them to one side on a metal tray to be catalogued. They made a thud as he dropped them, only from a height of a few inches. Electra found it a satisfying noise in a strange way, but not one that she would want to hear on a regular basis.

Electra recalled this to Augustine on the phone. "Gus, it's been pretty standard up to a point. The organs didn't look or feel any different to the other post mortems I've been to. But something felt different. There was something in the air. I can tell you..." Again, the reception stymied the conversation. Electra found a few seconds to add, "I'll Facebook message you the rest," with a chuckle in her voice. Augustine hated social media. He had always tried to avoid it. The trend of telling the world every aspect of your life was confusing to Augustine. He had joined Facebook under pressure from Electra and kept in touch with distant family members and colleagues over it. But he couldn't get to grips with people that would confirm what they had for breakfast or what they were watching on TV. For Augustine, it was like the least interesting soap opera you could imagine. Electra knew of his dislike and teased him about it as much as he could.

As the pathologist worked is way down the body Electra watched with some interest while he inspected the victim for any signs of sexual assault. She later recalled look in his eyes in the telephone conversation with Augustine.

"He looked shocked. The pathologist seemed genuinely frightened by what he saw. He was young, so it may have been his first time."

It was the type of look that she has actually been sent there for. It gave away a lot of information about her lifestyle, or at least the pathologist's view of her lifestyle. Electra didn't know it at that point, but the victim was unidentified.

And as she watched carefully, she could see there was something to pique his interest. His eyes gave it away to her. It was the coil that he removed from the body before placing on the metal tray. The click of metal against metal was a noise she wasn't used to in a post mortem. The clink of metal was matched by a look from the pathologist. Electra had got what she had come for.

5

Meanwhile, back at the station, the conversation was in full swing. Ash was leading proceedings, as he often did when Augustine was not around. The others in the team were listening intently to the way he saw it all happening.

"Listen, she died there and then in that alley. Even on a quiet midweek night, it was far too risky for the killer to move her to that spot after killing her somewhere else. So, we are looking at someone who took a chance with this girl, and carries a weapon around with him. He just happened to come across her at that time and carried out his whim," Ash lectured the rest of the team. The lights in the office were on and with the summer brightness outside it was a shock to the senses. Intense light seemed to produce intense conversation.

Lou wasn't quite so convinced. He had been on the force far longer than anyone else in the team and during that time he had worked on cases of sexual assault, drugs and low-level crime before transferring to the murder investigation team. He had seen far more in his years than Ash and was willing to contend with the view his colleague was currently putting forward as the gospel. "I don't think you can be totally sure that this is random and the guy just happened upon a victim. Not many people carry around a weapon of the size needed to inflict that wound and leave it to chance. If the letter left on her chest is significant, and I would hazard a guess that we all think it is, then he is looking to carry out more of these attacks. On that basis, why carry around a sword looking for a victim, when you run the chance of being caught and being locked up before you get the opportunity to carry out even one murder? It doesn't make sense," explained Lou. He wanted the rest of the team to use their experience and crunch the numbers rather than speculate at this time. They each had a forensics report sat in front of them and they were reading while talking. Various parts of the report sparked different conversations. By this time, Electra and Augustine were still absent from the office, so it consisted of

Ash, Lou and the other member of the team. They all spoke at once from certain parts of the report. It was as though they were reading precisely the same sentence at the same time, so the conversation went with the part of the report that they were reading. Each had slightly different experiences and often different views on the parts they were reading. If Ash saw the clinical nature of the weapon as reason to feel the attack was random, then Lou saw it as reason to believe that it was planned. The other one sat somewhere in between. But one aspect that they were all agreed upon was the fact that the murderer was good at what he did. The report pretty much gave then nothing in terms of cold hard evidence to track a killer and stop him before he committed any more. There were no fibres from clothing, no traces of bodily fluids apart from the victim's own and no fingerprints. He was good in this aspect. But obviously, he wanted them to know a little something. It was strange for the three of them to admire a crime like this, but if there was ever a perfect crime, this was approaching it.

"I think we should all go away and do our own reading, come up with our own ideas before the boss and Electra get back. That way we can influence this investigation for the better with our own thoughts," Lou urged the others. They all walked to their desks and sat with heads down. Lou strolled over to a desk that looked as old as he was. It had dinks and dents across the sides, but the surface was in good condition. If he could still work on it then Lou couldn't see any reason to request a change. The police had better things to spend their money on, he decided. The idea was to look through the report with a fine toothcomb to see if it threw up anything different, anything that could be a potential lead. The way that police work happened was by narrowing down the field of suspects until you had something to work with. It may be that the suspect was seen wearing certain items of clothing, or with a hairstyle or tattoo that rendered them different. This meant that the police could work with a pool of suspects that could be sifted through for alibis or motives.

In some crimes, the field is incredibly narrow already, but in this case, they pretty much had the whole male population to contend with.

Lou had seen it all before. He had worked for the police for longer than anyone else in the station. There were no records going back that far, so he could pretty much tell people that he had worked there for any length of time longer than 40 years, so he often settled on the figure 45, as it seemed to sound right. He had lost count himself. With the police falling in line with other professions and being unable to dismiss anyone just because they reached retirement age, Lou could stay as long as he was able to carry out the job to the satisfaction of his superiors. The fact that he could interject when others were getting carried away and bring an investigation to a real, functional level meant that Augustine and Marie were more than satisfied with his work.

Lou had nothing else to do. His wife had died of cancer a few years ago. This was the only time had had spent away from the police. He had looked after her himself day and night for the final 18 months of her illness. As she weakened to the point where all daily tasks were beyond her, he looked to the state for some help to maintain her dignity. She didn't want him to see her wasting away to nothing for the last of her days. She didn't want him to have to bathe her, change her underwear and all the other tasks associated with a cancerous bladder. For his part, Lou would have happily done whatever was needed to keep her happy and comfortable. But the lack of dignity is something that can never be undone. Once she allowed him to put himself in that position she felt she had nothing to live for. If he still saw her for that beautiful young girl she was back when they met, and what she wanted to feel like now, then there was a reason for her to fight. Not a fight that would end with an absolute victory, but the small victory of a few more extra days, maybe weeks with her darling husband. He found someone to help and it gave him the better side of the equation. The help dealt with the pain and embarrassment she went through, while he got to spend time making her laugh, talking about the past and distracting her from the time bomb ticking in her body.

Before that, Lou was one of those characters that just wanted to help. He experienced just about every department in the police and from this viewpoint he had a lot to offer. Now he still had the same experience, but only applied it in shorter bursts. Whether it was age or the passing of his wife, he didn't seem to be able to summon up the same consistency of help as he had in the past. But in a world where far too few people help each other, this was more than enough for the rest of the team. Lou was five feet eight with a little flash of grey hair around the temples and behind the ears. Apart from that there was the odd wisp of hair, but it was barely noticeable unless there was a strong wind blowing that pushing it out of place. The rest of the time he looked bald across most of his head to the untrained eye. Lou spent most of his time in the office. It wasn't that he had lost mobility or appetite to be out in the field, but that he did his best work sat in front of a desk. His recall was outstanding and if there were any cases that reminded him of the one they were working on, he could tell the name of the victim and the year straight away. This gave him or someone else in the team the starting point to look deeper into those similarities. Maybe it was a killer that had stopped for a few years and then started up again. Sometimes it might be a clue that ties together past crimes with one they had a prime suspect for now. On other occasions it came to nothing. But in all cases, this recall proved invaluable to rule people in or out, make links to past crimes or keep the current one separate. Lou was one of the first people asked when any serious crime happened in the force. He could give the investigating team a start. They were all thankful for it. He was glad to still be of use. In his mind, he had some thoughts of trying to keep doing the job until he went the same way as his wife. But at other times he just wanted it all to be over so he could sit at home and relax. But he felt deep down that he was never destined for this life. Another of the team with no children, he had little in retirement to look forward to. When he was growing up, Lou hung around with some of the seedier characters in his neighbourhood. They were into petty crime, and called themselves the Bravo Gang. Lou was never involved in what they did, but they never kept secrets from him. But when he started to move towards a career with the police, he lost contact with all the friends he had. Add to this the fact that he had no family apart from his wife, and a brother that lived in New Zealand, then Lou ended up pretty lonely outside of his work. He didn't have any hobbies or interests that would fill his life. He saw a retirement as punishment and couldn't see how he fitted into it. Lou was present at the crime scene earlier that morning because of his recall of previous crimes. He was told that his experience was going to be vital to Augustine and the rest of the team. But he hadn't seen anything like it before. It was a brutal killing, the type of which didn't happen when Lou started with the force. He was looking at the different angles though, when Augustine and Electra walked back into the office within a couple of minutes of each other. When he saw Electra first, he didn't stop what he was doing. He knew that they would all be briefed together by her. But when Augustine walked through the doors a few minutes later he knew that they would be called together soon. He wrapped up the two theories he was working on. He hadn't developed either to his satisfaction and would work on them later before discussing with anyone else. As Lou deleted the browsing history on his computer and looked out of the window to see what the weather was doing, he heard a call. It was the unmistakeable voice of Augustine Boyle, "time for a chat, guys. We've got a lot to discuss." Lou looked at the rest of the team and jumped up as not to be last into the room. He didn't want the others to think he was holding them back in any way. The brightness of the room was reaching the early afternoon peak and Lou wanted this to pass so they had a calmer conversation than what had gone before, but he couldn't see it with the characters assembled. He liked and respected Augustine, but thought he had assembled a group of parts rather than a functioning team.

6

The discussions of the team lasted for a full half an hour. Each had looked at the forensic report on their own, as Lou had suggested. The only ones that were a little behind in this were Electra and Augustine, but they were soon brought up to speed. Augustine had heard a preliminary report before he had even got to the station the first time that morning and the tests carried out in the meantime hadn't really added anything to the information he had at his fingertips. The rest of the team had scoured the report and, although they didn't know it at that time, the only one with anything to go on was Lou. He was looking at two lines of enquiry that might or might not go anywhere fast, if at all. Lou was working firstly on the assumption that the killer had been organised and was enacting some sport of ritual on the victim. Although midsummers night and all the rituals that were associated with it had passed a few weeks earlier, he knew that the police presence and monitoring on those with pagan leanings were tight at that time. If one of them also knew that they were being watched then they may leave their rituals, including sacrifice, to a later date when they are far more likely to get away with it. The fact that the victim was left with her head removed from her shoulders may have been accidental, as the perpetrator might have looked to cut her neck and watch the blood flow. Or so Lou understood the way that they did these things.

Across the world, it was incredibly rare that human sacrifice was used for any ritual of any belief or any religion, but it was something that Lou remembered reading about it in India when he was on holiday there with his wife some years back. A young woman had been found with her throat cut and blood everywhere at the site associated with historic sacrifice in the South of the country. Lou had been on holiday in Goa and read in the local English language newspaper the details. The police had a great deal to go on. The three people that sacrificed her had 'bathed' in her blood to honour whoever it was they decided wanted them to kill another human. They were not caught before he returned home, but they were not the brightest criminals in history and were locked up for life a brief time later. Even the fact that they were all men of a high caste, and the victim was a woman of a lower caste didn't save them from the judge and jury. This was one occasion that Indian justice was blind to money and status. That fact that it had been claimed to happen in the 20th Century in a country that was starting out attracting the tourist trade had shocked Lou and he carried out some research on it when he got home. It appeared there were a few crimes reported annually that might have been attributed to human sacrifice, but mainly in the East. He stored it with the rest of the information in his brain and hadn't had cause to access it until when he was considering what had happened to the girl in the alley. He wasn't sure, but he hadn't seen enough to rule it out.

The second idea mulling around in his head was one that he didn't want to think about. The woman had no identity at the moment. She had nothing on her that gave away who she was. The DNA taken from her at the scene didn't match anything that they had on the centralised computer database that all forces in the country had access to. It consists of the DNA taken from suspects and victims of investigations across the nation, and was growing at that point by around 30,000 samples every month. The amount of crime in the country was reported to be falling by the politicians. But with dwindling resources and a feel for what was actually happening on the ground, Lou, Augustine Boyle and all the other cops knew differently. The fact that the central DNA database was growing at such an alarming rate was testament to the soaring crime rate, much of it fuelled by drugs. At this point it contained the profiles of well over 6 million people - but not a match for the victim they had in the alley. Also, she didn't match any of the profiles given as missing people over the previous six months. When people go missing one of two things happen. They either turn up, dead or alive, within the first few days or they are never seen again. Going back six months was a precautionary measure, but Lou suspected that if she was noticed missing then she would have been reported as such within the last few days. No luck.

The fact that there was nothing to identify this girl usually meant one of two things - she was someone from outside the country that had entered illegally or she was a worker in the sex trade. The number of people that enter the UK without the proper authority frightened Lou. He had worked in the police for long enough to see a massive rise in these cases as time had gone on. They were found working for little or no money under the 'employ' of gangs of men who had smuggled them into the country. Then they were seen as a commodity, sometimes sold to the highest bidder as a housemaid, farm worker or worse. Many of them ended up in the sex trade, which is where Lou thought this girl might had been from. It was quite easy for someone who knew their way around prostitutes in the city to get one to visit an alley with him. Then he had her captive. From there he could do whatever he wanted. This was the only other way Lou thought this could have gone at the time, but he hadn't gathered enough evidence either way at that time to be confident enough to voice these theories out loud. He liked a lot more meat on the bones than he presently had to speak up to the rest of the team about his thoughts. But when Electra started to speak about what she found at the post mortem, Lou felt that one line of enquiry was stronger than the other. He looked as his colleague spoke. Her shock of hair never seemed to move. Lou wished he had enough hair to have the same hairstyle as Electra, in fact any hairstyle would do him.

"I watched intently as the pathologist worked his way around the body. Apart from the fact that she had her head removed from her shoulders, there was nothing to separate her from any other normal human being walking the streets. That was until he got to inspect her down below," Electra blushed slightly when she spoke. She didn't know why, but she had always felt a tinge of embarrassment talking about female genitalia, even with her sexual partners. She was brought up to pretend it didn't exist. "At this point I could see from his face that something unusual was present. He looked more intently at this area than any other part of the body."

"Don't we all, lads?" said Gary from the back of the room. He always tried to lighten the mood but it never had the desired effect. Somehow, he always ramped up the tension.

"Fuck off Gary," snarled Electra. She was embarrassed enough without any comments from the clown.

"Gary, shut up. We don't need your special brand of humour today. Electra, continue," interjected Augustine. He would deal with Gary later. Now was the time for the information. Then they could all get on with their work.

Electra had sat down when Gary made his remark. She wasn't comfortable anyway, and the way he spoke had made her want to leave the room and compose herself before starting again. Her cheeks flushed redder and she felt the well of her stomach fill with fluid. But after Augustine had spoken, she was confident enough to stand up again and resume.

"She hadn't suffered any injuries as part of the attack, but she had been incredibly sexually active. There were some old injuries from a few years back. And he removed a coil from her. We don't have the full details yet, but it certainly isn't one that is used in the UK. It looks European, he told me, possibly from Poland. I should have that detail later in the day."

Lou looked up at Electra with a strange smile on his face. If she didn't know him, she could easily have thought that he was gaining some sick pleasure from the description she had been giving. But she looked down at Lou and reciprocated. She knew he was working on a theory. She could see the hands moving as though in some kind of nervous spasm across his portly belly and realised he was adding her experience to a theory.

A few years earlier there had been a spate of murders of girls on the sex trade. A man had taken it upon himself to kill woman because of a rejection he had been dealt by a partner that he thought would be with him forever. When she left, he didn't feel specific resentment to her, but a general hatred of all females. At first, he started to frequent prostitutes and take out his anger with rough sex. But this didn't fully satisfy his anger and he moved on to killing them. He had killed seven before the police finally caught up with him. Lou could immediately see similarities here with that case. He would look further into it and see if there was a link to the letter 'A' that had been left on her chest. Maybe it wasn't the start of a message, but a coding system to classify his victims based on the sins he deemed them to commit or what type of woman they were. Lou feared that this wouldn't become clear until they had a few victims, but wanted to be ready to act of they got any opportunity to find the killer. He worked for the rest of the day on this. The others in the team went back to tie up any loose ends relating to the cases they were already working on. Augustine wanted their case load as clear as possible so they could divert resources to this as soon as possible. It might be a while before there was anything else to go on, but he needed his team to be completely ready to deal with whatever would come next. All the team went back to their old cases immediately after the meeting. All that is except for Gary. Augustine told him to remain in the office.

7

"I've told you before, Boyle, that I am trying to help. It is a serious subject and I thought a small crack would ease things for Electra, kind of take the pressure off her. It's not my fault she is so damn sensitive," Gary tried to explain in a passive-aggressive manner that typified the way he went about his business. His full name was Gary Hole, but others in the force referred to him as Gars - Gars Hole was an approximation of what most people thought of Gary when they had spent a little time with him. He didn't make friends easily and he really didn't give a shit whether he did or not. He saw his career as him against everyone else, and was willing to push others down to get himself up. Gary thought this was the way life had to be lived - that you only got on by seeing others suffer. Augustine didn't want him on his team, he didn't want him near any of his cases and he didn't want Gary to call him Boyle. But he didn't always get what he wanted. Gary was a short man with a complex about anyone and everything. He didn't like to be told what to do and had a reflex reaction of running his hands through his light hair one by one every time he thought he was being told off. His bright blue eyes completed a look that could have been Arian from the neck up.

"You need to be a part of the team. We are all relying on you to help us get these cases through. We are low on players as it is, without one person in the boat rowing in the opposite direction to the rest of us. I can see this case being a breakthrough for all of us. It might lead to promotions all round. Surely you want some of that?" asked Augustine. He prayed that this little pep talk would have a positive effect on Gary. He couldn't have been more wrong.

"Boyle, some of us are going to the top whether this case gets solved or not. I've been in the force half the time as you and I'm only one step behind you. Can you feel my breath on your neck?" Gary said with a sinister tone. As his boss, Augustine had made a personal rule to never call him Gars Hole but was about as close as he ever could be to breaking that rule. The anger in Gary's face was close to breaking out into an eruption. Augustine imagined his head as a volcano. The only way to deal with an eruption in nature was to get out of the way.

"OK then, Gary. As long as you do the work that is expected of you then we will all be fine," Augustine said as he tried to close down the conversation. Gary looked him up and down. He knew why he called him Boyle, because that was how he made his blood feel - boiled. He was a useless cop that was in his position because he had been there for a long time, not because he was capable of solving the difficult cases that he insisted on taking. Gary was sure that this habit would be the end of Boyle. Augustine was sure that with Gary on his team, he would have to spend too much time watching his back. Augustine wanted the focus of his entire team to be on the case in hand.

He wondered back to how he ended up with Gary on his team. Augustine Boyle had a reputation for getting everyone on board. Gary Hole had a reputation for pissing people off. He undermined his superiors, upset his colleagues and put investigations in jeopardy through his politics and games rather than getting on with the job in hand. Gary had passed through several teams without a great deal of success since he was promoted to the level he currently held. It was true in the way that he said to Augustine that he had made a lot of progress in a short space of time. What was also true was that he hadn't made any progress recently. He needed to break through to the same level as Augustine to have enough influence to dictate his own career. He saw Augustine Boyle and others of his rank as people that got in the way of his progress. But at first it seemed that Augustine and Gary were a perfect fit - the cop that didn't get on with anyone and the leader that got on with everyone. Surely they would meet in the middle somewhere and Gary would become a team player? Well, not so far thought Augustine.

It wasn't that he particularly waged open warfare on the rest of the team, but that he couldn't be trusted. Sometimes he just didn't come up with his side of the work and someone else had to step up to the plate and complete the missing tasks that Gary was assigned; on other occasions, he went too far along the wrong path, even though he was told to stop a particular line of enquiry because it was exhausted. Augustine wondered what Gary did with all the spare time he must have created by not doing all he was assigned. But he often thought that it was best if he didn't know.

But now he and his team were stuck with the guy. His reputation had travelled through the rest of the force and nobody else would willingly take him on. Augustine was stuck with Gary. He thought that he might just have to find some tasks to occupy the loose wheel on his otherwise happy team. Augustine sat his chin on his hands, and his elbows on the desk. He tried to determine if his head felt heavier than it was when he was younger. He would sit like this in university lectures and found it comfortable. The only discernible difference was that he thought he had more padding on the chin. A sign of reaching forty, Augustine thought before looking back at the reports on his desk. It felt like the beginning of a series of killings. He tried to shake this thought out of his head. He had to believe they would have the killer soon.

8

For the next few days the team busied themselves with their past workload. Augustine impressed upon them that they needed to clear everything they had to have all resources ready should this case develop further. He even managed to deflect some of the other crimes that his bosses wanted to give the team to deal with. He had a few days grace on these, but couldn't keep all work at bay forever.

Even though they were working on other parts of other cases, the whole team thought about the girl while working, while resting at home and even for some, in their sleep. It occupied their every thought. But only a few days later she was dropped to the back of their minds. Something else occurred that took over the events surrounding the unnamed girl in the alley.

9

Jeff Caine had been the leader of the far-right political group Britain Excelsior for around five years. He had taken over the leadership from the founders in a coup after he wanted them to take a more direct approach. They billeted mosques with posters asking for the people inside to 'turn in' people that the elders suspected of being involved with 'illegal activities.' He was always on the watch list for the police and Augustine had been involved in an encounter with him a few years earlier. Assigned to lead the policing team in the city centre when both the socialist and far right groups were scheduled to march in the same day, Augustine was pissed off with his commanding officer that he had been given a thankless task. As part of the policing programme, he was assigned a meeting with the leaders of the two groups to explain the policing structure and ask for some cooperation from the two sides. Augustine felt that he got very little out of the meeting with the socialist leader in terms of cooperation or resistance. But when he went to see Jeff Caine, he felt an air of hostility from the beginning. He asked questions and got no answers. He looked for cooperation and was told to 'fuck off' and he looked for a sign that Caine understood the way that the event would be policed. None came. When Augustine pressed him to confirm understanding, a tirade of abuse rained down that included the phrase 'fucking pig' around fifteen times. Augustine had heard it all before in the line of duty, but not from someone that was designated a leader in the community, even if it was the leader of a marginal group with a dubious background. The day passed with a great deal of effective policing, and Augustine made sure that he kept a strong eye and a tight rein on the far-right side after the way that encounter with their leader went. He wasn't sure what they were capable of but he intended to give them the slimmest chance to effect it.

Caine was a tall man at well over six foot, with one brown eye and one blue eye. This was the first thing that anyone noticed of him when they met.

They spoke about the fact that David Bowie had two eyes of distinct colours too. Caine lapped it up. He loved to be the centre of attention and was happy that it came to him in any way, shape or form. So, he was ecstatic when the press named him Hard Caine. It was meant to belittle him, but he just took it as another way to keep his name in the minds of others. It also kept his group in the news. He was the embodiment of 'any news is good news,' as the links of Britain Excelsior to beatings of young men from outside of the UK made him happy. He wasn't going to admit or deny whether he knew anything about it to the press that often camped outside the door of his three-bedroom home where he lived by himself. He was just delighted that he could have his face on the news again and use the platform to spout his rhetoric. He was a muscular man in the arms and legs, but carried a little too much weight around the middle. Caine told himself it was because he was so busy that he didn't have the time to eat properly and work out. But the fact of it was that he was lazy. He would rather go out for a three-course meal, at one of the top restaurants in the city for his profile, than to sit at home and cook for himself. He lived off an inheritance from his rich parents and a salary that he drew from Britain Excelsior, one of the reasons he courted publicity and went on frequent membership drives. The machinery of the party needed cash and Caine knew how to pique the feelings of those who blamed immigrants for their woes.

He knew how to work the fears of people to get then thinking that some outside force was responsible for the way they led their life. It wasn't enough that people could make their own decisions. He wanted them to think that the decisions were already made for them, the people that arrived on these shores were causing the problems of the country and that he had all the answers. In fact, all he did was point out problems. He had no answers of his own, but in the meantime, it gave him a good living.

10

He had studied his prey for some time. None of this was going to be left to chance, if he could help it. The second target was someone that he tracked the movements of for months to ensure that he could be in the right place at the right time. He found references from friendly faces so that he could get the job he needed in the kitchen of a restaurant in the city. He worked nights that he thought were perfect to carry out his second act, but it took some time to see the pattern. After a few weeks, he felt he had perfected what he was going to do.

It worked in the most efficient way possible. He was close to finishing a shift when the order came in for the table he wanted to target. It was the only single diner in the restaurant. He checked and double checked that fact. The last thing he wanted to do was to harm the wrong person. Each of his victims had to carry a meaning. They all needed to show what he intended, to complete his work. He knew it would take time, but he was willing to invest that to get the right outcome. There was no randomness to his work. That would send out the wrong message – one that had been sent out far too many times before.

He passed the Rohypnol from a vial tucked in the sleeve of his clothing, tucked under his watch, directly into the dinner. It was something that carried a lot of risk. If he was seen by any other member of staff then he could be found out there and then. The mission would be over before it had got interesting. As he had studied the customer in the past, he expected only one course to be eaten so he had to make sure the dose was measured correctly and delivered all in one go. Too little and there would be no effect. Too much and he might pass out before he even left the restaurant. Neither of those were going to allow the plan to work. He watched as it was taken out to the restaurant before letting the head chef he was done for the night. It was time for him to clock off. It was time for him to enact the next part of his plan.

In addition to working the odd night as a chef in the restaurant, he had set himself up as an Uber driver. He was rarely on there for work but kept up enough of a presence that he had a good rating and wasn't taken off the site for inactivity. He ran out of the restaurant and pulled a coat over his chef's whites. It wasn't that he was cold, but he felt it best that he kept the link to the restaurant under wraps as not to raise any suspicion from his prey. It wasn't long before an Uber customer came up needing a lift from the restaurant and only a few clicks later he had accepted the job and was en route. He had studied what to look for in Rohypnol victims; it was amazing the facts that you could find on the internet. He saw that the target was unsteady on his feet and looked unusually tired, even for this time of night. As he was told the address, he replied that there were roadworks between the city centre and there, and he would take a small diversion. The man offered no objection and he started his ride. If he had all his senses about him, Caine might have looked down his nose at the driver. The object was to drive until the man in the back of his car was out cold. Then he had control.

11

It was all over the news the following day. The leader of the far-right Britain Excelsior had been found mutilated in the street in front of their own party headquarters. Augustine had read all about it on the internet before he even left the house to travel to the station. The newspapers used to report news the following day, when it was already cold. But with the advent of 24 news on the TV and news websites for the daily papers, a murder that was interesting had already been discussed and dissected before the before the body was cold. Augustine hated the way that they had to fight the press to get to the bottom of the story. He hated the way that they needed to issue orders to stop journalists from publishing certain details. And he also hated the way that some murders were passed over, like the girl in the alley, while others were deemed worthy of great coverage, like Jeff Caine, the man that Augustine had faced before the marches in the city a few years ago and the man that was now on the first page of all the UK news sites. Augustine wondered if he saw this in the same 'all news is good news' manner as he had with every other part of his life. Augustine smiled, but he knew that he shouldn't.

Someone had tipped off the press, it seemed. In the modern age, detecting a crime gives the person who stumbles upon it a choice. They can go for the traditional method of calling the police so they can deal with it. Or they can get in touch with one of the tabloid newspapers to see if their discovery and associated story is worth anything. The person who found the body of Jeff Caine was now sitting in a luxurious city centre hotel at the expense of one of the national tabloids, with a nice holiday and stack of money coming their way to help the get over the grief of the discovery. It wasn't long before all the press was there and the story was given mass coverage. You could already see analysis on websites, talk on social media and rolling coverage on the 24-hour news channels with so much time to fill and so little to fill it with.

But the one thing that was significant to the police, that the press didn't know at that time was the fact that the killer had left a letter 'L' on a small piece of paper on the chest of the victim. Among all the open wounds and blood, this white piece of paper stood out as something pure and untouched. Set in such a scene of carnage, the pristine whiteness of the paper indicated that it wasn't left at the same time the man was killed, or it would have been steeped in blood. This could only mean one of two things for Augustine Boyle and his dedicated team – either the killer returned at a later time when the wounds were no longer seeping, or the person who left the letter was not the person who killed Jeff Caine. This got Augustine thinking. He was just arriving at the scene saw that the police cordon was huge. Although the horse had bolted, the stable door was well and truly shut. The fact that Jeff Caine laid dead on the street in front of his own party headquarters could not be changed, nor could the fact that the entire world already knew about it. But once the police were informed of the crime, they acted swiftly to seal off the area, remove the journalists and members of the public and restore a little piece of privacy for the deceased. In many cases when someone of public repute dies there are floral tributes and celebrities lining up to pay their respects. This wasn't quite the case with Jeff Caine because of the number of enemies he accrued over the years but there were still politicians wondering if this was aimed at them as a group.

Augustine Boyle had driven himself to the scene and met up with the rest of the team. The protocol of meeting at the station to discuss had to go out of the window somewhat with the fact that this murder was all over the news and the public expected to see detectives at the scene doing all they can to solve the case from the very outset. Augustine Boyle hated this part of the job. The politics of the role meant that public perception of the hard work you were doing was just as important to his bosses as the actual work itself. He ended up wasting time looking like he was being a good detective to show the face his superiors wanted the public to see. This was time that Augustine felt would be better used in actually making progress. The team would have been better prepared by letting the forensics do their job and discussing a plan of action. With the second piece of paper being found on the chest of a murder victim in a short space of time, Augustine and the rest of the crew knew there was a link. But an unknown girl in an alley and a well-known man in front of his own building didn't seem to have too much of an obvious link at that time. If their presence slowed the progress of the forensic team then this was another victory for public face over real detective work, thought Boyle. He looked at the building and shuddered for all it represented over the years, unashamedly racist yet finding a following from common people. The headquarters was built with sandstone and appeared white as the sun started to appear between the buildings opposite.

Caine would have found solace in the way the building stood out as white in a sea of dark buildings. Maybe it was symbolic that this was chosen as the headquarters for the pro-white party. He looked at the entire scene like he was scanning for clues, when he was really trying to rid himself of the negative connotations he carried in his mind about the building and the occupants. Anyone watching would think that Augustine was going about some important facet of detective work.

Not that there was much doubt over the cause of death. Controversial figures in politics rarely have the chance to grow old and die of natural causes. Their rhetoric attracts followers of strong belief both for their cause and against it. The 1960's in America saw many of the leading figures of the time not make it out of the decade, slain by people who though that their message was wrapped up in human form. The killers believed that death of the man would lead to death of the ideas. The words and messages of Martin Luther King and JFK in particular resonate with people today so the theory of killing an idea by killing a man doesn't ring true. The divisive message of Jeff Caine was not his alone, and they would remain long after his death. In many ways, if this was a political killing, then it made much of his ideology correct.

The wounds inflicted on his body were deep as Boyle and the team approached. The last checks on the body by the forensic team were taking place and as the investigators approached the forensics walked away and let them have a good look at the body. The face was left alone, but the rest of the body was covered in cuts and marks. The lacerations to the arms and legs were superficial and looked as though they had been delivered as Caine was trying to defend himself. The cuts on his torso were much deeper and had been delivered probably after the man was already dead. But there were little signs of a struggle in any other way. The blood was concentrated in one place which indicated that there was no movement throughout the attack or, as was considered with the attack on the alley, that the body was moved here sometime later. Again, Boyle looked around the area for CCTV cameras and again drew a blank. He thought that whoever had killed knew the camera coverage of the city in precise detail, or was a very lucky person indeed – at least so far. The wounds on the body were something else. The torso had deep cuts that exposed the internal organs and had broken ribs in more than one place. Augustine looked across at the rest of his team and saw a look of horror on most faces. Gary that usually faced anything down with bravado looked pale and about to be sick. The only one that kept a straight face was Electra, being used to the cutting up of bodies and probably already thinking about the post mortem that Gus would inevitably ask her to attend later in the day. Augustine decided that there was very little to gain from looking at the body any longer and motioned to a uniformed police officer to cover up the corpse of Jeff Caine. They would take their investigation to the surrounding area to see if anything came up.

"Gary and Lou, you take the left of the building while Ash and I look to the right," said Augustine, "there must be something here that gives us a clue to what we are working on. I don't like the fact that someone else is in control."

"We know that boss," replied Gary who was now getting over his queasiness and returning to his normal atrocious self. He smiled as well as he could with his stomach still moving around like he had a ferret climbing inside. Augustine just ignored him and carried on with his instructions. Behind his back, the rest of the team were smiling at the fact Gary had been passed over by Augustine. They all wanted to do the same to him.

"Electra, speak to the forensic leader and find out when the post mortem is likely to happen. Then go into the building and see what you can find. I'm sure Caine will have a laptop or other device in there. See if there are any emails, letters or anything else that might give us a clue," Augustine instructed. He loved the times when they could get down to business rather than push paper. Even though they were no further forward, it felt like something was happening. Activity always produced results, he told himself. He wasn't sure whether he believed it.

"Boss, the building is closed and we can't get access. We have spoken to the deputy of Britain Excelsior and he is refusing to come down. He doesn't want to end up in the same state as Caine," Electra explained.

"I don't give a shit. Break the fucking doors down if you have to. We need to investigate. It's the only way he will be safe in the long run. Tell him he's got 20 minutes to get here or we will 'unlock' the doors ourselves," Boyle shouted. The news helicopters were circling overhead and one came so close that the wind and noise made it difficult to be heard, let alone understood. "And get those bastards out of here," he continued. Then Augustine Boyle walked off. That was the signal for everyone to get on with their tasks. There were no specific instructions because there was nothing specific to look for. From the initial view, it looked as though the murder had taken place in one spot without a struggle. But the killer and victim must have travelled there and this might throw up some clues. Already Augustine had been watching the body language of the forensic team and it reminded him of the way they were in the alley with the girl. He felt that they had nothing to go on again, so it might be down to his detectives to find something that might give them a way in.

The four of them searched the area with torches to look for something that might produce a breakthrough. It was still dark in places, even though it had reached mid-morning and the torches allowed them to see what was on the ground. As with any major city, the streets were cleaned regularly and Electra had been told to find out from the city when the last clean had taken place while she waited for Caine's deputy to arrive or the 20-minute deadline to expire. That would give them a timeframe for the pieces of litter and stray coins they were picking up, bagging and cataloguing. Electra returned to tell Gus that the streets were cleaned the previous night at around midnight. So, whatever was present in front of the building had only been there a matter of hours. To the untrained eye none of it looked significant. The headquarters of Britain Excelsior was situated at the end of a long road, facing the direction of the breeze that was blowing the night before and was still present as Augustine looked through what they had found. But to someone who had done this before, there were a plethora of possibilities. The discarded sweet wrapper could have DNA from the killer, as could the cigarette butt. The 5 pence coin found near the gutter on the right of the building could have fallen from the pocket of the killer or the victim and have traces of body fluids on it. There wasn't a lot of pieces picked up, but there was enough for the forensic team to look at in the lab.

The 20-minute deadline passed with no sign of the deputy of Britain Excelsior. Little did Augustine know at the time, but he was travelling in the opposite direction. He had been through a series of blazing rows with Jeff Caine over the last few months and was looking to leave the party and set up on his own. Some of the secrets that he had learned about Caine while working with him were electric. The deputy had decided that this was the quickest way to set up his own political party and tied to extort money from Caine in exchange for his silence and the fact that he would leave the party. Jeff Caine decided that the best way to deal with this attempted blackmail was to ignore his deputy. They hadn't spoken in months and Caine was brewing in preparation for the next time they would be face to face. He planned and plotted the words that would come out of his mouth at their next meeting. The city wasn't that big as though they would never bump into each other again. And when they did, Jeff Caine was going to let him have it.

12

Scott Sharpe threw some clothes into a suitcase and went to the airport. He didn't know where he was going, and didn't know what he should pack, but he thought it might look suspicious boarding a flight without luggage of any description. The murder of Jeff Caine happened too late to be on the front of the newspapers but he was sure that other passengers would have seen it on the TV news before they left home for the airport or would be looking at it on their smartphones while eating, shopping or wandering around. Those with at least a little interest in politics would probably recognise him as the deputy or Britain Excelsior, or the acting leader now that Caine was dead. He thought about disguises, trying to leave the country under a different name or going into hiding. But after a little thought, Scott Sharpe decided that just getting out of the country was the best course of action.

He had always found airport lounges the strangest of places. Nobody was there out of choice, all they were doing was waiting for a screen to tell them where to assemble for the flight. He didn't like waiting around, and felt that he only had time to carry out all the necessary parts of his life, without the waits in between. It was even worse for him that someone else controlled the waits. It was like working with Jeff Caine all over again. He hated that bloke. When he first joined Britain Excelsior it was like a breath of fresh air. Scott had waited all his life to feel like he belonged. When he was young he never fitted in at any school. His parents moved around the country a lot so Scott felt like he was starting all over again at a new school every couple of years. He never got settled. He never liked being the new kid, but that was the role that he had to play time and time again. Scott watched while other kids played games on the school field in the summer months and the hard-concrete yard when the grass was wet. They enjoyed games that they had played together for years. Some were pretty obvious to Scott, like tag or football, but others in different corners of the country felt alien to him. He watched and tried to pick up the rules of the games but they seemed without rule. Some kids would be caught out by a particular move, while others would stay in the game for the same move. He gave up watching and waiting for someone to invite him into their game. Scott spent the rest of his playtimes inside. He read a huge number of books but couldn't tell you if any of it went in. Scott was the type of person to devour a book in a single sitting, but only be able to recall small parts of the book. Not everything in life had a meaning or a relevance to Scott. Much of it passed him by.

Working with Jeff Caine had become strained after around a year of being in the organisation. Jeff was welcoming of Scott's ideas to begin with. He listened and consulted others on what Scott had to say. For his part, Scott had looked for an organisation that thought like him and acted like him. Britain Excelsior seemed just that organisation. But with anything, there is a public face and a private face. It is the same with people. We all show the side that we want the world to see. It is only when you get to know someone and scratch the surface that you understand what they are like behind closed doors.

To the public, Britain Excelsior seemed organised, dedicated to their cause and ready to act at a moment's notice. Scott was attracted by this. In every job he had previously worked, Scott was always drawn to the people as much as the company. He would do his research and then meet with the person who would be his boss. This way he could get a feel of how they would work together and if Scott was comfortable with the people he would spend 8 hours plus a day with. Three jobs in a row Scott thought he had found someone who shared his views and his passion. Three jobs in a row, the manager that he had decided was the perfect fit for him announced the fact that they were leaving their job in the first week of Scott's employment. He was quite sure it wasn't him. People needed time to go through all the motions involved with leaving a job. People needed time to let Scott get under their skin and persuade them that working somewhere else was better than looking at his face every day of the week.

But behind the scenes, Britain Excelsior was a chaotic group of people, loosely gathered under the control of Jeff Caine. He had put a lot of money into the organisation and expected a lot of control in return. Those that didn't like it were quickly ushered out of the door. Those that wanted to stay had to toe the line and not steal any of the limelight from the leader. Those were the rules. Scott and Jeff were close initially but after Scott found out that none of his ideas were taken seriously, he pretty soon got pissed off with the way things were going. Jeff thought that Scott would be better inside the tent pissing out, and Scott didn't want to give Jeff the pleasure of ousting him. So, they drifted apart and ran their own little empires – Scott's much littler than Jeff's.

Scott walked through the terminal building slowly, keeping to the edges where there were fewer people and the light wasn't as strong. He didn't want to be seen, but thought that hiding in the toilets would just cause more suspicion. He wanted the next couple of hours to pass in the blink of an eye, so he could be on the plane and on his way out of here. When he arrived at the airport a couple of hours earlier, Scott Sharpe went to the booking desk for the first transatlantic airline he could find. For some reason, his mind kept telling him that Europe wasn't far enough. He wanted to get away before the press started to hound Britain Excelsior and rip it apart. There were so many stories to tell, that he wasn't sure which one they would go for first. Would it be the fact that he and Jeff were supposed to be leading the organisation and hadn't spoken in months? Would it be the numerous affairs that Jeff had been having with the married members of his team? Would it be his own addiction to sex, and the huge number of prostitutes he had been using in the city over the recent months? Scott had received a tip-off from an old acquaintance in the press that the story was out there, waiting to be told. He had no idea how the press found out about him and prostitutes, but he wasn't going to wait around to find out. Well, if these girls were willing to have sex for money, then they were also probably willing to sell their story for a bit of cash too. He had trusted them less and less over the previous weeks, but couldn't stop the urges. There was one in particular that he felt would sell her story for only a few quid. She was European and Scott was sure she knew who he was. It would be quite a tale for one of the leaders of an anti-immigration, anti-Europe political party to be sleeping with a European sex worker. The last time he saw her Scott made her pay for her possible loose lips. She wouldn't talk about him again, he was sure of it.

Scott Sharpe had a way with women normally, but as he got older he lost his touch. In his youth, he could have pretty much any woman he chose. Sometimes it was just for sex, on other occasions it was for a relationship. He wasn't controlling but had something that women found hard to resist. Scott loved the attention and thrived in any situation where women and alcohol were involved. As the years passed he just didn't know how to make the magic happen any longer. One of the issues was the fact that Scott aged, but his interest in women didn't. He was still targeting the women in their early twenties that he was so successful with when he was the same age. Now that he was in his late thirties the women he looked for in the past were married with kids, and the ones he went after in the present just weren't interested in a man nearly twice their age.

But he had aged well. He still had most of the looks that he carried around with him from his younger days, and with only a little extra baggage around the middle. Most of the people he knew of his time of life had succumbed to the ravages of age. Their faces had started to show the signs of wrinkles, their bodies were not as tight as when they were in their prime and their hair was receding at a rate of knots. For some reason, Scott had avoided all of these. When he went to the rare family occasion he was invited to attend, Scott always looked with great interest at the other men in the family to see where his genes came from. They all looked far older than their years and Scott looked far younger than his. Maybe he was adopted. Scott looked across at a group of early twenties who looked like they were heading for a hen do in a hot part of the world. If he wasn't trying to keep his head down, then this would be the type of women he would be looking to talk to and hopefully take it further than just a talk. While his wife was still asleep in their home, Scott was heading for the other side of the world. He had chosen the Bahamas from the short list that the lady at the airline desk had given him. It was somewhere he had never been, somewhere he imagined he wouldn't be known and was flying this morning. The last of these criteria was the most important of the three. He desperately wanted to get out of the country as soon as he could.

He went to the toilet to kill a bit of time and stretch his legs. He was well over six-foot-tall and this height meant his journeys by plane were uncomfortable to say the least. He looked in the mirror while he washed his hands. Scott had blond hair down to his shoulders and he could have easily passed for an Australian or Californian surfer if it wasn't for the clothes he was wearing. He looked in the mirror and the worry lines came across his face. That's the way to end up with wrinkles, he told himself. The only worry he had recently was the arguments he was having with Jeff Caine. They were not face-to-face any more, but across a series of emails. Scott had told Caine exactly what he thought of him to begin with. When Caine ignored everything that Sharpe threw at him, then he became angry. An email letting someone know that you don't think a great deal of them as a human being is one thing. An email threatening to kill them was quite something else. Scott Sharpe had let his emotions run away with him and let Caine have it all.

Airports showcase the diversity of the world community. People assemble there from all over the globe for a few fleeting hours at a time and then go. They are all homogenised by the same airport staples no matter where you are in the world. Burger King. Duty Free. Travel Money. Expensive sandwiches. Poor quality coffee and traffic that rushes everywhere but goes nowhere. Scott tried to guess what country other travellers were from based on the clothes they wore, the food they ate and their mannerisms. He didn't get close enough to hear their voices. Staying at a distance meant he had less chance of being noticed. Less chance of being kept in this country.

Scott looked across at the glowing lights on the shops, bars and cafes and wondered whether that was a deciding factor in the selection of somewhere to spend money. Did a neon light indicate an attractive place to put a hand into a pocket and pull out a wad of notes? Was this linked to nature? Did our ancestors feel more relaxed in the moonlight?

By this point he only had around an hour to wait before his gate would be shown and he could begin to board. Scott was torn between being the first on the plane and having everyone else walk past him, where at least he could bury his head in a magazine, or being the last on the plane and having to walk past everyone else. He settled for being in the middle, when the chaos of finding a seat, putting boarding cards away and making sure you have all you need for a flight seemed to distract others enough that he wouldn't be noticed in all the fuss. Then when the plane left the tarmac he thought he would be safe for a while at least. That was the plan, anyway. He went for a magazine all the same, so that he had something to bury his head in and keep away from prying eyes. Scott also thought it was a clever idea to buy a hat for the same purpose so bought something he had never owned before – a baseball cap. With that covering the top half of his face by being pulled low, and the magazine doing the rest, Scott hoped to have a peaceful flight away from people recognising who he was. He wanted to get away as fast as he could and leave Britain behind for a while. He may have been the de facto leader of Britain Excelsior at that time but Britain was the last place on earth he wanted to be. It held so many risks for him.

13

Back at the offices of Britain Excelsior, Electra had waited long enough. She had given the deputy of the party well over the 20 minutes Augustine had instructed. He was on her back again, and it was now time to gain access to the building. They had no idea what was inside. A last call to the deputy brought no answer, so he asked the police on duty to give her access to the building. The door was secure but no match for the methods of the police. They had been trained in these techniques – there was no use in trying to conduct a raid on a suspected drug den and taking five minutes to open the door. It was off its hinges and on the floor in ten seconds flat and Electra was looking through the entry of the building. It has a CCTV camera pointed at the door, but from the angle it looked like it wouldn't cover far enough to show the part of the street where Caine was killed, if indeed he was killed on the street. She had been told that the body was being moved and the post mortem would happen in around an hour and a half. Setting aside enough time for traffic, that only gave Electra 25 minutes in the building. She would have to work quickly.

After a quick look through the entry, she moved on to the offices. There were no signs or directions but from the look of the office at the end of the corridor on the first floor, Electra guessed that it belonged to Caine. The door handle was brass where the rest were chrome. That looked like the touch of a man who wanted others to know that he was in charge. As he opened the door it felt even more like a place that Jeff Caine would spend time. There were three photographs of people on the wall. One she didn't recognise, it might have been one of his family, but the other two were plain to see. The first was Enoch Powell, famous for a speech against immigration, and one of Caine shaking hands with Scott Sharpe, the deputy leader of the party whose headquarters she was now stood in. Sharpe was the man she had been trying to get hold of all morning. She had been briefed that Sharpe and Caine were not the best of friends at that time, nor for some time before, so she was a little puzzled as to why the photograph was still there. Sitting in the chair at the desk, she could see why it may have escaped Jeff Caine's attention. It was obscured by the coat stand when you sat at the desk. Jeff Caine had the photograph of one of his enemies sat looking at him all the time he was working at the desk. The funny thing was that he probably didn't know.

Electra could see that time was short, so she tried a few things that usually didn't work but might shine a slither of light on Caine's movements and potential killer. She looked in the drawer at the top of the desk to see if his diary was there. Amazingly the drawer was unlocked and the diary was present. Most people who are as busy as Jeff Caine took their diary with them wherever they went, or kept it online so they could access at any time. It appeared that Jeff Caine came from the old school with this, as he kept a physical diary. But there was very little in there of illumination. Electra palmed through the appointments for the last few days. Many of them were initialised and the ones that were not showed meetings in the office mainly. She bagged it and got ready to take it outside for one of the team to look over.

Just before she left the office to attend the post mortem, Electra tried one more thing. Now the diary was a long shot, but this was something that just never happened. Electra turned on the PC on the desk to see if she could access it without a password. To her amazement, she could. Not only that, but it immediately came up with the email inbox of the recently deceased Jeff Caine. The first few messages were the usual crap you find in any inbox – reminders about meetings, subscription emails and people trying to sell something. But by now it wasn't the inbox that had captured Electra's attention. She saw a folder to one side that had been named 'Scott Sharpe – evidence.' She knew at once this was the clue she had been looking for. A few minutes later she was on the phone to Augustine. He then made a call of his own. They wanted to speak to Scott Sharpe urgently.

14

The last few minutes of the wait before the gate was called felt like an eternity for Scott Sharpe. He had gone about hiding his face as much as possible for the hours preceding this but all he wanted to do now was to run up to the gate and get in the air. He was one of those people that always felt uneasy about a flight. He never felt comfortable from the moment the doors closed until they opened again at the other end. The worst part of it for him was the landing. If the plane crashed on landing then the last thing he would want was for the last few hours of his life to have been spent cooped up in a small seat on an aeroplane, which in itself followed a few hours pacing up and down a small terminal building waiting for things to happen. If the plane was going to have issues then he would much rather it was on take-off so he didn't have to endure airline food, airline staff and other airline passengers before his demise. And he'd love to see the headlines the day after. Sharpe always had a thing for wanting to know what others felt of him. The headlines after his death, assuming there were headlines, would be the perfect way to know exactly what people thought of him. Like the story surrounding Alfred Nobel and the negative obituary that prompted him to start the peace prize, Scott wondered if there would be words in there that would make him think he should have changed his ways. He gave up thinking of it all when he remembered that there was nothing he could have done about it.

He decided that the best way to kill time was to actually do something, so Scott Sharpe walked to the paltry arcade section and looked for a game to play that would take up some of his time. His grandmother always told him that a watched pot never boiled, and this was the same situation. He was watching time and it barely moved. The plan was to do something that took up time so he could rush to the gate and get on with his new life. He saw a shooting game and thought that might test his skills. It was one of those where you wait for the required images to pop up on the screen and then aim and fire to get rid of them. Every now and again something else popped up that you were not supposed to shoot, usually outlined in green, the colour that supposedly indicated friendliness. These games always choose their baddies and you get to choose from dinosaurs, pirates, monsters, military or something more sedate like animals. On this occasion, it was criminals and Scott played the part of a cop. He didn't feel at all home in the role and it wasn't long before he 'offed' several of the green-outlined characters that he had been sent to save. The game was over in a few minutes and Scott stood considering whether to put another 50p in the slot and continue, start again or just leave it.

He decided to leave it. He was never much good with a gun, anyway. A sword was far more his type of weapon. Scott had been part of the fencing team at university and reached a high standard before packing it up with all the rest of his university life after three years. He moved back home, lost the little contact he had with the people he studied with and just got on with his life. It was as though the three years spent at university were just an interlude. But the fencing always stayed in his blood. Whenever the Olympics made their way round on a four-year cycle, he would watch the fencing intently and try to imagine himself as part of the British team. His theory in life was that we can all achieve if we stay at it long enough. As others fall by the wayside and let life get in the way, then those that remain form the backbone of the British team, the Austrian team that he was watching at the last Olympics or any of the other teams. If he had stayed with the fencing then he was sure that he would be on that Olympic team and others that had given up would be watching him. Sharpe had no doubt that he was very skilled with a sword. Back in his university days he could make a hit without the other person even knowing it had happened. He imagined what it would be like if they didn't wear the protective suits.

After a few moments of looking at the screen blankly, he heard a voice.

"Excuse me, mister. Are you going to play on that?"

He looked down to where the noise was coming from and saw a kid that he estimated around eight years old. The child had unkempt hair and clothes that he had obviously chosen himself for the day without any parental input. That's what it was like when travelling with kids. Anything for a quiet life. "No, I'm finished. Are you old enough to play on that?"

"Yes. I've got my money here."

Not quite the question he asked, but Scott didn't want to draw any attention. He looked at his watch and saw that the gate would be displayed soon. Scott left the arcade and looked for the nearest information screen. They flicked between adverts and information so he knew he might have to wait a while. Advertisers were evidently more important than passengers in the modern airport. He wandered across to a screen that he had seen earlier in the darker corners of the terminal, and decided might be the best place to check out the flight times. It was hardly an untouched piece of the terminal, but was much quieter than any other. By that time there was a lot more light shining through as the sun rose overhead, so Scott walked the long way round to ensure there was no attention on him. He felt self-conscious even walking the extended way around when all the other passengers were congregated in the middle of the building, passing through the light and smiling at each other as they prepared for their holidays or trip home. But he wanted to remain as anonymous as possible for the next few minutes until he could feel the wheels of the plane lift from the runway and off into the air.

The gate was displayed as number 18, and a quick glance to his left told him that it was five minutes away. There was 45 minutes until take-off, so Scott banked on giving it ten minutes and then making his way to the gate. By his rough calculations, this would put him in the middle of the set of passengers and he could sit down while all the fuss of boarding an aeroplane was happening. What he would do at the other end was still up in the air at that time but the first step of the journey was always the hardest.

Scott walked along the small corridor towards the gate, the plane and his escape. He looked around the terminal one more time before he left the main part of the building and didn't see any sign that he was being watched. The terminal was now awash with light from above and many of the occupants had donned sunglasses to counter this. Scott thought this was the start of a holiday. The first time you put on sunglasses was when the holiday began; the last time you took them off was when it was all over. People were spending time eating, drinking and shopping rather than looking at the news. One aspect of going on holiday was to get away from it all, and Scott could see people focussed on each other rather than the news they were leaving behind. He took a deep breath and walked on towards the gate. A new life was waiting for him.

As he showed his boarding pass and passport at the gate to the airline staff, Scott noticed that there were a lot of staff present. He was used to flying in and around Europe and hadn't seen quite so many staff all in the same place. They were stood behind the gate, just leaning against the wall and chatting to each other. He put it down to the fact that it was a flight over the Atlantic in a bigger plane than he was used to and there were bound to be more people working on that flight. Scott recovered his passport and boarding pass and started to put them into his hand luggage as he walked. He didn't notice the woman who has taken them from him had turned around and was signalling to the two men chatting that this was the passenger they were looking for. As Scott stepped forward towards the plane, the two men blocked his path.

"Scott Sharpe, there are a few people who would like to speak to you." He flashed his badge. Sharpe dropped his bag and thought about running but realised his run was over. He said to the men, "where are we going?" but neither answered. Scott Sharpe took off his sunglasses.

15

The car journey to the police station was slow going. It was July and there was summer roadworks everywhere. All the local councils go their new budget in April and were afraid that if they didn't spend all they were allocated the year before then they would see funding cut. So, the summer was always the time of year when the streets were littered with patched up holes and men sat by the side of the road reading a newspaper in a transit van. Getting the road budget spent early was a priority. This was only matched in March at the end of the year when councils were frantically trying to use up the last pieces of cash on small projects. Where they went the rest of the year Scott had no idea. Curiously for the situation he was in, his main concern seemed to be what had happened to his luggage. Even though he had just thrown anything in the suitcase, he didn't like the idea that the case and its contents were making the trip to the Bahamas that he was supposed to go on. He asked the driver several times but the only answer he got was that it was taken care of. Sharpe hadn't a clue what that meant. It felt like he was getting the silent treatment. He had been on enough training courses to know that people like the police and interviewers used the power of silence to prompt the other side to fill the holes in the conversation with chatter. The idea was that they would offer up information more easily if it wasn't directly sought. The police left little to chance with this. Neuro Linguistic Programming and other specialists were hired to train their officers to use their words (and lack of words) to elicit the answers they needed. In the modern world of measures, getting a confession half an hour earlier would free up at least 2 officers to carry out other tasks in that half an hour. Every minute counted. Scott Sharpe wasn't about to play their games and decided to get some rest.

Once inside the station, he went through the routine of having his pockets emptied and his belt taken away from him before being escorted to a cell. The desk sergeant asked him for the name of his solicitor ad he paused for a few seconds before naming the solicitor who was on the board of Britain Excelsior. His ties with the organisation were shaky to say the least, and he had no idea what Jeff Caine had been saying about him behind his back but he had known Cal Green for a long time and thought he could trust him. The desk sergeant made a call and then told Scott he would have to wait for a while. Once in the cell, Scott sat on the edge of the seat to think about what to say to the police. He wasn't sure he wanted to give them anything.

16

Augustine Boyle had been told that the suspect was in custody and that he would soon be able to speak to him. Augustine didn't work well when he was hungry so he decided to go and get something to eat while waiting for the solicitor to arrive. He had dealt with Cal Green in the past and wanted to be totally ready for the tricks he was capable of. Cal Green wasn't corrupt, as far as Augustine was aware, but he didn't make it easy for the police to get the information they needed. Augustine was going to have to be on top of his game.

He went over the road from the station to a small café that many in the force used. In fact, it was so frequented that criminals were known to avoid it just in case they spilled some information to a whole bunch of police officers all at once. Augustine knew that many of the people in there switched off when they were not on duty. The conversation was about the football match the night before, the latest events in the Big Brother house or what they were eating rather than any conversation about the crimes they were investigating. Augustine liked it as a place to get away from his work for a short while.

"August, come and sit with us," called a voice from the back of the café and Augustine placed his order at the counter before joining the voice. There was a table of three. One face he recognised immediately, while the other two were new to him. The face that he recognised matched the voice that he thought he heard. Augustine didn't want to sit with him but he was one to keep the peace. He had dealt with him before and, although he was an arsehole, he was harmless enough. Most of the crap that came out of the mouth of the cocky colleagues was like water off a duck's back. Augustine sat down and waited for his food. He wasn't going to start a conversation here, but he wouldn't avoid one. That might get the voice thinking that he had something to hide. Then he would never shut up.

"You two," started the voice, "have you heard of August? He's the one that takes on all these cases and then has to let them go. He thinks he can solve the biggest cases on the force but has to crawl back into his shell when he realises that it is above him. Do you know why he is called August? That's because August is the time of year when he first solves one of his cases!"

Augustine wasn't bothered what the voice thought. He couldn't even remember his name, let alone what he did. He just treated it as banter and came back with something that he hoped would defuse the situation.

"Nice one. Is that your one joke for the year?" Augustine replied. He didn't want to get into anything too deep with this prick. He still had Cal Green to deal with and thought this was best approached with his powder dry. If the two new recruits were dumb enough to listen to this guy then they get all they deserve, Augustine thought. "Don't you have work to do? If you are better at this crime-solving business than me, then don't you have people to arrest?" Augustine could see that the voice was a little pissed off with this and was working out what to say in reply. The slight tension that was building was taken away as Augustine's food was brought over. He put his head down and tucked into his lunch. He pictured the voice looking puzzled and working through his repertoire for a response but if he had managed one, then it wasn't loud enough to drown out the faint music from the radio behind the counter and the light conversation of the rest of the room. Augustine could feel the three others at the table sit back and then return to whatever banalities they were discussing before his arrival. Much of it was punctuated with the voice telling the other two that they should follow him if they wanted to get on. Augustine managed a smile as he fed ham, egg and chips to his stomach. He washed it down with a cup of tea before rising and returning to the station without any further interaction with the rest of his table. He could be like that when he wanted. He had bigger things on his mind. As he walked over the road back to the station, he could see Cal Green get out of his car and walk to the front desk. He knew it was time to talk.

17

As soon as Augustine walked into the room, he could see that there was some tension between the lawyer and his client. He wasn't quite sure what it was straight away but saw it as a way to progress the enquiries. He would ask questions as normal but try to keep an eye on the reactions and body language between the two. He was sure it would give away some clues as to what was going on. He was glad that he had Electra sat beside him; she was the expert in picking up all of this.

"Do either of you want a drink?" asked Augustine after he had gone through the formalities. He always wanted the people he spoke to in the course of an investigation to be at ease. He thought that all that 'good cop – bad cop' stuff was for TV shows only. The more relaxed the person you were speaking to, the more you were likely to get anything out of them. That was his theory, anyway. Augustine wanted to get on with things, but knew he had to build to this. This was one occasion where he had to keep his cards close to his chest, no matter how tempting it was to throw them all on the table and declare that he was the winner. Cal Green was too long in the tooth for that game.

Cal Green was the lawyer of all the seedier characters in town. As soon as a suspected gang member or repeat criminal was arrested, Augustine already knew the answer to the question, "who is your lawyer?" The man who tried to make all of the criminals in town look as innocent as possible was Cal Green. He had files on his clients of all the charity work they had done, the people they had helped and a group of accomplices that were willing to provide an alibi for anyone caught in a sticky situation. It wasn't that none of his clients ever got sent down, but that it was rare and it was a difficult case to investigate. In fact, Augustine and Cal had been in the same interview room together so many times that it felt like they were talking to each other. The different accused sat between them every time changed month by month, but a similar conversation ensued. The words 'no comment' were the most frequent uttered from the mouth of those he represented. But this didn't feel like all the other interviews to Augustine. Cal was flustered and it was obviously something that had been said between the two before Augustine entered the room. He was dying to find out what it was.

"Where were you on the evening to early morning of 1st July?" asked Augustine in the matter-of-fact tone that he had perfected in these situations. It gave nothing away.

"I was at a business awards until 11pm. After that I don't remember. I'd had a few drinks and I probably just went home," replied Scott Sharpe. He could feel the eyes of his solicitor boring holes in the side of his skull. I was obvious to Augustine and Electra that this wasn't the answer that Cal Green wanted him to give. Scott's eyes were twitching. The bright blue flashed on and off like a switch as his eyelids covered and then uncovered them. Electra couldn't take her own eyes of them. He looked like a poster-boy for the political party he represented. It surely wasn't chance that Jeff Caine had chosen him to be second in command. But where had that ended up?

"And how about last night? Where were you last night between the hours of 11pm and 4am?" asked Augustine in the same manner. He wanted to get these two dates and times fixes in the mind of everyone in the room from the outset. The whereabouts of the suspect at these two times was crucial to Augustine. If he could throw enough doubt on that then he had something to go on.

"I went out in the city for a while. I drove around and spoke to a few random people. It is what politicians do, isn't it?"

"Not at that time of night, Scott. That isn't my experience of politicians, anyway. Were any of the people you spoke to prostitutes?"

That set Scott back. He knew that the press had their story about him but for some reason he didn't think that it was common enough knowledge to have reached the police too. He didn't' really want anyone to know anything about it. That was the best way he could keep control of the situation, but when the story got out he consoled himself with the fact that it was only the press. He might be headline news one day but the next, something else would come along and he could crawl back under his stone. The press loved to build people up, knock them down and build them up again. He could do the whole redemption thing in the public eye. He may have more problems looking in the eyes of his wife and kids but he could deal with that in private. But now he knew the police had all the details about his private life, it was only a matter of time before he would discover friends knew all along, Scott thought to himself. He felt in control up to that point. He thought that he could take his time, toy with the police and give the answers that he wanted. It wasn't until his solicitor turned up and tried to tell him what to do that he felt any pressure at all. Now that the detective sat opposite him was asking about prostitutes, he felt like the weight of the world was pressing down on his forehead. He stalled as long as he could but was painfully aware that the rest of the room were looking for him, waiting for an answer. He just wasn't sure what the right answer was any more.

"Yes, they were among the people I spoke to. They have a vote too. You never know when the next election might come along and I need to garner all the votes I can get," Scott replied in a manner that showed he might be back on the offensive again. But it was short lived. His solicitor saw to that.

"I told you before we began that you don't have to say anything. I suggest that your standard response is 'no comment' from now on," Cal Green explained to Scott as if he were a four-year-old that needed guidance to answer the basic questions that were being put to him.

Scott wore a resigned look on his face for the rest of the interview and plainly ignored the instructions from his lawyer. He was open and honest with every answer and confessed that he was a frequent visitor to the red-light district of town. He told the detectives that he had a habit that he had never been able to kick since his charm wore off but his libido didn't follow. He and his wife had drifted apart in the bedroom since they had children. Scott Sharpe treated the interview as though it was some kind of confessional. From the look on his face as he spoke about the number of times a week he went to the red-light district, the amount he spent there and the last time he was there, Electra felt he was absolving himself of all the sins he had carried out. If he admitted to this, then what else was he willing to admit to. She wanted Augustine to go both barrels at him, but just as they got to the interesting part he stopped. He said that he was going to go outside and get a cup of tea. He offered Scott and Cal the same privilege. Both declined. Electra followed Augustine out of the room and headed to the vending machine down the hall. The coffee there was shit and the tea was even worse, but it was wet and warm. They really didn't have much choice without leaving the building. Neither had the patience to stand next to a kettle while it boiled.

Electra took her first sip. She knew just as well as Augustine the number of times Cal Green had been present in the interview rooms, so it was no wonder he declined when offered a drink. He probably tried it once years before and still had that horrible taste in his mouth. She knew it was a difficult taste to remove but wanted to keep Augustine company and find out what the hell he was doing walking out when it just got to the interesting part. She had resisted the temptation to try to keep him in the room. She had even bitten her tongue when they got out into the corridor. But with a fresh cup of, well something, in her hand she took him to another vacant room and closed the door behind them.

"Gus, what the fuck?" she cursed. She hated to swear but he had made her feel like they were letting him slip through their fingers. Especially with that slimy lawyer in the room with him. He was probably briefing Scott now to keep his mouth shut for the rest of the time they had left. Cal Green knew the way that the system worked and could get his client out before they had enough time to get the answers they wanted. Questioning the suspect the first time was always far easier. They were often not expecting the questions, would not have had as much time to prepare their answers and didn't have slimy bastard lawyers like Cal Green in their ear for weeks before. She knew that and Gus knew it too. She was desperate to get their killer and draw a line under this.

"Something doesn't feel right," Augustine slowly replied as though he had to put a great deal of effort into putting those four words together in a coherent format. He was looking out into space as though he was trying to grasp something that wasn't quite real. Electra was confused but let him have a few moments to reach out for the thing only he could see before trying to start the conversation again.

"Gus, he feels perfect for the killer. He has a sex habit that wouldn't be out of place in a porn studio and has sent threatening emails to the man we found murdered this morning. Not only that, we caught him trying to leave the country without his wife even knowing that he was at the airport. He doesn't sound innocent. He doesn't feel innocent. Even if you take that lawyer out of the equation, he still looks guilty," she spoke in rapid fire in direct contrast to the laboured speech that Augustine was delivering.

"So why is he so open? Why is he telling us all the things that lead us to believe it is him? Guilty people don't generally do that. Guilty people who have Cal Green as their solicitor definitely don't do that. And we haven't even asked him about Jeff Caine yet. It doesn't make sense," Augustine bounced the words off the wall as though they would make more sense to him when out in the open. He wasn't looking at Electra and she wondered if he even remembered if she was in the room. She kicked the desk just to remind him.

"You saw it in there," Electra volleyed back. "He was confessing to his sins. It was like he was bathing in holy water the way that the light returned to his eyes when he told you of his habit. He wants us to know that he is guilty. He wants us to know that he is done."

"So why did he run?" Augustine used this sentence to end the conversation. Electra knew him well enough to understand that it was pointless going any further. Once Augustine Boyle had made up his kind it was always going to be made. He had to finish the interview and go through the motions but even if Scott Sharpe would confess to everything, which was incredibly unlikely now they had left him alone with the lawyer, then Augustine still wouldn't be convinced he had the right man. She followed him back to the interview room.

As soon as Augustine's backside hit the chair he began speaking again. But to Electra it wasn't the same man in the chair. He was asking the questions but without the same level of inquisition or clarity as before.

"What was your relationship with Jeff Caine like?" Augustine started. He had moved on from the prostitute and towards the celebrity politician in much the same way he lamented the attention of the press. He was just like them, he scolded himself. But he was too far away in terms of thought to even be upset by the realisation he was the same as the rest. He wondered if they were wasting their time questioning this guy when the real killer was probably still out there plotting the next one.

"I understand that you have had dealings with Mr Caine yourself detective," Scott retorted as he looked towards his lawyer. This time Cal gave him nothing but a smile that displayed he was pleased with the answer.

"I'm not sure how that is relevant, but I have dealt with him. But nothing on the same level as you."

"Then you will know how difficult he is. When you last dealt with him did you leave with the feeling that you wanted to hurt him? He left most people with that feeling. Over time he left me feeling like I wanted to hurt him more. But kill him? I don't have it in me."

Augustine was taken aback that Sharpe had gone straight at the subject. Earlier in the interview he seemed as though he would dance around the houses all day. Now he was taking the conversation along to the conclusion when Augustine wasn't quite sure he wanted to go there.

"You have sent him emails threatening the exact same end he came to overnight. Does this feel like a coincidence to you? I don't believe in coincidence Scott. I live in a world where the most likely person to commit a crime usually is. I have done this for some time now," Augustine continued saying the words that suggested he was pressing a suspect for details. But there was little tenacity in those words. Electra knew he was resigned to going through the motions.

"I can see why you have to question me over the death of someone that

I have fallen out with spectacularly. But the simple fact is that I didn't do it. And I don't know why you have brought my liaisons with ladies of the night into this. I am assured by my lawyer that this has nothing to do with the death of Jeff Caine and I will be making a formal complaint," Sharpe announced as though it was a matter of upmost importance.

Augustine and Electra looked at each other. Was this a bluff or did he really have no idea a prostitute died with a connection to Jeff Caine? Electra thought the former while Augustine thought the latter. But no matter how much he tried to listen to his doubts, the evidence looked pretty damning against the man he was sat opposite. He was suspected to have frequented the woman who was found in the alley. He was known to have a preference for his paid sexual conquests to be wearing a suit and he had told the man they found dead that very morning that he was going to kill him.

Augustine cut to the chase to test his theory of innocence. "You have visited this sex worker many times before, we believe. She was found dead with similarities to Jeff Caine. I have to say that you are the only person we are speaking to in connection with this. It doesn't look good Scott," explained Augustine as the shadow of innocence washed away from Scott's face. Electra reached over with an envelope. Augustine lifted the flap and removed the contents. He slid it over the desk in the direction of the suspect and his lawyer. The two of them looked at it and then looked away. It was a photograph taken as tastefully as possible that showed the face of the first victim, the girl in the alley.

"Do you know this girl?" asked Augustine in the gravest voice he could muster. He had practiced the voice for years before perfecting it. The first time he heard a senior detective using a grave voice he was impressed. He had spent hours in front of the mirror since to get it just right. He felt as though it was delivered perfectly this time. The practice had paid off.

"Yes, I do know her. I have been to see her. I believe that she was the one that sold my story to the papers. We had an argument…"

"Scott Sharpe. I am arresting you on suspicion of the murder of this woman and of Jeff Caine. You will be taken into custody now," Augustine repeated his grave voice. The only other voice heard before Scott Sharpe left the room was his lawyer.

"I told you to say, 'no comment' didn't I?" Cal Green added in the most unhelpful way. This was a case where he had lost the first round. He wasn't used to it. And he didn't like it one bit. Cal Green muttered under his breath as he left the station that he would be back and that Scott Sharpe would walk free. Augustine didn't hear him. By that time, he was sat back at his desk mulling over the last few days with a feeling that it might not all be over. Although his bosses would be happy that he got his man, Augustine would only be happy when all the evidence was dragged out in court and Scott Sharpe was shown to be guilty beyond all doubt. There was a long way to go before that would happen.

18

The next few days for Augustine were ones where he had time off work. He hated these days at the best of times, but when he had something going over and over in his mind, they were even worse. He was searching for the piece of information that would confirm the suspicions he had about Scott Sharpe being innocent. But without the case notes, the evidence and someone to sound off, it was never going to happen. Augustine had always worked better with others. Even back to his days at university, he didn't thrive when working alone. He sought out someone else to sit and write with whenever there was an essay due. This way he could ask questions, test theories and develop his ideas. He was never quite sure what the other person got out of the situation, but he knew that it worked incredibly well for him. And this continued to his working life. He could ask people what they thought, check some of his theories and listen to how other people saw the situation. This way he could develop his thoughts to a point where they felt sharpened to him. They felt as though they were fully developed and ready to use. Without the benefit of conversation and discussion he didn't have a lot of faith in his theories. With the light of discussion thrown on them, he believed in them totally.

But over the first two days away from work he wasn't able to do this. The ideas came and went. Something at the back of his mind kept on telling him that there was doubt but he never quite saw enough of the thought to draw it to the front of his brain. He gave up on the third morning and went into the office anyway. It was as though he was expected. Nobody batted and eyelid when he walked through the door. They knew he couldn't stay away for very long.

"Morning Gus," Electra greeted him without even lifting her head from the work she was doing. She didn't even need to turn around as his gait and aftershave gave him away. After years of wearing a different aftershave every day he had recently decided to settle on a favourite and stick to it.

Obviously that decision meant that his presence was obvious even when he wasn't expected and when the other person couldn't see him. He knew that he would make a lousy criminal, and this just confirmed that for him.

"Morning Electra. Anything new going on?" Augustine replied almost as soon as the last words had left Electra's mouth. He had practiced the small talk for two days so he could get straight to the point.

"With the Scott Sharpe case closed we have been assigned new investigations. Nothing quite as interesting as that one looked, though," Electra explained thinking that Augustine may have let go of his grip in Sharpe's innocence over the previous two days. She was partially right. He still had nagging doubts but was willing to concede that he was guilty if he could have a full discussion about it with someone. That someone was Electra.

"Do you fancy a coffee? I know a quiet place where we could talk." Asked Augustine. Electra reluctantly grabbed her jacket. She knew that the only way to get this over and done with was to have the conversation with her boss. That way he could either develop or destroy his thoughts and they could all move on.

It was a short walk to the coffee shop and on the way Augustine made all the kind of small talk that he usually hated from others. He asked how her parents were, if she had booked a holiday this year and how her dating was going. Electra didn't engage with him much. She wasn't bothered what he knew about her, but she understood that all of this was just to pass the time of day. He was neither listening to nor interested in her answers. She wanted to save her breath for the conversation he was building up to. She wanted to get to the coffee shop and put him out of his misery.

When they arrived, he made some joke with the server about a mocho-choca-skinny-latte-ccino and she smiled as though it was the first time she had heard it. Augustine then ordered two real drinks and brought them over to the seat Electra had chosen far at the back of the café with a view out onto the main road. She knew he wanted somewhere quiet and that was as close as they could get at that location. Not that they would discuss anything confidential or controversial, but that they could speak freely.

"I don't know why, but I'm not convinced that Scott Sharpe is the killer. It seems too clean," started Augustine. It was clear that the small talk was over and it was time for the matter in hand. Electra didn't mind because since he walked through the office door she had known this was coming. The wait only increased the tension. The small talk cranked it up another few notches.

"Well, you kind of made that obvious the other day. He fits perfectly.

He knows both of the victims and had a reason to kill them both, if you take the fact that he thought one had gone to the papers about him and the other was ruining his career. He even told Caine that he would kill him. He tried to leave the country in a rush and we only just about got hold of him before he boarded the plane. Nothing else nor anyone else has even been identified as a suspect. I can even tell you that he had shaved off all his pubic hair. Something may not feel right to you, but you must admit that there are a lot of factors that point to his guilt," Electra tied to talk him round. She also knew she needed to listen.

"Only really, really stupid killers send an email to a victim explaining what they are going to do. He doesn't come across as that stupid to me. The emails were a heat of the moment thing, but the crimes didn't feel that way. They felt planned and well executed. If he fires off emails in anger, why does he kill with such calmness and precision. We have found nothing forensic to attach him to either crime scene," Augustine monologued as though he was sat on his own. It was the same set of words that had bounced around his head and his home for the last few days. The difference now was that there was someone there to speak when he stopped.

"People can be cold-blooded in one situation and hot-blooded in another. The calm politician we see on the television obviously has another side in the ranting lunatic of his emails. Why can't he have another hidden side in the cold-blooded killer. Nobody has murderer stamped on their forehead, although it would make our job a hell of a lot easier," Electra cracked to try to get Gus thinking differently. As massive grin came over his face as she said that line. He had heard it from her before but it was never as pertinent as now.

"So, you think I've got the wrong end of the stick?" asked Augustine as he looked deep into his cup of coffee.

Electra wondered if he found the answer in there that had been staring him in the face since Scott Sharpe was arrested a few days earlier. "I don't see any other conclusion to this, Gus."

They drank their coffee while Electra filled him in on the other cases they had been assigned in the wake of the Sharpe case being well on the road to trial. There was still a lot of work to do in the meantime on Sharpe, but it wasn't going to take up their every working hour as it had initially appeared. The other new cases didn't appeal in the same way, and maybe it was that. Augustine imagined a long-winded case where he would get to pit his wits against a serial killer and build a reputation for success on the back of it. All he got was a cheap politician with a sex habit and a grudge. He was surely worth more than this?

After finishing his coffee Augustine decided that a day off was probably the best idea. The case had been solved and he could relax. The idea that Sharpe wasn't guilty of the murders seemed more incredulous by the minute. He could get the rest that the days off were designed to do, but this hadn't happened because of the way the case had preyed on his mind. It was now time to refresh and reload for the next few days. At least stopping the murderer from going about his killing spree early was to his credit. Simple policing and crunching the numbers had lead them to Scott Sharpe. Who knows what the next few days will lead to, thought Augustine. Who knows indeed.

19

Over the next few days, the team gathered the bits of evidence and information they needed to support the case against Scott Sharpe as well as taking on the new workload assigned to them. Where the killings had brought the team together, with the notable exception of Gary, the fact that these were now smaller cases meant that they tended to work on their own again. Augustine had enjoyed working closely with Electra and felt that she had the same feelings. Now they were just two people who happened to work in the same office. He felt lonelier than ever with nobody to work with and nobody to go home to. Maybe he would start with the online dating sites again. At least that gave him something to pass a few hours a few times a week. The days passed and the team just got their heads down. Augustine felt the doubts over Scott Sharpe pass as time moved on and nothing new came up to throw any real uncertainty on his guilt. It probably was him after all, Augustine conceded to himself.

20

This man has it coming. He can't have expected the world to just let him carry on with his way of life. He has to be punished for the way that he promotes greed for some at the expense of others. There are many things in life that have many losers providing the spoils to one winner. The unfairness of modern life means that every now and again one of these people must be singled out and punished. It means that one of these people must signal a warning to the rest of them, even to those that are considering a similar way of making money. The immorality of it all is too much to bear. That is why he is here with me. That is why he is struggling to breathe. That is why he will soon die.

I can tolerate this no longer. His wheezing only reminds me that he is still alive. There is no reason to keep him on this earth. I could not look myself in the mirror any longer if I let him go back to his work, his family, his life. He would cause more pain and devastation to others if I let this happen. It must end here. Now.

21

Augustine was bored. He sat opposite a very attractive woman who he guessed was in her early forties, not the early thirties that she had suggested on her profile. But that didn't matter. She didn't look any older than her claims. It was just when she spoke that she gave away her age. She knew far too much about the seventies then any self-respecting thirty-something would reveal. She also had two kids from a previous relationship and they were about the age that meant she would have been very young when she had them if her profile was correct. She didn't seem the type to have two kids before the age of twenty so Augustine deduced that she wasn't what she claimed to be. The fact that she had mislead him in her profile was of great intrigue to him at first. As someone who tried to work out the reason behind someone's lies for a living he was always interested in the fabrications people told and how it reflected on them. People told the most blatant lies to cover up some pretty irrelevant truths in his line of work. He thought that maybe she didn't think people would check out her profile if she was actually the wrong side of forty. It wouldn't have bothered Augustine. He was looking for a particular type of woman. He wanted someone that was tall, with long brown hair and that worked in fashion. He wanted a replacement for the girl he fell in love with at school and never quite got over. She hadn't fallen in love with him at all, in fact she barely knew he existed. Augustine watched her from afar and fell deeply in love. She left school and went into fashion design and he went off to university with some vague notion that if it was meant to be then they would bump into each other somewhere and live a happy life together. He had lost touch with her completely and regularly searched Facebook to see if he could catch up with what she was doing but whatever that was, it was more interesting to her than updating the internet about it and he had no idea where she was or what she was up to.

So, the one sat in front of him ticked the boxes he was looking for. Her profile stated that she worked in fashion. Augustine didn't know whether he was looking for a replacement or whether he was looking for someone that knew her. After his conclusions about her age, he also didn't know if she actually did work in fashion. But her profile picture couldn't lie. She was tall with long brown hair. But she just wasn't holding him in conversation. After a day at work where he questioned people for a living, he wanted someone at the end of the day to question him, to lead the conversation. But that just wasn't happening. The small sparks of conversation that did happen were all instigated by him. There would be a flurry of interest and answers before it all fizzled out to nothing and Augustine had to make all the running again. She was called Sandra, or Susan or something beginning with an 'S' but Augustine had lost interest completely. He wanted to finish his meal and get home. He wanted to get back to that dating site and look for someone else that ticked ALL of his boxes and didn't twist the truth. He could get someone like that spun him a lie, every day of the week at work. After hours, he wanted something a lot easier.

The conversation had completely run dry and Augustine was looking for something to get it going again. He prayed that the waiter would fall over and spill scolding hot soup in the lap of the man sitting on the table to his right so that the two of them would have something to talk about. But it was evident after waiting for such an event for a few minutes that it just wasn't going to happen, so Augustine went through the motions until it was all over. He was nearing his dessert and from there he could see the home straight. The last few mouthfuls of his main course were taken bite after bite so that he could see the finish line. He felt bad about seeing the meal in this way but consoled himself that he had given it his best shot.

Just as the waitress came over to ask them about their dessert, Augustine's phone rang. He would normally have been tempted to ignore it if the date was going well but that was far from the case. He picked it up and looked at the caller ID. It was Gary. On other occasions, this was another reason to ignore the call but even Gary would be more interesting than this, he thought. He swiped to answer the call and put it to his ear.

"Boss. You need to come to the station right away. He has killed again."

22

It didn't take long for Augustine to get out of the date, pay up and disappear, but not before making sure his date was safely in a cab. He didn't think much of her conversational skills, but wanted her home safe and well. Especially with what now looked like a killer still on the loose. He had been drinking red wine, so decided that a walk to the station, which was only about twenty minutes away, wouldn't be the best of ideas. He ordered a second taxi when she left and saw it come around the corner only a few minutes later. Midweek, the best time to call for a cab, Augustine thought to himself.

The taxi driver was one of those that wanted to talk the whole journey. It was only a few minutes ride but by the end of it Augustine felt exhausted. He was trying to make it clear he didn't want to talk, even pretending to fall asleep at one stage, but the driver just talked incessantly as though it wasn't important whether the recipient of his wisdom was awake or not. Of course, a taxi driver being asked to take someone to the police station at that time of night was always going to ask what it was all about but Augustine just blanked him. When he realised he would get no answer, the driver just continued to talk about the cricket match he watched the night before, the state of the economy or whatever dross was coming out of his mouth. Augustine hardly offered a word and the cab driver hardly noticed. He was probably the perfect passenger in that respect.

Augustine was greeted at the door by Gary, which was a strange sight. It was as though Gary was excited by the potential of events yet to unfold. Augustine had worked with him long enough to know that there could well be an ulterior motive behind the smile and greeting. It didn't take long to find out what that was. As they walked the corridor to the briefing room Gary started.

"Fucked that one up didn't you Boyle? While you have one man charged with the murders, you have let someone else die. I was going to say someone innocent, but this one is a banker. Nobody believes that they are innocent of anything anymore," Gary sneered the words through his teeth. Augustine thought that he was practicing a ventriloquist act the way he contorted his face into a flat shape that wouldn't give away the fact that he was talking.

"I had my doubts, but yes, I went with the rest if you in believing that it could have only been Scott Sharpe that committed those murders," replied Augustine.

"The rest of us? If you look carefully at the notes, my name isn't mentioned in there once. To anyone looking from the outside, and believe me they will, I wasn't part of this shambles. That was entirely up to you and the rest of your precious team."

"Gary, I'll personally make sure that everyone in the force knows that you were involved even if I have to drive around the country and speak to each one of them myself. You'll be in the reports, don't worry about that." They reached the door of the briefing room and found that all but Electra were there already. The two sat down in absolute silence among the rest of the team. Gary sat with a big grin on his face just looking around the room like he knew something they didn't. Augustine found the preliminary forensic report on his desk and looked through the details that were contained in it. The report looked pretty much identical to the two others that he had read when looking for the same killer. No evidence left at the scene, a clear cause of death and a single letter left on the chest of the victim.

"It's not Scott Sharpe. Someone ring that bastard lawyer and get his slimy ass out of bed and down here. If I've lost my evening then he can lose his too."

Gary was more than happy to pick up the phone and call Cal Green. He had been in the station so many times that they had his mobile and home numbers as well as the one at his office. He told Gary he was only too pleased to come to the station and wanted Augustine Boyle himself to release his client to him. Boyle would have to suck this one up. There was a bigger issue at hand. The team were all assembled when Electra walked into the room. He would brief them on the scant details he had already received and then they would go together to the scene of the crime. It was almost exactly half way between the alley they found the girl in and he headquarters of Britain Excelsior, where Jeff Caine's body was left mutilated. Maybe that was a sign. Maybe the fact that the body was found at the back of the Museum of Innocence was significant. But the scene that was waiting for them was far from innocent. They spoke briefly as a team and then went to the museum.

23

Augustine decide to travel with Gary this time. He felt that some supervision might bring him in line. Too many times it had been too easy to let him go about his business in his own way. Too many times Gary had gone missing in action and left the rest of them to pick up the pieces. Maybe if Augustine shadowed him for the next few days he might find out what Gary was up to and what his problem was. Maybe. They sat in near silence in the car. Augustine was processing the events of the last few days but all that kept cropping up in his mind was the date that he had just endured. He thought about how he could rate her on the site without causing her any upset. It hadn't gone well but there was no need to put her down. His phone beeped. It was a message from the dating site. She wanted to meet him again. How would he get out of that one? Augustine was fine when it was his job, but he always felt a lot more nervous in social situations. At least he had something else to think about. The car pulled as close as they could get. It was nearing midnight and the museum had been closed for several hours. Augustine decided that they should park in nearby street as not to draw attention to anyone passing by that there was something going on. Gary almost collided with the kerb as he threw his car to its destination. Augustine held out his hand towards the dashboard as a natural reaction. Gary saw him try to pull his hand away and laughed.

"Boyle, you are easily scared for a cop," Gary sneered as though it was another victory for him. Augustine conceded that he was probably right.

"Let's go and see what the museum has for us today," chirped Augustine as he tried to make light of the situation. He had told himself that he wasn't going to be dragged down into Gary's way of speaking to people. He would just ignore the barbs and pretend he was working with someone nice. That was the plan, anyway.

They walked across the deserted street to the side of the museum to be greeted by a security guard. He was a huge man of around six feet seven and looked like he worked out twice a day, but the man looked broken. He was shaking as though he had a fever and his eyes were reddening. He had been the person to find the body on his normal rounds to make sure the perimeter of the museum was secure and free from the druggies that frequently jacked up in the alleys behind the museum. At one stage, they started installing security cameras to monitor the activity but there was simply too many dark areas and places to disappear from the view of the CCTV to have everything covered. It was far more efficient to have to guards, and have one walk the perimeter every hour or so. It kept a presence and they could work together if needed. One on the outside of the building, and one with access to the security cameras that were installed. It had worked fine to that point, anyway.

As they walked around the left-hand side of the building as you faced it, the guard explained what he had been doing in the moments before his grim discovery, the one that had so visibly shaken him. He was wearing one of the high visibility jackets that seemed to be compulsory in the security industry over the top of a black uniform from head to foot. Augustine wondered if a lighter uniform might have rendered the fluorescent yellow jacket unnecessary. The man wore steel-toed boots as though he was going to need protection on that part of his body more than any other. If there was a reason for this then Augustine wanted to know what it was. But now was not the time.

"I was half way through my checks. John, the other guard was talking to me on the radio about the price of fish and chips in the local area. It wasn't very interesting but when you have worked the same shift with the same guy for years, there is little new to talk about. I did notice in the alley that there were a few bags of rubbish left. It happens every now and again. I think it is the local takeaways that don't want to pay to have their bins emptied. Christ knows how much that would cost them, a few quid a week I suspect. So, I moved them to the top of the alley and I was going to put them in the bins as I finished. I never know what is in them and I want to get straight back and wash my hands afterwards. A bit of a cleanliness freak, I confess. There are the bags," he explained as they walked past three black bin liners that were stacked one on top of the other ready to be taken to the large bins that were now situated at the front of the building. Augustine assumed that they were ready for collection before the museum opened, in fact before the rest of the city had woken from its slumber and started to go back to business again.

The guard continued, "I'll get rid of them when we come back out. My name is Steve, by the way." The rest of them nodded at Steve. He stooped as though they would find it difficult to see him with all his height. "I turned back after moving the bin bags and started to walk to the far corner of the building. From there it is only a few more checks before I could come back, get rid of the bags and be back inside again. That was when I noticed something that I first thought was moving. It must have been the breeze that rustled his clothes or something. I don't know why I thought he was moving, so the first call I made was for an ambulance. I thought if there was any movement then there might be a chance he was still alive. But when I took a closer look…." his hands shook. Then his whole body. He took a deep breath and continued, "the lady on the end of the phone told me she would call the police as well. They arrived together and I showed them back here in the same way I am showing you. The man from the ambulance was only here a few seconds. The body was a body and no longer a person."

As he finished speaking they reached the far corner of the museum. The guard asked to be excused and walked away. It was clear to Augustine that he had seen more than he wanted already and just escorted the police there out of duty rather than any desire to follow those footsteps again. The team all looked at each other before stepping closer to the body.

The body on the ground had been killed and cut, but it wasn't clear whether the cutting had been done before the killing or vice versa. It was clear that it was a man, but there was little else to give away the identity. The face had been cut in a horizontal direction around six times. Two were deep. There had been some teeth pulled and the blood from the gums was all over the bottom half of the man's face. He was wearing a suit of some description, Electra thought it looked expensive and she knew a little about fashion and a lot about spending money on clothes. The man's fingers had all been cut off and were scattered around the body like a garnish to a meal. It was as though their killer had started to enjoy his work. Close to the museum was a body that was arranged as though some sick mind believed it to be a work of art.

"Don't throw those bags away," shouted Augustine to the guard as he walked back along the alley at a snail's pace. Augustine Boyle had a thought that they might contain some clues. Best to leave the crime scene as it was. Not just the part that forensics had marked, but the entire alleyway. He'd love to close the whole museum, but knew that was a reach too far. Augustine hated the fact that they had a Museum of Innocence in a town where he saw so little innocence. Even those that were killed were more often than not far from being without their flaws. He had opposed the plans from the museum from the very start, quite vocally until his bosses put pressure on him to remain impartial. If he went for the jugular now, then he would be accused of bias. The end of the alley was as far as he could go in terms of protecting the scene. He asked one of the forensic team that were left when the body would be removed. He had some time. The rest of the team were sent out to take a look at the surrounding area, Electra was assigned to accompany the security guards to look through the CCTV footage while he grabbed a forensic and opened one of the bags. The contents of the bag were all connected to each other. Not the takeaway rubbish that the guard expected. They all led to the identity of the man laid at the end of the alley. Dental records confirmed that early the next morning.

By this time, the word had got out and there was a growing crowd assembled at the front of the museum. The fact that several police cars had arrived at the building with an ambulance and then some activity along the side of the museum had been reported on social media and this had been given legs by the quick way of sharing news. Augustine scanned the scene. He found it disturbing. It was like the masses that gathered to watch people thrown to the lions in ancient Rome or those that assembled at the stocks to throw rotten food at a criminal. But they wouldn't be able to see the body. People were congregated so they could tell their friends on social media that they were there. This was another reason that Augustine spent as little time as possible on social media networks. It was full of people who wanted the rest of the world know to know that they were close to danger or celebrity. It didn't impress him. He was sure it impressed nobody except the vacuous. As Augustine surveyed the area directly around the body just to double check that the forensic team had been as thorough as he would expect, he heard a voice shout out from the crowd.

"Detective, what did you find back there?" the voice came from the middle of the crowd and it was in dark shade, so Augustine couldn't make out where it was coming from exactly. He looked intently but knew it was a futile act.

Augustine stepped forward and tried to make out the place in the crowd where the voice was emanating from. The voice walked along the back of the group of people to shout out something else from a new location. He knew exactly what the detective had found in the alley. He had been responsible for the body.

"Detective why haven't you solved the growing number of murders in the city?" he shouted from his new vantage point. He wanted to play with the detective that he saw in front of him. The voice was deciding whether he would want to involve the man he had come to learn was called Augustine Boyle in one of his future killings. He was deciding if Boyle would live or die at an unspecified point in the near future. He circled back to where he had just come from. The voice looked carefully at the surroundings. He had already seen the other detectives disappear to where they had been sent and looked over his shoulder for any other police in the background. He had one more thing to say before he left. There was nobody to be seen.

"Detective, what is the meaning of the letters left on the chests of the victims?" he said as he began to walk away from the crowd. It would have been a throwaway comment but for the fact that these pieces of paper hadn't been released to the press.

Augustine ran towards the crowd of people at the end of the alleyway. The details about the letters left weren't in the public domain at that point and he looked across the crowd as he ran. If the man who had shouted knew about the letters then maybe he knew something about the murders. Augustine rushed to the crowd but there seemed to be nobody who knew the identity of the man who was shouting towards the detective. By this time, he was back in the shadows a street away. The voice had decided that the games he had been playing were not enough. He wanted to toy with the lead detective. But he now knew that any spectators to a murder investigation would be watched carefully. He knew this was probably his one and only chance to decide whether he was going to kill detective Augustine Boyle. He smiled as he made up his mind. The decision made him happy.

Augustine knew that he had to follow the voice. There was only one possible direction that he could have escaped in and not be seen. The street across the back of the crowd was long. If he had run left or right, then Augustine was sure he would still be able to see him. It was early in the day and Augustine was deprived of sleep, but the adrenaline kicked in and he started to run towards the road directly behind the crowd. There was no traffic. The police cordon had seen to that, so he got his head down and sprinted. Augustine had some catching up to do. As he reached the end of the first building on the road, Augustine noticed that there were scores of options for the voice to disappear into. Even at that time of the morning, he could have access to buildings, given the right code or pass. There were more side streets and alleys appearing with every stride. Augustine though that the voice would try to get as far away as possible, so kept on running hard along the same street. It was only when he was starting to flag that Augustine spotted someone else running about 100 yards in front of him. By this time Augustine was breathing heavily and had nothing extra left to pick up the pace. He opened his stride in an attempt to maintain speed and concentrated his vision on the man squarely in front of him. Augustine regretted wearing work shoes as the heels banged on the paving slabs underneath his feet. This would alert the runner if got near. But he had no choice but to keep chase.

The voice looked over his shoulder and spotted Augustine behind. He quickly darted right at the next intersection and crossed the road into the shadows. It wasn't the ultimate in protection, but made it much harder for the detective to see his quarry. Augustine took a deep breath as he turned the same corner, desperate for one last effort. But as he turned right, he saw nothing. There was nobody in sight. There was no movement that caught his eye. This could go on all day, he thought before deciding that he should head back to the museum. Augustine had defeat etched all over his face as he stood back over the body. He could feel the sweat running down his back and his heels ached from running hard in the wrong shoes.

Augustine looked back at the letter 'L' laid on the chest of the man on a small square of white paper. It wasn't as pristine white as the letters left on the other two victims, but the body had been attacked in a far more brutal way. There were etches of red seeping through the paper but the letter was unmistakeable. It was another message for the police. But what could it be? Augustine sighed and swore under his breath. This hadn't ended. He only hoped it wasn't just the beginning. He had to do something to break this cycle of death.

24

"What we have here is someone that wants to fuck with us," Augustine raved. He wasn't at his best on no sleep at all and the events of the last 24 hours were catching up with him. He had a headache from the lack of sleep and the last of the red wine leaving his system. From the museum, he had returned to the station to release Scott Sharpe into the ready arms of his lawyer. The fact that the transfer from the prison had taken longer than expected, even in the middle of the night with no traffic on the road, meant that he had to sit in a room with Cal Green for far longer than he wanted. Cal made no attempt to hide the huge grin on his face. Augustine tried to make small talk but the slimy lawyer had only one topic of conversation. He wanted to celebrate the little victory that he had over the detective that he had running battles with over the years. He wanted to rub it in as much as Gary Hole. It was a painful experience but Augustine's mind was working towards the ongoing investigation and where it would go from there. Like the other killings, there was no forensic evidence and no CCTV footage. It was obvious by now that the killer wasn't lucky. He was very good at what he did.

The three bags that were found in the alley were filled with possessions of the victim. There were some of his clothes, bank statements, his wallet filled with ID, bank cards and with a wad of notes. So, they knew it wasn't linked to money. Any self-respecting criminal would take all the cash from a wallet. This killer had bagged it all up with a whole other load of stuff from the guy's life and left it near to the body. And the body told its own story. It was quite simply a mess. The cuts and marks left signified some frenzy but the scene didn't offer any clues to the attacker. How could he kill someone in such a way but not leave a single trace of hair, fibre or anything else that could identify him? Was he a ghost?

Augustine lead the team in their discussions about the investigation. He wanted to know their thoughts on what was going on. More importantly he wanted their thoughts on where to take this next. The voice that shouted from the crowd clearly had some information. Was it time to go public and appeal for some help with this? The murders had been reported in the papers but hadn't really been linked at that time by the journalists. They were diverse people from diverse backgrounds but Augustine and the team of detectives sat in front of him knew the connection. They had a fair idea that the same killer was responsible for all the murders. In fact, Augustine relied on the fact that it was one killer. The thought that there were a group of killers out there made his blood run cold. If that was the case, then Scott Sharpe could have been involved after all, no matter what his instincts told him.

"Boyle there is nothing to go on," Gary shouted in the middle of the discussion. The rest of them already knew this but they wanted to look for solutions rather than wallow in the issues that they knew were already present.

"Gus, he's right. The post mortems gave us nothing, the CCTV images were crap and it seems like the guy that shouted at you from in front of the museum knows more about it than the entire police force put together," Electra highlighted the issue that Gary was trying to put across, but she delivered it with a lot more style and grace.

"So, we need to look at it from a different angle. What are the letters telling us? We now have two victims with the letter 'L' on their chest. They are linked in the mind of the killer. How are they linked to us?" she added with a lot more positivity and direction than Gary. He had left her feeling undermined and vulnerable the last time they had discussed the case and now she wanted to make him feel the same way. Gary sneered at her. She knew she had got to him and looked over to Augustine with a sense of satisfaction that didn't often come around Gary.

But before Augustine could speak, a voice came from to the side of him. He had forgotten that Lou was in the room just because there were louder voices. Augustine hadn't heard what was said the first time, but by the look on the faces of the rest of them, he was the only one.

"I think it is liar," Louis repeated for the benefit of Augustine. "I think that the 'L' stands for liar. We have a banker and a politician. Not exactly the kind of people that are known for telling the truth in the current climate. Jeff Caine has been exposed on many occasions for stretching the truth just about as far as it goes. The banker that we now know as Martin Doggett is one that has made his way up in the bank and was investigated recently for insider trading. It isn't much of a leap to believe that the killer lost money that was perhaps managed by Doggett. I think that these two with the letter 'L' on their chest are being marked as liars."

Augustine stood and looked into the eyes of Lou. He could see the years of experience in those eyes and listened intently as the most experienced member of the team explained why he thought that the letters were a classification rather than a message, as they had previously believed they were being given. While this made a lot more sense than being given a message letter by letter, it also meant that they were no further forward in the investigation. What could they do to protect all liars? Who did the killer believe were the biggest liars in society? How could they protect all estate agents, he thought to himself and chuckled internally? He was as convinced as Lou but it did nothing for the investigation.

"So, where do we go from here?" asked Augustine. He was practical to the extreme and although this was an interesting conversation, it did nothing at all for the way that they were going to catch the killer.

"I say we warn the public. Maybe this is the line in the sand that stops everyone from lying," cracked Ash. He hadn't said anything for a while and thought that he needed to speak up. He knew it wasn't helpful at all, but wanted the others to be reminded that he was still there. He continued, "but seriously, there has to be a way to work this out. A killer with a message that only stays between him and the police isn't really getting that message across. What could he have expected from us? There were no reports of the letter on Caine's chest even though the press got to him before us. If he had any idea about the way we work, then he would at least suspect that we wouldn't make this public. He is so organised in other areas. I think that he would know how we work."

"In that case, the message is for us and nobody else," Augustine and Ash finished the sentence in unison, as though they had been rehearsing it for weeks. But what had actually happened was the two men had thought of the same idea at the same time. It dawned in them both that the letters were for them to decipher, not for the public. It was the only way.

"I think we need some help," Augustine explained to the team. He had someone in mind. It was a fellow alumnus of Lancaster University that he had first met at a party for the great and good that had come out of that institution, a few years earlier. Augustine told the rest of them to crunch the numbers and check all angles. Speak to all the local newspapers to see if someone had been threatening violence or complaining day after day about the liars in society. This may have given them a clue as to who might be angry enough to do this. If Lou was right then this maniac wouldn't restrict himself to just killing. His anger would come out in other ways too.

Augustine picked up the phone and dialled, "Hello. Can I speak to Tim please? Hi Tim, it's Augustine Boyle. You know you said to call if I need your help? Well, I think I could do with a chat. How are you fixed tomorrow morning? Yes, ten sounds great. I'll come to you. We don't want the professor of psychology walking into a police station now do we? It might cause all manner of headlines, especially with a serial killer on the loose. Great. See you tomorrow."

After the discussion and the telephone call, Augustine felt energised again. It felt as though they were making some progress, even if it was only activity at this stage. The enquiries with the newspapers might bring something. It was more than they had already. Augustine spent the next few hours on the phone to different editors that he had befriended over the years in the job. His team did the rest with some of the reporters that the detectives inevitably bumped into when their jobs were focused on the same place at the same time. They might have to be a little exchange of information in return for the details they were after but at least there might be something to go on. One editor said that he recalled something a while back about letters coming into the office regarding the number of liars in society but would have to get one of his team to look into whether it was something they kept hold of or trashed. There was so much coming through, and this wasn't the only nutcase as the editor put it, that they didn't always keep hold of what they received.

By this time, Augustine felt the ordeal of a sleepless night catch up with him. It was two in the afternoon. He had been up since five the previous morning and those 33 hours had seen him do a full day's work, go on a date, have a few drinks, lead a murder investigation and have to put up with Cal Green and his triumphalism. It was time to catch up on some sleep. Augustine asked all the others if they needed anything before trudging off in the direction of the front of the office. He had asked Electra to drive him home and she would pull the car up for him to jump in. He had a couple of short conversations to have on the way out and felt that it was best to meet Electra rather than traipse all over the station or keep her waiting in the meantime. He spoke to his boss, Marie about the mess with Scott Sharpe. She had a press conference later and wanted moral support more than anything. It looked like Cal Green was going to file a complaint and make their life as difficult as possible for as long as he possibly could. She just wanted confirmation that they followed procedure to the letter. He then had a quick chat with his equivalent officer in the vice team to see if they had any more information on the first victim. They had been asking questions regarding this but hadn't found out a great deal when Augustine checked. He then ran through to the front of the building and met Electra. She was ready to take him back home. He was ready for bed. There was little conversation in the car. Electra was deep in thought about what the letters might mean and how they could get ahead of the game rather than receiving a call when a body was found, and Augustine was so tired that he kept nodding off. She dropped him off and he barely had enough energy to close the curtains before falling into bed fully clothed. He stayed there until the next morning. He slept like he hadn't for years. But his dreams were filled with new bodies. The prostitute, the banker and the politician were all present. He was sure they would remain there until he found out who had killed them.

25

"Just wait there, Mr Boyle," said the receptionist at the psychology department at the local university, "I'll let him know you are here."

Augustine looked around. It was typical of a university, he thought, that they didn't even have a system where she could call through to him. While the rest of the world had moved on, this corridor looked like the one that he had sat in during his days at university some twenty odd years earlier. It still had the carpet that looked like it was reclaimed from a pub, the yellow walls (why did universities insist on yellow walls?) and the fittings that looked like they should be in a museum dedicated to 1950's life. Augustine knew that universities didn't want to spend money frivolously but surely a lick of paint and a new carpet wouldn't cost the earth. He waited in a chair that felt like it was the only thing in the vicinity that didn't predate the 1970's and that included all the people he could see. It was exam time so around a third of the university were either deep in study or in deep shit in the exam room. Silence. Nobody leaves in the first or last half an hour. No smartphones or looking across at the paper of the person sat next to you. We shall begin now. And it was party night at the local nightclub for the rest of then, so the 9.30am start that Augustine chose had meant he was on campus well before those suffering from the night before had got up. He had agreed ten o'clock with Tim, his psychology contact, but decided that seeing as he was up, he might as well be early. The worst that could happen was that he would be offered a cup of tea and be made to wait for a short while. But people generally didn't make him wait. The fact that they were told a detective was sat waiting for them prompted most to put down what they were doing and be available. Tim was no exception to this.

A few seconds after the receptionist had returned, Tim followed. He hadn't really lost any of the looks that Augustine had noticed the first time they had met. Added to this he had searched him up on the university website, which by that time had put all the yearbooks online, and he hadn't really changed at all since he was at Lancaster University. Tim was around six-foot-tall with no noticeable fat on him. He had worked out one way or another all his life and this kept him lean. At that point in time it was swimming that took his fancy and he used to get up and swim fifty lengths every morning before coming in to work. It was easy to do on a university campus with swimming pool and sports centre attached so he kept it up. Tim knew it wouldn't keep him interested for more than a year and he would have to find some other way of keeping fit. But in the meantime, he loved to swim.

"Morning August. How are things? I expect not so well if you've come to see me," Tim started the conversation. Augustine didn't reply. He looked at the receptionist who was listening intently to what was going on. He didn't want her to think that he was here for a therapy session. He stood up and Tim turned on his heels and walked back in the direction he had appeared from. Augustine thought this must be the signal to follow and so he did. He looked the receptionist square in the eyes as he walked past so she was fully aware that he knew he was being watched. Augustine didn't really have any idea why he did it, but it made him feel a little better as he walked down the short yellow corridor to the room with the professor's name on it. They walked in and sat down. Augustine looked for a chair that wouldn't look like he was being analysed but couldn't find one so just sat where his eyes were shielded from the worst of the sunlight. As he sat down he felt a presence in the room. He looked over his shoulder and saw the receptionist had followed the two of them. She asked if they wanted a drink. Augustine was going to decline so he could have some privacy but as Tim had asked for a coffee he thought it better if he joined in. Augustine asked for a cup of tea. He had never got into the whole coffee thing and he got a massive headache a few hours after drinking the stuff. He began to speak to Tim.

"We have a killer who is playing with us. He leaves a letter on the chest of each victim. A single letter. At first, we thought it was a message, but one letter at a time that could take forever. We now think that the letters are a code. We think he is classifying his victims in terms of why they were killed. I'd like your input on it, if you don't mind, I'll wait until the drinks are here and then we can look at the photographs. They may take a strong stomach and I don't know if your receptionist..."

"Vera? She's fine. She has seen all manner of things. We aren't squeamish here," Tim interrupted.

"I didn't think I was until this case," Augustine lied. He suddenly felt very guilty about lying to a psychologist. He didn't know if they had some sort of magical power where they could detect a lie. He decided that the truth would be his only currency from then on in. The tea and coffee arrived and Augustine still waited until the receptionist was out of the room and the door was closed before he opened his case and spread out the images of the brutal deaths on the floor between him and the psychologist. The blood stains on the bodies picked up the red flecks in the carpet. The two men studied the images for a few minutes without speaking. The air was thick with concentration. Both men looked as though they were seeing these for the first time. Tim actually was on his maiden run through the photographs but Augustine was searching. He was searching for something that he hadn't seen at the scenes or hadn't picked up when looking at the photographs since. He wanted to see if there was another clue besides the single letter. They offered nothing in terms of the investigation. As Augustine looked at each picture he remembered the location where the body was found. He remembered the smells that had invaded his nostrils and left him feeling sick. He remembered the bodies appearing in his dreams. Tim was looking at the cuts on the victims more than the letters left on their chest. Once he had seen this detail once, it became irrelevant to him. As Augustine had already found, it gave up no clues to the police investigation. It was fascinating from a psychological point of view but needed no further study at that point in time.

"What did these people do," Tim asked to break the silence.

"The two L's were a banker and a politician. The A was a sex worker," Augustine tried to give away as little as possible. He wanted a fresh pair of eyes on the investigation and didn't want to lead Tim along any line of thought. He took a long sip of his tea with his eyes pointed out of the window.

"And I assume that you have considered the possibility that the 'L' stands for liar?" he asked without breaking his stare from the images laid out on his office floor. Images of extreme brutality that showed a killer, if it was only one, that seemed to have no boundaries. Missing fingers and a severed head were only part of the rage he inflicted on his victims. The question of whether these injuries were inflicted before or after death was the main one on the mind of Tim but he didn't dare ask. Augustine decided that the question was rhetorical and didn't answer. He was still sipping tea.

"They could be codes from different killers that are working together. 'A' could have killed one person and 'L' could have killed the two others. Instead of classifying the victims, they could be a means of classifying the killers. Have you thought about that?" Tim enquired. This time it was clear that the question was not rhetorical.

"I don't dare think like that," replied Augustine as he put his tea cup down on the floor next to him. He hadn't quite finished but never really got to the bottom of the tea. He hoped he would get to the bottom of this case.

Tim took up the slack in the conversation, "so, apart from giving you things to think about that you don't want to contemplate, what have you come here for? What do you want from me?" He had plenty of questions, aside from the one he dared not ask, and decided to start with this one. The answer might lead to many more.

"I want to see if you have a breakthrough. I want to know what type of killer..." Augustine paused. It wasn't for effect. His mind had disappeared back to his dreams. He wondered what bodies would appear in them that night.

"What type of killer leaves a note for the investigating police team on the chest of the victim? I would say that the calculated nature of that act mixed with the frenzy that the injuries on these bodies suggest, that you are dealing with a dangerous man. He can be calm enough at times to plan these attacks but wild enough to leave a body looking like this," Tim explained. He considered the question but then drew back from it. He couldn't figure whether it was relevant or just his inquisitiveness getting the better of him.

"His planning goes much further than that. He has left us nothing. There are no traces of fibre, no footprints, no fingerprints and not even the grainiest of CCTV images. It's like a ghost has committed these crimes," Augustine explained in the most pained of tones. He wanted to give his fellow alumnus something to go on. But that wasn't possible. He had laid all his cards on the deck. His grandfather wouldn't be pleased.

Tim stopped for a few moments to consider what he could say next. He felt the pain from August and wanted to deliver some good news but there wasn't much. If the killer was as organised as it appeared then this could go on for some time until he slipped up or the police got lucky. He looked across at the face opposite him. It was like the face of a child that really wanted something. But he couldn't deliver. There was so little given to work with. He could only delver a warning.

"Be careful. This guy could kill for some time and may even become involved in watching you work. You need to watch your back at all times August.," Tim told in a slow voice and Augustine felt shivers run down his spine and into his boots. He knew that this was going to be a case that would affect him personally. And this time it would be far more than lost sleep and visiting corpses in his dreams. This time he had a feeling that the killer was watching him. He had felt it since the day before at the museum and the voice shouting from the back of the crowd. He just hoped the voice would return and watch some of the other investigations if he killed again.

They would be ready for that.

26

The days went by without anything else from the killer. The only hook the team had was the return call from one of the editors that had been asked to look back at the letters the paper was receiving. He had called back only a few hours after first speaking to Augustine Boyle but by that point the lead detective had gone home to bed and the editor wouldn't speak to anyone else. He wanted something in return from Boyle and thought that dealing with one of his underlings wasn't going to give him access to the juiciest gossip. Boyle learned when he arrived back at the station after speaking with Tim that the editor wanted him to call back. He made it his top priority when he sat at his desk. This happened only a few minutes after walking in the door. He first checked that the team were OK. He then scheduled a meeting with Gary to keep him onside and in check. He had neglected to do this as things took a turn for the worse and resolved to get him back tightly under his wing again. He knew Gary wouldn't like it but what else could he do?

Augustine sat down and dialled the number. He had no idea why he insisted in using the landline when he walked around with a mobile phone in his pocket all day but it felt right for police business. It felt formal. It felt as though that was the way he should be working.

"Hi Sam, I was returning your call. Do you have something for me?" Typical Augustine. Straight to the point. He didn't bother with the small talk and just wanted answers. He had been like it all his life. It was little wonder he turned out to be a cop.

"It could be something, it could be nothing. There is no name or address but we did get a lot of letters regarding the liars in society a while back. All typed on the same cheap paper. It seemed like it was part of a series of rants. They were mixed in with similar rants about people being amoral. Who uses the word amoral anymore? Surely he means immoral?"

There was a short pause at the other end of the phone before Augustine said, "I'll be right over." And he put down the phone. Gary would have to wait. The editor didn't even get a chance to ask what was in it for him. Perhaps that was where Boyle was going, to dig up something juicy for him. He would find out when the detective arrived at his office. He guessed by the rush in Boyle's voice that he would see him within the hour. He was half right. It only took Augustine Boyle half an hour to knock on his door and take a seat. And he had brought with him another detective. Much nicer to look at than Boyle, thought the editor. Why can't I get visited by more police that look like this? He added.

In the meantime, Augustine had collared Electra and got her to drive the two of them to the offices of the newspaper. They were a striking old building that had been used by newspaper in one form or another for over a century. The Daily Gossip, as this one called itself, was the latest and didn't use all of the space to its fullest. The last occupants had moved out well over ten years ago and had sold all the presses at that time. With the digital age, this was no longer necessary and the Daily Gossip sold more copies online than they did in the newsstands of the city. There was a small parking area at the front of the building and Electra pulled up to be allowed entry. The guard in duty asked their business and Augustine leaned over to explain that he was coming to meet the editor and he was expected. A quick flash of the badge sealed the matter and the guard pointed to a space at the far end of a row of six cars. Electra pulled in and the two of them sat for a few moments

"I've dealt with this guy before and he will undoubtedly want something from us. He won't withhold what he has but it is nice to keep the channels of communication clear. Is there anything that we can give him to smooth things?" asked Augustine. This was one of the reasons he had asked Electra to come along. She was great at this kind of thing. She could come up with an inventive solution while he was still scratching his head.

"Does it have to be about this case? We could throw him a line about something else we are investigating," suggested Electra. She was very protective about the work that they had been doing on these murders. She had seen the post mortems and been first hand witness to the brutality of the crimes. The last thing she wanted was for it to turn into a feeding frenzy for the media, especially the press. The victims deserved better than this. The killer didn't deserve the bright lights of publicity for the sick scheme he was putting together.

"I think it does. He isn't stupid and knows the crimes that are going on in the city right now. There isn't a chance he won't at least suspect I am investigating the series of murders over the last few days. The press is still all over the Jeff Caine murder, especially with Scott Sharpe courting as much publicity as he can," Augustine explained in a way that got Electra thinking. She stopped thinking about how they could hide as much as possible from the editor of the most read trashy tabloid in town and started to think about how they could use the paper to send a message to the killer.

"How about we tell him something that will prompt the killer to be pissed off. How about we talk about his tiny prick and the fact that he killed the prostitute because he couldn't get it up. That might bring him to us," Electra said half in hope and half joking.

"Maybe not those exact words, but you might be on to something Electra. Let's go and see the editor." Let's see what he has for us."

27

Augustine and Electra sat on the floor of his office. The rescheduled meeting with Gary went as well as could be expected and then Augustine spent the rest of the afternoon sifting through photocopies of the letters that had been sent. The originals went with Electra as she and the contact she had in the forensic department checked them against the letters that were left on the chest of the victims. The same paper and the same ink. Not that this was proof that they were from the same hand, as this paper was sold all over the country and the ink was as common as a resolution in January, but it was a sign that there might be a link.

The empty pizza box was shoved into the corner of the room with similarly empty pop cans stacked on top of it. The rest of the team had gone home but these two wanted the silence and the seclusion to look at these documents fully. The letters all had titles that would spell out the contents of each letter before they looked further into them –

LIARS – The politicians that tell us one thing and do another

LIARS- The bankers that become rich off the back of our misery

LIARS – The tax collectors that rob from their fellow man and give to the powerful

AMORAL – Men that sleep with other men and think they can look God in the eye

AMORAL – Women who sell their body to the highest bidder and remain unclean forever

AMORAL – Those who don't follow in the word of God

UNCLEAN – Those that spread their diseases to their fellow man

UNCLEAN – Those that have intercourse outside of marriage

UNCLEAN – Women who pretend to be a virgin to their new husband

Obviously, this guy had a problem with a large sector of society. Augustine and Electra sat on the floor and stared at the letters now they were laid out together. This was all the editor had been able to give them, but he said that there were probably more that had been misfiled, shredded or that members of his team had taken home with them to show their friends or laugh over. It was a tirade that had lasted for around four weeks, with a letter every single day and then it all stopped. There were no requests to put the letters in the paper or threats related to the letters, just a stream of anger and then nothing. From the date of the last letter to the day Augustine and Electra collected them was just over 4 months. The killer, if this was their man, had obviously been angry for some time. He had obviously looked for another way to express that anger and found that it didn't satisfy his obsession. He had then probably gone on to making all the plans for the expression of anger that the pair of them were dealing with at that very moment in time, sat on the floor of Augustine's office at 7.30pm on a light evening.

"We've both had a look at these in general, why don't we take one each and look in detail for any clues that the words might bring us?" Electra asked her boss without it really being a question. She just picked up the one nearest to her and read to herself. Augustine followed suit. Both sat facing each other only a few feet apart but they might as well have been on different planets. Each was lost deep in the words and the meaning of the words that were laid out in front of them. They had both picked up one of the 'A' for Amoral letters because that had thrown the most intrigue on the case. The 'L' for Liars they had started to figure out for themselves, but nobody had come up with the word 'amoral' which seemed quaint and outdated. Not quite the word they would have associated with the killer they were having to track. He didn't seem quaint or old-fashioned at all. His attitudes might have come from times past where sin was observed from every angle but he must have had knowledge of some cutting-edge information if he was to evade the CCTV cameras and kill three people without leaving a trace. Augustine read every word as though it could shine a light on the case and reveal the identity of the killer but they were just the rant of someone who was clearly desperately angry at the way society was headed. All of the letters had been postmarked at the same sorting office in the same city the killings had happened. So far nothing exotic or different was showing in relation to the killings. So, far Augustine and his team had nothing. They knew what they were up against but hadn't the first clue who they were up against.

They both read the letters and the same words were used over and over again. The word 'God' was referenced in every letter, often more than once.

The words 'fellow man' were also a common entry. The feeling that something religious was entwined with this was something that both detectives felt but it was very different for Augustine than it was for Electra. Augustine was brought into the world by parents that knew nothing about religion. They were both atheists that had no interest in the teachings of any religion. They steered Augustine clear of anything religious in his early life and he hadn't encountered much since. He just closed his eyes to it all and carried on as though nothing had happened.

Electra was the opposite. She hadn't practiced religion for well over ten years but her early life was filled with visits to church and reading the bible. She was a regular visitor at church and spent a long time speaking to the vicar about the theological issues that entered her head as she grew up and saw more of the world. The feelings of right and wrong that were an integral part of that discussion stayed with her all her life. She felt that was why she had joined the police and become a detective. She had a powerful sense of what was right and what was wrong. She felt her duty to protect those that were in the right and find those that had done wrong.

To Augustine the words had a distinctly religious feel. To Electra they didn't quite ring true. They were not the words of the religion she had encountered as a child and though her teenage years. The messages of love, hope and devotion that she was brought up on were not present in the letters she had looked at for most of the day. There were religious words included but it didn't feel right to her.

"Gus, this doesn't feel like what we thought it was to begin with. The word God plastered all over these letters isn't the God that I know. I can't see how any mind can take the teachings of my religion and turn it into this. This isn't religion. This is hate," Electra spoke as though her life depended on it. Augustine could tell when she was trying to be her most sincere. He trusted her implicitly and when she spoke in this way, he listened intently.

"Electra, we have to look at this as evidence. All of the signs point one way. But I am listening. I want to believe you," Augustine tried to replicate her sincerity but in his own mind it just felt contrived. He hoped she knew he was being honest.

"We have to do something differently. As it stands we are waiting for him to slip up or give us a clue. People will die unless we break this cycle," Electra continued the conversation as though nothing was wrong. Augustine smiled and watched her lips mouth the words. He took them all in before replying. He wanted to shake things up as much as she did, but they didn't have a lot of options.

"Maybe the article in tomorrow's Daily Gossip might change things."

28

He washed his face in icy water before getting ready for the day. He had read that cold water on the face was good for the health. It was linked to the cold that our ancestors felt when they lived away from the central heating systems and city tower blocks that so many people resided in now. He had something to eat and then left the house for the day. The work that he had carried out over the last few days deserved more publicity than it was getting. He had worked hard at selecting the right people and delivering the right messages but the newspapers and the television people had got the wrong end of the stick. They were reporting that there was some nutcase on the loose that was killing at random. They made no report of the careful selection of the victims, the wickedness that these people had carried out and there was no mention that he had left a single letter on the chest of each. He knew that the police would interfere with his message and try to dilute it, but they had to let the truth come through eventually. Without the clarity of his message the public wouldn't understand.

He left the front door of his house and walked along the short road that lead to where life happened in his neighbourhood. It was as though everything stopped when it entered his street. There were only a handful of houses, and many of these were empty. Some of the others were rented out on Airbnb so the people living there changed regularly. It was the ideal place for him to make his plans and retreat after the murders without fear of recognition or detection. The rent was a little more than he wanted to pay but with the secluded nature of the location he was willing to stump up that extra cash to live in an unturned part of town. The fact that the landlord accepted cash several months in advance meant he wouldn't be disturbed on that front.

He walked down the main street to the series of shops that provided for people in that suburb. The café sold food that he just could not eat and consequently he had never been in there. The florist seemed a waste of time. Why buy flowers that would just be dead in a few days' time? The small supermarket, or was it a grocery store, gave enough provisions for people in the days between visiting the bigger supermarkets that were a car journey or bus ride away. The newsagent was his chosen destination. Since he had first killed, he went and bought all the local and national newspapers every day to see how his masterpiece was being reported. He wanted to get the press working on his behalf to tell his story and appeal to the millions of right-minded people that he thought were ready to understand. They were ready to turn away from society as it was and move with him to a place where people stopped living as sinners. He picked up an armful of newspapers and headed for the counter, where he was served by someone that might as well not have been there. They didn't acknowledge his existence with as much as a hello, an amount to pay or a goodbye. He was sure that he could just pick up the papers he wanted and walk out of the store without the worker even looking up from whatever celebrity dross magazine they were reading but that would draw unnecessary attention. He had to box clever if he was to keep under the radar of the police.

He walked back along the row of shops and ducked back into his quiet street. Only a few moments later he was sat in the living room of his flat with a pile of newspapers stacked up by his right leg. He reached down one by one and flicked through for any mention of his work. It had been a few days since the killing of the banker and by now the press was moving on to other things, but there was still the odd mention here and there.

It wasn't until he got to the Daily Gossip, which was near the bottom of the pile because it made him sick to read it, that he found anything of note. There was a small caption at the top of the front page that read 'Exclusive on the killer loose in our town. Turn to page 5.' He turned the page and almost at once his face turned to rage. He slammed his fists into the arms of the chair and felt something give on the inside. He had only just bought the chair but didn't care what state it ended up in. He hit it several times more just to make sure that the piece he dislodged the first time was well and truly broken.

He read the headline 'Serial Killer Bungles Murders' and couldn't believe his eyes. He hadn't bungled a single thing. The murders were carried out with expert precision. Each person had been hand-selected and had been killed exactly the way that he had imagined and planned before he set out. He had looked at the diverse ways in which people could die. The internet was his research tool, but not the ordinary internet where his records could be traced and everything he did could be monitored. No, that would be a particularly stupid way to set himself up for a fall. He had learned about the dark web from a contact and took it from there. It allowed him the freedom to talk to others, plot what he was doing and find out the most efficient ways to kill. The first was a learning curve for him. After that it was real fun. He enjoyed every minute of watching videos of others taking the head clean off. He found out that he would need to sharpen his blade to make sure it worked in one swoop. He also made sure that the person on the other end of the blade didn't have anything in the way that would soften the blow. No clothing around the neck, hair out of the way and arms under control. That way he could make sure that this person (not victim – they had brought this on themselves by their actions) would be killed with the minimum of fuss in the shortest period of time. It wasn't him that had bungled anything. If there was any bungling then it was done by the police. He had left them a small clue at each scene. He has even revisited one to watch them at play. On top of this he called out to the lead detective to see if he was alert enough to catch him. The bungling was done by the police.

When the rage cleared from his head and he was able to think again, he read through the article. Phrases such as 'victims killed in unusual ways' and 'the lack of a pattern' were supposed to be strong indications that he hadn't planned this out in advance. The fact that he didn't have a pattern was supposed to mark him out as an amateur. It made no mention of the number of people he had killed while the police were no nearer to catching him. Now that would mark him out as a true professional.

He sat and contemplated what he would do next. The plan was to lie low for a few days but he really needed to send out a message. He needed the police and whoever wrote that newspaper article to understand that he was the ultimate professional, that he could carry on with this for years and never be caught. He was monitoring many people all at once to decide who would be next and who would be spared. The anger that rose up in him when reading that article caused him to change his plans. He no longer felt the patience to lie low and let it pass for a few days. His lust for blood was stronger by the minute. He checked his notes on the potential whereabouts of the next person who needed to be dealt with. It followed well that this next person was someone whose movements were much easier to track. He didn't have to wait until he could follow them again. He knew exactly where to find them. And exactly what to do.

29

Augustine sighed as he stepped out of the shower. His date from the other night had been a bit of a shambles from start to finish. But with the persuasion of Electra after they got talking on his office floor only a day earlier, he decided to jump straight back on the horse and look on the dating site for another match. It didn't take him long to find what he wanted. Worked in fashion. Tall. Long brown hair. If he was going to jump back on the horse straight away then he would have less trepidation if it was what he was looking for.

She responded almost immediately with the offer of a date that night. She said that a girlfriend had let her down and she had tickets to go and see a stage show in the city later that night. It was a one-man show and had received some great reviews, the message stated and Augustine didn't feel inclined to say anything other than yes. He knew that if he told Electra of all this then he would be lectured about it for hours on end for the next few days. She had persuaded him to just get back on with it and he just felt this was the right place for him to be. The wet steam of the shower was replaced by the dry warmth of the bedroom as he walked in to get dressed. Augustine Boyle looked himself in the full-length mirror. He had no idea why he had bought it at the time, and even less idea now. It wasn't that he looked in it very often. Perhaps he had a future in mind where he would live with someone who would want or need a full-length mirror. Perhaps he was going to meet her that night, he thought.

He dressed in a suit. It wasn't what he normally wore on these occasions, but he didn't really know what to wear at a show and had a feeling from her profile image and messages that she wasn't his usual type of woman. Something a cut or two above what he had attracted in the past. Maybe this meant she was in high-end fashion. Maybe it would mean he would reconnect with the girl from school that he longed for. He sprayed some aftershave and looked in his wardrobe for a suitable watch to go with the outfit he had put together. Most of his watches were battered and old because he wore them when he was at work. He looked across at one that used to belong to his grandfather and had been given to him after he had passed away. It wasn't the most expensive watch in his collection by any means, but seemed to suit the outfit and occasion better than any other. He imagined his grandfather wearing it to a show when he was in his prime and this was enough to persuade Augustine that it was the right one for the occasion. He had agreed to meet her at the bar over the road from the theatre. He picked up his phone and dialled for a taxi. They told him it would only be a few minutes, but it was more like fifteen. Augustine waited in a seat neat the window so he could see it arrive. And then he jumped into his shoes and walked towards the front door. He always double checked the door before he left. Maybe being acutely aware of the amount of crime in the world had given him a sense that he should double check everything. Maybe the fact that so much of it happened anyway should have given him a 'who cares' attitude instead. The taxi driver said, "evening mate," though the lowered window and Augustine decided that this was a good cue to get in the back of the taxi instead of the front. It might dull the driver's need to talk incessantly, Augustine told himself. He didn't think that it would have any effect at all. He was right.

30

He set off in the direction of the city. Once again, he walked out of his obscure road and headed to somewhere with bright lights, the potential of being seen and CCTV cameras. But he had decided to meet the next person in his plans at this same location. He knew that this person spent a lot of time there. The fact was that his name was splashed all over the building. He knew that there were some grainy-image CCTV cameras if he went in and out a certain way but pretty much nothing if he went another carefully planned route. He followed the path that he had planned and walked over time and time again. He hadn't arranged to do it that night but it seemed as good a time as any.

31

Augustine had already downed a few drinks by the time his date arrived. It wasn't a confidence thing, but he just felt readier for a date if he had started drinking; the dates seemed to go a lot better. Whether that was the same experience for the date wasn't something he ever bothered to ask. He didn't get blind drunk, but merry enough to have a fun time regardless of how things went. Maybe that was what was missing with the date the other night. He had picked her up in a taxi so they both started drinking at the same time. He didn't want to appear as though he was knocking them back so he had drunk at her pace. This meant that he never really got into that merry mood. The effects of one had already worn off before he started the next, like the hospital patient that waited until he was in agony before he asked the nurse for another painkiller.

But this was different. The effects of that date had persuaded him that he needed to have a drink or two. He had only arrived a few minutes earlier than the arranged meeting time but she was obviously running late and Augustine ordered a pint with a whisky chaser so he could get in the mood for whatever lay ahead. The fact was that he was a little nervous about the 'show' that he had been invited to. He looked out of the taxi window as he was dropped off and there were a few places near to the bar they were meeting at. None of them looked like a place that he would have chosen to go, so he was a little out of his element. The solution in Augustine's eyes was a few drinks and a positive attitude. The events at work the previous few days had left him feeling low. One of the reasons he agreed to the date was to put this behind him for a few hours.

As she walked through the door he spotted her straight away. It was what he had been looking for in a date. Unlike the one a few days earlier, she hadn't lied on her dating profile. Or at least it didn't appear that she had lied. Augustine was most pleased with himself and thanked Electra under his breath for persuading him that this was a promising idea. He sipped the last of his second beer and stood up. She must have spotted him as he stood because she walked right over with a little flush of embarrassment. She felt conspicuous that he had stood for her, but the rest of the bar were enjoying themselves and hadn't really noticed, not that there were many people inside.

"Hello, I'm Augustine. It's really nice to meet you."

"I'm Christine. We can be the -ine's together," she replied in a way that put Augustine off his stride. He had expected to lead the conversation and the fact that she had made the first quip wasn't what he had anticipated. He cursed himself for not going on enough dates as this would have given him some warning that he wasn't in charge. This wasn't work, he had to remind himself. They both laughed. It was nervous at first but there was a break of tension too.

"I'd like that," he said as though it was an invitation that he could call her in on at any stage. She smiled to cement the laugh they had already shared and sat down. Before she touched the seat, she shot up again.

"I'm sorry, I forgot my manners. Do you want a drink?" she asked Augustine while looking him in the eye. He always found this reassuring. After dealing with so many people that told him a lie during the day he missed eye contact. He only really got it from his colleagues. She was refreshing to him and he warmed to her charm without delay.

"I'd love one. What are you having?" he asked. She looked at the empty glasses on the table and wondered if he had chosen a table that hadn't been cleared or if he had had a drink or two before she arrived. Not that it mattered.

"I'll have a beer. Is that what you've been drinking? What do you recommend?" she asked by way of finding out if he had needed a drink to calm the nerves. On a first date, she was always looking for the little signs that gave away what was going on. It was all part of the game.

"I've had a beer. The Nastro Peroni is good, but I've had a San Miguel. It always reminds me of the sunshine on holiday. Sometimes we need a bit of sunshine no matter what time of day," Augustine replied in a way that sounded as though he needed cheering up. It hadn't been his intention but was probably the effect of the work he had been carrying out. And the frustration that he wasn't able to resolve the situation. He hated loose ends but left too many of them in his job. That was why he was visited by the bodies of those he couldn't help in his dreams. Augustine tried to smile to counter the effect of the words he had just uttered but it made him feel even more pathetic.

"I'll get the drinks," she said as she walked over to the bar. He hoped that he hadn't set things off on the wrong foot after a promising start. He really liked her. The bar was quiet and she was back within two minutes. While she was gone, he contemplated how early in the evening he should ask about the show. He was incredibly curious about it but didn't want it to sound as though he was having second thoughts.

She sat down next to him rather than opposite and Augustine caught the smell of her. She had the mix of perfume and cleanliness. It was obvious she was in the shower only a short while before she left and the clean smell was still on her skin. He took a surreptitious breath and looked across the bar. He wondered if people would look at the two of them in this strange seating pattern but again the bar was minding its own business. He took another breath as he looked across to her. He muttered 'thank you' for the drink and then waited for her to start the conversation. He thought that after the way she had spoken when she first came in that it might be best if she led and he followed. A few seconds passed. He thought that she might say nothing and his vocal chords would be paralysed. What a night it would have been then. But relief was close at hand. The silence literally only lasted a few seconds but it could have been ten years for the way Augustine felt about it.

"Do you visit this part of town often," she asked. It was what most cities would call the theatre district but there were only a handful of them and they were scattered around. He knew what she meant.

"I don't really know enough about culture. I only come here for work usually," he replied. His profile made it clear he was a detective, but he could have been detecting almost anything for all she knew.

"Well, we have a treat in store for you today. Someone I went to college with puts on a show a few times a week at the place straight over the road. It's a one-man show, or you might call it a one-woman show. Whatever you call it, he starts in about half an hour. Then if you like, we can go and see him backstage afterwards. He has given me these tickets and he would be most upset if I didn't attend. That's why I invited you," she explained. By this time their chairs had moved apart a few inches so they could both see each other while they spoke. Augustine felt more comfortable with this arrangement but missed the smell of her.

"So, what does he do?" Augustine asked with the innocence of someone who hadn't picked up on the hints Christine had given him when explaining. It was amazing how perceptive he was during the day compared to how naïve he was at night.

"He sings, he dances and he works the crowd. I'm sure you'll love it."

32

He walked the route that he had planned and monitored over the previous few weeks. Nothing looked or felt any different to the last time he had been through a rehearsal. He has plenty of time on his hands so walked along the routes to the scenes of where he did his work several times a week to make sure that nothing was there that would cause him any problems. He was looking for new CCTV cameras, regular police patrols or obstacles that would slow him down in his escape. It was part of the masterplan. The more he knew about an area, the easier it would be to get in and out without fear of capture or detection. That was his theory anyway, and he hadn't been caught so far.

The night was just starting to show signs of appearing. It was one of those summer days that cooled off to give some respite from the intense heat that had been before and was sure to come again the next day or maybe the day after. He had taken the printed letter from his wall and had this securely in his pocket. He would need this after the killing. He would need this to show the world that he was professional and not the bungling killer that the Daily Gossip had portrayed him as. He would show them.

He had some time on his hands and didn't want to appear as though he was hanging around so he walked most of the route back home again before turning on his heels and starting back on the same journey. He was excited about getting on with his work and found himself outside the building much earlier than anticipated. He must have walked at twice his rehearsal pace with all the excitement. He was going to have to kill some time. He had around an hour, so just sat in one of the dark alleys near to the building. He was sure that he wouldn't be disturbed there. If he was seen then he would probably be dismissed as a junkie or drunk and left to sleep it off. He sat and waited with his eyes closed and thought about the task ahead. He knew in his mind that he was ready.

33

Augustine and Christine crossed the road hand in hand. He knew it was early days but she grabbed his hand and he let her. It felt more like a mother leading her small child across the road than anything romantic or physical. But it felt good to Augustine. The mix of the alcohol, the night air and the physical contact that had been missing in his life for so long all joined together to give him a sense of being. Outside of his work he often felt like he didn't amount to very much. He just filled in time until he was on his next shift. But with Christine he felt alive and wanted to milk it for all it was worth, even if it was only for a few hours one summer evening. The theatre they were approaching was lit in neon pink. This matched the image Augustine has made in his head when she was explaining the show. Even with scant detail he could picture the neon pink. Even when he didn't really know what the act was, he thought that there would be a lot of neon pink. He mainly pictured it inside the theatre as an assault on his eyes when he was trying to concentrate on the show, the person sat next to him or whatever else entered his mind. But the fact that it was all over the building desensitised him to it. He was so taken in by the display of colour that he no longer thought that the same colour on the inside of the building would have the same effect on him. He was now kind of looking forward to the show and prepared himself by resolving to drink no more. As soon as the air had entered his lungs when he left the bar, he could feel the effect of the alcohol in his system, on his inhibitions. He wasn't drunk, but he was more than merry. He wanted to be able to remember this in the morning, especially if she went back online in a few days and told him that this was only a one-off. The potential for this being a single experience inspired Augustine to imprint the tiniest details on his mind. The noise of a car as it passed behind them when crossing the street. The look on a woman's face as he first saw the neon pink, maybe it mirrored his own. The smell of garlic from a dozen restaurants further down the street – Indian, Italian, Mexican and more.

They went through a side entrance to the theatre and bypassed the small queue that was forming along the front of the building. She showed the man at the side door her tickets and he smiled and stepped to one side to let them both through. He added an "evening, sir," to Augustine as he walked by but it was so fleeting that he didn't have the time to respond. He was already bathed in a pink glow that signified he was into the main lobby of the theatre. It felt as though it was another way to awaken his senses to supplement the alcohol and fresh air. He stopped in his tracks and just stared at the bright display that was nothing like any he had seen before. Augustine wondered if this was what every theatre was like. He couldn't believe that he had reached this point in his life and this was his first experience. He hadn't even been inside a theatre as part of his work. This truly was the first time he had stepped foot in one. He wasn't sure whether he would do it again.

By this point, Christine was a few steps ahead of him and looked back in silence as he took it all in. She wanted to rush to their seats but just couldn't bring herself to stop his amazement. It was like watching a small child walk into Disneyworld for the first time. It was as good as the show for her, she could have stood there and watched Augustine all night instead of going through to where the actual performance would be starting in around twenty minutes. A huge grin snaked its way across her face and mirrored the smile that Augustine had since she sat next to him in the bar earlier. As he looked around at all of the colour, razzmatazz and symbolism, Augustine caught sight of his date and quickly remembered what he was there for. He skipped a few steps to her side and then asked where they needed to go next. She enquired if he needed a few more moments to take it all in but he declined and they joined hands again to walk through to the seats she had been given by her friend. They were great seats. Not too far back but not right at the front. She wanted to take it all in and a seat to near the front meant she couldn't see it all at once. Her friend knew this from conversations they had in the past and had selected the seats himself. He wanted Christine to have a great evening. He would invite her backstage afterwards and tell her his news. He had met someone and they were going to emigrate to Greece. They had found a home there and they could keep a few lambs, grow olives and spend a perfect life together. This was going to be one of his last shows and he wanted his friend to be there. He wanted her to know how happy he was.

"These are our seats. Do you like them? I'm sure I can get them changed if not," Christine asked.

"You know far more about this than me. I'll go with the flow. Is this the best place to see the show from?" Augustine replied more out of courtesy than with any interest. He would have taken it all in from any seat in the room. He was happy at that time to see what he had let himself in for. His curiosity had taken over and he now wouldn't miss this for the world.

"I think these are perfect. They are the seats I would have chosen myself if I had the chance. You get to see it all," Christine explained to Augustine who she noticed was now looking around at alternative locations. He was the type to assess every angle and her offer to re-seat them had got him thinking. He was also a planner. He wanted to know here the fire exits where and how easily he could escape if there was an issue. Not that he foresaw one, but it was always good to know how to get out of any situation. He was the type that still listened intently to the instructions from the crew at the start of a flight. He listened to the number of emergency exits and always made sure he knew where the nearest exists were in case he had to evacuate. His time in the police had taught him that almost anything can happen and those that were prepared would stand the best chance of survival. By this point he noticed that Christine had already sat down so he joined her. The seats had plenty of room but she was draped over the arm that was between his seat and hers. He loved the way that she had no inhibitions about close contact on a first date. He was under no illusions that this meant anything, but he loved her touch and her smell. It had been far too long since he had experienced this from anyone.

The lights slowly started to fade and then the loudest boom sounded the start of the show.

"Fuck!" shouted Augustine. He had just sunk into relaxation with Christine when the noise came as a shock. His natural reaction was to curse and then he went bright red because he seemed to be the only one in the whole room that had been surprised by the noise. Maybe it was because this was his first time in a theatre. Maybe all shows started like this. Maybe everyone else knew that it was coming. Christine was laughing so much that a single tear ran down her face and collected in the folds near her mouth. She was enjoying herself too much to wipe it away. Augustine felt his embarrassment wash away with her laughter and joined in. He was determined to make the most of the evening.

The music began and the curtain rose to reveal the silhouette of a single figure at the back of the stage. It wasn't clear at that point who the figure was or what they were going to do. They remained perfectly still for ten seconds, twenty seconds, thirty seconds before they started to dance with the music. At that point, the dancer still hadn't left the back of the stage and was some distance from the audience but Augustine could see that they were a talented dancer. He and Christine swayed with the music and movement. Augustine looked to his right and saw that another couple was doing the exact same thing. It was mesmeric and all eyes in the room were firmly fixed on the dancer. They still had their back to the audience but was moving closer all the time. The music was accompanied by singing and as the dancer turned around, Augustine and the whole audience were completely captivated. The figure on the stage filled the eyes and ears of the whole room. He was giving his all because he knew it was nearing the end. He wouldn't do this anymore. He spotted his friend in the audience a few rows back in the seats he had secured for her and a friend. A tear welled up in his left eye and those with a good ear for it could detect a slight trembling in his voice for a few words but the professional came out in him and he resumed his show in his normal style. Just a little bit louder, a little bit stronger and a little bit more emotional. He wanted to finish in style.

As the break neared, the singer dedicated the last song before the interval to his dear friend Christine. By this time, Augustine knew the artist as Betty Black and he was proud to be sat next to Christine as she smiled and blew a kiss to the performer. After he finished the song, the lights came on in the audience and a flurry of people left to visit the toilet, get another drink or just stretch their legs. Augustine and Christine let the others get up and go. They chatted while they waited for the queues to die down a little and then they would go and do whatever they needed to do in the interval. Augustine felt the pressure of the drinks he had in the bar on his lower abdomen and knew that a visit to the toilet was in order.

"That was beautiful of your friend, of Betty, to dedicate that song to you," Augustine started the conversation as people milled all around them. Christine was crying.

"It doesn't feel that way," she replied. Until that point, Augustine had thought that the tears were those of happiness. But maybe he was wrong.

"Why is that? It seemed really touching," Augustine tried to make her think happy thoughts. He wanted the date to be a contrast to the unhappiness he saw at work all day long.

"I've been to see his show many times before and he has never dedicated a note to me, let alone a song. It feels like he is trying to tell me something. It feels like he is saying…" Christine paused. She had a horrible thought in her head but didn't want to let it develop. She certainly wasn't going to let it out in the open where it could grow as an idea and become reality. "The queues for the exits are disappearing. Shall we head out now," she said as though the sentences before hadn't ever existed.

"Let's," said Augustine. He wanted to say nothing but thought it rude. He settled for a single word instead. As the two of them walked towards the exit from the hall and back out onto the neon pink lobby they both were thinking about what was going on. Christine wondered if her friend was saying goodbye. It certainly seemed that was to her. If he was, then what was the reason? Was he ill, was he leaving or had they fallen out? She didn't know what to think. She needed to see him after the show. He had invited her backstage, so she was not far from finding out. Augustine was thinking about whether the performer would spoil his date. He was having a wonderful time up until then but now faced an evening with someone who was clearly upset. Maybe another drink would help. Maybe that would be the worst thing he could do.

34

He knew time was about to deliver him another body for his portfolio. He was about to show the newspapers, the police, the public that he was organised, disciplined and able to deliver what he promised to himself. He knew the way into the room he needed to occupy. He joined the cleaning staff as they entered the building away from the lights and people of the main street. The crew changed so much as they were employed by a contract company so nobody thought anything of the new guy following them into the building. But he didn't stay with them for long. As they walked to the cleaning store to get their mops, sprays and cloths for their work that would start soon, he disappeared into a dark corridor. He would only need to stay there for around a minute, by his calculations until he could enter the room he needed to be in. Then he could sit and wait for his next victim. He could wait until they came to him. As a figure walked past, he heard a noise from the other end of the corridor and knew this was the time. The door had been left ajar and he walked in and chose his spot. In the shadows so he couldn't be seen; close to the door so he could stop his victim from escaping. Now to sit back and wait. It wouldn't be long.

35

By the time Augustine and Christine, the two -ine's, had taken their seats the music was just starting up and it was clear that the second half of the show was imminent. In the break, they had both gone in their opposite directions to the toilets before meeting up again at the bar in the far corner of the lobby. Augustine was still undecided whether to have another drink when she returned. He bought a Jack Daniels and coke for her and a coke for himself. He made sure the barman put them both in the same type of glass so it wouldn't look as though he was a lightweight. He then sat back with Christine and readied his mind for the second half of the show. Now he knew wat he was letting himself in for, it felt like he should be prepared.

"So, what do you think of it all? How is your first visit to the theatre?" she asked him in a teasing way that made him feel like an outsider in someone else's world.

"It was really good. I loved it. Your friend is very talented," Augustine replied as though he was a theatre critic for the school newspaper. He had nothing insightful to say, but felt as though he should.

"He has been doing this for long enough. We met at uni and he was heading down this path then. I used to make costumes for him, but he never wore them outside of his own room. He had the talent then but not the confidence," Christine recalled. Augustine wanted to know more but knew they didn't have a lot of time.

"So, you can say that you started his career?"

"No, not really. He never wore the costumes I made in a show. I couldn't persuade him to come out of his shell. That was down to someone else."

Augustine could sense a jealousy in her statement Someone else had managed to do what Christine has tried and failed. He didn't think that was something that happened very often in her life. She was a set-your-mind-to-it type of girl. He admired that in a woman more than he could say. It was the girl that got away when he was in school, it was the promising detectives that outgrew him and moved on to pastures new when he had taught them all he could.

"But he must respect you. He has given you tickets and dedicated a song to you. It is clear that you mean a lot to him," Augustine tried again to steer the conversation in the direction of the positive. He hoped that she would put her worry behind her and be the woman that had taken his world by storm only a few hours earlier. She smiled. It was a vacant smile as though it had been conceived a long time ago in a distant place but it was a smile nonetheless. Augustine was satisfied.

"Ladies and gentlemen, can you please take your seats for the second half of the show," the announcement came over the speakers and the moment was gone. The smile was lost, Augustine was confused and Christine got up and walked aimlessly towards the entrance to the hall. Augustine jumped to his feet and held her hand while they walked. She didn't fight it but he didn't feel the same level of warmth as before. He hoped that the music and dance would get her back in the mood to be close – and happy.

It took a few minutes, but Christine draped herself over the arm of Augustine's seat again and the closeness resumed. He smelt her hair and skin once more and was taken back to a few hours before when he first smelt them. He was lost in the occasion. The scents of the beautiful woman, the soft music and the strength of the voice of Betty were all hitting his senses at once. He hadn't had a drink for some time but felt intoxicated with all the experiences he was having. The second half of the show was part glitz and part soul. He could see what Christine meant by this being a goodbye. It was like a performer at the top of their game leaving to do something new. Betty was amazing. As the show closed the audience got to their feet and applauded. Augustine didn't know if this was what always happened but it felt as though something special was going on. He held Christine's hand as they sat down. The two of them felt emotionally drained at the end of the show. They sat in silence for a few moments, each deep in their own thoughts.

"He always needs a few minutes to get ready, wind down and dress in a manner that he feels comfortable in with guests. He told me to wait for around ten minutes and then we could come backstage and sit in his dressing room. I'm looking forward to it, but I'm afraid he is saying goodbye. Maybe it would be better if he had already said it on the stage tonight," Christine wondered. From a selfish point of view Augustine wanted to go backstage and soak up the atmosphere. His first visit to the theatre had been exciting from start to finish and like a schoolboy at his first football match, he didn't want it to end.

"I think that if he invited you backstage, even if it was to say goodbye, then that is the way he wants to do it. If you walk away now then you don't get a second chance at this.," Augustine replied half in support and half with his own enjoyment in mind. He knew he was right, though. And so did Christine.

"I never want a good thing to end. I don't want to ever say goodbye," Christine said wondering what it might be that would take him out of her life. She was living in the same city as him but hadn't seen enough of him recently. A pang of guilt entered her head. She looked at her watch to see how long she had given him. It wasn't nearly long enough.

"Wherever he is going in the world, you will be able to just hop on a plane and see him. There isn't a goodbye any more on our planet. Travel and the internet have made it too small for that," Augustine consoled her.

"But what if where he is going isn't on this planet," Christine spat out the thought that had been bugging her all night. Augustine was thinking the same thing but hoped that his date hadn't cottoned on to the fact. He was wrong. She got to her feet and walked towards the centre of the stage. She had been to see Betty backstage a few times before and had always just wandered through the curtain and walked around until she found where he was. The first time she knocked on half a dozen doors and found all manner of people getting ready to clean up, practising for their act to come on to stage the next day or that had been working on the show. After a few trips, she sort of learned where Betty would be sat and how to find him. Augustine followed as though he was on duty. Walking to the areas of a building or scene that others didn't normally enter were all part and parcel of being a cop. He developed a sense of scrutiny in these areas, especially places that had served him food and drink. Augustine wanted to know that they kept the highest standards. His stomach demanded no less from them. But as he realised that the catering facilities were in a different part of the building he switched off again and followed his date. He was transfixed by her and the narrow corridors meant that they had to walk in single file in case someone came the other way, so he focused his attention on her hair. He remembered the smell of it and was now taken by the condition. It had a sheen that he had never mustered in his own hair, now receding. He debated whether it was in her genes or from a bottle. Maybe he would get to ask her what gave it that shine if they went on another date together. It didn't feel like a first date question.

They dodged a few people who were busy sweeping, carrying what looked like laundry and generally looking busy. Augustine could tell by the way she rushed that Christine was nearing the dressing room that they were heading to. As they made it to the last corner, someone came bunding around it in the opposite direction. He wore a hoodie pulled low over his face and looked down to the ground. It was dark in the corridors anyway and he almost bumped into Christine. He was a muscular man and did knock into Augustine as two of them passed in the narrow corridor. Augustine felt a large bump on his side, but thought nothing of it. Obviously, the man had somewhere to go. Augustine took a quick glance over his shoulder and saw the man with a hoodie on and some gloves, so he was probably one of the cleaning team racing through their tasks so they could get out of there as quickly as possible. Augustine thought maybe he was a cleaner that needed to get a lot done before the end of his shift or maybe he was a stage hand that needed to carry heavy equipment before he headed home. It was already late and Augustine thought that if he was at work at that time that he would be rushing to get it done and get out of there.

He looked forward to where Christine was stood before he bumped into someone and she wasn't there. He panicked for a few seconds before putting his head around the corner. She was there looking at her watch, deciding if she had given Betty enough time to receive visitors. It wasn't her that was the problem. She had known him for long enough to see him in any condition. But the date she had brought with her was having his first experience of the theatre. She felt that it was her duty to make sure he wanted to come back and seeing Betty in a state of undress might put him off for life. There was so much padding and flattening involved in making Betty transform from his male form into the shapely female on the stage that it looked as though he was cutting off bits of his body and attaching bits from someone else. Christine decided that she could wait no longer and headed for the door. If Betty wasn't in the state to receive visitors then Augustine could wait outside the door for a few moments. He'd just have to be patient.

As Christine approached the door, she noticed that it wasn't closed. Betty would be getting undressed and wouldn't want someone to see what was going on, even through the crack in a slightly ajar door, so she wondered whether he was actually inside at all. Maybe he had gone to see someone else for a drink before he came back to his room. He was a sociable animal and always liked to have a wind-down drink after a show. Christine pushed at the open door but it only moved two inches. She looked back at Augustine who was watching over her shoulder. She pushed again but there was only the smallest movement as the first time.

"Betty, are you there?" she asked. There was no response so she asked again in a louder voice. Still no reply. She looked back at Augustine who by now was thinking that he might just have to give the door a hard shove. She stepped to one side and he pushed. The door moved a little further than it had for Christine but still hadn't opened. There was just about enough space for Augustine to get his head through and peer around the corner. He wanted to know what was blocking the door. As he looked down he saw the body of Betty in a small pool of blood with the letter 'A' printed on a square piece of white paper laid on her chest.

"Christine call an ambulance. Get some help. I'll see what I can do," Augustine spoke as though the life of Betty depended on it. But in reality, he already knew that it was too late to save him. He checked the neck and wrist but there was no pulse.

"You're bleeding Augustine. There is blood on your jacket," Christine said as he considered what he might do next. He had been feeling weaker since he bumped into the cleaner in the corridor. He wanted to get up and chase the man in the corridor. Even if he wasn't the killer, he would have been the last person to walk past that room. He would surely know something. He looked at the blood on his jacket and felt a small pain in his side. Augustine felt dizzy and sat down. The room was spinning around him.

36

He opened up his stride. He was sure that the man he passed in the corridor was the detective he had viewed and shouted at when they were investigating one of his pieces of work at the museum. What the fuck was he doing there? Was he following him? Was he on to him? If he had been alone then he could maybe have killed the detective too, but three bodies in one night was too much. Plus, he had only come out with one letter. He had read a lot about killers and they got caught when they started to improvise. The detective and the woman he was with were not part of the plan, so it was best he left them behind. But that was one hell of a bump he gave that nosy detective. He hoped that he would be well enough to receive his punishment when the time came.

He didn't know if the alarm had been sounded. He didn't know if there would be other police officers waiting for him outside of the theatre. So, he waited until he saw someone else leave. He put his foot in the exit door as though he was following but waited for a minute just to see if the person in front of him was stopped. It looked as though the coast was clear so he headed out of the building and back along the route home. He knew that route well and was sure that he could be safe from the prying eyes of the CCTV cameras that were starting to invade every corner of the big cities. The fact that conservation was an important thing in his home city had meant that many protested against these cameras being mounted on buildings that had been in existence for hundreds of years. It was his salvation in many ways and he scoured the planning permission part of the city website to see when another planning application was made for another camera. He would stoke up the passion of people online so that they organised an opposition to these 'eyesores' and kept him with as little surveillance as possible.

But he had some thinking to do on the way home. He didn't know whether to go home and lay low for a few days, or whether that was going to be a risk. He had no idea why the detective was there, but the fact he didn't stop him in the corridor and smelt like he had been drinking was an indication that it perhaps wasn't on business. Was his home now under watch? Did the detective let him go only to be picked up when he got home? He didn't think that this was anything other than a coincidence, but wasn't willing to take a risk. He headed towards his home street but didn't turn down it. He stopped in the shadows for a few moments and looked to see if there was anything unusual in the street. He couldn't see any cars that were not already there and thought that if the police were waiting for him it would be in a car. The risk was too much to take. He started walking again. He knew a place that would offer him sanctuary at any time of the day or night. It was only a few minutes away and he could stay there for as long as he needed.

37

There was nobody in view when he got there. It was past midnight when he arrived and he just opened the door and slipped inside. It was always like that. The door was always open for those that were in need. He found a place to sit and tried as best he could to get comfortable. What he had seen and enacted on someone else that night would be enough to stop most from sleeping for weeks. But not him. It was all part of his work. It was all part of his mission. The person that he finished off that night deserved everything he got. The detective deserved the same fate too.

It was quiet and he knew that he wouldn't be disturbed for hours. Nobody else would enter the same building unless they were in the same need as him. If someone else walked through the doors he would greet them as a kindred spirit. Otherwise he would just get some rest and think about going back home. How long would he need? Would it be safe in the morning? Would he need a few days? Or would it never be safe to return home? His home would give the police all the clues they needed that the occupant was the killer, but very few to his identity. The computer was encrypted beyond anything the police could lay their hands on quickly, but he was sure that they could work on it over a matter of days to reveal some of the secrets inside. The walls were covered with every last detail of his plans. Maybe the police could search though records and link him to the home, but it was paid for in cash with no names asked. There were weapons, but they were immaculately clean and who didn't have a weapon of one sort or another in their home? A kitchen knife in one pair of hands can be used to make a meal but in another pair of hands can be used to kill and maim. A ceremonial sword looks innocent on the wall of a home but can look deadly when taken down from the wall and put into the hands of someone. He was sure that if they were able to connect the property to the killings, it would be more difficult to connect him to that property. He had done his homework. He had carried out his research. He was diligent. At least as diligent as he could be. As he closed his eyes, he saw the detective that he had encountered in the corridor of the theatre. He felt no remorse for his act that night, but couldn't get the image of the detective out of his mind.

38

Christine paced up and down outside the hospital. She hadn't smoked for years but the events of that evening had driven her back to that bad habit that she had carried out from the age of 17 until her early thirties. As she walked up and down the smoking area, Christine tried to remember what made her stop. Most ex-smokers she spoke to had a story that they could tell about what had driven them to stop smoking. For some it was a health scare, for others a close friend or relative that had passed away from smoking-related illnesses, but everyone had a story. She had been in shock so much during that night that she clean forgot what her story was. She racked her brains but the more she tried to force the memory to the front of her mind, the more her brain resisted and buried it deep beneath a mound of other information that was of no use whatsoever.

She had all kinds of thoughts come to the front of her mind but not the one she wanted. For some reason, she thought about prime numbers, an episode of EastEnders she watched about fifteen years earlier and the exact name of the colour of the paint in her living room. But none of these gave her a way in to why she stopped smoking. Why she had started again, only half an hour earlier, was easier to work out. She didn't need her brain to work with her on that one. She was worried about the fate of the person she had accompanied to the hospital. She admitted to herself that it didn't look good. He has been taken there by ambulance with a single stab wound to the side. It had punctured several of his organs and the fact that he moved around after he was stabbed had made the bleeding worse.

A figure walked outside. He stopped and looked at Christine. He didn't want to deliver her the bad news, but she had to know.

"He's gone. There wasn't a great deal that could be done for him. A stab wound to the side doesn't feel like much at the time it happens. People think that they have been punched or just bumped into, and they often don't notice the puncture wound until it is too late. I think that is why I ended up with his blood on me. The man that killed him must have had it on his clothes when he bumped into me," Augustine reached out to take Christine in his arms. He felt like he had a duty to explain to her, but it was more than that. He felt like he had a duty to protect her. To protect all of the people in his city. The murders didn't just affect the person who was killed. Their friends had to cope with the grief. Their family had to cope with a massive hole in their life. The person who finds the body has to deal with that vision. The rest of the city have to deal with feeling less safe in their own home. They make decisions that they don't go out at night, or that they cut back their life in some way. Augustine had a duty to all of the people in his city to catch this monster and make sure that they could go back to their normal life. He sighed as he held Christine in his arms. The trip to the hospital and the attention of the doctors was all just in case. He had already died in the dressing room and there was no real chance of him ever coming back. Augustine knew that from the way that the eyes looked. Although he checked the pulse to make sure, the eyes gave it all away. He had seen so many pairs of eyes on people that had passed away that he knew what they looked like. Show him a pair of eyes and Augustine Boyle could tell you whether that person was alive or dead. If he had found the body on his own, then Augustine wouldn't have made a great deal of effort to try to get him back. Because he clearly meant so much to Christine, he made every effort to make it look like he was doing something. She had a feeling that Betty was trying to say goodbye. But it was never meant to be like this.

They walked inside and he got two cups of tea from the vending machine. He already knew they would taste like shit but they both needed a hot drink. The teas and coffees in the vending machine weren't drunk for their quality, more the fact that they were there. In times of crisis, people reached for a hot drink. It is comfort blanket that makes us all feel better about the world and the worries we face in it. Augustine and Christine sat in the relative's room together. He had been overwhelmed by the evening that had gone before in so many ways that it was difficult for him to take stock. From the smell of his date, to the visual bombardment of the theatre right through to finding another victim of the serial killer. The alcohol, the neon pink lights, the emotion and the blood on his shirt all added up to a night he would never forget. Christine sipped the tea like it was medicine. The taste obviously appalled her, but she took the medicine as if it would do her some good. The two -ine's sat at the end of the night, by now the early hours of the morning, next to each other having a drink. Just like it all began. What went in between was something that both wanted to avenge.

39

"Excuse me…Excuse me. Are you OK?"

He was woken by someone who shook him gently and spoke in the softest tone. It wasn't the best way to wake someone up but as he was found in a chair where he wasn't expected the person who discovered him wasn't entirely sure what he was doing there. He had taken some time the night before to clean up. As much as this was a place of sanctuary and no questions asked, he didn't want to raise suspicions. He didn't visit the place all that regularly but he was bound to know someone if he stayed there for long enough. That was just the way it was in this community. He had washed off the blood from his arm and the little that had got onto the sleeve of his hoodie. There wasn't much, but it would have been enough to get tongues wagging. This was a place he had chosen to be a safe haven. He didn't want to spoil that by causing people to wonder why he was there. The jacket was on the back of his chair and was pretty much dry by that point. He knew that he could leave at a moment's notice and just disappear. But first he wanted to let the passage of time pass. He wanted to be in this safe place and work out whether his home was somewhere he could ever go again. It would take at least a day for him to catch the news, speak to a few people and see if they were on to him. The next day at least would be spent in this place. He looked around. It was a place that he hadn't really been in many times before but it was still familiar. He knew what he could expect in a place like this. He knew that he could sit there, talk to people and pass the time of day. He wouldn't be asked to leave and would be provided with food and water if he needed it. He hadn't eaten much over the last few weeks. He had been in training to operate effectively without the requirement that he ate three meals a day. The research he had done on the internet gave him plenty of examples of people who could survive for extended periods of time in conditions that were alien to modern day humans. Hunger was just one of these. He didn't crave food and drink in the same way that the rest of society did. He just wanted to survive. He had no need for anything other than the replacement of the calories he had burned off. Nothing more.

"Are you OK?"

The voice was still there, stood a few feet away. He opened his eyes fully and sat up from the chair. He had also adapted to sleep in any conditions, so the discomfort of a chair that would stop most from getting a decent rest was no obstacle to him. The only thing that interrupted his sleep was the face of the detective that he couldn't shake out of his mind. He was desperate to know what he was doing there, but his haste to prove something had already nearly ended in disaster once, so he told himself that patience was the key. He knew the voice was about to start again. He could feel the man stood only a few feet away start to prepare himself to speak again. He couldn't bear the same question to be asked again, so he spoke before the voice could ask if he was OK.

"I'm fine, thank you. I just needed some rest. I knew I would be welcome here," he said to explain his presence and prompt for some patience. The voice smiled at him and spoke gently. It was so low that a passing bus drowned out most of what he said. He wondered whether there would be any point in asking him to repeat what he had just said. He knew the drill. He would be told that he was welcome to stay as long as he liked. He would be offered fresh clothes and something to eat and drink. He would be told that he could talk if he wanted to. He wanted none of these in reality, but also didn't want to raise any suspicions. So, he said, "thank you," and laid his head back down on the seat. It would be some time before there were more than the odd one or two bodies in the room and he wanted to make the most of the quiet time.

He nodded off again and tried to look beyond the face of the detective that he had bumped into in that corridor. He wondered if the detective had the same visions in his sleep. He wondered if the detective was thinking about him right now. It wasn't sleep that he got, but he felt rested with his eyes closed in the relative quiet of that room. He thought again about the detective. He wondered what stopped him from getting to sleep.

40

Augustine Boyle sat looking at the wall in his bedroom. He had tried to get some sleep after making sure Christine was safely home, but it just wouldn't come. He was sure that he had been close to the killer that evening. He was now sure that the man who brushed past him in the corridor was that killer, but the fact that he had almost passed out had stopped Augustine from chasing him down. The alcohol, the heat of the building, the exertions to open the dressing room door and the sight of the blood had all worked together to make Augustine feel dizzy. It had come over him all at once, so for a few fleeting seconds both him and his date thought that he might have been stabbed by the fleeing assassin. Thankfully that wasn't the case. The blood on his shirt was nothing more than a stain left by the killer. A stain that would probably never come out. A stain that Augustine wasn't sure he wanted to erase. The blood on his shirt was visible in the early morning light on the hanger that was sat across the top of his bedroom door. He looked at it and thought that the shirt should go with him all the time so that he could be constantly reminded of how he felt when he was holding Christine at the hospital earlier that morning. He wanted to bottle that feeling and use it to lift him when he felt down. Maybe if he took a photo of it on his phone, then it would always be a few clicks away. Maybe.

Augustine wasn't due in the office that day. He had planned his date around the fact he was due a day off and didn't have to get up the next morning. But he was awake, thinking about nothing but the killer and ready to make a difference. He knew the day off wouldn't happen.

Augustine set about getting ready for the day. He stepped into the shower before it had warmed up and felt that the cold gave him a burst of energy. He finished the shower by turning down the dial and rinsing with more chilly water. It wasn't something he had done before, but it gave him a spring in his step that he didn't think possible after the night he had been through. He walked to the kitchen and looked through cupboards to see what there might be. The erratic hours of the shifts he worked plus the number of times he was called out in the middle of the night meant that he rarely ate breakfast at home. He knew that he should, but it just didn't really happen with any regularity. He found some cereal in the cupboard next to the oven and ate it dry because the only thing that resembled milk in the fridge was curdled. He remembered why he didn't eat breakfast at home. Because there was nothing there to eat.

All the while he was eating, the radio was on. The local radio reported that the performer Betty Black had been found killed in his dressing room after his show last night. Augustine listened with one ear to hear if they had any information that he had told the rest of his team to keep quiet. They said very little in terms of detail. Augustine was happy that Gary was on holiday that week and hadn't been there to snoop around and brief his friends in the media. Augustine was sure this was where they got a lot of their information from. But not this time.

He finished off what he had cobbled together for breakfast and then went back to the bathroom to clean his teeth and have a shave. Then he stumbled back into his bedroom to get dressed for the day ahead. Augustine preferred it when he was on the beat. Back then he didn't have to think about what he had to wear. He was just provided with a uniform and expected to wear it. Now he had to make his own decisions. His bosses told him that he needed to be smart, but there was no need for a suit. Without a woman in his life to dress him, Augustine agonised over what message he might be sending out with any given choice of outfit. This got even worse as he got older. He felt as though he was still wearing the clothes that he bought around twenty years earlier. They still fit him, on the whole, and they didn't show any signs of wear so he saw no reason to replace them. Except the fact that he now felt like a forty-something wearing the clothes of a twenty-something. Maybe it was time for a change, he thought as he looked in the mirror. Maybe it was time to buy some new clothes.

Augustine jumped into his car and set off on the familiar route to work. He had driven this same journey at all times of the day and night and in all weather conditions. It was close to rush hour so it took him far longer than he wanted to get to work. With the energy given to him by the cold shower, he wanted to get in to the station, talk to people, hope they absorbed some of his enthusiasm and then get down to work. But the frustration of sitting in the car for longer than he wanted was starting to play on his nerves. Augustine out the radio on. He moved away from the AM stations that he usually listened to. There was going to be too much on there about the murder he so nearly witnessed the night before. Instead he went for the music stations on the FM dial. It was warm so he wound the window down and tried to balance the air outside with the noise that came with it. The traffic was fighting with the music. It wasn't until he came to a stop at the front of a queue of traffic at some lights that he was able to make out the words in the songs that were playing. Some kids crossed the roads at the lights and listened in to the music as it was playing. At that point, Augustine felt older than ever. He felt like an imposter. It was a small sports car, with his twenty-year-old clothes and he was listening to pop music. He wound the window back up and cranked up the air conditioning. He hated to spend money on aircon when he could just wind down the window but he couldn't hide his embarrassment in any other way. Augustine wondered what other men of his age dressed in, what other men of his age listened to and what other men of his age drove around in. The lights went green and he stepped on the accelerator. He wasn't far from the station. He would have bigger things to worry about there.

41

"Morning boss. What are you doing here?" was the first thing he heard when he walked through the door. It was Lou's way of greeting him. Lou wasn't at the theatre overnight, unlike the rest of the team. He had been working late anyway to help out with the investigation into the letters sent to the newspaper. He wanted to speak to the editors that had received the letters and they all worked late shifts to ensure that the paper got the latest news even in its early editions. Lou stayed around to speak to all that had seen the letters. It wasn't more than a matter of routine but he took every part of his job seriously. Whatever task he was given, Lou did it by the letter. He had finished around the same time Augustine was leaving the theatre armed with a set of statements that might come in handy if they ever caught the person who did the killings, and if he was also the person who wrote this abuse.

Lou had seen a great deal during his years in the force. He started out dealing with the smallest crimes and keeping the streets safe. Community policing it is referred to now. But now he didn't spend much time at all on the streets – he didn't know many police officers that did. Their role was to decide which crimes needed their attention. The murder would always see more resources than the theft, that hadn't changed since his day, but now there were so many crimes that were just left. People reported a burglary because they needed a crime number to claim on the insurance, not because they thought that any amount of resources would be put into catching and punishing the person who committed the crime. But Lou carried out his duties in the most diligent fashion. Everything deserved his full attention if he was asked to investigate. If that meant he worked several hours unpaid, then so be it. That was just the way it was. The fact that he was at the station before Augustine was testament to his dedication. Most others would have taken the hours back in the form of a lie-in the next day. Not Lou. He had a murderer to catch.

"Morning Lou. I guess you've heard?" Augustine asked in a weary tone. He still had the energy flowing through his veins but he didn't want to use it all on the first conversation. He thought his might be a long day.

"Yeah. You okay?"

"I think so. I'm too tired to tell really," Augustine pretended.

"The rest of them are here, and Gary is due back this afternoon. Shall we have the meeting then?"

"No. Let's all sit down together now. I can fill Gary in later."

Lou spoke to all of the others one by one and arranged that they all meet around fifteen minutes later. Augustine was ready to get the team going again and they all wanted to know what had happened at the theatre. The first thing they wanted to know was what was Augustine Boyle doing at the scene of the murder, but each was willing to put that to one side and listen to their boss tell about the encounter he had with the killer. He wasn't going to disappoint.

After the meeting, they were all energised and ready to go. The fact that Augustine was so close to the killer, even though it was by chance, gave them all hope. He was out there and active. He wasn't the ghost that they all thought he might have been after leaving no trace at the other scenes. If they upped their presence, got out and about then they too had the same chance that Augustine had of bumping into the killer. The letters sent to the newspaper looked more and more like they were connected to the killings. This victim had the letter 'A' on his chest which linked to the ranting letters claiming that homosexuality was 'Amoral' and linking this victim to the prostitute they had found in the alleyway at the start of the investigation. It followed that the code being used was the same one for all the four crimes that they were linking together. Although there were no more murders that had the same letter left on the chest of the victim, Lou was looking back through murders for the last 5 years to see if there could be a link established. Maybe the killer had grown tired of killing and the link between his victims being ignored or not understood by the police. He could have expected the police to make the links, but when they didn't the killer gave them prompts in the form of these letters. Maybe he had only changed recently to gain the publicity he craved.

The CCTV was down to Electra. Based on the way that the killer had managed to evade CCTV images for the last killings, the whole group didn't leave much hope of finding the murderer by this method. But they went through the meticulous parts of the job as though they would find what they were looking for. The reports were back from the forensic team and once again there was little to go on. Augustine wondered how he did it. The guy was killing people on a regular basis and leaving no clues. He even bumped into the killer and had nothing to go on. The hood on his clothing as pulled so low that he didn't get any view of his face at all. Christine's statement said exactly the same thing.

Ash was sent out to the theatre to speak to all of the workers there. Augustine had spoken briefly to some of them the night before, but they wanted full statements and a longer conversation. Ash was always the right man to do this kind of work. He was enthusiastic and patient, so he could sit there all day and listen to the same story. He was skilled enough to spot the subtle differences in what people were telling him. He knew which strings to pull on that gave him more to go on and which strings would just pull and pull with nothing at the end. Augustine admired Ash for the way he went about this part of the job. All Augustine wanted to do was ask the glory questions. He wanted to know what the other person knew. He didn't have the time or the patience to draw it out of them slowly. Ash was the opposite. He could play all the games that people wanted to play when being questioned by a police officer or detective. He could patiently let them have their little piece of spotlight before pulling the rug out from under their feet. If there was anything to learn from the people at the theatre, then Ash would bring this back to the investigation.

And that just left Gary. He would be back in a few hours and would want to know everything that had gone on in his absence. And Augustine was sure that he would make great hay out of the fact he walked straight past the killer close to the scene of a murder and didn't stop him. Augustine had no fears that he had done anything wrong, but he knew that little prick would try to make him feel bad. So, he had to plan something that kept Gary out of his hair, away from the more sensitive parts of the case and actually working for a change. He wondered what that might be. Then a thought struck Augustine. He knew exactly what he was going to get Gary to do.

42

He had sat in the same seat for hours. The man that had first come and spoken to him gave him food and drink, which he took out of the need to be left alone rather than hunger or thirst. He saw the man leave the room and not come back, which he decided was a good sign. The rest of the day had been his own. All he had was his thoughts. He could access all the information he needed again from any computer in the world, he just had to make sure that the encryption was strong enough to keep out anyone that might want to see what he was planning. There was no issue there, but it felt like he was starting all over again. He wanted to go back to his home and see whether there was any chance of him getting back to familiar surroundings. He wanted to rush back there every time he thought about it but knew that rushing wasn't going to help.

It was in the middle of the afternoon by the time that anyone else entered the room. By this time his hoodie was dry and he had covered his face again. He listened on his phone to the radio news and there was no indication that the police knew anything about who might have killed the performer at the theatre the night before. There was no name, no warning that he was armed, no instruction not to approach. If they knew who he was then perhaps the police would ask people for help. The fact that they hadn't made him feel like he was safer.

There was some movement near the glass doors that were opposite his seat before a man walked in with his head bowed. He looked as though he visited the place on a regular basis, but wasn't there in an official capacity. He let the man go about his business without being disturbed. It took him some minutes to practice what he had visited the room for before he was finished. After he looked over. The two men met eyes and both walked towards each other. They hadn't met before but it felt like they should both go through the motions of speaking to each other and exchanging pleasantries.

"Good afternoon. I've not seen you here before. I hope you are comfortable. What is your name?" The man asked. He looked as though he was just passing the time, but it wasn't certain whether he entered the room with any other motive.

"I'm Al," he said. He decided that the shortened form of his name was as good a name as any to use with a stranger. He hadn't been called Al for a long time, preferring his full name. He had killed enough strangers over the last few days to wonder what their names were too. If anyone asked him from that point on, he would just call himself Al and leave it at that. It was pretty much the only thing he hadn't planned during his mission, an alias, but now he sort of had one. And he had the stranger in front of him to thank. He didn't want to know the man's name so didn't ask.

"Well, Al. You are welcome to stay here as long as you like. Do you have enough food and drink? Do you need anything?" the man asked. It was the same experience as speaking to the other man in the same room earlier that day. He didn't actually want anything but someone just turning up and turning away all offers of help would raise suspicions, even if the suspicions never left their head. Al accepted the offer and took the food and drink that he was brought. It wasn't much but these kind gestures got him thinking about his mission. He had looked at the worst in society and tried to make them stand out in his work as a message to others. He wanted the acts and behaviours that he saw to stop. The only way he could see that happening was to show people the consequences of their actions. If people saw others just like them killed as an act of retribution then maybe they would change their ways. He hadn't seen much sign of it up to that point, but that was his plan, his mission. But sitting in this room he had now twice seen the best of humanity. He had seen people that had never met him before stop what they were doing and get him food and drink. He didn't actually want food and drink, but the act in itself was something that made him feel warm inside. It was his people that were the good of humanity. The others that he had killed did not belong with him. They had to pay the price.

As he sat there, he thought more about his mission. He had identified many people that would serve as a lesson to others. He knew that the banker and politician wouldn't be missed. They had chosen a life of lies and tried to make their money and reputation on the back of it. Even if the press coverage for the first few days was about the nature of the murder, he knew that people everywhere would be secretly thinking that they got what they deserved. But he knew that people would have a harder time in understanding the work he had carried out on the other two. Society loves to blame itself for the problems that people have. The newspapers that gave coverage of the prostitute were full of lament. They wondered how society had let her down in this way. They didn't understand. These were her choices. He hadn't seen the coverage of the man last night, but he was sure that the press would find some way to wash him of all blame. The choice he made to love another man instead of a woman was his. It was wrong. Society had been bent out of all reasonable proportion. Al longed for the days when homosexuality was taboo again. He wanted it all to stop. It made him sick to think about it. At least he had made sure there was one less on the planet last night. Hopefully he could get back to his work again.

He knew that others were trying to do the same thing. He knew that they had the same end in mind as him, but they didn't understand how to pull it off. He would complete his work where others had failed. They had failed in the planning. They didn't choose their targets correctly. They had failed in the execution. His way was better. It would bring the right results.

43

Augustine was looking through the images and statements from the four murders they were investigating when Gary walked back into the office. He had obviously been somewhere hot as he was several shades darker than when Augustine had last seen him a few days earlier. He still had that same look of smugness on his face. Not even the sun could wipe that. He strolled around as though he was still on holiday for a few minutes and Augustine let him. He didn't want to upset him quite yet, but he didn't want him to get too comfortable either. Gary asked a few questions and then had a whispered conversation with Electra for a few minutes. She hated him and he made her skin crawl but she thought he ought to know that there was another murder and one that Augustine was close to while he was away. He huddled down next to her desk and was listening intently to what was being said. A soon as he finished talking to Electra he sprung back up and marched into Augustine's office. He was already in the room when he decided that a little protocol was needed and he stepped back to knock on the door.

"I hear you let our murderer go? Another fuck up by the great Augustine Boyle. I guess you will be leaving this investigation soon? I'm sure they will give it to someone who actually knows how to catch a criminal," Gary spat out all of this in a manner that told he couldn't wait. He didn't have the guile or intelligence to let the conversation flow naturally and go in for the kill. He just wanted to throw everything he had at Boyle. Augustine's grandfather would have a field day at cards with this character.

"Obviously I didn't know he was the murderer when I walked past him, but yeah, I was this close to the guy," Augustine held up his hands before narrowing them, "in fact no, closer. He bumped into me."

"And you still couldn't catch him. Talk about bad policing."

"I was off duty, on a date if you must know, and there was no investigation at the time. What are you trying to insinuate here, Gary?"

"Never mind. I'm sure I'll work better with your replacement."

Although there was never any indication that Augustine had done anything wrong or was indeed going to be replaced on the case, this pissed him off. He wanted every case to go right, even if it was just so he could get some sleep without being invaded by new bodies in his dreams, and the fact that Gary was so openly hostile put his back up. But he played the long game. He held all of his best cards while Gary had thrown all of his down on the table.

"Until that happens, I am in charge of that investigation. And I have a little job for you. One of the forensic team has noticed that the murders have all taken place near to the drainage system. I need you to go down the sewers at the first three murder sites to see if there is anything there. We might be looking for blood, clothing or a weapon. I have arranged for a guide to show you around. You will meet someone from the city's water department outside the front of the Museum of innocence in around half an hour. I'm sure you'll enjoy it," Augustine spoke slowly and drew every possible piece of enjoyment out of the statement. He never took his eyes off Gary while he spoke so he could see his face change from glee to pain. It was worth listening to all his shit earlier. Gary paused as though he was trying to think of something clever to say. It wouldn't come.

"Let me know how you get on," Augustine added as a final 'fuck you.' The message wasn't lost on Gary who was starting to go pale and reduce the effects of his recently-earned tan.

They would all meet and discuss their findings the next day. Augustine was looking forward to hearing Gary tell the rest of the team about his trip to the sewers. That would just crank up the embarrassment and make this assignment all the sweeter for Augustine. He heard Gary mutter, "fucking Boyle," as he left the room. It was the most satisfying curse he had heard in his life. Augustine Boyle rocked back into his chair and grinned. He thought it might be some time before he smiled again after the night before but there it was. As wide as his face.

44

Al left the building the next morning. He had given it long enough and listened to the radio on his phone as much as the battery would allow. There was no mention of him. In fact, there was no mention of any progress at all relating to the murder of the performer at the theatre, so he felt as though it would be safe to at least go and take a look at his house. The police weren't very subtle at what they do, so he knew they would be sat in an obvious car in the street if his home was under surveillance. He left around quarter past five in the morning. This felt like the optimal time as there would be no commuters quite that early and all signs of people coming back from their drink-fuelled night out would have been over for a few hours. He would have the streets to himself. But he felt like this anyway. He knew the CCTV systems well enough to understand how to move around without being watched. He had the streets to himself. He moved in the shadows and wasn't noticed by others that were going about their daily business. He had the streets to himself. He didn't recognise those who carried around their sins as fellow humans. He saw them as an inferior species that needed to mend their ways or be wiped off the face of the earth. He had the streets to himself. He hadn't any friends or family to speak to or share his life with. He had the streets to himself. The narrow road that he called home was almost derelict and had gone unnoticed to the rest of society. He had the streets to himself.

Al walked past the end of his road. That was part of the plan. The first step was to look like he wasn't headed there at all. He wanted to look like someone who was going somewhere, even though he was clearly the only person that was going anywhere at that time of the day in that part of town. There was a car in the street opposite his home that he didn't recognise but it looked like nothing the police would own. Even with their reduced budgets, he was hard pushed to believe that the police would take out his home in a beaten black Mitsubishi Colt that was losing its trim and was well over ten years old. The disgusting orange/red seats that went with it were another sign that nobody in their right mind would buy a car like this. He walked around a hundred yards past the end of his road before cutting down a side street and doubling back. He now pulled his hood down and changed his gait – his attempt not to look like the same person as he walked back. After killing a handful of people and evading all capture, Al started to believe he had chameleon-like qualities at times. He had even walked straight past the lead detective trying to capture him without being noticed.

As he reached the end of his road, Al looked left and right before crossing. Nothing looked any different to when he was there a few minutes earlier. In fact, nothing had changed for years. It was a forgotten part of town – that was the beauty of it. Even the police had forgotten about his street. Al loved living in absolute obscurity there. The neighbours rarely showed their faces, especially in the early and late parts of the day that Al operated in. He only knew a few of them, even after years in the street. Most were elderly and discarded by society and their own families, it seemed to Al. He didn't ever see people come to visit, or take them out for the day. There weren't many social care visits that he had seen. Local authority cuts had made sure that certain parts of society were just hidden away from sight.

Al felt like he should after two nights sleeping in a chair. He ached and wanted to get home and have a wash. This was the pressing thought on his mind. He decided that if he was being ambushed here, that getting taken to the police station for another night or two without access to running water would be the worst part about his capture. It was making him feel like he would run away from the police just to have the chance to jump into a shower and get clean before giving up.

He slowly walked along the street before his curiosity got the better of him. Al walked towards the Mitsubishi Colt to take a closer look. It was clear that it hadn't been cleaned inside or out for many months, if at all. The trim, the seals and the door handles were all falling away. This gave it the impression of a car that needed a lot of care and attention, where some general maintenance over the years would have stopped it ending up in this sorry state. As he got closer still it was clear that there was no one inside, unless they were very small and stooped in the foot well. He breathed a sigh that was half relief and half confirmation that he was right all along. Al planned every step of his operation and didn't like to leave anything to chance. Now that he could see that the car was empty he was ready to move on with his plans again. There was nothing else for the police to hide in, nor anywhere else for them to wait as far as he was concerned. He was stood looking straight at the rear window on the passenger side of the car when he heard a screech of tyres behind him and a flash of lights caught his eye. Al was stunned to see a police car roll around the corner and pull up between him and his home. The officer inside didn't get out. His window was already wound down and he leaned as far out of the car as possible. It was still very early in the morning and he didn't want to shout over the hum of the engine. Al didn't want to make this any easier for him. He was looking for a way out. He considered killing the police officer, running out of the street and trying to see if he could jump start the Colt all in a few seconds before deciding that he would wait it out. He had been caught on the hop once by the police arriving when he thought he'd avoided them. The last thing he now wanted was to act rashly and find out that there were more around the corner.

"Is this your vehicle, sir?" the police officer asked in a voice that gave nothing away that he was suspicious. Al guessed this was all part of the training and he could ask any question in the world like this. If he turned up at a scene where someone was stood in a pool of blood with an axe in their hand, Al was sure that he could ask "have you used this axe recently, sir?" in a similar manner.

"No, I've never seen it in our street before, which is why I was taking a look," Al replied, trying to emulate the police officer's way of sounding neutral. "I suppose people can park here and walk to the city if they like. It may be a commuter."

"The only people up are the likes of you and me. It's a bit early for a commuter if you ask me," the police officer continued the conversation even though Al was now thinking about how to get out of it and get away from this part of the world as quickly as possible. The police officer was called Andy Lane. Al wanted to disappear, but knew that would pose more interest that continuing with this conversation – if it was just a coincidence and nothing to do with his crimes.

"I suppose. Is there a problem with this car?" asked Al. He thought that steering the conversation to the car was far more likely to keep it off him.

"It has had a bit of history over the last few days. The car was reported missing around four days ago and then reported as abandoned here last night. It's the first chance I've had to come and take a look. It seems strange that as soon as I turn the corner to look at this reported car that I find someone staring through the window. But you wouldn't know anything about that, would you?" PC Lane was now starting to lose the air of neutrality.

"Well I actually would," Al was great at thinking on his feet and bet from his experience of this neighbourhood that the report would have been anonymous. "I was the one that made the call. I was just checking that I had given all the right details over to you guys. I couldn't sleep thinking about it."

The police officer looked him up and down. There had been no name attached to the report but something didn't feel right about the man stood in front of him. He could well have been the one that reported the car, but the fact that he was stood in front of it when he turned the corner just raised his suspicion level. He wanted to ask a few more questions. The car wasn't involved on any crimes as far as they were aware at the time, but there wasn't a great deal else going on at that time of the morning. It had been a couple of days since anyone was killed and the chief had asked for a greater presence on the streets as part of the reassurance of the public. This was all a part of that reassurance. He wanted to let the people who were concerned about the events know that they were being looked after. He wanted to let the criminals know that they were being watched. Officer Lane felt that was how it went. They couldn't catch the man that was killing all these people on the streets of the city, so the smaller players ended up getting caught for things that they were getting away with in the recent past. The killer was making it difficult for everyone else in the city, not least the petty criminals that usually worked under the radar – or at least only popped their head up onto the radar screen every now and again.

"What concerned you so much about this car then? It looks like any other car in the city. It's bashed up from the busy streets, just parked here, not doing anybody any harm. Why call it in? Why not just leave it? Most people think that the police have enough to do without chasing abandoned cars," the police officer was deciding whether to get out of his car and stand with the man he had found staring into the empty vehicle. He had a sneaking suspicion in the back of his mind that he might try to run, but he wasn't entirely sure why he felt that way.

"It just stands out in this street. We have all lived here a long time and I suppose we don't like anything different coming into our little world. It doesn't belong to any of us, so I wondered why it had been left here. Some cars come and go in a few hours. This has been here for…"

Al slowed as he didn't really know how long it had been there. It wasn't there when he left to deal with the entertainer in the theatre. It could have arrived at any time after that.

The crackle of the police radio interrupted him anyway. The police officer disappeared back inside the car and listened intently to what was being said. From the outside of the car Al could pick up the odd word.

"…break in… damage…city centre….immediately…"

"I'll get it taken away," the police officer said as he drove off. The fact that some low-grade criminal had saved the man who the whole police force was chasing with a passion was not lost on Al. He laughed all the way from the car to his home. He walked back to his room and laid down to sleep, but not before having the shower that his body and mind had craved for some time. It was a restful sleep. For Al, this encounter confirmed his belief that he was in total control. It confirmed to him that the police were no closer to knowing who he was then when this all began. The brush with the detective in the corridor outside the performers room was coincidence after all. He could begin his plans again. This time he would not be rushed.

45

After dealing with the break in, the police officer, Andy Lane, spoke to the transport department to get the vehicle towed away and taken to the impound for the rightful owner to be reunited with it. Something nagged away at the back of his mind about the man stood in the street at that time of the morning. He wasn't sure that he was involved with the theft of the car, but still didn't feel easy about the conversation or the answers he was given in that short space of time they were face to face. He vowed to go back to the street and take a look in more detail when he had the time. It would all be part of the high profile policing he was asked to carry out. He could justify it to anyone that asked, not least of all his boss. But he would keep it to himself for the time being. PC Lane didn't want to bother anyone else with it. He just had that nagging doubt that you get about certain people at times. It might come to nothing, but there could be something in it.

46

The room was silent. Five people all sat with their guns trained on each other. There was a tension in the air. Nobody knew who would shoot first, and what would happen after that. They all had a great deal to lose at that moment in time. Augustine Boyle looked across at the other four, one by one and tried to determine a way out of this that would work for everyone. But he knew that no words would make things better. It was time for action.

Laser tag always ended up like this. The five on the team had gone for a bonding session and they were all close on the scoreboard with almost no time left. Gary was in the lead and didn't see the need to back down. 'Why him?' Augustine thought. He could cope with anyone else winning this. They would see it as fun. But Gary would see it as a further sign of his superiority over the rest of the team. Augustine could see the clock ticking down. They had all tried to get to the base and fire the shot that would catapult them into the lead. This was probably the police way of thinking that had brought them all together at the base. Cut to the chase, find the most important part of the situation and deal with it. But when you have five people that think in the same way then the result is they all stand facing each other in a standoff.

Twenty seconds left.

Augustine wondered if anyone else was going to make the first move. His next team bonding session would be something less competitive. Or he would do it when Gary was next on holiday. No, that wasn't right. He was the one that needed these more than the others. He looked at Lou who was on the lowest score. Some might see this as a 'nothing to lose' situation but not Lou. He looked resigned to defeat. It wasn't that he was easily beaten, but he preferred to save his efforts for the real world. Lou had never understood the focus on video games of the younger generation. Why waste all that effort on capturing imaginary bad guys when there were enough real ones to catch on the streets of their own city? Why not go outside and play a real game of football than sit in your room and play an imaginary one? Augustine decided that Lou wasn't going to be the one to defeat Gary.

Fifteen seconds left.

He looked at Electra. She would give anything to defeat Gary. She didn't want him on their team from the start. She was professional enough to have tried to make him welcome but his attitude got in the way. He saw women as servants or potential sexual conquests. When she made it clear to him that he wasn't going to get her to make him a cup of tea on demand or drop her knickers for him ever, he lost interest in her and treated her like shit. She dealt with him in the same way.

Augustine wanted to make eye contact with her to see if she was going to work with him to finish Gary off. But she had her eyes locked on her prey. She was zoned in on Gary. Augustine wondered if she was trying to hypnotise him into inaction. The stare was so strong and hard that Augustine gulped. She could lock anyone in her stare for whatever reason she wanted. Gary was forcing his eyes open so he didn't blink first. Every action, every situation was like a competition to him. Electra would want to win with every ounce of her being, but wouldn't be reckless in her pursuit. Each action would need to be calculated. But she didn't have much time.

Ten seconds left.

Augustine looked towards Ash. He was already looking back. The two of them had developed an innate understanding of each other during their time together. Ash felt the same way about Gary as the rest of the team. He was in second place and was probably the most likely to overtake Gary in the scoring. Just one hit more or one damage less than Gary would put him into the lead and take the day.

Augustine was trying to think of how to communicate that they go for Gary together. Two of their hits on him meant that Gary could only respond to one of them. This would lose him the game. The clock was ticking and the time for the final action was nigh. Augustine closed his eyes for a second while deciding what to signal. When he opened them again Ash had a broad grin on his face. Augustine knew that he didn't need to make any signal. As the last few seconds ticked down, the triggers were pulled and the flash of the vests the players wore pulsated so many times that nobody could be sure who was being hit and who was making those hits.

The screen with the scores went off and the tension grew again to the level it was at when the five of them were facing each other. Augustine was pretty sure he had hit Gary but saw his vest flash too, so he was also pretty sure he had taken at least one hit. They went to the cool down room and waited for the screens to show the scores. It was all part of the theatre of the activity. The short wait for the scores meant that the excitement levels were still set at maximum even after all the running around and shooting. Most of them sat looking at the floor, while waiting.

"Fuck it," shouted Gary. They all knew this meant that he hadn't won. For Lou and Electra this was enough. They could sit in the bar afterwards and be satisfied that it wasn't Gary, no matter who it was. But for Augustine and Ash, there was more to it than that. They both arrived at the laser tag with only thoughts of winning on their mind. They looked at each other before looking at the scoreboard on a small television screen in the top right-hand corner of a dark and dirty room.

"Yes! Gotcha Gus!"

Augustine sighed at two things. Firstly, he had lost to Ash. Secondly there was now someone else that was calling him Gus instead of Augustine. He would have to wait until the next time to deal with one. But he couldn't fight the other. He had grown to love his name Augustine since he left school and could walk away from the teasing over it. Even the pricks in the force that used the August part of his name to mock him, didn't bother him now. But he much preferred Augustine over Gus. He felt that Augustine gave him an air of authority and set him apart from others. Gus could have been just about anyone – there was only one Augustine that he knew of.

They all got up together and left the small room before the tension grew again. The next stop was the pub and a few drinks, but most of the team decided not too many as they had to be back at work at various times the next day. Gary would be the first in, but you wouldn't have been able to tell that from the number of beers he was pouring down his neck. The defeat had obviously hit him hard and he wanted a few cold ones to numb the pain or move his mind on to something else.

Augustine always tried to keep the conversation as far away from work as possible on these occasions as they were designed to help build the team and get to know each other but the high profile of the case that they were working on and the fact that it occupied the whole team all the time meant that this was an impossible task on this night out. He first tried telling people to talk about something else if he overheard them discussing the case with each other, then moved to the tactic of steering the conversation in a different direction before giving up and letting them talk. He thought that maybe it might help them process the information and be closer to a breakthrough. The only thing that was even close to a breakthrough at that point though was the fact that he has accidentally bumped into the man he thought was the killer while off duty one day – not much of a breakthrough as far as Augustine Boyle was concerned. While others talked about the case with a great deal of discretion (they were sat in a public place) Augustine withdrew into himself. He started to think about the life that he had lead that ended up with him sat in that bar at that particular time. He often used to disappear into his own thoughts and try to analyse the path that lead him to that exact point.

He wasn't the type of person that believed in fate. He didn't for one second think that he was born to do this job, live this life and end up here. Augustine Boyle believed that his life, and the life of anyone else for that matter, was a series of choices, with each choice steering the person one way or another to the next choice and the one after. He believed in essence that life was one huge decision tree with one choice leading to two potential second choices, four on the next level and so on. With scores of these decisions to make every day, the lower levels of the decision tree went into their trillions and beyond. But Augustine thought he could boil all of these decisions down to a few important ones. Sure, the choice of what to eat for lunch might lead to a higher fat intake and the raised chance of heart disease in the long run but it wasn't a decision in isolation that would have a major significance on his life. But the decision of what to study at university or what promotion to seek in his profession was something that would impact his life for a very long time in the future. These were the decisions that would influence his life and lead him to the point he was at.

So, while the others chatted, Augustine dipped in and out of the conversations to make it look like he was present, when he actually wasn't. He thought about the last change in job he took. It was several years ago and at the time felt like a natural progression. But now it felt like a mistake. It felt like one of the major decisions that had pointed him to this seat, in this bar with these people. It wasn't that he was desperately unhappy with the people, the place or the job he had, but that there might be better out there. If his decision making in the past was different then his situation would be different too. He knew that bad decisions could leave him far worse off than he was at that point in time, but he also believed that better decision making, especially those important ones, could have given him an easier life. Not that he would have any idea how to cope with an easy life. It was just a thought process that he had to go through.

"Gus, what's wrong?" Electra interrupted his thoughts. She wanted him as part of their conversation. He was the facilitator in the group as well as the de facto leader. He was the person who could weld together the different ideas of the group unto something cogent that would stand up to some scrutiny. She thought that he could get a great deal from the conversations they were having. Plus, she wanted some protection from an increasingly drunk Gary. He hadn't said anything that was inappropriate or offensive but it could be close at hand.

"I'm OK. Just mulling over the last few weeks. We need a break in this case and I nearly had it by chance. I bumped into the guy but for some reason he got away. I want all of this to end," Augustine looked from the distance, where his thoughts had been for some time, to the foreground where he found Electra looking straight in to his eyes as he spoke.

"I think you might get a lot from this conversation. I know I'd get a lot from you being part of it," Electra spoke as though she needed him more than ever. It was a way she had with words that was incredibly persuasive to Augustine. He wanted his team to get along and be as one. He wanted them all to feel safe and happy in their job. But he had a soft spot for Electra. He could see a bright future for her. He didn't want her to become disillusioned in any way. He joined in.

"So, where are we now?" Augustine spoke across the group. If he was to be part of the conversation then he had some catching up to do. The rest of them were only too happy to fill him in. Augustine listened, questioned and argued. He wanted to put all of their thoughts to the test. Discussing a case over a few drinks was an effective way to find consensus and examine theories. But it wasn't one that could be found in any policing manuals. The rest of the evening was as interesting for Augustine as any he could remember for some time. They would all go away with different thoughts and come back the next day. It could be the change that they were looking for in the way they approached the case. The conversations with the aid of alcohol meant that nobody was afraid of saying something wrong and all theories were listened to. The answers might come from this, thought Augustine. Even if they didn't, the team felt stronger – even Gary who didn't need a few drinks to speak his mind.

47

Al had been sat in his home for days since the last killing. He wanted to regroup, catch up on lost sleep and make detailed plans for the next person who needed to be taught a lesson. In fact, he was working on a few at once. He felt as though he had let himself down with the last murder. It had gone to plan up to a point but the risks involved were far too great to do it like this on a regular basis. Part of the reason he was doing this was to prove a point to some of the people he had argued with in the past. He wanted to prove that his way was correct and they were wrong. But to do this he had to kill a lot of people without getting caught. Taking risks like the one he had felt compelled to by the newspaper article questioning his ability would leave him closer to detection and arrest. That would make his plans look foolish. He wasn't prepared to do that again.

He walked to the bathroom and got out the shaving foam. This had become more than just part of the way he went about his work. It had become a ritual that he would go through every few days. There was little if any growth of hair on any part of his body but he had to keep it free from hair. His bathroom was tiled with mirrored tiles on every surface, including the floor. It was well lit so he could see every part of his body. He didn't want to run the chance of leaving any trace of hair next to any of the people he killed. He was sure that if anyone ever entered the property and looked in the bathroom that they would find him very strange indeed. But he didn't care. Everything about his life over the past few years had been geared up to the work he was carrying out at that point. He had tiled the bathroom himself so it did what he needed. Planning and attention to detail had always been a part of his life. He was known in school as someone that would pick up the teacher or one of his classmates on the tiniest detail or fact that was out of place. And now he was using that attention to detail to create something that would teach people his way of life. He looked at his reflection in one of the tiles and caught the smirk that was working its way from his mouth to his eyes. He loved doing what he was doing. It made him feel fulfilled.

Al finished his ritual and then washed his sore skin with water and a harsh soap that he had found at the local chemist. He wanted his skin to feel the effects of the shaving and the soap exacerbated this. He wanted his body to know that something different was happening. It did when the sting of the soap hit the open pores that has just been shaved. He was practised enough to be careful and not cut himself, but he shaved every part of his body whether it showed signs of hair developing or not. He felt invigorated and dried off to get dressed. It would be a few days at least until his next target could be identified, tracked and established fully, but he wanted to stay on top of his skin. Al dressed and went back to his room to look at all the research he had done. He looked across the walls. Each was dedicated to a different element of his work.

The one above his desk and computer was for the people that he was targeting. This has photographs that he had taken from afar, name and address details as well as proposed places to end their life based on the research he had carried out on their daily routines. In many ways, it was the wall of the damned. These were the people who led a life that Al had identified should be marked as unacceptable. They had chosen a path that he did not agree with and they must pay the price for this decision. It was the ultimate price to pay. In good time, he would take their life. Al sat at the desk and looked around the room. He looked up at the wall that contained the people he had personally selected. He wondered if they had any idea if their time on this planet was coming to an end. They had made a poor choice at some stage, in his eyes, so they must have foreseen that this choice would wind them up in a great deal of trouble. Al was that trouble.

He looked to his right and saw what started out as an empty wall start to be populated with pieces of paper, newspaper cuttings and yet more photographs. These corresponded with similar gaps on the main wall. This was the wall of people who he already taught a lesson. These were the people that had travelled from the wall of targets to what someone in the police would call the wall of victims. Not Al, however. He saw this as completed work. Once he had been successful in converting someone from the main wall, he would remove their details and photographs before placing them on the wall to the right. This would be accompanied, often a few days later, by a newspaper clipping or two about the murder. This reminded him that all of this was real and not some giant video game that he was playing. With the amount of research and preparation Al went to for any murder, it sometimes felt like he was at the computer in front of him rather than occupying the real world. He went into some kind of new world when he was killing the person, so he could be sat at home thinking about what had happened with a sense of detachment. The newspaper articles were confirmation for Al that he was there, he had killed those people and he was building his work. It was his reality check.

Al listened at the window to his left. He was as astonished as always that in this big city he lived in a place where there was almost no noise pretty much all of the time. It made his work a lot easier and allowed him to prepare in privacy but is was an amazing thing to hear, even after being there for a few years. Just a few hundred yards away the streets would be filled with people and traffic and the noise would be incessant for all the daylight hours and many of those in darkness too. But he could sit there and the whole world wouldn't know he existed. But he was sure they would soon. He saw a day in the none-too-distant future where news reports across the world would speak about what he was doing and the message he brought with it. He could see days where he was the top trending topic on all social media outlets as people tried to guess who he was and what he was trying to build. This made Al excited. He had a message to deliver, first and foremost, and the more exposure he got the better. That was what pissed him off so much about his reaction to the article in the Daily Gossip. He wanted people to talk about him, write about him and discuss him. It was the best way to spread the word. He wasn't naïve enough to believe that everyone would understand the importance of his work.

He looked around the window at the rest of the left-hand wall and the work that it contained. It was essentially a large map of the city. It was expertly drawn on a white board wall that was sat to the left of the window. He had marked all the CCTV cameras, the areas where he could walk uninterrupted and there were also colour-coded dotted lines that signified the routes his targets took. These were cross-referenced by dots of the same colour on the top right-hand corner of the sheets and photographs that corresponded to the targets. This was something that wouldn't have been out of place in a military operation. Al was ready for whatever came his way. He would be able to locate the likely whereabouts of any of his chosen victims at any point of the day and act accordingly. It was this level of detail that had allowed him to kill the entertainer in the theatre that night. He just knew where he would be. There were over twenty more identified at that point in time. Some had more details than others attached to them, but all were in the process of being stalked. Their information was being gathered without their knowledge. All so Al could use them to send his message to the rest of the world.

The wall directly behind Al and the desk didn't have anywhere near as much detail as the others. It was where the door was, so there was a big part of the wall missing. The rest was filled with a series of letters printed on small white squares of paper. He turned and looked at the wall. Al knew that each of these four walls was an integral part of his plan. He had missed the proximity to his research when he spent two days away from his home. It comforted him when he had the tiny doubts that would sometimes enter his brain. But he had been back for a while now and was trying to make up his mind which one of his targets was next. He thought long and hard about this and nothing else for a few hours. It was a big decision. He wanted the next one to go perfectly again so he could get the feeling that he was in control again. He decided. This person was the perfect choice. Al looked again at the details he had gathered on this person. They had the right kind of profile to take his message to the next level. Al grinned again. It was time to enact the next plan.

48

Sally Archer sat on the sofa trying her best to ignore the dog. It has been in and around her feet for at least ten minutes. She knew that Jojo wanted to be taken for a walk but she didn't feel up to it. It was drizzling outside although it was still a warm late summer evening. The first signs that summer might be over soon were appearing in the skies with a cooler wind and the odd rain shower. Sally didn't want to acknowledge the fact that the world was changing in that direction so she buried her head in the sand as much as she could. The grey sky and falling rain were just a step to far for her at that moment. But the prospect of cleaning up after Jojo was something more persuasive than facing up to the changing seasons.

"Alright Jojo. Give me a minute to get ready," exclaimed as she got to het feet. The first thing she would need to do was visit the toilet and she knew that the reaction from her dog would be that she was running away. She swerved her body towards the front door so Jojo would head that way before walking off quickly in the other direction to visit the toilet in some peace. She got the toilet door closed behind her before the dog has even realised she wasn't at the front door. It was as close as Sally was going to get to peace, but she was happy at that small victory. She washed her hands and opened the door to stop the sound of scratching and low barking coming from behind it. She looked out of the window again to confirm that the rain was still hanging in the air before picking up her summer coat, the one without a hood, and set about opening the front door. She wasn't totally comfortable in that part of town but it was all she could afford. She lived on her own and had no idea how single people could afford the rent in any part of the city without having to make sacrifices somewhere else in life. She worked full-time in the planning department for the city council and still had to cut her summer holiday back to one week instead of two and go out once a month with friends just so she had enough cash left to pay all the bills and keep decent food on the table. Sally longed to have enough money to relax and even look forward to retirement but with the ever-increasing state pension age, she couldn't see far enough into the future to even contemplate her retirement. The money she had in her pension would provide for something reasonable, but not even up to the standard of living she had now. It was a nagging worry at the back of her mind but she tried to get on with life and ignore the distant future wherever possible. She didn't know if she would make it there anyway.

The front door was growing more locks and security devices all the time. Every time Sally heard about another murder in the city or break in near to her home she saved a little money every week until she could afford another lock, chain or spy hole. She wanted to be able to see whoever was near her door and stop them from entering if needed. One lock, two locks, three locks and more were added over the four years she has lived there so it always took a few seconds to check the coast was clear and then get all the security devices unlocked to get out into the world. Sally hoped that Jojo hadn't developed a desperation to go to the toilet in the few minutes or so she had been stalling. Finally, the door was open and the two were out in the miserable summer evening.

Sally looked around and there was no sign of any other beings in her neighbourhood braving the damp weather. It was way past the time that the few commuters in her street came home and before any strays would return from the pub that was situated only around 400 yards away, if you turned the corner and walked in the opposite direction to the city centre. Sally had owned Jojo for nearly ten years and they both knew the area well. She didn't feel the need to keep her dog on a lead anymore because of this. She would just wander along behind wherever Jojo took her. The walk wasn't usually far as Jojo would do what a dog does and then want to be back inside again, especially on a wet night like this one. It was a call of nature rather than a ramble through nature for the dog. But on this occasion Jojo started to walk a little faster than usual. After a few minutes Sally was left behind and was starting to shout the name of her dog in between phrases like "stupid dog" and "don't do this to me." Sally was ready to go home. Obviously Jojo was not.

After walking aimlessly for a couple of minutes, Sally spotted a white flash along a side street that looked like her dog. Jojo was mainly brown, but with a white marking that ran for around 8 inches along her back and tail. This made her easier to spot and Sally was sure that there wasn't anyone else mad enough to be walking a dog in this weather. She headed down the side street and then followed the likely route of first right, because only around 50 yards further on was a main road. Sally knew that Jojo didn't like the sound of traffic and main roads. There was the odd slush of tyres from cars and buses going along that road. Sally bet that was enough to put her dog off. She knew vaguely of the streets they were now walking but had rarely been down them herself on foot. The main road was one of the bus routes into the city centre but not the one she used. The buses seemed dirtier and as for the fellow passenger, well there wasn't much she was willing to say about them.

She was now closing in a few steps behind Jojo but didn't feel the need to rush. The dog was far too short for her to walk alongside with the collar in her hand and she hadn't brought a lead. She just admonished the dog for running off and walked beside her. Sally walked along. She assumed that Jojo had done her business in the few minutes that they were apart but couldn't be sure. The fact that the dog was continuing to walk away from home suggested that this wasn't the case. As they neared a rare piece of woodland in the city, Jojo scuttled off again. Sally waited at the kerb to give the poor dog a minute or two to visit the toilet in privacy, the same way that Sally wanted privacy in the loo back at home. She could usually hear Jojo in the leaves and grass looking for the ideal spot to leave something behind. But silence was all that greeted her. Sally wanted to give it one more minute but the creepy nature of the streets she was on and the lack of a signal that there would be any end to the rain prompted her to follow in after the dog. She wanted to get back home, dry her hair and fall asleep in front of the television. A regular weekday evening as far as she was concerned.

"Jojo, where are you?" Sally asked as though she would receive an answer. She thought it better than walking silently and wanting the dog to know she was cross. The tone in her voice was angry but resigned too. She didn't know whether dogs could pick up these small signals so resolved to speak again, but this time without the resignation in her voice.

"Jojo come out here at once. It is time to go home. Time for bed," Sally was pleased with the way this went in her own mind, even though there was no sign of the dog reappearing.

Sally tiptoed in the way that cartoon characters do. She made deliberate slow strides with her knees raised so that anyone who saw her would know that she wasn't trying to disturb them. She would rather have walked through the wooded area with her dog at the end of a lead so any passers-by could see what she was doing there, but exaggerated movements of her legs were the best way Sally could think of to let people know she wasn't there to do any harm. She was now whispering the name of her dog and to keep the noise level to a minimum. Sally was just as concerned that she would be in peril if someone else came along and spotted her as she would be if she was spotted looking suspicious in this area. Sally became very aware of every noise and potential movement that came from behind her. The rain falling onto cars on the road she had just left was pitter-pattering away and was fairly constant, but it was small noises like a splash from a bus passing on the main road or the wind blowing through the top leaves on the trees made her jump slightly, even if it was barely noticeable to anyone else. All along she was trying to find Jojo with the minimum of fuss and noise so she could get away from the streets that she was starting to fear and get back behind the several locks of her front door.

Sally walked further still into the wooded area. It was only around a hundred square yards and was probably the remnant of an ancient protection order but with the grey from the sky it started to look dark and Sally wasn't happy in just wading in to look for her dog. She walked slowly further all the while hoping that Jojo would bound out in front of her and start the journey home. But there wasn't even the sign of the white flash on her back and tail. Sally knew she would have to walk deeper.

Even though the wooded area had been protected when the rest of the neighbourhood has been built on, there was no maintenance carried out. The undergrowth grew thicker the further Sally stepped in and what was at first swallowing her ankle at every step was now fast approaching her knees. It was alright for Jojo. She could just find a way in and out, even under, the plant life and keep going. Sally had a more difficult time of it. She was about to give up and turn around again when Sally thought she saw Jojo's white flash in front of her. Around five yards ahead there was a cleared area, which looked circular around seven feet in diameter. But there appeared to be a block through the middle of the circle that hadn't been cleared. In the near-darkness under the grey sky and the canopy of the oak trees it looked like a primitive crop circle. The darker area in the middle was occupied was where Jojo was now stood with her tail wagging. Sally fought her way through the last few strides to join her pet.

Jojo was very excited about something that was in that circle, and Sally was eager to find out what it was. As she made the last few strides, she looked for her mobile phone to use the torch function and shine some sort of light on Jojo's find so they could get it over and done with and get back home. Sally was sure that the rain was still in the air, even though by this stage she was covered by the trees and didn't feel any. Her jacket was wet and she wanted to get into the dry for the rest of the night. Whatever she found on TV was bound to be better than walking through the rain in a neighbourhood she didn't totally trust. As Sally looked for the right button to push on her phone, she looked around again at the neighbourhood. It struck her that she couldn't be seen by anyone from this exact point. It wasn't in any way possible to view the place where she and Jojo were stood from the street, the road or any of the homes. 'Where else in this city can you get that?' Sally asked herself. She then turned to where her dog was, now only around two feet away and shone the torch.

"Holy shit." Sally dropped the phone. Jojo barked and then let out what might have been mistaken for a howl. When Sally recovered the phone from the deep plantation by following the light of the torch she stepped towards what looked like a person laid directly along the middle of the cleared area. Sally got closer still and looked at the strange shape. The light from her phone was poor and she needed to get very close to the shape to identify what it was. When she was only a few inches away she realised that she was looking at the leg of someone. It was a body. The person was dressed in shorts and Sally guessed it was a woman by the shape of the legs and the fact that there was no hair at all present. She shone the light along the body, up the right arm and looked at the face. She was right. It was a woman. Sally assumed she was dead because there was no sign of life and this wasn't the type of place where someone would have a lie down. She checked the pulse on the wrist and then on the neck and found nothing. But there were no signs of an injury. The cause of death wasn't immediately obvious. Sally called 999 and told them what she had found. She explained as best she could the place where she was and told them to send an ambulance and the police. She didn't hold out any hope that the person could be saved but didn't give up on anyone.

Sally wasn't afraid of dead bodies and was incredibly curious so before she went out to the street to flag down the emergency services, she thought that she would take a look at the body and see if she could establish why it was lying in that place. She found two plastic bags in her pockets that she always kept there to clear up any mess Jojo left when they were on a walk. She had already touched the body in a few places and wanted to keep her fingerprints off the lifeless victim as much as possible. She had nothing at all to hide but knew that not all police investigations found the guilty party. She called Jojo over and the dog for the first time that night did as she was told.

"Jojo sit. Jojo stay. Good girl," Sally said now in a voice that was clear she meant business. Jojo wouldn't mess with her now.

Sally put the bags on her hands and touched various parts of the body. She wanted to find out if there was anything obvious that would allow her to give the police or ambulance service something to go on. She started with the two most obvious places – the head and the chest. The head wasn't showing any signs of damage. Often a blow to the head would cause something to distort, either inwards or outwards, and the signs were pretty obvious. Sally had been trained in basic first aid a few times in the past with her employers and knew some rudimentary things about the human body. She was confident that she would be able to determine if something noticeable was apparent. Then she went to the chest. Blows here could leave tell-tale signs too. There was a piece of paper on the chest that might have been covering a puncture hole or other wound so Sally removed it and put it in her pocket so she could see what was going on. She checked the chest and found nothing obvious there either. The sound of sirens in the distance was becoming louder so Sally called for her pet and the two of them made their slow progress to the street again. Sally stood between two cars looking one way and then the other to see the flashing lights that would mean some sort of help was on the way. She could then unburden herself of what had happened and get on with her life. That was what she told herself anyway. The reality was that Sally didn't let things go easily.

The sirens came from both ends of the street. At first from the left, she saw a string blue light at a height and knew instinctively through the drizzle and darkness that this was an ambulance. She stepped out half way into the road to flag it down and point them in the right direction. She glanced over her shoulder and saw a police car only a few yards behind in the race to reach her first. The police officer in the front was looking left and right to see if there was a safe place to park the car but none presented itself. So, he backed up a little to give the ambulance crew all the space they needed and got out some tape to make sure the area was sealed as best it could be. The sirens and flashing lights were bound to alert others in the neighbourhood to the fact that something was going on and he wanted to get some sort of control before the detectives arrived and started asking questions.

As he finished the rudimentary barrier between the area of attention and the rest of the street, the policeman saw someone talking to the ambulance crew who were looking deep into the wooded area on the other side of the street to him. He didn't want anyone inside the area so crossed the road and approached. As he did, the woman finished talking to the paramedics and stepped toe to toe with him.

"Nobody is allowed in here, can you please step outside," the policeman asked in as firm a voice as he could manage while still trying to maintain calm. He had received a warning about the way he spoke to people about a year earlier and had since tried to add some niceties to his speech. It wasn't always evident.

"I was just letting the ambulance guys know where I found the body. Is there a problem?" Sally replied. She wanted to help and knew that they all had a difficult job to do.

"I'm sorry. I didn't realise it was you who had called it in. You are soaked through. Do you want to sit in the back of the car while they do their work?" the policeman could feel another complaint coming on so added helpfulness in droves at this point.

"That would be good," Sally said while looking up at the sky. The light rain was forming a sheen across her face and it had already penetrated her jacket to reach the clothes underneath. She continued as they walked towards the police car, lights now off, "Would you like to know what happened?"

"If you feel up to it."

"Yes, I'm fine."

Sally and Jojo followed the police officer to the car and she told him all that she had seen. It took far longer than she had anticipated because he wrote down everything that happened word for word and asked her to read it back. By the time she was finished Sally was ready for bed, but the police officer had been asked to keep her there for a little while longer. Someone called Detective Augustine Boyle would soon be there and he wanted to talk to her.

When Augustine arrived, the body was being loaded into the ambulance. He looked at the two paramedics and one shook their head to let him know the news. Sally was sat in the back of the police car to the left of him and saw the motion from the paramedic. She was sure that the body was just that, but wanted someone else to make the final decision. She looked into the distance and wondered if the veneer of rain was going to cease that night. Jojo was curled up beside her and looked as though she wouldn't stir again that night. Sally wanted to do the same.

"Good evening, I'm Detective Augustine Boyle. I know you have given a full statement, but I'd like to ask a few questions if that is alright. Then we'll make sure you get home safely and out of the rain. Is that OK?"

Sally looked up and saw the detective smiling down at her. He had obviously dealt with things like this before. She wasn't squeamish and was able to look over the body before returning to the road but this was something completely different. It was as though he was enjoying this. She imagined him taking the call while sat at home and rushing out to see who had been murdered now. But his demeanour was so welcoming and calm that she couldn't help but like him instantly.

"Only if you're not too long," Sally said with a wink, "I have a bed to get to."

"You'll be there before you know it," replied the handsome detective. Sally didn't want to go over the statement for a third time, but was willing to answer any questions the detective had. He was probably better to look at than anything she would find on television at that time of night.

"How did you end up all the way in there," Augustine asked while pointing at an arbitrary point in the distance that he thought would signify the location of the body.

"I followed my dog," Sally motioned in her own way to the seat beside her. Augustine had taken his position in the passenger seat at the front of the car and was looking over the back corner of the seat to Sally who was sat in the rear seat behind the driver. He hadn't noticed the dog curled up asleep until Sally had nodded her head in that direction.

"So, he found the body?"

"Yes, he darted off in there and when I found him he was over the person. I checked their pulse and called for you guys – and the ambulance. I knew they were dead, I just thought there might be a slight chance with medical science that if they had been there only a few hours…" Sally stopped talking and started to cry. She had felt her voice breaking when speaking to the detective and thought for the first time about this as a human being rather than a body. She looked at the detective through the tears and wondered what she must have looked like. Out for far too long in the drizzle and now crying. She knew that she would be quite some sight.

"It is OK. Take your time. I only have another one or two questions for now. I just want to get a few details," the kind detective spoke softly and slowly like he had all the time in the world. Sally thought that inside he must be raring to find out what had happened to the person she discovered. She could see he was ready to speak again.

"Did you see anything else around the body, on the floor? Take your time. It is important that we get this right." Augustine Boyle asked in a deliberate tone. He wanted to make sure that the state of the body taken by the paramedics was the one that she saw when she arrived at the scene. Boyle had sent the police officer that was comforting Sally when he arrived into the undergrowth to see if there was anything else left around. A murder weapon would be a great start to this investigation, even if Boyle was going to hand it over to someone else very soon. It didn't fit the pattern of the murderer that his team were chasing and that was now seen as the highest priority in the city at the time. If this didn't fit the pattern, then he could pass it off onto someone else. He would be much happier passing the body over with a good chance of solving the case. Although many of his fellow detectives had given up on Augustine Boyle as someone who only ever took on helpless cases. He hadn't given up on them.

"There was just a clearing in the woods and the body in the middle of it. My dog was there first. She just stood on the body until I got there," Sally looked the kind detective straight in the eye as she spoke. She wanted to look for clues to see if he had any idea what had happened. She was pretty good at working out what people were thinking, but she hadn't come across anyone like this man before. He would make a great poker player, she thought. She had no idea that he struggled to keep his cards close to his chest.

"Thank you Sally. You have been very patient with us. I can see the police officer approaching. He has been to the scene. I have one more question and then I need to speak to him for a minute or so. Then we'll get you home – is that alright?" Augustine explained in a manner that made Sally think he would make a great father. She had rarely seen such a display of patience in a man. If only there were more like him out there.

"Yes, detective. That's fine."

"Oh, Sally. That wasn't the last question, you know, where I said, 'is that alright?' There is one more question to do with what you found." Augustine was playing with her a little. He wanted her at ease.

"I understand."

"Now you were walking in this neighbourhood for the first time, according to what you have told the police officer. That's fine. And he said that you were a little scared about the neighbourhood and what the people were like around here. That's fine too. But when you started to walk into the woods, did you notice if anyone could see you? Do you think that someone in one of these houses or in a passing car could have seen you walk through? Was it like you were being watched?" Augustine Boyle wanted to know what it might be like for Sally, and thus the killer, to walk into the wooded area for the first time. He had already decided that the body in the ambulance hadn't ended up there of natural causes or by her own hand. Augustine wanted to know if there was the feeling of being watched, the potential of being seen. If Sally felt it then the killer might have felt it too. If there was a chance the killer could have been seen them he could put some of his resources into

"Quite the opposite, detective. It felt as though not a soul in the world could see me. I felt creeped out by the neighbourhood until I walked into the woods. Then I felt as though nobody could touch me."

Augustine Boyle thanked he for her time and then asked if she minded waiting a few seconds while he spoke to the police officer. Sally could hear parts of their conversation but nothing of sufficient clarity to piece together what she had seen. Sally was determined to find out what was going on with the body. She had never seen a dead body before and she was intrigued to find out what had brought it there. Jojo had opened a door in Sally's mind that would never be closed again until she knew what had happened to the woman in the woods. The detective popped his head into the rear of the car and thanked her for his time. He then left and the police officer jumped in the front. He took her home so she could get some rest. But Sally couldn't sleep. As she heard the faint snores of Jojo elsewhere in her home, she laid in her bed and thought of all the diverse and unusual ways the body could have made the journey from human to corpse. It took all night.

49

Augustine followed the ambulance to the hospital where the body of the woman was due to be given a post mortem and assessed for the cause of death. He much preferred Electra to do this for two main reasons. Firstly, he didn't get on with dead bodies. He didn't want another to visit him in his dreams. And he also didn't like the smells that accompanied them. In the wide open it was bad enough. But in the confined space of the post mortem room and with the body likely being cut open, he was going to find those smells even tougher to deal with. Secondly, Electra was the best in his team, the best he knew, at picking up those little signals that turned an observation of something mundane into a vital part of any investigation.

But he was on duty at that time and he didn't want to wake Electra for a post mortem on a body that they would be handing over on the morning anyway. It was now 2 in the morning and the coroner was there from a previous post mortem. He, like Augustine, didn't see the point in handing it all over to someone else so stayed on to complete the job. Augustine got ready and followed the lead of the coroner in putting large swabs of Vaseline over his nostrils. It hadn't made much difference in the past but it felt better that he was taking some steps to deal with the situation. The feeling that he was exerting control over the situation was comforting.

He watched intently as the coroner worked on the body. He worked diligently as though he had plenty of time and it wasn't 2 in the morning. Augustine watched his face more than his hands to keep his mind off what was going on and to see if there were any body language clues to go with the written report he would have in his hands later. But there was nothing. The woman seemed for all intents and purposes a normal member of society, a retired lawyer no less, and the cause of death was a single puncture wound to the heart. Augustine thanked the coroner, took the report and made a few notes himself. He was sure whoever took the case from him wouldn't thank him in the slightest, but he wanted to give over as much as he could.

Augustine was only around an hour from the end of his shift, so he decided that a quick visit to the wooded area might help him get a better idea of what had happened. He couldn't decide whether the victim had been killed there or carried there after death. The post mortem gave up no clues in this area, except for the fact that she had been dead for approximately 2 months. He drove the empty streets that always greeted the emergency services at that time of day and looked for the road that had been down earlier that night. The streets were narrow and all looked the same in the daylight, let alone the dark but Augustine slowed when he was in the right part of town and looked along the tops of the houses to spot the tall oaks that gave away the location of the woodland. It took him a few minutes of driving up and down and then a few minutes more to find somewhere to park. Augustine took a torch from the boot of his car and headed back to the woods. He had no idea what he was looking for, but the feeling of being all alone and hidden from the outside world was going to be a good start. He wanted to wind down from work and prepare for a sleep when he got home. Boyle took his mind off the immediate situation, which before entering the woods was one of trepidation. In the same way that Sally had described, the atmosphere in the neighbourhood was one that made you feel like something menacing was about to happen. Even when all the residents were in their homes and asleep, the place could have been only a few seconds from everything kicking off at any moment. To take his mind off it, Augustine tried to remember the name of the woman who had been found here. He had only heard it in passing once, said by the coroner as he got the fingerprint report through from the computer in the post mortem room.

Harriet, no, Hope, nah

Augustine stepped into the first few yards of the woods. He looked forwards then stopped, turned around and looked back. The first signs of dawn were in the air and he decided that the torch would bring attention that he didn't need. He walked a few backward steps, all the while looking up at the surrounding homes to see if he could have been seen.

Heather, nope, Holly, no

Then Augustine turned back around and relocated the clearing in the centre of the woods. He had to make it that far to see if there were any clues left behind. There was only going to be one post mortem, but plenty of chances to check this out. She had been there long enough. What difference would a few hours make?

Hazel, I don't think so, Hannah, never

Augustine reached the middle of the woods and looked at the clearing. It was shaded by the biggest oak tree in the woods, but he could still make out the cleared piece of ground. Augustine wanted to know if it was a natural clearing or one that had been made by hand.

Heidi, that's not it, Helen…. yes! That was it. Now what was her surname? Something is telling me it was a colour or shade.

Augustine got down on to one knee in the clearing and looked at the boundaries. Although it appeared to be almost a perfect circle, there were no signs that the plants had been cut to make it like this. He got out his torch and moved closer. The feeling that he was hidden away from the rest of the world took over.

Green, doesn't sound right, Brown, no I'd remember that

The plants on closer inspection backed up what Augustine had previously thought. There was no sign that this was manmade. He wanted to get out of there now he had discovered that, but him and his torch had one more task to carry out before he could head home.

White, black, grey, nope, none of them

The area around the cleared patch could have been hiding something sinister. The people of the neighbourhood must have been aware that something was going on with the flashing blue lights at either end of the street and sporadic activity in the middle. But none came out. Whether it was the persistent rain or the late hour, there was no audience to see the police do their work. But the next morning when things brightened up, there would be people in and around the site, even given the police tape across the front of the woods. Augustine wanted to check the area around the body before the souvenir hunters got there.

Blue, now you're just being silly, violet — yes that's it. Helen Violet.

Augustine found nothing and returned to his car, and then back home to bed. He had all the information he needed to give the new investigating officer as much to go on as possible at that time. All that was left for the day was to get undressed and drop off to sleep. Augustine knew that wouldn't take long. Whether he would be able to stay asleep with another potential body to occupy his dreams was another matter altogether.

50

Al sat on his haunches in his home. He had been out for only an hour in total, but had added to his body of work that had been growing over previous weeks. He was quite proud of the one that he had enacted in the few hours of dark that were available at that time of year. It was someone that he had been watching and studying for some time. They were a slight departure from the work that he had been previously carrying out, but he felt that a small change might prompt the police to release the details of the letters he had left on the chest of his victim. So far, this information hadn't been put out there in the public domain. Al was tempted to speculate about this on one of the message boards at the bottom of a news site so he could start to push this fact out there, but the possibility he was traced was too much of a risk. He had carried out one mission where there was risk involved and didn't feel safe at all afterwards. The work of that night took him back to familiar ground and allowed him to feel comfortable again. He was back on track and was ready to keep going until the police had no choice but to reveal what he was saying to them.

The walk back home was in stark contrast to the one he had made after killing the entertainer in the theatre. Then he was worried that he was being followed and too scared to return home in case it was being staked out. As there had been no visits to his home in the meantime and the only encounter he had with a member of the police force was coincidental, Al felt that he had no reason to fear coming home after a killing. He walked the dark streets from the park where he had met his victim without any thoughts that he could be seen or captured. Al was confident once again. That meant he would kill more often. But his confidence signalled terrible things for the city. People would suffer.

The person who he had killed might take some time to find. It wasn't the first time he had killed in this way. The park was on the edge of the city, on the same side of town as Al's home. The boundary of the park was under the flyover that brought traffic from the suburbs to the big city in the early hours of the day and took them back home again after the work was done. This was where he arranged to meet someone. During his time on the dark web, Al started to look in some detail at the activities of some groups that he disagreed with. One of them was the homosexual community. It wasn't just the fact that they were committing acts that he disagreed with, but they seemed to be far more promiscuous in his eyes than straight people. The fact that the straight people Al knew were all in and around him, and the gay people he knew were active users of a meet-up homosexual website didn't strike him as the reason for the difference he spotted. He just viewed the way people connected with each other on there as something that needed to be stopped. Again, Al was tempted to leave a message. This would be his way or warning all the other users of the site to stop, but the risks involved were far too great.

Al built up a profile on the site over the time he was observing. He thought it might come in useful at a later stage of his work. He was right, it was easy to isolate one user that seemed to respond to every request and he groomed him. He called himself TimidSam. It was to build up trust and develop a dialogue that could lead to a meeting one day. Or one night. And that night had just been and gone. TimidSam's last night on earth.

Al had arranged to meet him at the edge of the park under the flyover. He used the name ShyGuy123 and this seemed to strike a chord with his target. They could be timid and shy together. They were both a little nervous, so meeting in seclusion was Al's way of getting TimidSam to meet. It gave Al all the time and solitude he needed to go about his work. The target was identified and met. The last act was to kill and then cut. Al loved this part of the mission he had set himself. It meant that he could take out some of his anger on the person he had decided must be taught a lesson. After death, they were a punchbag for him. Al cut TimidSam in a few strategic places that were designed to show anyone who found him just what he thought of the man.

Al took some chloroform with him to render TimidSam unconscious so he could make the kill without a struggle. It was these tiny details that had given Al the run on the police for all these weeks. He could kill at will and never be caught, he thought as he stood there over the body, ready to deliver the blow that would finish them off. The detectives are like sparrows pecking away at the breadcrumbs I've dropped, hoping that one of them will be enough to fill their belly. But what has been left behind is carefully orchestrated. There's only enough breadcrumbs to leave them hungry for more, Al thought to himself. This time he suffocated the person laid in front of him. It was easier that way. There would be little in the way of blood and then he could tourniquet different parts of the body before making his cuts. This one was going to look like he had suffered. This one was going to be cut below the belt.

As he stood in the shower and thought back to his meeting in the park, Al decided that he wouldn't wait long for the next one. He had several targets lined up and knew their movements off by heart. The first thing he did when arriving home was to move TimidSam from the wall of targets to the wall of victims. It made him feel like he was making progress, in the same way that businesses set targets and then congratulate themselves when their goal has been achieved, Al tried to think of some way to pat himself on the back in the immediate aftermath of a killing. Moving the image of the target from one wall to another was a good start. It signalled that this was a job well done. He was still working on an addition to this celebration but for the time being it was sufficiently satisfying on its own.

There were three or four people that he could kill next. The police were not helping him in publicising the full details of his crimes, so more bodies would make them think about getting all the information out there so the public could lend a hand. That was his theory, in any case. Al finished in the shower and dried himself off. He had used antibacterial disinfectant to wash in after every murder on the off chance that there were traces of blood on him. The clothes that he wore were burned in the vegetable patch at the end of his garden every time. He was cautious to the nth degree as there was a lot more people to kill and he wanted to kill without being detected. It was part of the plan and was keeping him going.

Al looked in the mirror and then sharply pulled his gaze away again. He hadn't looked at himself for some time. He felt no reason to. He didn't know why the mirror was still there on the wall. He could shave with the use of a hand mirror and he didn't want to see what he looked like any more. The small face of a hand mirror only gave the smallest glimpses of his person at one time. He couldn't piece them together as a whole. Al was fearful that he would look very different now he was a killer. He knew the work he was carrying out was the right thing, but he was concerned that something might give the game away.

Ever since he was young, Al had believed in the power to know someone's secrets by looking at them. He first noticed that when he looked through a newspaper he could pick out the people that were dead just from the images. He would go through the paper page by page without looking at any headlines, captions or words, from the photograph, he would determine whether the person in the image was dead and put a mark next to the photo. Then Al would go back through the newspaper and read the details to confirm his thoughts. He was never wrong. Every image with a mark next to it would be that of someone who was no longer living.

He wondered if this was a skill that was common. So, at school he would ask others to do the same thing with the newspaper he bought on the way in. Nobody else was quite as accurate as him, but Al noticed that people were able to pick this out around 85% of the time. He had to investigate further.

But he couldn't find a way to test this theory any further until he reached the age of 18. He then volunteered to help in the local prison. He would go in and meet people, listen to them speak and generally be supportive. Al would listen to people for a few minutes and then think about what crime they committed to be in there. In his mind, he would split people into one of two categories –

1. Those that had killed someone

2. Those that had not

After making up his mind, Al would speak to prison guards and find out what these people were in for. As with the images in the newspapers, he would be right every single time. Al carried this ability with him wherever he went. It was easy for him to spot someone who had killed. It wasn't something he wanted to see in the mirror. He decided that he would take it down after the next killing to see if it would burn with his clothes.

And Al was concerned that others had the same ability as him. After learning that others could spot the dead in newspaper images just like him, he was now worried that others could spot those that had killed. When he walked the streets, he tried to keep his head down. If someone looked in his direction, then he immediately assumed that they had picked him out as a murderer. Al went out in the early morning and the late evening to avoid these looks. He decided that he was best to avoid all people rather than feel this way.

Al got dressed and had a decision to make. He had to decide whether to go to sleep now and further the chances that he became a nocturnal animal like the bats he had seen on the way to the park or the fox that had walked across his path on the way home or whether he would stay up, have some breakfast and live something like a normal life. Al went to the kitchen and put some breakfast together. He wanted to research in the day and do his work whenever it was most appropriate. Al sat down in front of the television and slowly ate his cereal. On the screen was the local news about a body found in woodland that had been there for several months. Al laughed and continued eating.

51

Augustine raised his head from the pillow and wondered what the time was. The days where he had an alarm clock right next to his king-size bed were over. He pushed back the silk-feel sheets and let the air of the room wash over the naked top half of his body. He went through stages of wearing bedclothes and then not. It didn't go with the seasons or any trends he picked up in the magazines he had delivered on subscription and browsed through from time to time. GQ was his favourite, and he wanted to know how to retain some degree of style now he was a little older. He shopped in the places they recommended, wore the clothes they said were in fashion and generally looked to these magazines for some inspiration. Augustine felt it was the substitute for having a woman in his life that would ordinarily do all of these things for him. He saw it as fall back when he didn't have someone to talk to about interior design or what clothes went with what. He still had no confidence that they were the right choices. He was satisfied that he had someone to blame, though. The sheets felt right to Augustine when he bought them. He had arrived at the store as a direct result of another set of sheets he had seen in GQ than were not available when he got there. He didn't fancy another visit to the store, let alone a 6 week wait for them to come back in stock so he looked for an alternative. While feeling sheets (was this really how people selected their bed linen?) Augustine came across the ones he was partially under at that moment. They still felt the same way now as they did when he put his hands on them in the store. Sleeping in them on his own and getting them dry cleaned had preserved the feel, Augustine thought to himself as he considered how long they had been on, how many times he had actually made it as far as his bedroom at that time, and when he needed to next change them. He couldn't decide, so Augustine made up his mind that he would swap them over that morning before he made it to work.

The alarm clock was a few feet away. He had moved it to the other end of the chest of drawers by his bed for two reasons. Firstly, the light from the clock was strong and when Augustine was trying to force his body back into sleep mode, the green glow from the numbers on the clock would illuminate the room and get his brain working again. The second reason was that he rarely needed an alarm clock. It was there, and the alarm was set, but Augustine was always up hours before the time he input into the alarm screen. He figured it had been months since he last used the alarm but he could have been wrong. Time was abstract for Augustine. With no regular monitors of his time like a family or a 9-to-5 job, he just lived until someone told him something had happened. It could be that one of his relatives were ill (there were few of them left) or that a colleague was leaving his team or retiring. This would send Augustine into thinking mode for a few days. He would stop, take stock of the last period of time before reverting back into Augustine mode. He was much happier in his own mode and found the times in between tiring. Considering what had gone on in his life before was a drain on his resources. Just going about his daily routine and living from event to event was where Augustine would get his energy from.

He thought twice about actually checking the time before just getting up and getting ready. He wanted to be early anyway to hand over the case he was dealing with the night before. He was sure that his boss Marie would have already decided who he was giving it to, and briefed them. Marie worked in the same efficient way that Augustine did. Maybe it was why he was still there even though his figures looked poor in comparison to others in his role. She appreciated the fact that he took on all the crappy cases that the rest of them didn't want and she felt that he got closer to solving them than anyone else on the department would have. Marie was protective of Augustine when she explained what was going on to her bosses. They didn't get close enough to the investigations to see what was going on. They just looked at the figures and saw an underachiever. Augustine wanted to do more, but didn't stand much of a chance while there were paper-pushers in the higher echelons. He'd just have to keep plugging away.

Whether the case he was handing over was going to be easy to solve was a matter for much debate. The body had been there for several months and the post mortem threw up nothing that would give the detective in charge a lead. Augustine thought for a few seconds that it was no different to the ones that he was working on but parked that thought in case it came out in the handover. The last thing he wanted was another detective giving him the brush off because of their figures. He wanted to hand this over with as much enthusiasm and attention to detail as he would expect from anyone else.

Augustine arrived at the station to see several pairs of eyes all fixed on his. The rest of the team hadn't heard about the body until detective Jon Foley arrived asking what time Augustine would arrive in an aggressive voice. When Lou told the detective that Augustine wasn't expected for at least a couple of hours, Foley said, "fuck it, I'll wait in his office." He was still sat there 90 minutes later when Augustine walked through the door. Before Lou could warn him, Augustine had seen the other detective in his office and guessed what had happened. Foley was up on his feet and at the door before Augustine could think or act, so he walked straight towards the other detective to get him back into the office and away from the prying eyes and ears of the team.

"What are you fucking playing at…" were the only words heard by Electra, Lou and Gary – the three members of the team that were at the station in their office that morning. The rest was muffled by the door, but they could all guess what was happening. Electra wanted to protect Augustine from the shit that he was thrown by the other detectives. If he didn't take on so many of the 'lost causes' that they pushed aside then they would all suffer. Augustine was doing them a favour, she thought. Electra has always had a soft spot for Augustine Boyle from the first time they met. She was young and had just got her first break moving out of being on the beat and to investigate higher level crimes. He was someone that had been around a few times and she developed a sort of crush on him. Not physical, but that she wanted to work with a detective just like Augustine. It became her mission. She would listen out for cases that he was involved in and try to see if there was an overlap with what she was doing. Electra wanted to capture the attention of this man and she wanted to work on his team. She thought that being an attractive young lady and him being notoriously single would help things. She wasn't the type to sleep her way to the top but there was no harm in using the obvious attractions that she was given by nature. After a while they bumped into each other more often. She blushed each time they were close to each other and Electra was sure that he noticed. She didn't want others to see her emotions, but it was a natural thing. Again, she consoled herself, it can't hurt if he thinks I'm smitten. Electra thought about when she finally joined the team. She was ecstatic and wanted to hug and kiss Augustine all over. At times, she was like a giddy schoolgirl inside but Electra almost never let that side of her out. She was guarded as could be. As Electra thought about her emotions, she heard the noise coming from her boss's room. On the other side of the door there was a row continuing, but the tone made her feel it was running out of steam.

"Boyle, I'm sick of shovelling your shit. You've managed to convince Marie that you can let this one go, but you have to convince me too," Foley was trying to close rank on Augustine, but with no more authority and less years in the force is wasn't going to wash.

"I don't have to do shit," Augustine fought fire with fire when he knew he would get the backing of his bosses. Even the disparity in detection figures wouldn't get Foley out of this one. Augustine wondered what the problem was. It had to be more than being handed a case that he didn't want. Foley did that in reverse all the time.

"I don't want the crap that you picked up on last night's shift. You're making no progress at all with the case you have now, so why would you not have time for another dead-end investigation? You and your team of fuck-ups seem to specialise in them," Jon Foley continued to bait Augustine to respond. It was a classic tactic that would work with a criminal but not another detective. Augustine slowed it all down.

"I have researched as much as I could. All my notes are on the file. You can pick it right up from there," Augustine tried the classic tactic of deflection. He wouldn't get drawn into an argument where the outcome was already determined. He had won the argument already by passing the case over with the express authority of their line manager. What would he gain from getting angry with this prick?

"I'll tell you what," Jon Foley sensed a gap and went for it, "I'll let you deal with this one and I'll take the others off your hands. Does that sound like a deal?"

Foley had cut to the chase. Augustine had kept his cards close to his chest because he didn't feel the need to play any, but the result was that his opponent had revealed everything. Maybe his grandfather had something with this tactic. Augustine Boyle had waited for others to circle around his investigation. It didn't feel like it was going anywhere, but the publicity was too much for the other detectives to bear. They wanted the high-profile case, the one that all the newspapers were covering and the one all their friends were talking about. The fact that Augustine Boyle had the case was enough to make their blood simmer away for hours on end. The plots were going on behind his back to relieve him of the investigation. Boyle would stand firm. There was no chance of him giving this one up.

Foley could see that it wasn't going to be that easy. But he wasn't going to give Augustine the easy win of walking off with his tail between his legs. "I'll get one of my team to come and pick up the notes later. Some of us are busy," and with that Jon Foley opened the door with a wild swing and stormed off out of the office.

After Detective Jon Foley left, Boyle sat and thought for a fleeting time. He wondered how long he might have to produce some results with this before the noise from people like Foley would get louder. He thought that maybe one or two more murders with no progress might see the case handed to another detective and him relieved of his command over this killer. Augustine wanted desperately to find a chink of light in the case. As it was, the only unnatural light in the room came from the door that was still wide open from Foley's exit. The glare of a torch was shining straight at Augustine's face. At the other end of the torch was Gary Hole. He looked pissed off. He was looking at the back on his upturned monitor with the light half shining on the subject of his anger and the other half shining directly at Augustine. If it had been anyone else it would have been a complete coincidence. As it was Gary, Augustine was sure it was contrived. Of all the people in the building, Gary was the one that would have loved the conversation he had just been through with Jon Foley. Voices were raised, but Augustine was sure they were quiet enough for even the likes of Gary to not overhear.

He walked out into the office to see what was going on. As he got closer Gary lifted the light and it shone fully in Augustine's face. Like before, he thought, 'if this was anyone else…'

"What's up Gary?" Augustine wanted to show that he cared. In some ways, he did care. He cared that Gary didn't go off telling other detectives that they had made no progress. He cared that Gary didn't piss of the productive members of his team. He cared that Gary didn't get the upper hand with him. He cared that he was still able to control his movements. But Augustine really didn't give a shit about the state of Gary's monitor. He did precious little with it anyway.

"I don't know. It just went off, "Gary replied with the torch still shining full in Augustine's face. The rest of the room had now stopped what they were doing to see if Augustine was going to have his second confrontation in ten minutes but he seemed resigned to help rather than argue. As Augustine approached he could see a light from the downturned monitor screen and wondered what was going on. Gary looked at where Augustine's eyes were and quickly put the torch away. "I think I've got it now," he said with a smile and put the black monitor screen back on the desk. Augustine, baffled, returned to his office without offering any more on the subject. Perhaps he should be worrying about what Gary was up to this time, but Augustine had long since decided not to waste time on him. He couldn't be arsed.

The trip to the sewers the day before had delivered nothing of note for the investigation but had satisfied the rest of the team that Gary had been given this unenviable task. For his part, Gary played the role he should have. He stayed there all day and filed a report to Augustine at the end of it. He didn't want Augustine to derive any satisfaction from giving him the shit jobs. It wouldn't be long in Gary's eyes before he would be at least Boyle's equal, if not his superior. He was willing to play the long game.

As he sat back at his desk, Augustine decided that he would read through the report one more time before one of Foley's underlings arrived. If he was going to be abused for it, he might as well make sure it was as good as he could leave it. Another thought entered his head. What if he was taken off the serial killer case? He might end up back with the case if he didn't make any progress with what he was doing, so it could be in his best interests to make sure that the file in his hand was as complete as could be.

While reading, and urge to call Sally came across Augustine. There was nothing in the notes or the interview that caused him any concern but something was tapping him on the back of the head all the time about her. He decided that after a cup of tea he would probably do that. Electra was getting up out of her seat just as Augustine walked through his office door with eyes on the exit. She walked alongside him for a few strides without saying anything. She knew this face. She knew his destination. Without a word, she walked with him to the café over the road from the station. She was happy to sit in silence with him if he wanted.

On their return, Gary told Augustine that someone had come to collect the file from his office. One of Foley's team, he thought. Augustine saw the file missing from his desk, but the single sheet he had been studying before the trip across the road was still on top of the filing cabinet that sat behind the modern ergonomically-designed chair behind the large dark-wood desk that could have easily been mistaken for a dining table because of the size and the quality of the wood. Augustine had inherited the desk from the previous occupant of the office and loved the solidity it represented. He hoped that anyone who met him in the office would feel that he had the same solidity of character. It obviously hadn't happened for Jon Foley around an hour earlier.

The piece of paper was beckoning Augustine to the cabinet and he walked past the desk and brushed it with his hand. He wanted to feel the quality. Augustine Boyle took the piece of paper between two fingers as though it was dirty and placed it on his desk. For some reason, he didn't want it to look as though it had been hidden or well-used. When it made its way back to the rest of the file he didn't want it to stand out in any way. He hadn't kept it back with a purpose but it felt like it had one now. Augustine had a telephone call to make.

52

Sally had only been up for a short while and Jojo was already agitating to get out for a walk. Sally slept well after she had managed to doze off and was still in sleep mode on her second cup of coffee when Jojo first began. Sally loved her coffee. It was only cheap stuff that she bought from the local pound shop, but she would go through a couple of jars a week. She knew people that would drink as much as she did but in the expensive coffee shop chains and spend hundreds of pounds a month on coffee. She just wanted a strong black pick-me-up and didn't mind too much about the flavour. Jojo would have to wait until she was dressed and presentable. Walking around scruffy in the dark with a dog was one thing but walking without getting dressed properly in the daylight was another thing altogether. Sally went to the bathroom and looked at herself in the mirror. She wasn't much impressed at what she saw. The rain from the night before had given her hair that frizzy look that the humidity of holidays only usually delivered. The bags under her eyes were reaching towards the floor in a manner that she had never seen before. And this is what sleep does for you, she thought.

Sally took her time over getting ready. The sound of the shower, the electric toothbrush and the hair dryer drowned out the agitation of the dog and allowed her a little time to do what she wanted. She wasn't going in to work. She had texted her boss and he understood. Official company policy stated that she should ring within half an hour of her shift beginning but he wasn't the type of manager to get worked up over the occasional absence. She told him briefly in the text what she had seen and knew this would buy her a few days at least, not that she needed them. In all likelihood, she would be back in the following day and would be the centre of attention as her colleagues would want to know what she had been through. She was quite private with many parts of her life but this was an opportunity that she couldn't miss out on.

Jojo had enough of waiting and began to bark and whine to go with the scratching at the door. Sally knew the game was up, but she was almost ready by that point. She grabbed her coat and slipped on her shoes as she left. It had stopped raining and was a fine day by the time the two of them had walked to the edge of the property and joined the pavement. Sally immediately regretted putting her coat on but Jojo was off and away. She tied the two arms of her coat together around her waist and followed her dog. This time Jojo walked in the opposite direction to the one that they followed the night before. Sally was torn between getting away from the events of the previous night and getting a closer look as part of her intrigue. She decided to follow her pet and then maybe see if she could steer her towards the road they found the body in later in the walk.

Sally took her time ambling along behind Jojo, who now found every aspect of every part of every inch of pavement interesting. Sally couldn't help but wonder if it was the find from the night before that had sparked this intrigue from her dog or whether it had always been there and she hadn't noticed. In any event, Sally couldn't get Jojo to walk where she wanted. The dog was off on a mission that only she could decipher. Her owner was just there to follow behind.

After a short while Sally noticed Jojo walk across the road and on to the shaded side of the street. They had walked in the sun all the journey to that point so Sally hadn't even considered that there was anything in the way of shade present that day. As she walked along the street shaded by the buildings above and hemmed in by the cars parked along the side of the road, Sally felt a cool breeze and decided to put her jacket back on. The slight chill that told her summer was starting to fade and autumn was on its was enough to persuade Sally to put her hands in her pockets. She had heard of Reynaud's Disease and wondered many times if she had it. The cold on her knuckles and her feet was painful and once it began she found it almost impossible to shake the feeling. After a few seconds when the numbing had died down a little she felt a piece of paper in her pocket. Sally remembered that she had removed it from the body she found to check for any injuries. It was too dark to see the night before. Sally looked at the paper. It had a single letter imprinted on it – I.

She thought this was strange and put it back in her pocket. It couldn't have anything to do with the body She had found. It must have been from a printed document and blown there before landing on the body. There is no way that someone would print a single letter and leave it on a dead body, would they?

Jojo was heading towards home and Sally just followed. The traffic at this time of day was light as most had already begun their day's work. The few others that she saw were on foot as the weather was pleasant out of the shade. Sally returned home and put the kettle on before she did anything else. Jojo was still itching for a bit of activity, so she opened the back door and let the dog run around the garden. Sally listened to the increasing churn of water in the kettle until a click went and the sound died down. She poured the scolding water over the cheap instant coffee powder and stirred vigorously. It took a bit of work to get the granules dissolved but Sally felt that a cheap coffee habit was better than an expensive coffee habit. The detective in Sally wanted to know what had happened to the body she found. She sat down and put on the 24-hour news channel to see if there were any reports for her to go on. There was a row going on in Brussels about something to do with the Euro and this dominated the news reports and discussions. It was on in the background while Sally let her imagination go wild about the body of the woman.

It was a love triangle and the other two have run off into the sunset together.

It was suicide and she left the letter on her chest to denote that 'I' did it.

She was hunted and killed by an alien species and the body fell into the undergrowth from their space craft.

Now she knew she was getting too carried away with it. Suddenly the phone rang. Sally threw all thoughts of the body to one side and answered.

"Hello…." She never really knew what to say on the phone so just hoped the person at the other end would take the lead.

"Sally? It's Augustine, the detective. We met last night. I just wanted to see if you were OK. It can be quite a shock to see a dead body."

"I'm OK, I think. I'm not really awake, but I think that it might be the disruption to my sleep pattern rather than the shock of seeing the body. It didn't feel real."

"I'm glad you're OK. I suffer badly when seeing bodies and I have seen a great deal of them. If you ever need anyone to talk to you have my number."

"Thank you, Augustine. I'll bear that in mind."

"I was calling to talk through your statement from last night. Nothing to worry about, just checking that it was all correct, now you have had time to sleep on it. I have handed this case over to a colleague, who will be investigating from here. His name is Jon Foley and he is very good at what he does."

"That's a shame. I was kind of hoping to deal with you in the future, detective."

Augustine blushed. Sally blushed. Neither could see but they both suspected that the other was going through the same physical reaction to her comment. Augustine waited for a few seconds before speaking again. He wanted to retain composure. After the short wait, he went through the different parts of her statement again, as he remembered it, just to be thorough. He started with the journey behind her dog, he couldn't remember the name, so he was sure how she approached the wooded area. He wanted to know if she had the same feeling of being alone in the world that she described the night before. She did.

Augustine checked the other parts of her account, like the number of times she touched the body, what her dog was doing at the time (Sally reminded him the dog was called Jojo) and how long it took her to call the police. He made no notes whatsoever as he saw no reason to pull her up on any of her account. He just felt that he should keep her talking.

At the end of the account, Augustine asked Sally if there was anything else she had remembered after a good night's sleep. Sally paused for a few seconds.

"Sally. Is there something else?" Augustine felt this was the time to prompt her. She had given him nothing new up to that point but he was compelled to push he on this question. Her hesitation was enough to pique his interest.

Sally replied, "I don't know if it is connected or even if it is important I forgot last night and then I found it again this morning. On the centre of her chest was a piece of paper with a single letter printed on it. Do you think it might be significant Augustine?"

But the other end of the line was dead. Augustine had already shouted out of the office to Ash who had now started work, and he was on the way to see Jon Foley. Ash was sent on a mission to retrieve the file and was asked to meet Augustine outside the back of the building. They were on their way to see Sally.

53

Sally sat and waited. She had worked out that the piece of paper was important and went to the kitchen to get some rubber gloves to pick it out of her pocket with. She shut the back door on Jojo, she would be happy in the garden for hours. What had the dog unearthed? Sally looked out across the garden and thought she should have made more effort with it before the detective arrived. He hadn't said he was coming but she was sure he would be here any minute. The lawn hadn't been mown in over a week and she hadn't dead-headed the flowers that had passed their summer bloom and were wilting in time for Autumn. She was proud of her garden when it looked its best but a little ashamed when she got lazy and let it all drop a bit. She was sure the detective would have bigger fish to fry but the garden was nagging away at Sally.

As she looked once again and wondered if she had the time to mow the lawn the doorbell rang. She walked from the kitchen, looking at the state of her front room as she travelled the short walk to the front door. Sally rearranged the cushions on the sofa before seeing her coffee cup on the floor next to the right-hand leg of the same sofa. They would have to wait a few seconds. She had to move the cup to the kitchen and out of sight. Sally skipped back to the front door and opened it. She felt a push against the door from the other side straight away. It wasn't what she had expected. The security chain was on, she didn't feel totally comfortable in the city, and there was a hand pushing from the other side of the door. She looked through the gap but the body was so close to the door she couldn't see what was going on. Sally said, "who is it?"

"My name is Ash. I'm with the police. There are a couple of reporters out here. I'd like to get in if I can."

Sally opened the door. She saw a man ducking under his jacket to keep away from the photographer a couple of doors down who was snapping away at his camera, over the bushes. She followed suit and covered her face before slamming the door behind the two of them.

They stumbled into the hallway in the rush to get out of sight of the reporters. Ash tried to stand up straight and look dignified but the time for that had passed. He looked at the woman who had let him in and recognised her from the brief description that Augustine had given him. It was one of the rare occasions that Augustine had volunteered to drive. He was already waiting in his car when Ash returned from visiting Jon Foley's team for the file. Foley wasn't there, the rumour was that he hardly ever was, but the guy who had picked up the file was only too happy to hand it back. As they pulled into the street where Sally lived, Ash could see reporters up and down the street. Obviously, someone had made a call. Some of the reporters were in the wooded area while others were knocking on doors. Augustine made the decision for Ash to jump out and for him to do a few laps around the block before returning. All he wanted was for Ash to ask a few questions and get the piece of paper. That would be enough for now.

"You forgot about the piece of paper when you spoke to the police last night?" asked Ash as he nodded towards the paper that was sat centrally on the coffee table in the living room.

"Do you want a drink? Tea, coffee?" Sally enquired hoping that Augustine would be following behind soon.

"No thanks, I won't be here long," Ash shuffled into the living room hoping that Sally would follow and offer him a seat. He was never comfortable taking the lead in someone else's home, even in his professional shoes. Ash was relieved that Sally took his hint, followed him in and pointed to a chair. He could get on with the matter in hand.

"So, what happened with the piece of paper?"

"I was looking for wounds. I didn't know if she was alive or dead to begin with. It seemed odd that there was a piece of paper on her chest, and I removed it to see if there was a cut or puncture wound underneath. I had checked her head and the rest of her body and found nothing. I put it in my pocket while I checked and then forgot about it. I went for a walk with Jojo, my dog, this morning and I found it in my jacket pocket again. I still didn't think it was connected to the body until I spoke to your colleague, until I spoke to Augustine," Sally was aware that she was being watched while she spoke. She had assumed that it was the same the night before when she spoke to first the police officer and then Augustine, but it was dark and she was consumed by the events. But now in the light and with a sleep behind her she was more sensitive to this. The detective who had introduced himself as Ash was watching her face as she spoke. Sally was uncomfortable and sped up her speech to stop him doing this.

"I understand. It may or it may not be connected to the body," Ash lied. The information about the letters hadn't made it into the public sphere until then and he wasn't going to be the one that let it. He was sure that Gary was more than capable of that. "I have an evidence bag, I'm going to put the piece of paper in that, in case it is of any use to us."

"I see. I'd love your job. I'd love to be able to follow the clues to find a killer," Sally found herself speaking her thoughts. It happened far too often for her liking, but she had grown used to it. Sally was aware that she was being watched again and stopped. Ash wasn't totally comfortable with her and would be advising Augustine to have another chat with her. She had missed vital evidence once; there was nothing to say that she knew more that she hadn't told them yet. But for now, he knew that Augustine would be driving up and down trying to hide from the reporters. Ash wasn't that well known to the journalistic community, but Augustine had been around long enough to attract the attention of every newshound in the city. Ash said his thanks to Sally and headed for the door.

"If you think of anything else - anything no matter how small, then please get in touch. You have Augustine's card. Here is mine," Ash handed over his business card. They were all produced on the same software in the same way, so the only difference between Ash's business card and the one that Sally had received from Augustine the night before were the name and number. She didn't see a lot of point in having cards for two people that probably sat only a few feet from each other at most, but she took it anyway.

Ash walked out of the front door and saw reporters from his right, pretty much exactly where they had been when he walked in, and Augustine's car moving slowly along the street to his left. He held up both arms at once. The left to let Augustine know he was ready and the right to shield his face from the photographers. Augustine pulled up with a screech of tyres and Ash ran across the street to get in. They both pulled the sun visors in their respective side of the car down and Augustine drove carefully to the end of the road. The last thing he wanted was for one of the reporters or photographers to jump out into the road in front of him. He indicated right and turned left at the end of the road to put them off his trail. It was only a few seconds before he looked in his mirror. There was nobody to be seen.

"Do you have it?"

"Yes."

"Does it look like our man?"

"Yes."

Not another word was spoken on the journey back to the police station. Both men were deep in thought.

54

Augustine and Ash updated the rest of the team on what had happened. Electra guessed that there was some sort of developments at the way the two of them left quickly but hadn't expected it to be news of that magnitude. It got all of the team thinking differently. They had assumed that they were all dealing with a murderer who had been killing people for only a few weeks at most, but this indicated that it had been going on far longer than that.

Gary just sat there with a grin on his face. Augustine could tell that he was enjoying the fact they had been barking up a tree that wasn't entirely wrong, but wasn't entirely right either for a while. Augustine wanted to take him to one side, but decided that he could have his smirk. It cost nothing and was worth nothing either.

The rest of the day went away in relative silence. They all worked but the mood was as downbeat as it ever had been. Augustine let them get it out of their system. There was still a long way to go with this investigation, it seemed, so he knew there would be some bad days to go with the good.

55

Police officer Andy Lane was walking the beat on a quiet shift. It was hot. The kind of late summer day that the television weathergirls called the Indian summer, but he had no idea what that meant. All he knew at that point in time was that he wanted someone to talk to. The day had dragged. It was several hours since his last call and that was just to break up a few kids hanging around in front of a shop. They had been setting alight the contents of a bin and then putting it back out again with a dustbin lid taken from the side of a local shop. They had done this a few times and the shop owner wasn't very happy. He didn't want them in front of his shop in case it put his customers off, so he called about the fire. Andy Lane had been trained extensively in 'community policing' but after all that training, he found that he was a natural at it anyway. He just listened to people and calmed them before going on his way.

The hours since had been spent walking up and down the streets. The police presence had been upped in and around the city centre since the killings and he was part of this reassuring presence. PC Andy Lane was a friendly face on the streets for many. The evening was starting to show signs of taking over from the afternoon. The sun was lower in the sky and the intense brightness had faded. Insects were slowing down their activity in preparation for the coolness that would reach the city over the next few hours. People were starting to return home from school and work so the number of cars and bodies near to Andy Lane was getting higher.

He walked almost aimlessly around the streets on days like this. He would just walk around and make sure people could see him. The actual aim of his duty was to reassure and to provide a warning not to misbehave. Andy saw the best way to do this was just to be present. The more streets he was seen on, the better he had done his job. He turned a corner onto a street on felt the full glare of the sun in his eyes. He raised his right hand and decided that he would turn into the road on the left around 100 yards in front of him. PC Lane listened to the sound of children playing in the park at the end of the street. When he was younger it used to be football in the winter and cricket in the summer. But the money in football had made it something that was played all year round. But the local kids had just got into cricket in a big way. He could hear he unmistakeable sound of ball on bat and raised a smile. Perhaps there was a future for the England cricket team after all, he chuckled to himself.

It felt like it took an age to reach the road he had planned to walk down to shield his eyes from the sun. The insects that were still bathed in sunshine hadn't given up quite yet and several bit at his neck as he walked the last few yards to the road on his left. The sound from the slaps he delivered to try to kill them reverberated along the streets with no wind to carry it away. In the end, Andy Lane slapped his neck a few times even when he didn't feel a bite from the insects. For one thing, he was trying to pre-empt them, and for another he liked the sound it made.

Finally, he reached the street and turned left. He was happy that the sun was now out of his eyes. It took a few seconds for his eyes to adjust. When they did he cursed himself that he had walked into a cul-de-sac. He was going to have to turn around again to face the sun. Andy looked up and down the street and something felt familiar. He was new to the city and didn't know if all of these cul-de-sacs looked the same. He turned on his heels and tried to remember if he had seen another escape route from the glare of the sun any further down the road. His brain told him to slow down. He had no idea why, but something told him to stop. It was after a few seconds that he realised what his brain had been trying to tell him. It was the street where he had investigated the abandoned car. It was the street where he had spoken to the man who was staring into the car. It was the street that he had told himself that he would return to and investigate.

PC Andy Lane walked across the street towards the place where he had seen the car. He recalled his conversation as best he could, but checked back though his notebook to recall exactly what was said. The man that he had spoken to wasn't connected to the theft of the car. That was a bunch of teenagers and they had already dealt with that. But he made Andy feel uneasy. He looked back through his notebook to try to find some clarity. It was several pages back before he could find the notes he made while he was speaking to the gentleman. Although it wasn't that long ago, PC Andy Lane took notes all the time. He relied on them for occasions like this where he couldn't quite remember what had gone on. He took them in case one of his superiors asked him what had gone on in a given situation. It was always handy to have notes relating to every encounter as a policeman, Andy thought.

The notes were good enough for him to recall what had gone on –

'Car reported as abandoned in Auriel Close. I got to the address at 5.15am. As I arrived there was a male stood looking into the car. When questioned he said that he had reported the car himself. He was vague about the car and the street, but seemed to know his way around. I asked him where he lived and he gestured towards the opposite side of the street. I think he lives at number 12.'

That was enough to get Andy Lane interested in this again. He recalled the early morning and the surprise that there was a man stood looking into the car that had been reported the night before. There was another call that stopped him talking to the man further on that morning, or even getting his name, but being back in the sunshine at that location made Andy decide to investigate further. He crossed the street and looked at the property that he had identified as the possible home of the man he met. Now he could feel the sun in the corner of his right eye every time he stepped between the houses on that side of the road. It was low enough to be hidden by the homes, but still had enough warmth to tingle on his face as it hit him for a few seconds at a time.

It had been far too long since he had anything interesting to do that day and Andy Lane had decided that a chat with the man he had to break off his conversation with a few days earlier was a good way to get his interest levels back up again. It was far better than just walking around, waiting for his shift to end.

The insects had disappeared from the street as there was now more shade than sun. Andy thought that they might have gone back to the street where he was blinded by the orange-red brightness. At least they had a few more minutes there. This part of town felt so quiet, so abandoned. Just like the car, he thought. The people who lived here must have been left to rot. They are hidden away from the world, with no prying eyes to see them. Andy noticed that many of the properties looked empty. This that showed some signs of life still had the curtains closed and looked for all the world like the people inside relied on help to do anything and everything. He couldn't shake the feeling that he was in a lost part of the city. It was as though he had walked into a black hole that kept all its secrets locked away from the rest of the city, the rest of the world.

He looked straight ahead now at the property with the number 12 stencilled on the bin. He was sure from the nod that he was given that this is where the man lived. If he did live at this address, then he was probably the only active member of this cul-de-sac, Andy thought. The property looked as though it needed a lot of care and attention. It was typical of the type of properties that landlords rented out to tenants who had no choice.

There was no scrutiny on these landlords and they could just leave people in the worst conditions. It was usually people who didn't know how to complain or didn't want to complain in case they drew attention to themselves, Whichever way, these people needed some help rather than being screwed over by unscrupulous landlords. Andy reached the drive and looked up and down for any signs of life. If there was someone home then nothing gave this fact away. Andy stopped for a second and radioed to his control where he was. He was going out on a limb to start knocking on doors, but if he ended up chatting to this guy for a while then he wanted his base to know the ground he had already covered and where he was. That would keep his boss off his back when he returned to the station later in the day. He walked up the drive and knocked on the door.

56

"It's time to go. There's nothing else to be seen or done here," Augustine told his team of people. They had been at their desks all day, except for the short trip to Sally's house for Ash and Augustine to pick up the letter laid on the chest of the latest victim of the serial killer – or that probably should have been the first victim. They had crunched the numbers and taken as much information as possible about the victim. Something reminded Lou of the first victim. He wondered whether these were experiments. He wondered whether the killer tried out his techniques on these first, knowing that one couldn't be identified and the other would take some time to find. He wondered a lot of things where the void was that usually gave him a clue to the identity and motive of the killer. If he was trying to leave the detectives a message, then it was a very narrow one from where Lou was sitting.

"Augustine, I'm going to stay a little while longer," Lou explained. He wanted to test a few theories and carry out some research. Also, he had nowhere else to go that appealed to him.

"No, Lou. We all need a break from this. You're coming with me. I need a drink and you could do with one too. No arguments," Augustine countered before opening up to the rest of the group, "you are all welcome to join us."

A few mumbles went around the room. Nothing that was particularly enthusiastic, but also nothing that was negative either. Augustine waited by the door for two reasons. Firstly, he wanted to make sure they had all left and secondly, he wanted to see who was coming with him. It was the whole team. Augustine looked up at the poor-quality strip lighting that his team had to endure all day long. It flickered every now and again, but not that any of them noticed while working. The lack of quality light in the room was a concern for Augustine. He read a lot of architectural magazines out of personal interest and they all talked about the benefits of natural light. Even in the offices of Scandinavia, where the sun didn't rise above the horizon, they had taken into account the need for natural light. Augustine couldn't get his head around any point in time in the past where this wasn't considered important. Obviously the 1960's, when this particular police station was built didn't feel the needs of the people on the inside.

Even Gary had hit the floor during the day. They all thought they had some form of containment on the killer with the relatively recent nature of the crimes. But the possibility that this new body brought of the killer being active for several months and having hidden a body changed the way they had all been thinking. Up until that call to Sally, they had thought that killing significant (to him) figures in public places where he modus operandum and the body count was at 4. But now this could be any number and all the people of the city were potential targets. They all lined up by the door to go for a drink. Augustine told them all to leave their cars at the station. They would walk to the nearest pub and get a taxi home. With pressure on the team to provide a solution he couldn't afford any scandals of drink-driving in his small but (mostly) dedicated bunch of people.

They set off together across the road while there was still no sign of nightfall. Augustine looked up to the blue of the sky directly above and looked for the first sign of stars in the sky. It had been night when all of the previous murders had happened, as far as they could tell. He wondered where the killer was and when he would strike next. He also wondered how many bodies would visit him in his sleep that night. Then he looked down, through the orange brightness of the near horizon and through to the rest of the team walking in front of him. Augustine wanted a result in this case for them as much as him. He was the one that took on all the obscure cases with a small chance of success. It was his decision that led the rest of them to the low point they were feeling then. It was his responsibility to lead them from this to a success or two every now and again. Solving this case would be the biggest success any of them would have experienced in their career, including him. They turned right into the beer garden of the first pub they came across. Augustine took the orders and went to the bar with Gary. He was being unusually helpful and this made Augustine even more nervous. Like having children – when they are quiet is the time you should worry most about what they are up to. The two of them carried the drinks back to the rest of the team and they all took a long sip before any conversation began. Augustine could see this might be a long night for him.

57

Andy Lane stood in front of the door. In his early days in the police force, he had been taught that you should always knock on a door rather than ring the bell. Using a bell could leave you wondering. If you didn't hear the bell, you might think that it wasn't working, or it wasn't very loud or it was only heard inside the house. This inserted a delay and prompted a repeat action. You might end up listening very close to the door to check out whether the bell sounded. There was no such ambiguity with a knock. You knew that you have rapped hard on the door and that the sound would travel into the property. Andy Lane knocked so hard that the door opened. At first, he wondered whether he had broken something as the door swung slowly open, the hinges giving a creak of desire for oil on the way. But on closer inspection, he could see that the door hadn't been locked. Andy looked through the hallway in front of him. It gave him a view of most of the house from one vantage point. PC Andy Lane looked straight ahead and saw a small kitchen that was in need of modernisation, as the estate agent's patter went. But it was clean from what he could see and there was nothing left out of place. Andy wondered whether there was anyone living there at all, whether the person he met in the street had given him a false idea of where he lived to put him off the scent. On the right was a living room that had wallpaper that was peeling on the top edges. It hadn't got so bad that it needed to be ripped off but it could have done with some wallpaper glue and a bit of pressure. PC Andy Lane had learned that a bit of pressure resolved a lot of issues. In his line of work pressure on the wound of someone he found after an emergency call could very well keep them alive. It would stop them from losing too much blood and provide a window of hope for the medical team. Pressure on a suspect when questioning would often lead to them giving up answers that they hadn't intended. 'Keep them talking' was a motto he had heard used a lot in his basic training, but once on the job he found that there was more to it than that. Let someone talk and they could go on about the weather, he latest football results or the state of the economy. Apply some basic pressure and you can get someone talking about what you want them to talk about.

"Where were you at 3PM yesterday?"

"How many times have you been to this area?"

"Where did you get that watch?"

These were all questions that when repeated, often yielded different answers. The cracks in a made-up alibi would start to appear and you could eventually drive a lorry through the gaps left. Pressure would change the balance of power in these situations. The pressure on the wallpaper would only need to be applied for a few seconds, but would bring the room back to life. Andy couldn't help but feel that the neatness of the kitchen felt different to the slightly ragged edge of the living room. Maybe the person who lived there didn't use the living room. There was a seat that didn't look sat-in and the absence of a television was another clue that this room wasn't in regular use.

To the left was an empty room. It was too small to be a dining room and too big to be a study, so it was probably difficult for the person who lived there to decide what to do with. Andy saw that they had decided to do nothing with it. The door was open and there was nothing in the room. The walls were painted magnolia, a sign that the property was rented, and the carpet was cheap cream one that was mirrored throughout the areas he could see in the house. Where it was on the stairs, it was starting to pull and looked saggy. Cheap carpets always do after a few years of even the lightest wear. The room had nothing else, not even curtains. PC Andy Lane could see that this was a house that wasn't lived in by a family, more likely a single person. It could be his man.

Up those stairs was a door that was halfway open and he could see the room in front of him from a low angle. He could make out a desk of some sort and what looked like several monitors. Without moving he tried to scan all that was there to see in the room. The walls we covered, but not with receding wallpaper like the living room he had just looked at, but with what seemed like post-it notes, newspaper clippings and pieces of paper. It looked like an office rather than a bedroom. He looked around the ceiling of the hallways and tried to estimate how many other rooms might be upstairs out of his view. He estimated 2 or 3 bedrooms plus a bathroom. If his theory about only one person living there was correct meant that this room could be a study or office and the occupant would still have space to have their own bedroom. PC Lane stood and thought about his next move. Walking back out again would leave him with many questions unanswered. He had been at the door of the property for around a minute but wanted to know far more about what he could see. As a child, he had been a story writer. He would meet a person or see some aspect of life and then write a whole story around it. He still did it in his head to that day. He would see a room, a photograph or speak to someone for a few seconds and then write their whole life story behind it. His imagination would construct a backstory, a series of events and contact with an imaginary set of characters. The questions that the rooms he could see in this property would conjure up would give him a whole novel to write in his head if he let it. Stepping further into the property would answer a lot of these questions for him.

The other option was to explore further. He had already radioed back to let the control room know where he was, so it wasn't as though he would be expected anywhere else. If nobody was in it would only take a couple of minutes to look at what was inside and satisfy himself. He wanted to see a photograph of the man he has spoken to or to find a utility bill lying around so he could call back and check his identity. Anything to resolve the unanswered questions in his mind. He decided that he should find out if anyone was there, so he called in a midrange voice, "hello. Is there anyone here? Can you hear me?" Andy Lane realised at that point that there was no sound at all. There was nothing from the house, from the neighbourhood or the streets that would be crisscrossed by cars only a few hundred yards away. It was eerie. He asked again, the same words but a little louder. Still nothing. He walked into the hallway and made a decision. He turned off his radio. He didn't want to be disturbed. The upstairs room that had all the items on the wall was a better prospect to find the information he wanted than the rooms downstairs that were empty. He slowly walked up the steps with his eyes down on his feet. The carpet was worn through in places and it was clear that the tacks underneath were not holding it in place. It was the kind of staircase that you expect to creak with every step, but there was no sound at all, continuing the silence Andy had observed and then broken a few seconds earlier. He listened out for the sound his muscles and bones might make when exerting the pressure on his feet to climb the stairs but nothing.

As he neared the top of the stairs, PC Andy Lane slowed to make sure he wasn't disturbing anyone. At the top of the stairs was another window that had no curtains and he peered out of the window in the direction of the street. In the garden of the next-door neighbour was the bike of a young child, turned upside down and rusted from several years exposure to the elements. Andy wondered what the child might be doing now, in his usual manner. He thought for a few seconds that they could have fallen off the bike and been injured, grown out of it and just discarded it or something more sinister might have happened. It felt like the kind of neighbourhood where something sinister could have happened in the past, swallowed up by the silence. Andy Lane pulled himself back into the room – he didn't have the luxury of being able to go deep into his imagination at that point. He wanted some information and then to go. There were two other rooms to his right as he got to the top of the stairs in addition to the one he could see from the front door. He walked towards the two rooms that sat adjacent at the end of the corridor. He walked past the room that had made up his mind that he should go upstairs. Andy wanted to investigate them all but the lure of the room at the top of the stairs meant that this had to be the first one to enter. He turned back and walked towards the door.

As PC Andy Lane walked into the room, the enormity of the information struck him. There were newspaper clippings, notes, printouts and maps all over the walls. There was so much information that PC Lane went into overload and didn't take any of it in initially. He thought that the occupant might have been a train spotter and was collecting masses of information. He looked at the map on the wall, drawn on a whiteboard and considered what all the lines and dots might mean. The map was of the city and there were colours all over it that must mean something significant to the person who drew it. They were a talented artist, as the map was as good as anything that could have been printed. Andy stood for a while and admired the artwork. It was a sight to behold for someone who could barely hold a pencil. In art classes at school nobody wanted to sit near Andy. Not only was he nothing of an artist, he was also by far the most likely in the class to knock over the pot of water or spill paint on whoever was sitting next to him. The talent to draw a map of the city, presumably freehand, was something way beyond his comprehension. He studied the detail that he could figure out instantly from the map. He had never been great at reading maps but could see where the hospital was that he had taken his mother to time after time as she fought the cancer in her lungs that finally took her life. He saw the police station where he began his work every day. He saw the Museum of Innocence that his father took him to several times a year, where his interest in the world stemmed from. The museum was marked in red, as was the theatre where he had been sent in the aftermath of the killing of the entertainer. PC Lane found this odd. He looked for more areas marked in red on the map. There was a small wooded area near to the street he was at now, as well as an alleyway off the main street.

While he was looking at the map, something caught the corner of his eye. At first, he thought it was movement but soon realised that the sun glinting through the window was catching on a photograph that was pinned to the wall. On closer inspection, there were many photographs. With each one was a series of notes that seemed to describe details about their life –

where they travelled, at what times, something interesting about them and then something nasty about them. For instance, under the photograph he had first noticed was a note that said, '8.45am home to work @ Sand Street, arrival at 8.55am. Return journey from 5.10pm to arrive home at August Road at 5.20pm. Monday to Friday only. Never uses an umbrella. Ties her blonde wavy hair up in the rain and exposes her throat. Slept with 6 people she works with.' It was the last sentence on every note that made Andy Lane feel uneasy about the wall. There were comments that made him feel judgement was being passed. The person who wrote these, and all were in the same handwriting, was setting targets, that much he was sure of. There were a few gaps on the wall, where it looked as though pins and Blu Tack had been used to secure more photographs, more notes, more abuse.

He wondered why those people had been taken down. He wondered why the abuse had been removed, but he didn't wonder for long. As PC Andy Lane looked to his right he could see a wall that was roughly the same dimensions. The squareness of the room had escaped him up to that point but it was now obvious. In the exact same places as the gaps on the wall where the desk was placed were photographs and notes on the wall to the right. The first photo was someone he recognised. It was Jeff Caine, the politician who was killed a few weeks earlier. Lane looked back across the room to the wall opposite and saw the red mark in front of the building of his political organisation Britain Excelsior. He quickly put all of these pieces together and assumed that this was the killer they had been looking for. He wanted to check his assumption was right. One more face from the wall. Again, the photo he checked was one he recognised. It was the entertainer from the theatre. He already knew here was a red mark there. He already knew that this was the scene of another killing. Slid behind the photographs were newspaper clippings. They were placed neatly so the photo held them up against the wall and they could be accessed at any time. Andy Lane took one from behind the image of Jeff Caine and it was a newspaper report about the killing. Along the border were the words 'killed because he oppressed me' and the political party underlined wherever it appeared in the article. There were six mentions and, along with the words in the margin, all stood out in red ink against the black and white of the newspaper.

PC Andy Lane started his radio up. It was an old model that he was given when his went in for repair. It always took a few minutes to charge up and be ready for use. He would wait for it to charge and then call for help. This was something that he couldn't handle on his own.

58

Augustine and the rest of the team were drinking slowly. None wanted to be the first to leave but also none wanted to get drunk. They had moved from the beer garden to the inside of the pub. The beer garden had been great to begin with. The smell of barbecues from those that were making the most of the warmth wafted across where they sat and mixed with the alcohol and the last of the evening heat made for a pleasant combination. Augustine found that it made him hungry and got a few packs of crisps with the next order. This hadn't filled the hole and he considered asking the rest of them if they wanted to join him at the nearest curry house. Then he decided that they all had better things to do without even asking them.

Inside the pub was a mix of the old and the new. The carpet looked like it has been there for decades, with a swirling blue pattern. It had stood up remarkably well to the test of time and the patter of drunken feet across it, not to mention what had been spilled over the years. Augustine was impressed that it didn't show signs of wear in any part he looked. Even near the bar, where he assumed the most number of feet would have walked, it looked as though it was new. Maybe that was the idea behind the pattern – it drew your attention away from any wear. The atmosphere inside the pub was less summery than outside. The building had been there at least as long as the carpet and the light was almost non-existent. Another building that the Scandinavians wouldn't have put up with, Augustine thought to himself. And as such it felt cold. The summer clothing that was evident outside was replaced with jackets and long trousers. People who had been to the pub before, and the clientele looked like they were regulars, knew that the weather outside had little bearing on the conditions inside. All came prepared.

The conversation meandered everywhere except what had occupied their minds all day. Unlike the last time they had all gone out together, Augustine didn't feel the need to steer people away from subjects and be the facilitator. He just listened and added a comment where he felt necessary. Talking about the latest hit celebrity television show left Augustine without a great deal to say. He never followed these things, and hadn't heard of any of the celebrities either so he smiled a lot and nodded where he felt appropriate. It was like being in a nightclub and not hearing what the other person was saying. But Augustine's hearing wasn't crowded out by noise, it was just that he switched off his hearing in between comments.

Electra held court for most of the evening. She could switch between being in the background and being the centre of attention with ease. She would play many distinct roles in life. She had got to her limit with Gary and decided that the best way to keep his mouth at bay was to take control. She lined up the conversations, she dictated when they changed and she asked questions of others. Gary would just have to dance to her tune.

"Who has something to tell us about themselves that we don't already know?" Electra asked as she looked across the rest of the people sat around the table. She was trying to make eye contact. She had learned (or was it she had been taught?) that eye contact went a long way in these situations. She wanted someone else to take the floor for a little while, but she would remain in control. She saw her role in this 'confession' as interviewer, so whoever stepped forward would answer what she wanted to know. Gary was game.

"I've got loads of stories that none of you know about me. I'll start with a tame one and see if you can handle it before we move on to something a little juicier," he loved the attention and wanted to wrestle it away from Electra. Perhaps that is why the two of them clashed so often.

"I used to be a criminal," Gary made the statement and then paused. He wanted it to have maximum effect.

"I can see that all of you are having a tough time believing that someone as innocent as me could ever have a criminal past," he said amidst the sniggers. "You may wonder how I got through the background checks to join the force, or how I have managed to cover it up for so many years, but I am sitting here now telling you that I have a criminal past," he spoke with a glee in his voice that made it sound as though he was proud of it.

"I suspected this for some time, but haven't got all the evidence together yet," joked Ash. He made light of any situation that made him feel uncomfortable. He then sneaked a glance at Augustine before returning to gaze at Gary for a response.

"You'll never catch me, cop!" Gary replied at what was now nearing the top of his voice. The rest of the pub turned around but Gary had his back to them; he was on a roll and wasn't going to stop.

"I started early, it was petty crime to begin with, but I could always see a future of bigger and better things. The first few times I can honestly say that I did it for the rush. The feeling I got was something else. I didn't want it to stop. Then after that I needed bigger hits to make me feel the same level of exhilaration," Gary continued with the pub behind his back as much of an audience as the table of colleagues in front of him.

Electra wanted her control back, so she started to ask the questions, "So you were young when you started? How young were you?"

The first time was a few months after my 17th birthday," Gary replied while staring straight into Electra's eyes. He was trying to unnerve her, but she wouldn't be deterred.

"And you carried this on until when?"

"I sometimes still do it now. Not very often, but when the mood takes me I just can't help it. It's like a drug," Gary was being more cryptic now than at the start of the conversation. Augustine smelt that they were being played with but wanted to see how this all panned out so sat back and just listened.

"I started at 31, 32 and then this wasn't enough. I then thought about going to 35 for a few months before doing it. Sometimes I got way over 40, before calming back down again. My highest is 55. But I have always campaigned against the 30 miles per hour speed limit and I don't think it works," Gary finished with a massive smile on his face. The others joined in with the laughter. Augustine was delighted with how it ended. The rest of the team could have taken it in a very different way, but it felt to Augustine like they were bonding. Maybe Gary could be a valuable member of the team after all. The more they got to know him, the more they might like him. The stories went on. There wasn't a lot of drinking done, but the time together was going to get them all working together in the coming days. That was the hope anyway.

59

PC Andy Lane was excited. He had worked as a police officer for over a year and had been involved around the fringes of some major crimes. But his desire was to become a detective. He wanted to solve complex crimes and deliver hope to people. That was the whole reason he joined the police force. Some of his friends had cut him off when he joined. He was told that when you are in the police, your only friends are the police. They weren't exactly hardened criminals but hung around in circles where being friends with a policeman wasn't accepted. He just had to learn to live with it. When he went to parties, people who didn't know him asked what he did. The response always made people warier of what they said. People tended to drink less around him and act in a different way. It felt good that he was respected, but he didn't feel that others relaxed in his company. Sometimes he tried too hard to make people relax and ended up getting quite drunk himself. His desire to help people always came out in his actions.

His radio was making a small screeching sound that indicated the battery was warming up, in the same way the flash used to warm up on an old camera in the days before digital and smartphones. He would be able to speak to someone in a minute or so and get the help he needed to gather this evidence, find the occupant and make the biggest splash of his career so far. As he listened, the silence was still there, still taking up every spare space in the world around him. Andy looked out of the window to his left without moving his feet. He wanted to see if there was any movement in the neighbourhood. How could a part of such a bustling city be so run down and so quiet? There was a slight breeze that was moving only the tips of the leaves on the trees near to the house. If he hadn't been looking directly for a sign of movement then he would never have noticed it.

The room was amazing in many ways. That someone could have such a detailed plan of the city and the people in it stunned Andy Lane. He wasn't expecting anything of the sort, even when he imagined the killer that most of the police were hoping to find. He thought of the killer as someone who was good at what they did, but didn't consider the planning that went into being that good. He wasn't involved directly in the case, but had heard that the killer left no clues behind, no fingerprints and no hairs. Now he knew how someone could kill who he wanted and when he wanted without a great deal of fear of capture. But not now. His killing days were over. Andy would bring him to justice and end the fear that was in the hearts of the people of this great city. The end to this particular brand of evil was near.

PC Lane turned around and stepped towards the door. He wanted to get outside, away from the stifling evil to call for backup. As he turned, he saw a series of letters on the wall in front on him. They were contained in plastic sheets, so they could be removed if needed. The first few letters were in a lighter colour, as though they had a different meaning or purpose, while the rest were on 4-inch square pieces of white paper. Andy Lane stepped back so he could see all of the letters at once. The spelled out a message –

'IN ALLAH WE TRUST TO DELIVER US FROM EVIL. LET HIM GIVE ME THE STRENGTH TO CARRY OUT HIS WORK. ALL INFIDELS MUST DIE.'

PC Lane went cold. He could feel blood drain away from his head and feet on its route to his vital organs. He retched as his body responded to the shock in his system. He looked again at the radio and realised it would be around 30 seconds before he would be able to speak to anyone. He put his hands on his knees and tried to breathe deeply. His body needed oxygen and fast. He gulped as much air as he could but didn't feel any different. Andy stepped out on to the landing to make his way downstairs.

"Good evening officer."

He looked to his left and saw the outline of a person in the darkness that was now taking over the house.

60

Augustine and Lou had made it as far as the curry house. This was Augustine's favourite cuisine and he would visit any curry house that showed a decent hygiene rating on the door. There was so much to choose from as the menu was around 15 pages long that the two of them asked the waiter for a while to make up their minds. Both men were hungry from working a long day and then taking in a few drinks at the pub. Lou had ordered the two of them a Cobra lager each while Augustine went to the toilet. He found that as he got older, the chill of the night air would work its way to his bladder before it reached anywhere else. He wondered if this was something that would pass in a few years. Clearly it hadn't affected Lou in the same way.

When he returned, Augustine sipped a large gulp of Cobra and asked Lou what he thought of the evening. Augustine valued Lou's opinion after his many years in different departments in the force.

"I think we are coming together as a team. But that doesn't get us any closer to catching this bastard," Lou commented. It was the comment Augustine had expected, but not one he wanted to hear. He knew the killer felt as far away now as he ever did, but wanted someone to tell him it would be alright. If this was the answer he wanted, then Lou was the wrong man to ask. He always told it straight.

"Do you think that we will catch him? He feels so distant," Augustine wanted the conversation between the two men to focus on the killer, in contrast to the conversation the whole team were having earlier, which he wanted to be about anything but.

"We have to keep doing the right things. We are relying on him to slip up, but if you look through history, these guys always do. It might be on the next killing, or you might have to wait for years, but he will slip up one day," Lou offered as many words of comfort as he had. Augustine didn't feel any comfort at all in the situation. He was a man of action. He had patience (why else would he take on all the lost causes?) but he also wanted results.

The waiter came over and spoke in soft voice that belied his large frame, "do you want poppadums?" It was so quiet that Augustine had to ask him to repeat himself.

"Do you want poppadums?"

"We'll have a few, don't you think Lou?"

"Yes, Gus. It will give us time to work through the menu. I didn't think I would have to read this much just to order my food."

All Augustine heard was another person in his team that had called him Gus. It was too much to fight. He resigned himself to the fact that he would now be Gus and not Augustine. His mother hated names being shortened and always called him by his full first name. When his friends came around to his house and called him 'August' or 'Gus' she corrected them and the name that she had given him sort of stuck with him all his early life. She wasn't around anymore to protect it for him. He didn't have the energy to protect it himself. The name Gus was going to take over, he thought.

As the meal went on, the two men found a lot of common ground on the killer they were trying to catch. The one thing they agreed on was that they were missing a major piece of the jigsaw in the motive and meaning of the letters left on the chest of the victims. It meant something to someone, so should mean something to them. The fact that the killer had left these letters meant that he was giving them a message or classifying them in some way. There were five letters so far, and two of them had been repeated. That is what made Lou so sure that the victims were being identified as having the same characteristic in some way. The links to the newspaper and the letters they had received from what appeared to be the same person lead Lou to believe that people were being categorised by their perceived sins. But Gus wasn't convinced. He felt that there was something more to this. Whatever the case. He resolved to spend more time on it as a team the following day. It might provide a big step in the right direction. It might just keep him on the case.

61

"I said 'good evening' to you. Why don't you reply?"

PC Andy Lane couldn't move his lips. He had no idea that there was someone present and even less idea how long they had been there. But he felt as though this was a situation he had to get out of quickly. He looked down the stairs but felt the presence move towards him and close off that escape route. The man breathed heavily and Andy Lane could feel his breath against his face. It was even warmer than the air in the house and the police officer stepped back. He wanted to put space between himself and the man. His backward step put him in the centre of the room where the message was clear to see written large across the wall.

The man stepped forward and moved the policeman further into the room. As he stepped across the threshold the light from the window illuminated his face. It was then that PC Lane realised it was the same man he had spoken to in the street.

"Forgive me if I don't give you my full name, but I'd like to be known as Al. You will by now have grasped that I am holding a gun and you have no means of escape," Al spoke as though all of this were pure fact and couldn't be changed. Andy hadn't seen the gun until it was pointed out. He pretended to look to his feet, but was checking the radio to see if it had sprung into life. No such luck.

"You have seen far too much for me to ever let you go. My work is nowhere near finished, as you can see from the walls, so I can't run the risk of you interrupting me so early in the piece," Al didn't take his eyes off the police officer for one second. When he was young his brothers used to challenge him to staring contests, but Al always won. He had this uncanny ability to fix his eyes on a spot for minutes at a time without the prospect of blinking ever reaching them. He had used this power later in life to attract girls in bars, but for now it was keeping the policeman in check. Al quickly checked the side of the policeman's uniform and noted that he had no gun. It was rare to see armed police on the streets of the United Kingdom, but Al knew there were some out there. He had probably prompted more of them himself with the actions he had taken over the previous weeks.

Andy Lane had lost the ability to talk. He was working out his options but kept on coming up with a blank. There was only one viable escape route and that was blocked by a man with a gun, so he would have to take a risk to get out of this one. He decided to let Al talk and see what he had to say. At some stage, he might lose concentration and give him a chance.

"You must be impressed with the research I have put into this. I'm nothing like the image that the Daily Gossip put out there. I am organised and ready to kill at any time. You police have got nowhere near me in all this time. You have no idea who might be next," Al taunted the police officer who looked like a rabbit who had been caught in the glare of headlights and had no idea where to go. Al wanted the police officer to ask him questions. He wanted to explain the idea behind his work. It became clear that the police officer was going to say pretty much nothing at all, so Al imagined that he had been asked the questions anyway.

"All of this? It is the work that my life has been leading up to. For years I have watched my Muslim brothers try to rise up and repeat the success of 9-11. But driving a car into a few innocent people might get some headlines, but it does nothing to deliver our message. We don't want terror, although that has its interesting side. We want to teach you the error of your ways. The people of this country are bathed in sin and corruption. They are following a way of life that will only lead to damnation. I don't want to kill innocent people. I want to use guilty people to save the lives of the rest of us," Al was in full flow by now and was looking across the room for an audience that appreciated his words. But he found none. PC Lane was looking over Al's shoulder at the stairs and the only possible escape route.

"There is no way out. You can look beyond me all you like, but you can't look beyond the will of Allah. Your people need a leader, they need a new Moses. I will lead them to the promised land. I will lead them to a life free from sin," Al resembled a television preacher who had got carried away with the message. He was no longer trying to convince the police officer that he was right, he was trying to convince himself that he was right.

PC Andy Lane decided he could keep his silence no more. The good people of the country would never know his final words if the man stood between him and freedom pulled the trigger, but he felt compelled to say them anyway. "You are nothing but a killer. The people you are killing are more righteous than you. They have never killed. They are on the side of right. You are the sinner," Andy Lane spoke with the same level of conviction in his voice as the day he accepted his role in the police.

Al's eyes filled with rage. He stepped towards the policeman and raised his right hand with the gun in it. The police officer saw this as make or break and tried to stop Al from raising his hand. Al sidestepped him and kept on going with his right arm until it was high above his head. Then in one movement, he brought down all the force of his arm and the weight of the gun on the back of the police officer's head. He slumped at Al's feet and lay there lifeless. A beaming smile hit Al's face. He pulled on two plastic gloves from his pockets before grabbing the police officer's hands and dragging him face first down the stairs. He turned 180 degrees at the bottom of the stairs and took him out into the back garden. The trees around the garden had overgrown so much that he wasn't overlooked on any side. He flipped the policeman over before returning to the house. Al was gone for only a minute or so and returned with two items. The first was a knife that he used to make a cut on the man's trousers. Al made a few piercing cuts to his upper thigh before pulling the trousers back over to hide the wound and stop the blood that was now spurting out from getting on his own clothes or skin. The second item was the letter 'H' from the wall of the house. He placed it on the chest of the prostrate police officer and walked off into the house. A few minutes later he emerged from the front door with a case and a pocket filled with the rest of the letters and a briefcase filled with some of the other effects of his study. Al walked with a spring in his step and made his way out of the street he lived in. As he walked away the smoke from a downstairs window started to billow out into the street. He glanced over his shoulder and smirked at the scene that he had left behind. He was happy that someone would find the mess there because it might prompt them to finally reveal the fact he had left letters on the bodies of the people he killed. It might finally get his message out there.

62

The emergency operator had received no calls in the last half an hour of her shift. It was one of the most unusual days, but she though that the time of night coupled with the warm late summer weather had meant people were more engaged in having a wonderful time or sleeping than they were in creating emergencies. That was the part of the job that she didn't like and that she found others overlooked. When she told someone what she did for a living they would think that she would be proud she was helping others. But she was more concerned with why people called the emergency services.

Sam had been doing the job for around 8 months after her training but was reaching the end of her time there. She could no longer deal with the destruction that humans performed on each other. Just about every call she received was as the result of one person causing harm to another or to themselves. The ambulance calls she took, particularly at the weekend, were mainly drink and drug related. The police calls were pretty much the same, but with robbery thrown in too. The calls for the fire brigade were the result of arson or neglect. She thought that her time might be better spent stopping people from drinking, rehabilitating people away from crime or educating building owners that they need to keep on top of fire safety than it was clearing up the mess that all this made. She didn't feel any joy in her job, even on the odd occasion she got 'feedback' that she had saved someone's life. All she could picture was the person that had put them in a life-endangering situation in the first place.

It was near the end of her shift and Sam rejoiced that she only had a few minutes to go. She had taken no calls in half an hour and hoped that she could escape from any more for the next few minutes. Even the room she occupied was depressing. It was a small office with a few operators in. They had been arranged in the call centre style, so each had their own space, made by temporary screens and rarely saw each other. They were sat only a few yards apart for hours on end and didn't meet eye to eye. The modern drive for efficiency in every aspect of work life had overshadowed the need for people to feel valued and happy in their work. Sam was looking at what she could do to help in the real world and not in her 8-hour prison. She had considered counselling and education but was still to make her mind up. She knew that whatever lay ahead, this job was soon to be behind her. There would be a lot of work and studying to make a difference in her life, and some expense she might add, but it had to be better than this.

Sam looked at the three walls her screens had made and the effort she had put into making it feel more like a place she could spend time. The walls were filled with photos of her on holiday with friends and family. If one thing was bound to raise her spirits and remind her why she worked then it was the holidays she had been on in the past. They were a signal that there were more holidays to look forward to in the future, funded by her income. She looked over the pictures that were grouped together of the holiday she had with Tom, her brother and the mix of friends the two of them had in Iceland a few years earlier. It was such a laugh and she was concerned to begin with how it would go. Tom's mates were adventure seekers and her friends were generally those that liked a bit of luxury and pampering. But they hadn't been on holiday together since they were kids and had always agreed to visit some of the world with each other one day. They just invited people and let them decide if they could get on. Even if it meant that the brother and sister went together. But they were all game and signed up within days of the invite being sent out. The whole group had a whale of a time, relaxing at night after some adventurous days. It was the summer so there was a party atmosphere already on the island. All vowed to go back one day. The photos were of Tom rock climbing and the girls enjoying the thermal waters. Another group of photos still remained although the person featured in them didn't feature in her life. It was an ex-boyfriend and although she would like to wipe him out of her memories (he treated her like shit and fucked off with his ex) the holiday was too good to take down. She has always wanted to visit California. She had feelings for California like others around her had for Australia. For Sam, it had the same vibe. It was relaxed, baked in sunshine and filled with beautiful people in her mind. When she arrived, it lived up to expectations in every way. She loved every second of the three weeks they spent there and had looked into gaining a Green Card to live in the United States every year since. But it was more and more difficult to get into America permanently. Sam thought she would have to go back one day as a tourist again and live that life for a fleeting time again.

The phone rang. She had hoped that she could avoid that for the last small portion of her shift. She consoled herself that she would only have time for one call.

"Emergency services. What service so you require?"

"Uh, fire......and I guess the police. Do they usually come together?"

"It depends on what the cause of the fire is. I'll get them both out to you. Can you give me your name?"

"It's Fred. There's a fire at the house opposite me. I need someone to come quickly. Somebody lives there, and I haven't seen them come out of the house. I'm worried. I can't get out and about myself or I would have gone to see if I could help. If I was twenty years younger I'd have been in there like a shot."

Sam sent the fire brigade and the police to the address. She then clocked off for her shift with her thoughts split between Fred being 20 years younger, her next trip to California and what she would do to get out of this job and into one that made a difference, in her eyes. Thoughts of her next job took over and Sam walked home with a view of herself in a few years' time. She could picture life as a counsellor.

63

The fire crew arrived at the scene and quickly assessed the situation. Fred watched as best he could from the house over the road but couldn't really see much. When he was young the fire brigade used to arrive, douse the place with water and see what happened. Now he could see someone taking charge and discussing the situation with people. Fred blamed it on health and safety ('health and safety gone mad' was a phrase he used far too often) but could see that it wasn't taking long. The fire crew assembled while the police looked around at the rest of the neighbourhood for signs of what might have started it or to see if the fire was causing a stir. In other parts of the city, a fire this big would have attracted a crowd of thousands by now, but this quiet forgotten part of town saw nobody stop to watch the hypnotic flames start to rise up the building and reach into the night sky.

Fred watched some more and noticed that one of the fire fighters was trying to kick down the side gate and gain access to the garden. It took a few blows, which made him wonder why the man opposite had taken so much care of the security of his back garden. The fire fighter walked through the broken gate and ran back out of the same gate a few seconds later. He spoke to the man that appeared to be in charge and then the radio was used. By now Fred had managed to get in a better position and he saw the rest of the events unfold.

The fire fighter returned to the garden and then walked back out with someone over his shoulder.

The police at the scene looked concerned with the man who had been retrieved from the garden.

The fire fighter handed something over and this was bagged up by the police officer he first spoke to.

An ambulance arrived and the man was put on a stretcher and taken away.

The fire crew worked on the house for a few hours before it looked as though the fire was extinguished. The orange flames stood out against the darkening sky and Fred felt like it was bonfire night. But there was a sinister element to the show. Someone had been taken away from the scene by an ambulance. Fred hoped that it wasn't his neighbour. He hadn't seen much of him since the new neighbour had moved in and he didn't even know the guy's name but Fred didn't wish ill of anyone on his small sphere of contact. He slept in his chair hoping that it wasn't the neighbour. If it was the neighbour he hoped that he would be OK.

64

Augustine Boyle beat the rest of the team into the office the following day. The conversations he had been through with Lou at the curry house had got his mind going. When that happened, there was little chance of sleep. He wanted to test his theories on the rest of the team, and that meant some time at the computer. He thought best when it was written down. He delivered his words best when it was written down and he wanted to talk to the rest of the team about the different ideas he and Lou brainstormed the night before.

But the second Augustine walked into the police station he could sense that there was something in the air. The people working there were unusually down and he was told that his boss was waiting in his office. Augustine rushed through to find out what was going on. The person at the front desk offered to bring him through a hot drink and he asked for a black tea. Over the years Augustine had moved away from his usual strong tea with only a splash of milk because others didn't understand what he meant by a splash of milk. He didn't really like the taste or smell of milk at all. When he asked for a strong tea, here was invariably a load of milk in it and a strained teabag. When he asked for tea with a tiny amount of milk in it, the result was more often than not that the other person had used enough milk to last him a week. To avoid this hazard, he drank black tea when it was made by anyone else. He walked to his office while trying to decide what the news might be.

As Augustine walked through the door, he could see Marie sat at his desk looking for all the world like she had received a shock. Augustine knew that she wouldn't be there unless absolutely necessary so dragged in a chair from the nearest desk so he could sit too. There were other chairs in his office but none nearly as comfortable as the one behind his desk that was occupied by Marie.

"There has been a major development with the killer you are tracing. He has struck again. A police officer. Andy Lane, I don't know if you know him. We think we may soon know who the killer is," Marie explained but she could immediately see that Augustine wasn't taking in the information she was conveying. He had gone into deep thought and from experience, Marie knew it could be a few minutes until he came back again. She gave him time.

"So, he has killed one of our own? How did this happen? How did we know?" Augustine looked up and down as though he was searching for answers. He was trying to avert his gaze from Marie and work the tears away from his eyes before she could see them. He thought that if he didn't let her see then he could maintain a strong front and work the situation through rationally.

"We were called to a fire. One of the fire brigade went into the back garden to assess the fire and found him in the back garden. He had been hit over the head by the looks of it. I have asked Electra to go to the post mortem instead of coming here. I thought this is what you would want to happen. I can call her again if you have someone else in mind," Marie spoke to Augustine with two hats on. She was his boss and wanted to help the investigation as much as she could. It wasn't just Augustine that was feeling the pressure of multiple killings and no indication that they had any idea of who the killer was and where they might be. But her other hat was one that wanted to take control. She hadn't woken Augustine when she was told of the killed police officer a few hours earlier because she wanted time to make plans and think about how this might play out. She wasn't ready to take Augustine off this case yet, but wanted to conduct things more closely than ever before. Who knows, she may not have been in a position to have the final say on whether he would be allowed to continue looking for this killer that has now taken the life of a police officer to add to all the others found dead.

"How do you know it's him? Was there a letter left on his chest?" Augustine asked as if the answer would change any of the emotions he was feeling at that time. He had come across PC Andy Lane a few times in his work and always found him to be an upstanding member of the police force. He could see a day where he became a detective and maybe they would even work together. But now all Augustine could see were the tears welling up in his eyes. He didn't know what to do or say next. He looked to Marie for the lead.

"There was a letter left on his chest. The fire brigade has stopped the fire taking the whole building out and there is some other evidence in there. We can go look with the rest of the team when they arrive. The information we want is upstairs, so there is a little work going on to secure the stairs. The next call is yours. We go as soon as they get here, or wait for Electra," Marie spoke in a way that sounded inclusive. She didn't want to step on Augustine's toes too much. She wanted him to still feel like he was making decisions.

"We go when the rest of them are here. Electra will catch up in no time. I can't wait," Augustine looked at Marie for the first time since he had been given the news. He was ready to start looking forward and getting his teeth into the information. It had taken the death of a colleague, but it seemed like some progress was finally about to be made in the search for the killer.

65

As the group arrived at the scene of the fire and the finding of the body of their colleague, the fire brigade had gone and there was a joiner on site repairing the staircase so they could see the information Marie had referred to in the short briefing. She didn't go into detail as to see it in situ was probably going to explain everything they would need to know. She hadn't seen it herself, only been told the broad brushstrokes, and was intrigued as to the finer details. The fire chief had told her what his men had seen through the window while making sure the fire was extinguished and he had been able to get up there and quickly survey the scene himself. But it was nothing like having a team of trained detectives at the location. Marie was first there and she had waited for the rest of them to arrive. It was a quiet neighbourhood. At the front of the building, Marie held court and explained a few of the facts, as she knew them, while the joiner was finishing off the work on the stairs. 'Only about ten minutes,' he had shouted when she first arrived. That should give me plenty of time, she thought.

"PC Andy Lane radioed from here at exactly 7.24 PM yesterday. It appears he turned his radio off at that point. We have no record of the signal being live for the next half an hour or so. A neighbour called the emergency services and initially the fire brigade and police were sent. They were both on the scene before 8 PM. It wasn't until a firefighter entered the back garden at around 8.15 PM that a body was noticed and the ambulance service was called to assist. PC Andy Lane was pronounced dead at the scene at 8.25 PM. The post mortem is being carried out now, Electra is there, but it appears he was struck on the head and there are cuts to the thigh area. We will know more when Electra is back in the office later today. Do we have any questions?" Marie spoke to the whole team by creating eye contact one by one and then moving on to the next. This was her way of knowing that they had all listened to her. There were no questions. They were all champing at the bit to get inside the building and see what they had been brought there for.

"We can go in shortly. I just want to remind you that this is the person we suspect has killed all these people. I will remind you to wear gloves and touch as little as possible. We go in, see what is contained on these walls and then get out so forensics can do their job. I have pulled a few strings to get us here first. Don't fuck it up. The person who this address is registered to is called Alaaldin Hussein but we still can't be 100% sure it is him yet," Marie was looking directly at Augustine to see how he was taking all of this. She was sure that he would rather be giving the briefing but he didn't seem to be out of place with the rest of his team. She wondered if this was how he lead them.

"I'm ready now, love," the joiner shouted as he walked out of the front door, "it's all yours."

Marie looked at the team of detectives stood in front of her. It was like training new recruits again. They all looked eager to learn. It was the type of response she wanted. She stepped to one side and let Augustine lead the way. He bounced the first few steps to stay at the front and walked through the front door, looking directly ahead all the time. The rest of the team followed with Marie at the back. It was a narrow staircase but opened out into a wider landing at the top of the stairs. There was a charcoal taste in every breath that made it an unpleasant place to be, but the further up the stairs they went, the more obvious it was that the fire damage was mainly contained to the ground floor and front of the building. The room they were about to enter on the instructions of Marie had largely escaped unscathed.

The scene was one of confusion to begin with. The walls looked like they were randomly filled with pieces of paper, photographs, newspaper clippings and notes. But once the detectives were stood in the middle of the room, they could survey everything in one go and quickly realised that this was more organised than at first glance.

Augustine was looking at the map on the left side of the room, as they entered. It was detailed and the red marking stood out above all else. Augustine knew the locations and pictured himself stood there after the murders. He could see himself with the body, like in his dreams, as he surveyed each of the red areas. The theatre, where he had felt dizzy and had to sit down. The Museum of Innocence where they worked around the side of the building to find the body. The headquarters of Britain Excelsior, where the politician Jeff Caine's body was found and where he had to break into the building to look at Scott Sharpe's computer. He felt cold that the murders had been plotted on a map as though they were tourist sites. There were always macabre people who went in for visiting mass graves or the sites of a serial killer, but this was the closest Augustine had ever got to this phenomenon.

Gary was looking at the opposite wall, where he found images, notes and newspaper articles about the people who had already been killed. He recognised them from sight, but the details that the killer had left in his notes gave Gary more of an insight into their lives than he had ever imagined. There were comments about their habits, their supposed sins and a lot of information about their activities. No wonder the killer could slay them at will when he had their shift patterns and route to work studied and written down.

Ash and Lou stood and stared at the array of people on the wall in front of them. It was a level of detail only matched by that on the wall in front of Gary. Each target had been noted for their sin, their lifestyle and their accessibility – Lou could put it no other way. Those people with a lifestyle that would expose them to danger were the easiest to select. Those were the people that were on this list of 'sinners' and chosen to be killed. Ash looked over at Lou and mouthed the words 'fucking hell,' at him. He didn't know whether Lou was looking or not. He just needed to say it.

All four turned around as Marie coughed. She was looking at the wall that contained the door they entered by. She was trying to take it all in and had wandered until she was back to back with Ash. The enormity of the message on the wall was too much to take in from close quarters. She counted 94 letters in the entire message after checking twice. They had five victims so far. There was one letter unaccounted for, the 'N' in the first word. This left 88 victims left before the killer completed his work. She took the deepest breath of her life. She sucked in air as though her life depended on it. By this point, the rest of the team were stood alongside her, all reading the message. These were light grey letters, not the black letters that had been left on the bodies of the victims they had so far found but the message was still stark and clear. He intended to kill a lot more people. They had a group of potential victims identified on the walls in front of them, but there were nowhere near 88 people there, maybe around 25. Others were at risk. The killer was not finished.

66

Al had another address on the opposite side of the city, under the name of his brother who had returned to Pakistan a few years earlier. There was little to link the two brothers, they came to the UK at different times, had different surnames and didn't see a great deal of each other. The alternative of sleeping rough or staying in a hotel were options Al had considered but they felt as though they carried even more risk than using a home that hadn't been linked to him before. A hotel would want some ID and a nosy owner might call the police if he suspected Al of being linked to any criminality. There was a chance by now the police could have some information on him and possibly circulated his name to the press and there would be those looking to catch him. Sleeping rough had the frequent hazard of being in contact with the police. His description would definitely have been circulated there and this was a risk he was not willing to take.

But Al knew that the whole exercise as fraught with risk. He couldn't kill all those people without taking a risk or two. He had taunted the detective at the Museum after killing the banker. He had bumped into the detective after killing the gay entertainer. But his work was far from done and taking too many risks was going to lengthen the odds that he would prove his peers wrong and get all his work carried out before detection. He had listened to enough shit from people who wanted to become famous by driving a van into people and maybe cutting a few up before the police arrived and shot them. He had a message to get out there. They were just small-time idiots who wanted a bit of fame in their one community. The people who had blown up others and killed the odd bystander were known in the radical Muslim community as warriors. But Al had much bigger ideas. He wanted the name Alaaldin Hussein to be known away from his community. He wanted the name Alaaldin Hussein to strike fear into the people of the United Kingdom and the Western world. He wanted people to know that he was different to the rest of them. He wanted his name to be synonymous with Muslim terror. Most of all he wanted to be the poster child that inspired a new generation of extremists. Those that held political views against his people, those that lent money and exploited the poor, those that practiced homosexuality and those that sold their body should not sleep easily. Those were the first line of people that should live in fear of Alaaldin Hussein and those that followed him. All the other sinners of the western world should change their ways or face the same end.

Al walked the two miles to his brother's place and opened the door with a key that had rested in his wallet for the past two years without ever being disturbed. He had some plans he could access from the laptop in his bag, but the rest would have to be started from scratch. He hoped that the fire had destroyed all the information he left on the walls in his study, but had to assume that the police might be able to gain some information from the charred remains. He would have to start again. But there was one target that Al could easily reach. He knew a little about the target and could add the rest of the data needed to make a clean kill soon. Al sat on the bed in the upstairs room of the apartment his brother still owned. It was the only piece of furniture in the place. Al closed his eyes in deep thought. He wanted to kill again before the week was out.

67

Lou was thinking about retirement. He had worked way past the age he was going to retire but hadn't found anything else he wanted to do with his life. The passing of his wife left him with no direction and few ideas about what the future might hold. So, he just kept on doing what he knew. It was easier that way. A life where you don't have to make any decisions always felt easier for Lou. As he sat, he wondered if this was one of the reasons he joined the police and stayed for as long as he had. At home, his wife would tell him what to do. It wasn't that she was bossy, but that he would get home and she would tell him what they were going to have for dinner, she would let him know if they were going somewhere at the weekend and she would arrange the rest of his life too. It was to the degree that she would get his clothes out of the wardrobe and have them on the bed so he could just get dressed without having to make any form of decision regarding what to wear. It felt the same at work. His daily work life was dictated to him by the criminals that had committed a crime the day before. He turned up, found out what was needed of him and then got on with it. He didn't have the time to make decisions, just process information and then move on to the next one. Because of this he didn't get emotionally attached to the work. He felt sorry for the people who had been the victim of crime and their family too, but didn't lose sleep over it like many of the people he worked with. Lou wanted a change. He sat and thought about the different things he could be doing with his life instead of being a cop. None appealed that much that he jacked his job in straight away but there were a few options that might sound good enough if he put more thought into it. He parked these ideas for a while and got on with his work. It was a few hours since they had come back from the scene of the latest murder and the fire that accompanied it. Electra had given them all a briefing from the post mortem. Brief was the operative word. The police officer had been killed by a blow to the head and it appeared that the wounds on his thigh were carried out after he was already dead. That shone a light on the way that the others were cut. But that was the only light from the post mortem. There was little else to say.

From that point on, the whole team threw themselves into finding out as much as they could about Alaaldin Hussein. They wanted to know where he had lived, where he had worked and if he had any family that they could contact. The idea was that they spent that day looking for as much information as they could and the day after would consist of following up on these leads. So far Lou had found 2 places where he might have possibly worked but nothing on the family side of things. Electra was working with Ash and they had a good idea about a couple of places Alaaldin might have lived so would follow that up with the current occupants and the landlords. All the information they could gather was getting them further ahead with an investigation that had seemed dead-end only the day before. Gary had the task that none of the rest of the team wanted. He was going to knock door to door and ask the neighbours all they knew about the man who they suspected of killing several people already and plotting the murder of many more. These conversations always ended up with phrases such as –

'He kept himself to himself.'

'He was quiet.'

'I didn't see much of him.'

But someone had to have these conversations in case a gem came up. Every now and again someone might mention something that would change the course of an investigation. Gary had spoken to someone at the door once who just happened to mention that they had hidden CCTV cameras along the side of their home. This lead to the images being used to catch a rapist who had dragged two women into the bushes across the street and raped them systematically. The conversation about the crime didn't bring out anything from the person who had these cameras. It was just a general chat about the state of society as Gary was breaking off the conversation when it came up. Gary could see the potential benefit of this way of gathering evidence, but he just wished that it was someone else that was given this task.

The team worked diligently for hours without a break. The only time one of them came away from their desk was to come into Augustine's office to check a detail or to add another person to his list of contacts. Augustine was in his element gathering all the information they had on a spreadsheet and making sure that it all tallied. He wanted to stay in touch with them all the following day and found that this was the best way to do it. He had several goes at getting the columns right, but had finally settled on the order of –

- Name
- Contact number if known
- Category of contact (colleague, landlord, family, friend, neighbour, new tenant)
- Town
- Who was going to speak to them

This meant that Augustine was able to keep a record of what was going on and monitor it as the day went by. He could take the sheet with him and phone the rest of his team to ask questions and collate information. He would accompany Lou, Electra would work with Ash and Gary would do the house to house stuff on his own. Augustine worked with a renewed vigour, so much so that Marie left them to get on with their work. Her only insistence was that Augustine called her every 2 hours at least to let her know the progress that was being made. She could still feel the heat of her bosses on the back of her neck, but was more able to go back to them with reports that they were making a breakthrough. That would buy her and Augustine some time.

Marie was acutely aware of time in her job. She had worked in what she now regarded the lower levels of the police force for many years before working her way up. She no longer saw her role as that of someone in the police force but as a go-between. She stopped the pressure from those at the top who only wanted results quickly from reaching those at the bottom who had to work on a limited budget. This pressure, if not buffered, could crush the people at the bottom and cause them to leave the force. She would slow down the rate of change and deliver the highlights of the success to those above in order to keep the wheels in motion and everyone happy. For Marie, it wasn't the role she thought she was applying for. If she had known at the time, then she would have stayed where she was. The extra few thousand a year were not worth the hassle. But as she jumped with her eyes closed and landed, Marie quickly grew into the role before she fully had the chance to realise what it was all about. She became an expert in diplomacy, which was the opposite of her time as a detective. When she worked directly on crime Marie had no patience at all. She wanted results the same day she was given a case. That was how hard she tried to work her team. But over the years she found out this wasn't realistic. Once you are in a role and doing the same thing day after day it becomes difficult, if not impossible, to change. This isn't always because of the people around you. Sometimes it is your own self-consciousness that stops you from changing your behaviour. The move to the next level of management allowed Marie to change without anyone really noticing.

She looked across he office and wondered how it was different to any other in the building. If someone walked into the police station for the first time would they know that she was a higher rank than Augustine just by comparing offices? She looked at the dark mahogany of her desk and thought that this was a sign of quality that was easy for anyone to spot. She looked at the carpet on the floor and how this contrasted with the vinyl that ran into Augustine's office from the rest of the room around him. She thought about the horrible strip lighting that was in Augustine's office and was also a feature of hers until she had it replaced with subtler downlighters. The whole interior of her room looked and smelled like it was made for someone of a higher stature in her eyes. She had added little touches here and there from the potpourri in a bowl by the window to the photographs of famous city landmarks hung on the wall. Marie was proud of her office. She spent far more time awake there than she did at home, so this was the place where her small inclination to interior design took hold. It wasn't much but made Marie feel like she was marked as one of the 'big bosses' in her force in the future. She vowed that she would treat people with more patience than the bosses she was used to dealing with, but she also presumed that they had their own pressures from above and a demand for results that she didn't comprehend at that time.

She wondered who would take her place if she was promoted, not that it seemed likely at the time. She already knew that she could work well with Augustine and had all the secrets that made him tick. She knew what to say and when to say it to get him working longer hours and delivering better results. More importantly she knew when to say nothing at all. The motivation and communication courses that Marie had been booked on always failed to deal with that side of things. The course would let the people sat in the room know about body language, the use of words and how all of this worked together. But in her eyes these courses always failed to address the times when you should say nothing at all. This was an incredibly powerful way to deliver a message. The power of silence often trumped the power of the spoken word. Especially when so many words were spoken during the course of the average meeting.

Marie had no idea what would happen over the next few days, but that was the time she estimated both her and Augustine had to make some major progress with this killer before the pressure became too great and he had to be shuffled off to an easier set of assignments. He got away with missing the odd case when it was a single killing of someone that didn't have a public profile. But when he was unable to catch a killer that was bumping off people in the limelight and had been successful on several occasions, there was no wriggle room for Augustine this time. He had to get deep into this case, so deep that nobody else could rightly take over effectively. Marie could see that he was on the right tracks after the killing of a police officer, but the fact that 'one of their own' was killed before real progress was able to be made would alienate Augustine Boyle with many of the other people who worked for the police. They had a duty to protect each other. This was a duty that some might think Augustine had failed.

68

Al studied the notes he had made on his laptop and stored deep in the dark web. He had notes all over his walls back at his place, but they were either burned beyond recognition or in the hands of the police by that point. He would love to walk back in there and check the damage but that was only going to get him caught and thrown behind bars. He still had a lot of work to do and was in no mood to stop where he was. The message on his wall was long. He hadn't really counted how many letters there was in the whole message but he knew that there was a long way to go if he was going to finish his work. He knew that it couldn't be long before the police let the first few letters out. By the look of it they still had one body to find before they were up to speed. Al didn't intend on letting them catch up at all. His next victim would be the high profile one that would force them to reveal his message. Al thought that maybe the politician would prompt them to reveal more information than they already had, but it hadn't worked out that way. He would now up the ante and take the game to them. He was saving this particular victim until near the end of his masterpiece, but it would have to be accelerated.

Al looked at the notes several times. He was excited by this killing in a way that he hadn't been so far. The notes talked about a man who was around 6-foot-tall with dark brown hair cut in a traditional short-back-and-sides manner. The man was to be found alone in public and private places regularly but didn't keep regular work hours. This was the thing that was making Al hesitant about this potential victim. The others that he had killed in the past were all to be found at certain places at exact time several times per week. That made it easy for Al to hunt them down and finish them off. But this one might work early one day and then late for the next four or five days. He might be at his place of work for 6 hours or for 14. He could have a couple of days off, together or apart, during the week and work all weekend. The more Al looked at the notes, the less he saw a pattern that he could use. It might be back to the drawing board. Whenever Al got stuck with some planning, in his work life before or his mission now, he went away and thought about something completely different. Trying to crunch an answer when one was becoming less clear by the second wasn't going to work for him. Al went and made a cup of tea and tried to plan what he was having to eat for the next few days. He wasn't a creature that needed three square meals per day and could go all day without eating very much at all, but the meal planning would take his mind of the next victim. He could then come back to it later with a fresh mind and hopefully find a better solution. He didn't want to take risks with this one, but he had to step things up if he was to get that message away from the closed doors of the police and out to the public at large. Then they would understand he wasn't some ordinary killer, some psychopath with a grudge but a man with a clear message for the people of the world. This next killing was going to be the one that changed things.

Al planned out his meals for a full week. When he arrived at his brother's home there was nothing still in date in the kitchen. After clearing the cupboards of expired tins of mackerel and baked beans, he had grabbed a few things from the local store. There wasn't much on the shelves so Al picked up cereal, unexpired tins of beans and some teabags. After that there was nothing at all to eat in his brother's place. Al took the plan and developed a shopping list from it. There was still little chance that he would actually take this list to the shop, an even smaller chance that he would make any of the meals it contained and the slimmest chance of all that he would eat all of these meals but it was a means to an end. The exercise in planning one thing was supposed to clear his mind to plan something completely different.

The flat was dark and felt tiny to Al in comparison with the house he had just vacated and torched. He wanted somewhere bigger and more importantly somewhere with several exits in case he needed to leave quickly, but that just wasn't possible at the time. Lying low was the first step. Al hoped that by staying in this flat he wouldn't have to escape in a rush. He had sat on the floor or the bed since moving in because his brother had left almost nothing behind. Al wanted to keep his sleeping area separate from the rest of the house. If it had become a living room and dining room too then he would have got no sleep at all when it was finally time to rest his head. Two of the few items he had managed to bring with him were a can of shaving foam and his razor. He never knew when he would need them, so they were always spares stationed in his laptop bag. He had considered taking them out of there on several occasions in the past but something at the back of his mind had stopped him. He told himself that there was never going to be a reason to need them from his laptop case. He was always having these conversations backwards and forwards with himself. There was nobody else to talk to, so he replaced the conversations a man of his age might normally have with a wife, children, parents, friends and work colleagues with an internal discussion where he played both roles in the conversation. They could sometimes go on for several minutes while Al decided what the best course of action was. They were always trivial actions up for discussion. The status quo usually reigned.

Al returned from thoughts of food and meal plans and back to the matter in hand – how to plot the killing of the man in his notes. It was almost immediately that he realised where the problem lay. He was trying to identify when the man was at work, based on a work day that could go from early in the morning to late at night on rare occasions. But the constant wasn't his journey to work – it was his time at home. Only once in the month since he had watched this target had the man not come home at all. Rather than trying to look for the man on his route to work, as Al had manged to find most of the other victims, he could visit him at home in the hours running up to midnight or the early hours of the morning. He was bound to be home at that time. Al could carry out his work there.

The day was drawing to a close. Al looked across at the sun starting to set past the window in his brother's apartment. It took away the window in to his new life. Al didn't like the daylight hours because this was the time where others could see him through the window. He had stopped going out and getting the daily newspapers to see if he was the talk of the town. His only access to the news was the internet. There were sporadic mentions of the letters he had left on the chest of people on message boards related to the city. The people who had posted this information must have had inside information as those who had found the bodies or those who worked in the police. One was called Sally and was adamant that she had seen the body of one of the victims and there was clearly a message being delivered. Sally claimed that she saw a letter on the chest that had to have been left there by the killer. But others on the message board cut her off as a crank. They said that if this was the case then they would all know about it. Sally was shouted down every time she had something to say on the matter. Al looked up and down the message board and found that Sally had given up after a week or so of abuse.

Why didn't they listen to Sally? Why can't they understand that she is right? The message needs to get out there and maybe people like Sally are my best bet. The police don't let my words get out there. I can't publish them myself for fear of being caught. The way to reach people could be though those like Sally that have seen or heard the truth. I could do with more disciples like her. Even if she doesn't believe in the righteousness of my actions, she can still help to let as many people as possible know that I am here and I am talking to the world,' Al thought to himself.

The darkness was his comfort blanket. It was where Al did his best work. The cover that it gave him allowed the security that he could go about his business with less chance of detection. Al liked the way that the dark would send most people away behind their doors with their curtains closed. When they couldn't see past their own four walls they were less interested in what he was doing between his four. Al waited all day for the night to arrive. He was happiest in the winter when people disappeared indoors earlier and earlier at night. But this was in the planning stage. To effect his plans he needed people to be out early in the morning and late at night, so he picked mid-summer to put all of his plans into action. Now summer was passing into Autumn Al had a decision to make. Would he look to hunt out people from the few that ventured out in the coldest part of the year, or would he hibernate until the following spring?

69

"Yeah I think he worked here. We have so many people come and go, especially his type," the factory manager told Augustine and Lou. He was tall and slim and looked like he had been there forever. Augustine couldn't work out whether he was answering their questions because he wanted to help or because it gave him a few minutes away from the factory floor to roll his next batch of cigarettes while he was talking. Whichever reason it was, Lou wished he wasn't doing it. He stopped short of telling him to halt, but was looking intently at the pile of rolling tobacco on the desk rather than listening fully to the man in the seat opposite him and Augustine. He was an obvious smoker, even without the paraphernalia in front of him. Yellowing fingertips and red veins working their way from the bags under his eyes to his top lip past a nose that was too big for that face gave the game away. They say that your nose and ears are the only parts of your body that keep on growing through your life and this man was the living proof of that. The nose had been outsized for the face about an inch ago and the ears were accentuated by the lack of hair around the temples. Lou wondered how others saw him now he was getting older, but he was sure that he looked after himself better than the factory manager. He resisted the temptation to fake-sneeze and distribute the effects of the desk across the floor. How do things as light as tobacco and papers create problems so heavy? Lou thought to himself before being brought back into the room by Augustine's voice.

"I assume you keep records? You surely don't have to guess whether he worked for you?" Augustine asked as he took back the photograph of Alaaldin Hussein they had picked up from the home he appeared to have lived in and torched. There were a few photographs lying around the place and it was difficult to tell without records whether this was their man, but it was the best match they could find. A neighbour confirmed this was probably the man who lived across the road and kept himself to himself the evening before. Augustine was convinced enough by this.

"You know how it is. People like him are ten-a-penny. They come, they go. Too many questions and they just disappear," the factory manager replied, now seeming to take more of an interest when his record-keeping was brought into question. He was concerned that there might be another visit from the authorities soon. "I keep records when people come to work for me, but I don't keep them in good order when they leave. We go through a few hundred people a year here – this isn't the police force, you know. I can't be expected to have records for all of them going back I don't know how far." He looked at Augustine as the man in charge to see if he could read his eyes.

Augustine looked back across the desk. If there was ever a time to play an ace card early this was it. He didn't have to wait and play games with this one, after all he didn't have the time, there were other people to talk to that Lou had identified. The smugness that was present to begin with had worked its way off the face of the factory manager and Augustine felt the upper hand. Just to rub it in a little more he paused for thirty seconds so that he could watch the beads of sweat fall off the temples, past those ears and onto his blue stained overall. These 30 seconds went by in a flash for Augustine and Lou, but they could tell that time wasn't passing so quickly for the person who was facing them. He looked at the ceiling and the floor in turn around five or six times hoping that an answer would come to him. It didn't.

When the time was up, Augustine began, "why don't we start again. Shall we pretend that we have just walked in?"

"That might be a good idea," the factory manager replied. He wasn't in a good place.

"Do you know this man?" Lou asked in a laboured vice that made it sound like he was explaining something to a three-year-old child. He liked the position that Augustine had put them in. There was a little going-through-the-motions but after that a point needed to be made.

"Yes, I think I recognise him. I don't have the records to hand, but I can tell you what I remember," the factory manager answered as he swept the remaining tobacco into a pouch and cleared it with the papers into the top drawer of his desk. Augustine preferred the new version of the factory manager; Lou wasn't enamoured about either of them. He wanted to hear what was said.

"So, you remember him working here?" Lou pressed.

"As I said, there are a lot of his type who come here to work. Not many questions asked, cash in hand and they come and go as they please. I call them immi-wants. Immigrants who just want to take all the time. It is what makes the UK a popular destination for people from his part of the world. The government creates this problem, not me," the factory manager spat out the last words as though he was appalled by the presence of people from outside the UK. But he was quite happy to make money off their back. Lou knew he couldn't keep up the 'nice' act for long. He was back to type.

"What do you remember about this guy?" Lou asked the same question in a more direct way to cut through the bluster. He looked the factory manager in the eye and this sparked him into action. He stood up and walked around the back of the desk for a few seconds as though he needed this low level of activity to compose himself.

"He worried a few of the others. Nothing specific, but he wouldn't listen to the more experienced heads here. Some people take the newbies under their wing and try to guide them to our way of working. They told me he wanted to do things his own way. I told them he wouldn't be around for long and to just let it slide. I think he got into an argument with one of them in the staff room one day. A couple of punches were thrown and he didn't come back past the end of that week. I looked on it as another incident in the life of a factory. Nothing to get too excited over," he explained in the most forthcoming way he had been since the two detectives arrived there.

"Are any of these 'experienced heads' still here? I'd like a chat if they are," Augustine asked but without any doubt in his voice. He knew that the experienced members of the team would still be there. It was how the factory kept control of the rest of them. Augustine knew he would be there a while. As the factory manager took a couple of the cigarettes he managed to roll out of the drawer and headed towards the door, Augustine stopped him. "We are going to get a tea from the drive-through place over the road. Shall we bring one back for you? And what about the people we will be speaking to? how many of them are there? What do they drink?"

"I can't take them all off the floor at once. That would mean I have to close down a couple of lines. It will cost me money."

"You can use the time to get your paperwork in order. You never know when someone might be along to check up on your employee records."

Augustine left the building and formulated a plan of attack with Lou. They just needed a few minutes with each to gather basic information. If one of the workers in the factory had something more interesting to say, then they could arrange to speak to them in more detail over the next few days. The factory manager had identified six people that were there when Al was working there. They may have some information that could prove useful, even though he was only there for a short space of time.

They had instructed the factory manager to set aside two rooms to speak to the workers, so Lou and Augustine could work at the same time and get through them with as little disruption as possible. Although it was appealing to piss the factory manager off, he might be needed again in the future, so they would keep his downtime to a minimum. Augustine and Lou got back to the factory with a large array of drinks and a few packs of cakes. They distributed these to the men sat waiting outside the primary office and set about their work. Augustine wanted something juicy but all Lou wanted was to get out of there. He still had half his mind on leaving his job and wanted to get the details down on paper before moving on to the next place he had identified with his research the day before. It was becoming more and more like a job and less like something he enjoyed every day.

Each had their own story to tell about Alaaldin Hussein. None were particularly pleasant but at the same time, none would have warranted a call to the police. It seemed as though he was searching for people all the time he was there. He spoke strongly of religion and the need to clean up society. Al was always asking others if they wanted to help him. When he received a negative reply, he turned abusive. He spoke up against the wrong guy one day who responded to the abuse with his fists. That led to Al leaving without adding to his followers.

70

Gary walked around the neighbourhood like a naughty schoolboy. He was given a task that he thought was beneath him by a manager that he thought wasn't as good as him. This all lead to apathy. The doors he knocked on either were not answered or the person who made it to the door looked as though it had taken all their energy to do so. When he stepped back inside the house and sat with the occupant, they were so out of breath that they had little to add except the odd nod. With Gary's lack of enthusiasm, the conversations were devoid of energy and stuttered to a halt almost as soon as they had begun. Gary made a note of the words that were said, so he could prove he had carried out the task he was given, but there was nothing more in it than that.

"I don't get out much so I have only ever seen him through the windows."

"My carer has commented that he was out there at all times of the day and night, but I didn't think anything of it."

"I don't know when he moved in. One day he was just there. He didn't have a car and he didn't do any gardening."

To Gary this was all pointless. It didn't take the investigation anywhere. If one of the neighbours said, "Oh yes, I remember the day he was carrying a body along the street over his shoulder," then Gary would have something to go on. But all the people he had spoken to were of a generation that would have called the police if the guy had shown any signs of criminality. They would have reported him for dumping his garden cuttings or putting non-recyclables in his recycling bin. But they hadn't. Somehow this man had managed to go out and kill people without the world knowing.

The last house in the street was one that didn't look occupied during the day. Of all the properties in the street, this was surely the only one where the occupant worked for a living. By this time it was early afternoon so there was bound to be no one indoors, Gary thought and hoped. Gary was told to knock on every door and then to go back to the doors where he hadn't managed to speak to anyone in case they had arrived back when he was inside another property. But Gary had been able to see the street from every house he entered. It was a cul-de-sac and nobody could have got in or out without him noticing, on foot or in a car. He would make this his last house and then get off home. He had done a few hours that day and had built up a bit of lieu time over the course of the previous few weeks. He would just go back and let Augustine know the next day what he had done. It wasn't like he was in any position to stop him.

He knocked a second time and waited for a response. To his surprise and disappointment, he could see some movement at the back of the house, possibly the garden, so he would wait another minute or so before looking over the fence to the left-hand side of the house. The garden was the best kept on the whole street and Gary suspected he had finally found someone who might have been as active as their suspect. All the other gardens in the street were in a poor state, and this was reflected in the health of the people who owned the gardens. Many had carers coming in to help them with basic daily tasks like cleaning, cooking and getting out of bed so the garden was way out of their reach. Unless this was another infirm resident but one who had a bit of cash to pay for maintenance, Gary wasn't sure. But the whole property had a different feel to the rest of the street. The house didn't look as though it fitted in the neighbourhood. It was built on a bigger plot and the front door was facing away from the street as though it didn't want to be there. It was like a parent who pretended that the naughty child wasn't theirs. It was looking away and hoping that the rest of the street would bring itself back into line while its gaze was in a different direction. Gary wondered if it was actually part of the same street for the time he was standing at the doorstep waiting for the obvious occupant to make it to the front door. It was nowhere near the main road but wasn't really part of the rest of the street. Maybe it had an address all of its own. It was showing no street number on the door but someone had painted the number 12 on the side of the wheelie bin that was tucked half away behind a bush on the right side of the property as he looked at it. It probably wasn't the current owner who had done this, Gary thought, as it was not in keeping with the rest of the property. It was an eyesore on what was otherwise a pristine piece of real estate. The bin felt as though it belonged to the seedier part of the street – the part where a body had been found and where some gruesome details about murders and potential victims were discovered soon after.

The people on the walls had all been informed that they were on this target list and given some form of police protection in the aftermath of the discovery. This ranged from being put up in a hotel in a discrete location or being given an escort to and from work with a guard outside their home. They were probably not at risk because the killer had left their details behind. It was like visiting a city in the aftermath of a terrorist attack. In a strange way, it was probably the best time to go. Vigilance would be high and the police would have a much greater presence. The streets would be safer, certainly than they were in the days running up to an attack. These people were probably the safest in the city. They had been identified for one reason or another (Gary was there when one man asked why he was a target. He was distraught to find that it was because he visited prostitutes. He begged the police to not let his wife know) but were now more than likely safe because they were known to the police. The killer was too cold and calculating to target people that he had unwittingly prompted the police about.

There was movement in the house much closer to the front of the house now so Gary knocked for a third time, this time he banged on the door loudly. It rattled on the hinges as though it had been given a good hard knock before. Gary was ready to add a kick or two when he made eye contact with someone inside. It was a small man who appeared to be tidying up before he opened the door. Gary wondered what might be so important to clear before anyone came in and resolved to ask a few questions about this when he got inside. The eye contact lasted for a few seconds and the man moved out of sight before appearing at the glass by the side of the door. It opened a fraction and he asked for some ID. Gary obliged and then the door was closed ajar to let the safety catch off before opening fully and the man standing back from the mat to user Gary into the hall.

"Can you take your shoes off, please. It's a new carpet and I don't want anything on it. I mulled over the choice of colour and allowed the salesman to persuade me that light cream was perfect. I don't like it. Something darker would have been more suitable," the man took his time with the words as though the detective would be impressed by the expenditure. Gary looked him in the eye again, as he had done through the window. It was just to check that the man knew he was there on business, not to have a chat.

"Shoes off. Can I come in and sit down? I'd like to talk to you about the fire at the end of the street," Gary started but before he had time to finish his thoughts, the man was back on 'impress mode.'

"I know all about it. I am in charge of the Neighbourhood Watch in this set of streets. Did you know that?" Gary wasn't impressed at all. He was beginning to regret knocking three times. He wished he had just walked away when the first answer didn't come.

"What do you know about the fire?" asked Gary, now wanting to find out if this was fact or rumour. He had never been involved in community policing and didn't know what the connection between coppers on the beat and Neighbourhood Watch teams was. He suspected very little, but humoured the man all the same. He definitely had a case of short man syndrome and Gary could see he made up for his lack of height with his self-importance.

"I know that there was a fire and that Mr. Wilson at number 5 rang for the fire brigade and the police. I then saw an ambulance arrive a short while later. Someone told me that the ambulance took a man away, but I can't remember who it was that told me this," the man in the house that looked away from the rest of the street explained his knowledge. He was called Adam Martin and had been the type of man who collected information like this all his life. Becoming the leader of the Neighbourhood Watch was a natural extension of the way he was. It suited him perfectly to knock on doors and gather rumours and gossip (because that was all they really were) for his own end. He would sometimes report a few things back to the police if he felt that it was something he couldn't handle but most of the conversations at the doorstep were one neighbour bitching about another.

"Did you see that car parked overnight at her house. It's the third man she's had stay over this month."

"How many times a week does he wash his car? It's only a cheap thing, several years old but he treats it like it was a Ferrari."

"Those at number 2 have been using a hose to water their garden again. I thought there was still a hosepipe ban in place."

Adam Martin loved all the gossip and he was the friend of the person he was speaking to at that time and that time only. If number 16 and number 18 on the next street had it in for each other he would switch sides to who he was talking to. He just wanted to hear all the moans people had about each other. It was far more interesting than dealing with the Neighbourhood Watch paperwork and instructions.

"What is your name?"

"Sorry?"

"I need to make a few notes before we get into the interesting stuff. What is your name?" Gary knew that the promise of something interesting would get his attention.

"Adam Martin."

"And the address of this place?"

"Number 12, Auriel Close."

"How long have you lived here?"

"I moved in on the 12th August 1982," Gary wasn't surprised that he knew the exact date. He wouldn't have been surprised if he knew the exact time he first opened the front door either.

"And you know the neighbourhood pretty well?"

"I talk to most people whenever I can. One man who didn't really have the time of day for me was the man who owned the house that was set on fire. Was it him that was taken away? Is he OK?"

"We'll get to that later on," Gary could feel from that question that Adam Martin had something to tell him about Alaaldin Hussein, "so what do you know about that man?"

"I have been concerned about him for a while. He is the only person that has given me any cause for genuine concern all the time I have overseen the Neighbourhood Watch. He left early in the morning and came back late at night. This wouldn't be unusual for someone who works but I don't recall him ever having a job. I used to try to talk to him about the neighbourhood but he was very closed. I kept a file on him but I didn't say anything in case I was accused of…" Adam stopped in his tracks. It was clear he had a concept in mind but either couldn't find the right word to describe it or didn't want to use the word he had in his head.

Gary looked at Adam and his head was bowed. He looked to be in pain, so much pain that Gary considered calling for help in the first few seconds. As Adam looked up from the ground, Gary could see that is was a psychological pain rather than a physical one. "I didn't want to be accused of racism. The only person in our streets that was Asian and he was the only one I kept a file on. I was sure that he could play the race card at any time and I would be in trouble. I even looked hard at the other people in the streets I am in charge of to see if I could find someone else to start a file on. That way it would look like I had been fair. I'm sure I have been fair but I don't know what it would look like."

Gary could see a tear slowly fall down the cheek of the man he was talking to. It took some debris with it and Gary thought for a second that the man was wearing makeup before deciding that it was something from the back garden that Adam had been working on before he arrived. It wasn't a tear of sadness. It was a tear of frustration.

"I'm not stupid," Adam said trying to force his eye to suck the tear back up from where it came without any success. "I know that he is a bad man. I knew it all along but didn't want to cause myself any problems. It wasn't him in that ambulance, was it? It was someone he had killed."

Gary looked Adam up and down and tried to make sense of it all. The man was a conundrum and had presented himself in diverse ways in the few minutes they had been sat together. After the layers of show had been peeled away, this was the real Adam Martin had now been finally revealed. This was a man who had aspired to some responsibility but didn't know how to use it when it arrived. He used the position to listen to all the seedy side of his neighbourhood and when the one person in the streets he patrolled was likely to have done something significant, he wasn't able to act out of the fear of being called a racist. The way that society had evolved meant that Adam wasn't the only person who felt this way. He was gathering evidence on someone but was afraid to use it in case he was wrong. Society gave more respect to those that kept their mouth shut than those that opened it and made a mistake. If Adam had been wrong about the neighbour who he had been keeping tabs on, then he would have been vilified and lost his position as the head of the Neighbourhood Watch. Not the type of sacking that would have attracted national headlines but enough of a local scandal that it would have affected Adam for a few years. He hadn't reached retirement age, but wasn't working at the time, enjoying a payoff from a previous employer that was downsizing. He didn't have any direct plans to return to the workforce but if circumstances dictated it or if he got so bored at home he wanted to go back out to work then keeping his hand in with the Neighbourhood Watch would have looked like a positive use of his time on his CV then just sitting around at home doing very little. Adam didn't have any concrete evidence about his neighbour, but he has a strong feeling that he was up to no good and a list of comings and goings that the police may well have been able to use in support of their investigation. As it was, Adam had stalled making his suspicions public, after all they were just suspicions and the police are busy people, until it was too late. Adam looked a broken man at that point. His life for the last few years had been his patrol and he had been more interested in others dirty washing than he was in keeping them safe. Gary felt sorry for him. It was a voluntary role with no training and little support, so how would the police ever expect someone to get it right? he thought. He knew of police officers and detectives that made bigger mistakes and they had all the training, support and experience in the world. To console the man, he thought about telling him how close Augustine was to catching the killer when he walked past him in the corridor of the theatre, but that was a step too far even for Gary.

"I know this might be hard for you to hear, but we suspect that the man who lived at the end of your road might be the one that is killing people in the city. He might be the man responsible for a series of deaths. I'm sure you will understand in your role that discretion is needed with this information, and we are still working on this as a theory rather than fact," Gary's speech slowed dramatically towards the end and the volume dropped as he wasn't sure if the man sat in the same room as he was even listening. Gary felt he could have said anything at all during that time and the walls would be the only thing that absorbed his words. Adam was looking back down at the floor and the colour had dropped out of his cheeks. The debris from the garden was even more obvious against the whiter backdrop of blood-drained skin. This was why it was the only garden in the street that was in order. Not only that, it was in perfect order. Only a few hours a day could keep it looking like that.

"You look like you need some fresh air. Shall we step outside for a few minutes?" Gary asked with two motives in mind. He wanted Adam to feel better and be able to pass on the information he gathered about his neighbour, but Gary was also interested in what the back garden looked like. His father was only a few years from retirement and Gary pictured him spending most of his time in the garden. There would probably be as much time on his back with a beer or a G&T in his hand as the time he would spend tending his garden, but it would be good to see what he could achieve if he set his mind to it. As the two of them stood and walked towards the back door in knowing silence, Gary could see the back garden through the window for the first time. It was an oasis and felt even more out of place on that street than the house had. It was as though he had stepped into another dimension where his job wasn't to catch people who killed and the world outside wasn't dangerous. Gary was in awe of the work that this must have taken. Adam was oblivious to the garden and the reaction it engendered as he was of the words that were spilling for Gary's mouth.

"This is amazing. I would love a garden like this. How many hours a week does it take to get it looking this good? Does it always look this good? How long have you lived here?" the statements and questions just fell out of his mouth and zigzagged across the garden to nobody in particular. Adam wasn't going to respond, that much was obvious, so Gary imagined the answers that made him feel better about the work his father might have to impart on his own wreck of a garden. 'Thank you. Thank you again. Only a couple. Yes. All Spring and Summer. Only a few years to get it looking like this,' were the answers that Gary wanted to hear. He could then tell his father that he could replicate the effect with the minimum of effort. The truth was probably a million miles away but Gary just pictured himself at a barbecue with a beer congratulating his dad.

"I don't know what to do or say. Will I be in some sort of trouble?" Adam broke the bubble of Gary's dream garden with the first words he had uttered in minutes.

"I don't really know. You have records, but didn't have anything concrete to go on. I'm not sure how much more you could have done," Gary responded in consolation. He wanted to help Adam regain his connection with the world, give over the notes he had made and allow him to finish his shift and go home. With something in the way of information, he would have to call Augustine before he left, but this wasn't a case-breaker, so Gary still had plans to disappear off home to reclaim some of the hours he was owed.

"I want to help catch him. I feel like I have let people down," Adam said with some colour returning to his cheeks but still without any life in his voice.

"We all feel like that," Gary lied. He never felt remorse or guilt. It was part of the way he was made up. "If you let me have the notes you have made then I can pass these on to the rest of the team. This way you are helping us a great deal." There it was again. Gary was as adept at lying as he was at undermining authority. It was another underhand trick that just came naturally. Maybe he was always destined to be an arsehole.

"I'll get them for you," Adam told Gary in a way that gave away the fact he didn't believe the detective stood in his back garden with him. Adam had been around long enough to spot a lie and even someone as well-versed in it as Gary wasn't going to fool him. Now he wanted the papers out of his possession and the detective out of his house. Adam had some thinking to do. He wanted to catch the man from the end of the street himself. He felt as though he should make things up to the people of the city that had lived in fear because he let a man slip through on his watch, let alone those people who were killed. He handed over the notes he had made and showed the detective the door.

71

Ash and Electra had been to several places that their research told them might have been previous addresses for Alaaldin Hussein. They were all in run down parts of the city and all drew a blank. It was as though the lack of trust in the police from people in the poorest parts of town had also transferred to their buildings. Secrets were absorbed into the walls and ceilings of each address. If only they had a way of extracting them. Each of the properties that had been linked to his name in tenancy agreements or on the voters' roll were left abandoned and there were few neighbours in the adjacent properties, let alone anyone who knew him. Alaaldin was a ghost. He existed on the very margins of society.

There was one more place to visit and Ash drove the pair of them there. During the downtime between properties, Electra made calls to the landlords to see if the remembered him. Most were landlords that operated on either side of the line of the law so either accepted tenants cash in hand or didn't keep any kind of records. Electra got into policing to protect the kind of people who ended up in these situations with unscrupulous landlords who would throw them out with no notice if they found another tenant willing to pay a bit more money. She was appalled at the conditions one of her friends found herself in while she was at university and vowed to wipe this kind of landlord off the face of the earth. During her time in the police, she also found that landlords and employers who didn't keep records stood in the way of them getting a result. They really had no idea whether the tenant was Alaaldin Hussein or whether it was someone else completely, and that was partly down to the fact these people wanted to operate out of sight of the law. As far as she could make out, this was all in an attempt to save a few pounds here and there in tax.

But she wasn't chasing the landlords for their under-the-table deals, and was prepared to look the other way to get as much information as she could about the killer who was at large on the streets of their city. He was a bigger menace. But even when she told the landlords that they were not under investigation or suspicion, they had been through so many tenants that one in particular couldn't be pulled out from the scores of names and faces of the past. Some of the properties were in multiple occupation and the landlords may not have even met him. That was a fruitless part of the investigation as far as she was concerned. They would have to concentrate on the people who live there now, on the off chance that they met their man.

"It's the next right, I think," Electra offered. Ash already knew where he was going, but Electra didn't like handing control over to anyone else. This was a lead she had found and she wanted to ask all the questions and give direction to the enquiry. This started with leading Ash to the right address. He was happy to let her tell him the moves. He was thinking back to the last person they questioned and couldn't help but think he was hiding something. Most people when the police knock on the door will invite them in, particularly when the investigation doesn't involve them at all. But the guy at the last flat, Barry Garside, had walked out into the street and closed his front door behind him to talk. Nobody likes to be seen talking to the police in the small neighbourhoods that produce a large amount of crime in the city, but Barry was happier with that than he was in letting Ash and Electra through the door. They couldn't invite themselves in, but Ash wondered what he had to hide behind that door.

The right turn was negotiated without incident, much to the pleasure of Electra, and Ash slowed to look at the numbers on the doors of the houses to the right-hand side of the road. The first few had no number at all. They had doors that were facing each other rather than the street and looked to have been converted into flats by the same developer. The same red doors, the same tarmacked drive and the same cheap replacement windows were a real giveaway. Ash looked for something different in a property to break the monotony of cheap conversions, but there was none in sight and he had to return his attention to the road. He imagined magnolia walls, poorly-fitted internal window fixtures and the cheapest kitchen that Ikea could supply in flat after flat. He had seen it all before.

Electra was looking to the properties on the left of the car. She was looking for number 26, and had started with 148, so knew there was a little while to go. She looked dead ahead to assess the parking situation further up the road. If she reached the end of the road and couldn't find a parking space then she feared that the journey back round would be a bit of a pain. It was reaching mid-afternoon and the commute traffic was starting to build. It could add twenty minutes to her day, which wouldn't cause them any undue pain, but she would rather not drive around any longer. There could be far more productive things she could spend her time on.

Comparing notes after a day in the field with the other members of the team was one. Double checking all the references that they established the day before was another. Quite frankly anything that was moving the case forward was more productive than driving around the block twice because she missed a parking space. The sheer number of occupants had made the parking situation almost impossible. Electra looked at the houses and wondered what lay inside. They were mostly converted into flats on her side of the street too and this meant that there was little or shared outside space. Through the summer the people who lived there had three choices. They could go into a shared garden and try to find their own oasis among the bins, overgrown weeds and uncut grass that was always the feature of a garden shared by three flats, four flats or more. They could stay indoors and cope with the heat in their own way. Fans just pushed warm air from one part of the room to another while making that annoying creaking sound. It was a reminder that they were actually on, for those that paid the electricity bill but felt no benefit. The fan itself didn't produce chilly air but the constant groan that is made when moving backwards and forwards took your mind away from the heat and focused it on another annoyance instead. The third option was to go somewhere else to escape the heat. The pub or local park were always popular choices as far as Electra could see. She didn't have children and wasn't a big drinker so the appeal of either was lost on her, but from passing she always saw people gather there in droves. There must be something in it, she thought to herself. Electra contrasted this to the childhood she had. It was more free range than factory farming. Instead of the small flats that felt like cages in the summer heat, she was brought up in a garden, close to a wood where the days were filled with running. She didn't think it was possible from the viewpoint of twenty-odd years later but she used to run for hours every day. There was only the rest for refreshments that stopped her from being on the move from just after breakfast until just before teatime. They say that in New York, Central Park is the back garden of everyone in the city because they don't have one of their own. It offers a place to join others for a run, practice yoga or just have a picnic. In their city, Electra saw pubs and parks serving the same role. It just didn't have the same sense of style as New York. Little in their city did.

She nudged Ash when she saw a space around number 44 on her side of the road. He looked at her as though she was stopping him early but then looked down the road to see cars on either side of the road like they were lined up for inspection and pulled in quickly before he had the chance to indicate. He could see nothing else in either direction, but Ash liked to indicate when he turned. It wasn't something to warn others of his movement as there were no others there at the time, but it felt right. He has always done it, even in the middle of the night on a road where no other car had been (or would be) for hours. It was a habit that wasn't going to be broken now he had been driving for this long. The air was stifling as they stepped outside of the air conditioning of the car and out into the street. The sun had been beating down on this spot for almost ten hours by this point and the metal of the cars present was storing this heat and transferring it to anyone that walked past. The first signs of shade were edging across the far side of the road. It would be welcome relief on the return journey to the car if the conversation with the current occupant was going to take more than a few minutes. Electra wetted her lips with her tongue and contemplated the shade as they walked towards number 26, flat B.

They arrived and looked the building up and down as though it would give up its secrets if interrogated in the right way. If this was possible, it would make my job a lot easier, thought Ash. They sized it up and walked through the space where a gate presumably once stood, towards the disorganised group of letterboxes that had been stuck to the inside wall of the sheltered porch at the front door. There was a set of doorbells and they each had a sticker with a flat number on, but the time they had been there combined with the weather had made these stickers illegible. Electra went for the logical choice that flat B would be the second one from the top and pressed long and hard. The light on the buzzer went out for the time she held her finger there before slowly coming back to life after she took the pressure away. There was no other indication that the bell worked so they waited to see if a response was forthcoming. Ash stepped back away from the door and looked at the windows on either side. He was trying to decide which one he thought was flat B. It looked from the array of letterboxes and bells that there were five flats in total in this Georgian property that would have housed one large family in the past. By the look of the windows in the roof, which he had spotted when walking from the car, this meant two on each floor and one in the roof space. His guess was that flat B was to the right as he looked, but, it could have been any of them. Some of Ash's friends were property developers and he had been told all manner of stories about how they worked the system to get the most profit. Some properties were split into apartments and the surveyor would be shown the biggest apartment as 'A' so they could get the most value and biggest mortgage from their lender. As soon as the surveyor left, the letter 'B' would be attached to the same large flat so that another lender would give them the most money possible. This went on until all the valuations were in and the money was released. The property developer got the most they could for their money, while the lenders all lent on what was essentially the same flat. In this building, flat B could be any of them.

As Ash looked up and wondered, the door opened slowly. Ash returned to the front door and saw a woman stood looking at Electra. He smiled and coughed to gain attention but the woman and Electra were locked in some sort of staring contest and he couldn't break their concentration. He chuckled to himself as this went on for a few seconds more before kicking his feet against the step. Whether it was the noise he made, or that one of them blinked, he didn't know but the silence and inactivity stopped from the two women and Electra spoke.

"We are here to ask you a few questions, if you don't mind," Electra explained, "It is about the person who lived here before you. Did you meet them at all?"

"You don't remember me, do you? I have pictured your face every day for around 8 years. I thought that you would remember me. I suppose that you see a lot of people like me," the woman spoke to Electra like they were long lost friends. Electra had seen something familiar in those eyes, but wasn't able to place them. The woman was right, she did see a lot of people in her job and didn't find it easy to remember them all.

"I'm sorry. I am terrible with names and faces. I'm not quite sure how I ended up in this job!" Electra tried to make light of the situation and elicit some detail from the woman.

"My name is Babs Harvey. You protected me after my husband beat me half to death. He was a heavy drinker and I just happened to be in the wrong place one night. He had hurt me before, but that time was something else. I was quite a mess and you helped me when I left the hospital. I couldn't go back after that. You were the first person I saw that wasn't a nurse or a doctor and I needed a friendly face to tell me everything would work out alright in the end. That was you. I was only with you for a few minutes, but you got my mind in a better place. I haven't been able to thank you," the woman explained. Electra looked her up and down. This was a skinny woman, maybe in her late fifties with thinning hair and red blotches under her eyes. It was as though she had been crying. Electra hoped that she was living a happier life than when they had last met.

Electra felt bad. She loved her old role helping women who had faced domestic violence to break that cycle, but Babs was right, she literally only ever had a few minutes with people to assess their situation and get the relevant people to support the women. It was a fleeting moment in the lives of women who were thinking far more about what they were escaping and where they were fleeing to. Electra didn't think that anyone would remember her role in all that turmoil. Obviously, some did.

"I'm sorry. I don't have a great memory, but I am so happy that I was able to help," Electra replied sheepishly. It didn't feel great.

"I have always believed that we would bump into each other somewhere down the line. I thought that it was part of my destiny to see you again and say thank you. These last few years I have been fighting lung cancer, a fight that is almost over, and I was worried that you wouldn't show up again. But here you are. Would the two of you like to come in and sit down? I'm afraid I can't stand for much longer," Babs looked over her shoulder towards the stairs as though they were the first step on the way to the top of Mount Everest. She climbed them first while the two detectives followed. They sat together in a small front room above the window in the left-hand side of the building on the first floor. Ash's guess at which flat it might have been was on the wrong floor and the wrong side of the house, but he wouldn't have been confident enough to put any money on his guess at any rate.

"So, you want to know about the person who lived here before me?" Babs repeated the question back to the two detectives so the conversation was re-framed after what had been said downstairs. Babs had said what she wanted to Electra and wanted to help her out, but she didn't have much energy.

"Yes," Electra responded, "Did you ever meet him?" She too sensed the need to get on with things and thought that her connection with Babs would work through the small talk and get to the point.

"The place had been empty for over a month when I got here. The person who was here before left a lot of rubbish, which I had to deal with. The landlord wasn't overly helpful," Babs explained with a weariness in her voice that was as much to do with looking back at that time as it was her present lack of liveliness.

"You never met. In those possessions you had to sort out, were there any items that you thought might have been unusual?" Electra asked while looking at Ash. She wanted to know if he thought she was heading in the right direction. He looked dead ahead. She took this as a signal that she was on the right track. If he wanted her to move on then he would have made a sign, she thought.

"If you count someone leaving letters unsent and clothes unworn all over the place, then yes. And there were hundreds of disposable razors along with cans of shaving foam. The bath blocked a little while after I got here and the plumber took more hair out of the plug than you would normally see on a barber's floor," Babs could see that this was news the detectives wanted to hear. Electra's eyes lit up for the first time since she had been there. Ash was making frantic notes.

"Hair?" Ash spoke for the first time. He had been hooked by this revelation and was already linking it to the fact that they had found no hairs at any of the murder scenes.

"The plumber just kept on pulling it out of the sink," Babs explained and the look on her face showed that she hadn't found it a pleasant watch at all.

"I'll just have to make a call," Ash told the two women present, as he stood up and walked towards the kitchen. "Is it OK if I speak in here?" he asked out loud and closed the door behind him without waiting for an answer. Babs looked at Electra to explain his behaviour but she had no explanation ready.

"Sorry. Is there anything else?" Electra asked. She loved open questions, but could see that Babs was tired. If she had only a one-word negative answer then that was fine in the circumstances.

"I could go on all day. There were boxes of latex gloves, paperwork left all over the place. I got rid of just about all of it. From some of the writing I thought that maybe he was an author, but that would have been some creepy stuff," Babs closed her eyes as she spoke. Electra took this as an opportunity to look around the room. It looked like the home of someone who didn't have the energy to maintain it. There were several scratches in the wallpaper that could have been replaced, two door handles that were broken and the lightbulb in the lamp by the sofa had blown some time ago by the looks of it. The corners of the room were in need of a duster and the hoover had obviously not seen the light of day for some time. Electra noted that these were all tasks that couldn't be done easily and wondered what help might be available for Babs. She resolved to take a look into it when she had a spare moment, if that ever came. Babs opened her eyes again and Electra realised that she didn't have much time left. Ash strolled back into the room, mouthed 'sorry' at Babs before smiling at Electra and sitting back in the seat he had vacated a short while earlier.

"There were boxes of latex gloves and some creepy writing left too," Electra filled Ash in on the information he had missed while out of the room. He raised his eyebrows and considered getting back on the phone to Augustine before thinking better of it.

"Do you have any of this stuff left?" Ash asked. His usual patience was replaced by a kind of urgency after the call.

"I have some of the documents that looked official. I haven't looked at them in any detail, but put them in a kitchen drawer in case he came back, or the landlord asked for them. I asked the landlord what to do with the rest of the stuff and he never came back to me, so I got rid of them," Babs spoke with increasing weariness before directing her stare to Ash, "The kitchen where you have just been. Middle drawer, right hand side."

Ash took the instruction and got back to his feet. He searched past the tea towels and takeaway menus to a large brown envelope and slid it out from underneath the other contents of the drawer. He walked back into the living room and handed it to Babs. She didn't raise her hands and looked at Ash. He sat back down, put on some latex gloves of his own and opened the envelope. Inside were documents that could make life much easier for someone who wanted to evade the law. There were three passports, two British and one from Pakistan that were all in different names. They had been prepared for slightly different identities, so one had a full beard and head of hair, one had all this shaved off and the other was much shorter hair and beard. Ash guesses that he could have picked the one closest to his current hairstyle and use it to stay a step ahead of the game if needed. Augustine and Marie would have to let the transport police and airport security know that there could be a flight risk for this suspect. Also in the envelope were driving licences from the UK and Pakistan that used different names and addresses as well as some letters, all unfinished and unsent. The first two caught Electra's eye as the same style and tone as the ones she and Augustine has retrieved from the newspaper. This definitely felt like their man.

"This is all I have. You can take it, but I need you to leave," Babs spoke so softly that the two detectives could barely hear what she said.

"Are you OK?" Electra asked with the upmost of concern. She didn't want to impose on someone who was clearly so unwell. They had outstayed their welcome

"I'm fine. I just need to rest."

"Do you have any help? Is there anything I can do?"

"Right now, I have to sleep. But if you are around in the next couple of days, then I'd love some company."

Electra had a day off the following day. The morning was going to be taken over by the funeral of Andy Lane, but she would come back in the afternoon. Then the day after that she started late, so could come over before work. She smiled at Babs and received the warmest smile of her life in return. The two detectives got up and quietly made their way down the stairs and though the front door; Electra made sure it was closed before they walked back to the car.

Apart from Gary, the team sat together in the office and discussed their findings. The hair and latex gloves found at Babs apartment were the most telling find of the day, closely followed by the false documents from the kitchen drawer. They would all be attending the funeral the next morning, but after that the names and addresses on these documents would need to be double checked against the public records. As some were in the city, they could be visited to see if there were any more clues. But for the time being, they would all get a good night's rest and prepare to say goodbye to a colleague. Marie arrived as the meeting was about to close so she could thank them all for the constructive work put in that day. Augustine spoke to each team member one by one as they left. He sat with Marie after and discussed the progress they had been able to make.

"We've made a bigger step forward today than all the weeks we have been working on this. I'm still getting to grips with his death, but PC Andy Lane has brought us more progress with this case than all the detectives of my team put together. Tomorrow I will pay my respects and thank him for all he has done," Augustine could speak his mind to Marie without any filters. He had no need to think twice about the words that were coming out of his mouth.

"We need to back all of this up. The reports should be together before I go home tomorrow. I want to see that we have a growing file of facts on this killer – not more speculation and guesswork. Is that clear?" Marie didn't often lay down the law often but felt that this was a point that needed labelling. Augustine had to jump through a few hoops with her to keep this investigation. She needed to show something to those above to have any say in the matter of who would lead the chase for the killer.

"I understand," Augustine replied, "I think we are closing in. and I haven't thought that until now." He looked across the room to see if Marie was studying him. He expected her to watch his lips and eyes closely for signs of sincerity, but she was already somewhere else. He guessed that it might be the funeral tomorrow. She would have to speak to Andy Lane's family again and this was one of the worst parts of her job. She spoke no more, but Augustine imagined what was passing through her head. He could picture her sitting down with Andy Lane's parents, who had never thought for one second that their child would die before them. She would have to make attempts to console the inconsolable. That wasn't a job that Augustine would ever want to do.

The two of them sat in silence for a while. Augustine wanted to go but felt as though he should stay, to support her and be there should she need him. He looked down at the envelope of documents that Ash had handed him. It was filled with items that could blow this case apart, but he was ready to sit on them out of respect for the fallen PC. Augustine looked again at Marie. She was on her way home in her mind, but the body hadn't caught up with this thought. He would sit there as long as she needed.

72

Augustine pulled on his shirt and tie. He had a suit that he only ever wore for funerals. It was dark blue rather than black because he wanted some light on the day, even if it was the smallest gesture. The shoulders still had signs of the wood from his grandfather's coffin. His brother, cousins and himself had carried the coffin. Some of the wood had stained his jacket. Dry cleaning hadn't removed it. Augustine wasn't sure if he wanted it to be removed. The tie was black. He worried if it would show off the non-blackness of his suit, but it had never been commented on. He was trying to count the number of funerals he had been to. He had reached the number seven before telling himself to concentrate on something more light-hearted. There was going to be plenty of time to mourn later in the day, then after that work. The time while he was getting ready should be focused on something else, he decided. Augustine missed a lot of what others thought was normal conversation. He didn't watch much television and wasn't into sports. He liked to read, but found escape in obscure books he picked up from just about anywhere rather than the bestsellers that everyone else might be talking about. He was a conversation to avoid for most people because they didn't share the same background or culture. Augustine thought about the books he might like to read. He was heavily into the works of Philip Roth but hadn't made his way through the back catalogue. He stopped and thought about the ones that were missing and when he could get around to reading them. His life was consumed by the killer he was hunting, so reading anything of substance was out of the question. He resolved to buy a newspaper every day and do some reading there. This would keep him up to date with current affairs and satisfy his desire to consume something written. It was far better than getting his news from social media, like many of his friends. He had never understood the desire to read news from sources that couldn't be relied upon, even in his job. Yes, a newspaper would satisfy his desire to consume information. The time spent deciding what to do helped Augustine move away from the depressing thoughts that had begun his day and moved him towards a lighter frame of mind. He felt that someone to share this life with would help him keep this frame of mind for longer. He had thought the date with Christine was going well until they found her friend murdered. This was enough to scupper any date, but for Augustine there was always one thing or another that stood in the way of dating success. If it wasn't the mood he was in, then it was the way he perceived them. If it wasn't a bad meal, then it was terrible weather that might dampen an otherwise lively night. And if all else fell into place, if Augustine felt comfortable with a woman, then there was the death of her friend to finish off any lingering hopes that he might find happiness.

He was dressed and ready to face the day. The only problem was the clock still said 7.00 and the funeral wasn't for another 4 hours. Augustine traipsed down to the local shop in his funeral suit and bought the first newspaper of his new resolution. He walked back home with it under his arm, like it was a mission he had been given from a higher plain. Augustine made a cup of tea and sat at his kitchen table to read and drink. It was his intention to read for around an hour and then start to make tracks towards the police station. Marie had given instructions that they were all to meet at the police station. The funeral procession was to pass the station on the way from Andy Lane's home to the church and it felt fitting that they all joined the other mourners from there.

By the time Augustine first picked up his tea cup to drink it was already cold. He gave himself five more minutes and he would then get ready for the drive to the station. But those five minutes turned into an hour and he looked at the clock exactly as it turned to 10.25. Augustine jumped up and hunted around the kitchen for his car keys. He always told himself to put the keys in the same place every night so he could easily find them the next morning, but this determination at the start of the day was never matched by the appropriate action at the end of it. He looked under post that had been sat there for days, moved cups that had tea stains just as old and eventually found his keys on the edge of the draining board. He jumped in his car and made his way to the station. The car park was filling up, so he pulled into the first space he saw. Augustine usually deliberated over parking spaces looking for the perfect one. The first few he came across were usually labelled as too small, too far away or another 'too,' but that day he just had to find a space and get to the station as quickly as he could. It was gone 10.40 and the funeral was due to pass their doors at any minute. Augustine stepped into line with Marie and the rest of his team within 2 minutes and saw the funeral moving towards the police station from his left. He bowed his head and waited for someone in front of him to move. As they did, he stepped across Gary to walk with Electra. She looked up to the sky and Augustine could see a tear roll down her cheek and collect on the front of her dress. She was all in black, as would have been expected of someone who was a stickler for tradition. She had been passed down this sense of order by her grandmother. It wasn't going to change.

The funeral was a mix of the light and the dark. The passing of someone so young was never going to be an easy affair, but the youth of the people there brought a vibrancy that you don't normally find on these occasions. People were there to celebrate his life more than to mourn his death. Andy's friends refused to let the killer win, and the colour yellow was shown by many of them. It was his favourite colour. Someone in his circle had suggested they all wear something yellow on Facebook a couple of nights before the funeral. This had obviously caught on with those that were connected to him on a personal level. As for the people who knew Andy Lane on a professional level, the slightly lighter suit that Augustine wore was as close as any of them had come to colour.

The morning passed quickly and before they knew it, the team were sat back in the office together. There was a downbeat mood, as could be expected, as they went about typing up their findings from the day before and following up any loose ends. There were a few landlords to talk to and some ex-colleagues that they might like to speak to in the future. It all pointed to one man. They had suspected that it was Alaaldin Hussein for a few days but the final pieces of the jigsaw were slotting into place to give them the full picture of this character. Augustine sat with each of the team members in turn to make sure they had followed up all the leads from their research and were able to gather something that would stand up in a court of law when they found him. That was Augustine's view. He classified it now as a 'when' and not an 'if.' The team members were all as upbeat as Augustine about finding the killer. The morning had strengthened their resolve to deal with the man who had taken a colleague from them. One by one, Gary, Electra and Ash had sat with Augustine and talked about their leads. Electra had come into the office specifically for the conversation on her day off. She wanted Gus to know that he had her full backing and she was putting together the information that she and Ash had got – especially that from Babs. She assured Augustine that Ash was checking the addresses on the fake documents as they spoke before leaving the station to fulfil her promise to Babs.

The last member of the team through the door was Lou. He didn't share the same enthusiasm as the rest of the team. The others had talked up their chances of finding this man. Augustine could see negativity written all over Lou's face.

"What's wrong Lou? You are always the person who keeps the rest of them on track," Augustine asked the man sat opposite. It was the first time he had noticed Lou's advancing years. He looked like the world was moving too quickly for him.

"Not this time, Gus," Lou replied. There was that name again. Augustine thought about issuing a memo to confirm that he wasn't to be called Gus, but thought better of it in the circumstances. He watched Lou think very carefully about what he was going to say. This wasn't like the grandfather of the team; he usually had just the right words at the right moments.

"Watching Andy Lane's family today told me that my time here is coming to an end. I don't know what else I have in life, but I am sure that I don't want to be in the police any more. It is a life of mopping up the worst of society, while trying to protect the best. I'm afraid that the worst always win. How are we going to catch this killer? He is a ghost. We have got lucky now. Do you really think he is going to allow us to get lucky again?" the questions from Lou struck a chord at the heart of Augustine. He wasn't sure how much of his job was luck and how much was ability. He could go through all the procedures, but until Andy Lane stumbled on a killer, they had almost nothing to work with.

"Lou, there is nothing different we do now to what we did when you started this job. We work hard, follow all the clues, gather evidence and sometimes do a bit of hoping. This killer is no more of a ghost than any other we have searched for together," Augustine lied to his colleague. He didn't feel great about it, but wanted to get Lou back onside. He needed the support of his most experienced member of the team, even if it was just until this case was over. He had no idea whether Lou had to work notice or could just walk away at that moment and never come back.

"Augustine, this man walked straight past you. He controls us. I daresay that the killing of Andy Lane was part of his plan. He has been in total control so far – what makes you think that he wasn't up to the mark when he killed one of our own?" Lou wasn't going to be swayed in his opinion. Augustine could see the defeat in his colleague's eyes. It wasn't a pretty sight.

"Lou, why don't you go home and think about things for a while. We will keep up the work here and I can call you in a couple of days. I'd love you to still be here when we catch this guy. You have put in a lot of work to find justice for the victims and their families," Augustine tried to appeal to Lou's sense of fairness and thought it might have turned his colleague's head for a while.

"I'll sleep on it. Give me a few days," Lou replied. He wasn't ready to commit to staying just as he wasn't ready to commit to leaving. Lou was a man of balance. He quite accepted that nobody was ever 100% committed to anything in life. He had hovered around 50-50 for some time but was beginning to see more negatives than positives to working as a detective. If he got to 45-55 then he knew his time was up. Augustine watched Lou walk out of the door and wondered if it would be the last time. He sighed and thought about the career he must have seen. From the early days in the police when a thick ear or a slap on the wrist deterred petty criminals to today when they buried a colleague and chased a man who had killed at least six people. He could see why Lou didn't think this was what he had signed up for.

73

The day was drawing to a close and only Augustine and Ash remained in the office. Augustine was sat at the desk reading the notes from all the other members of his team. He had a meeting the next morning with Marie to discuss the progress made and the steps required to bring this guy to justice, so he had to know his stuff inside out. He didn't get into policing to read notes and sit in meetings but found it a necessary part of his role. If he didn't do this and shield his team from it then someone else would have to waste their time with it. He would rather they got to do the more enjoyable parts of the role and he put up with all the shitty bits like explaining what he was doing, looking at performance charts and attending meetings. It still didn't feel like they were effective, even after years of sitting through them.

Ash was looking again at the documents he and Electra had been given by Babs in her flat. She had kept them for some time without a real purpose. Ash believed that just about everything happened for a reason. He wasn't going to commit 100% to the theory of fate, but he was most of the way there. He thought about the different things that could have happened with the documents before they ended up sat on his desk.

Alaaldin could have taken them with him. He could have burned them. He could have thrown them away to sit in landfill forever. He could have hidden them somewhere that was still unfound. Babs could have thrown them with the rest of the contents of the flat when she moved in. She could have discarded them later after the landlord or the previous tenant hadn't claimed them. They could have been damaged by a water leak or a fire. They could have been lost or Babs could have forgotten she had them in her infirm state when he and Electra paid her a visit. Even after they arrived in his hands they could have been in a car accident and the documents damaged. They could have been stolen. They could have even been blank or faded over time. But none of these things, or a thousand others that hadn't yet entered Ash's brain, had happened and the twists of fate delivered them into his hands. After the funeral, he had been in a meeting with Augustine, had a catch-up with Electra before needing to leave the station for a while for a hospital appointment. It was a regular check on the state of his knee after a basketball injury and only took a couple of hours out of his day but left him needing to pull together the last pieces of his research before Augustine's meeting with Marie the next morning. He didn't feel it with the rest of the team, but he knew that this was a hugely important meeting. Being part of the team that didn't catch a major serial killer wasn't quite as detrimental to a career as being the lead detective, but it wasn't far off. Ash had to work hard that evening to provide all the answers Marie might want from his boss.

"I'm going now. Are you OK?" Augustine suddenly appeared on Ash's radar. He had a jacket on like he was going somewhere that might see rain. Ash looked him up and down to determine what it was all about but remembered that the weather report that morning suggested rain. Augustine was known to study the weather. If anyone in the office wanted to know one of two things, then they would only have to ask Augustine. The first was what the weather was going to be like and the second was what time the sun rose and set. As a man with problems sleeping, the rising and setting of the sun were always vitally important pieces of information to have.

"I'm fine. I want to make sure we have all the data from these documents," Ash waved them in the air like they were prizes won at the fair. He smiled along with it and Augustine was reminded of photos in the local newspaper of kids' football teams who had won division 9 of their local league and were as happy as the Premier League winning team, assembled for hundreds of millions, with their result.

"I've closed all the blinds, so you can get some peace. The car park is almost empty. Just leave it on my desk if you finish late. There's no need to come in early as well if you are here for a few hours tonight. I'll work out what you mean before I go visit Marie," Augustine explained. Ash knew he didn't like meetings at any rate, least of all when there was pressure to perform, so he smiled widely at his boss and friend to give some moral support.

"You'll be fine, Gus," he said, maintaining the smile so he spoke with his mouth open. The consonants had no distinct formation but Ash knew he was being heard.

"You might not be if you keep calling me that," he retorted with a glint in his eyes. Ash took it that this was a joke. If he was glinting then he couldn't possibly mean it. "See you tomorrow, Gus."

"Yeah, yeah. See you tomorrow."

As Augustine left the station, a pair of eyes followed him from the shadows across the road. The figure watched intently as the detective jumped in his car, and checked the registration on the car with the one he had already written in his notebook months earlier. It was the same.

74

Augustine took the long route home. He had several mapped out from the years of working and living in the same places. Some were better in rush hour, others when there was nothing on the road. He didn't want to get home quickly because he had a date. This was the opposite of his usual behaviour, but this date was with Christine. If he could have ended his previous date with her half an hour earlier then he would at that point have been racing home to get ready. But he was in two minds. She had called and asked him. He didn't feel able to say anything but 'yes.' She didn't want to be in the same part of town as before, so they arranged to meet in a pub near to her home. It wasn't going to be anything like as new or glamorous as the last date, but felt more suited to their current situation.

He made it home and looked at the large clock he had in the kitchen. It was something he bought on a whim without thinking about where he would put it. When he got it back to his house it didn't feel at home anywhere. It made too much noise for the bedroom. It was too large for the hall. And it clashed with the wallpaper in the living room. The kitchen was the least-worst option so Augustine hung it there, above the glass-topped table where he ate his breakfast on the occasional morning he had something in the cupboards to eat. It still felt out of place to him, but he had learned to not let it bug him as much. The first few days and weeks were a struggle to keep his hands off the clock and remove it. Only the image of the price tag stopped him from giving it to charity. Again, he thought that being with someone might have given him a second pair of eyes on big purchase decisions like this. He wanted a woman to help him in all the areas of life where he slipped up. Maybe this was a better way for dating sites to work than their current model. He could offer someone financial stability, suggested reading material, emotional stability, some basic gardening skills, problem solving, being a good listener and being great with pets. In return, he was looking for someone with an eye for interior design, a person who would help him spend his money wisely, a good cook and with an ability in DIY. Between them they could have a life where all bases were covered (at least all the ones that were important to Augustine) and live a happy life. They would be the two matching pieces of a two-piece jigsaw. But Augustine wondered whether the longer he waited, the less chance there was of that other piece being left over. He wasn't sure if the 2nd piece of his jigsaw had already settled for a near match, or maybe someone who didn't see them for the skills they could bring but actually did that 'fall in love' thing that had eluded him and dragged him down since school.

He headed for the shower. It was preparation for any event that he was anxious about. He would have another in the morning just before he left home to meet with Marie. It wasn't a cleanliness thing, more of a habit. As Augustine got out of the shower he heard his phone ring. In a state of undress and with wet skin, he would normally have left it, but with a date he didn't much fancy on the near horizon, he hoped that it might have been Christine letting him down gently. He picked it up without looking, pushed the green part of the touchscreen and held it to his ear.

"Augustine."

It wasn't Christine.

"Augustine are you there?" He didn't know why but he had gone silent when it wasn't who he expected. It took a few seconds to readjust and speak.

"Hi, Lou. Is everything OK. You sound different," Augustine replied. The wet was dripping from his skin onto the carpet and he wanted to return to getting dry. Augustine knew how to get to the point when he wanted to.

"Can I come over? I was cooking my dinner and…" Augustine could hear Lou crying. It wasn't a sound that he had heard before or thought he would ever hear. Lou regained some composure and started again, "I have had a chip pan fire. I wasn't concentrating. The fire brigade has been in. The place is a bit of a mess. I didn't know who to call. You are near the top of my list."

"Lou. I'm going out for a while, but get around here and you can stay in the spare room," Augustine thought about cancelling the date to be with Lou, but couldn't bring himself to do this any more than he could have said 'no,' to Christine in the first place. It was his duty after the way the first date ended. He would send her a text to say he might be bit late, but didn't feel in any position to cancel.

Lou was at his front door within 15 minutes – time that Augustine used to get dried, tidy up the place as much as he could and get the takeaway menus out. Augustine guessed that Lou hadn't eaten and he wasn't the man to cook for him. He was ready to go out when Lou arrived and had already called a taxi that was due within the next ten minutes. He didn't want to leave Lou on his own but the sight of him at the front door looking, well looking just like Lou always did, cheered Augustine up no end. He could have a chat with his colleague when the date was over or the next morning. It wasn't as if he had turned up in tears. Augustine left the TV on, £20 for a takeaway and the keys to the front door with Lou before walking down the road in the direction of the taxi office. He was sure they would come from there as it was now just gone 8 o'clock and he knew from an investigation into an assault on a driver a few years ago that this was the time they changed shift. He looked back at his house and could see the silhouette of Lou move about in the front room closest to the street through the curtains. He looked head and saw a taxi slowly make its way along the street as though it felt the same level of tiredness as a human. He stepped out into the road and the taxi driver slowed down. He recognised Augustine and unlocked the doors. The detective sat in the front seat, he didn't understand those that always sat in the back, and the car moved away.

75

In another part of the city, Al was making his way out. He had all the equipment he needed in his backpack. He didn't know this part of the city anywhere near as well as his own home, but that wasn't a place he could return to. He looked through the spy hole in the front door before he left. The fact that he had given both clues and extra motivation to the police by killing one of their own made him nervous. He operated better when he was calm and totally in control, but to return to this state would take months of work. He knew that one carefully chosen killing, perhaps the last of this summer, would bring him the headlines he needed. The coast looked clear, so he set out through the front door and out into the night air. The late summer evening felt like a battle between summer and autumn. The clear skies of the day brought heat, but this was soon dispersed by the cool breeze of night. As soon as Al stepped off the threshold of the building and onto the public highway he could feel it. He could feel the autumn and winter cold pressing against the sides of his freshly shaven head. He pulled up his hood and looked left and right before proceeding. It was as futile a gesture as there ever could be. If they were on to him, then there would be no escape. If the police suspected him of killing all those people and had found this address, then there would be scores of them, armed to the teeth. Looking out to see if he was being watched was something that happened naturally, rather than an act that would get him out of danger.

He smiled to himself. A life filled with futile gestures had found a meaning a few years earlier. He had spoken to people who had been out and fought for their religion. He had listened to soldiers who put their life and liberty at risk to learn about jihad and the role they could play in it. He was encouraged to follow the same path but always felt that the fight was right here, at home. The people that were a danger to his religion and oppressing Islam all over the world were in the Western countries that had invaded Iraq and Afghanistan. They were not the poor fellow Muslims that were suffering enough already. He watched with dismay the bombings in Manchester and London, the attacks across the United Kingdom that were supposed to spread terror. He didn't believe in terror. It felt like such an arbitrary act. Making people feel frightened wasn't going to change their lives. It made Islam look immoral and without guidance. He had a better way of changing lives. He believed that the world was heading in the wrong direction. Rights for homosexuals, the greed of the capitalist society and the corruption of politicians were at the top of his list of the modern day deadly sins. These were parts of society that had to be eradicated and Al believed that Islam showed the way. It showed that homosexuality was a sin. It showed that greed was the road to hell. It showed that politicians preaching peace on one hand while waging war on the other should be delivered the ultimate blow. If only he could get near to Tony Blair.

Al's smiled moved to gritted teeth as he recalled conversations he had with his brothers. They were all for the terror approach. They believed that killing people randomly would bring the West to its knees. But he knew they were wrong. He knew that targeting people for their sins was the right approach. He knew that this was the way to change the way people lived. And that night was going to be the time that he made a killing that would send his message out to the world. This would create headlines. This would see his message released. This would force the police to show the letters he was leaving on the chest of his victims. This would open the eyes of the world to the sins of their ways.

Al had a plan. He knew that he had to act that night. It was time to deliver the biggest part of his message so far. He had watched and knew where he needed to be. Another dead police officer would send the city into a tailspin. This time he was after a bigger fish than the one that wandered into his home.

76

Ash sat and looked around the office. He was fascinated by the cheap furniture that was bought by the police. There was so much to choose from out there, and yet they always seemed to end up with the cheapest, flimsiest furniture available. This stuff made IKEA look like high-end, he thought to himself. The hours spent assembling it too were a massive cost to the police. There were much better things that police officers could spend their time on, but with every new desk, chair or cabinet delivered, someone would have to take themselves off the street and assemble it. The instructions were usually in Chinese, as this was the cheapest place to get this stuff from, and in the end, there were as many parts left over as were attached to the piece of furniture. Without a way to check, the discards were placed in a room until it filled and was all thrown in a skip in one go. This resembled the way that most homes accumulated and discarded of their trash. It would go in a 'designated place' such as the loft or the garage until the loft or garage was filled to breaking point. It would then be emptied as the occupants would utter phrases like "I have no idea why we kept this," or, "I don't even know what this is off." This was replicated in homes, businesses and police stations across the country, probably across the world for all Ash knew. In the middle were the people with sense, like him, that would make alternative purchase decisions and find products that were already assembled and have no leftover arm A or bracket H to decide what to do with.

As Ash shook his head in disbelief at all this waste, his attention returned to the envelope sat in front of him. He hadn't really looked at the contents with any care and attention until that moment because the day had run away from him. Now with a fresh cup of coffee and silence in the office, he knew that he could look at what was in front of him with complete concentration. Ash had read an article in a newspaper a few weeks before that said if you turn up for work at 5am and work for 2 hours, then you would get as much done as an 8-hour day with all the distractions of the phone and colleagues. He could well believe it. He was sure that this was an exercise in dotting i's and crossing t's but it would help Augustine present the case in full the next morning.

Ash sorted the items into different piles. Driving licences in one, passports in another and then the other assorted bits of paper in a third, which included rent books, birth certificates and other pieces of paper that looked official but were not all in a language that Ash could decipher. The third pile looked he easiest to work through, so Ash took each in turn and made notes across a prepared piece of paper. It was printed from Excel with columns denoting name, address and notes. Ash hoped that this would help him to formalise any patterns that existed in the information. He was terrible at noticing everyday patterns and needed to have these pointed out to him. Sometimes he still didn't get it. So, with his work, Ash always used structures like spreadsheets to make these patterns stand out.

After around 20 minutes of checking each document, writing down the names and address as well as making notes, Ash had finally handled and assessed every document that came from the envelope in the flat he and Electra had visited. She was as excited as him to find out what might be inside and had even asked Ash to call her if there was anything interesting in the envelope. He had said he would but had no intention of calling her on a day off, which had now become an evening off. He respected Electra as a colleague and a person. He wouldn't want someone calling him when he was relaxing on an evening unless it was life or death. He was sure she had better things to do with her life.

Ash went to grab another coffee. The vending machine didn't usually stay on this late in the day and lurched into action as though it too was having a relaxing evening. Ash waited patiently before deciding that he should relieve some of the fluid that was already building up in his bladder. He knew that another cup of coffee was probably going to put more pressure on it later. He wanted to check the results and go for the night. He could leave a brief note for Augustine and be back in the morning fresh to go at it all again. Ash felt like the rest of the team that progress was being made. He was starting to feel that he needed to step into the shoes of Lou, who wasn't fulfilling his role as catalyst for the team as he had done over the last few years. Ash looked up to Lou, they all did, because he had seen it all before and approached every new case with the same calmness and authority. He got the rest of them thinking in exactly the same way. Human emotion dictated that you became angry or upset at seeing another senseless murder, but Lou allowed that to be processed before moving on to the practical side of things – what are we going to do about it? It was Lou's stock phrase, a kind of call to arms for the rest of the team to stop wallowing in the helplessness of human nature and to begin the steps to find whoever was responsible and bring them to justice. That was all they could do from that point. In Lou's eyes, this was the best method to stop another killing in the future. If potential killers see that other killers get caught, convicted and locked up for the rest of their life, then this was the ultimate deterrent. With Lou getting to a point where he may not be around for much longer, Ash was the one to step into this role; to point the team in the right direction.

With a fresh cup of coffee, and room for it in his bladder, Ash sat back at his desk readied for the task ahead. He had to put all his concentration into the document he had complied. If there were patterns then he was probably the last person on earth he would have chosen to analyse them, but he was alone without another soul to pass this on to. Ash sat and read line by line, first the names. There were different variations of the same names appearing on his list. Where Ash first thought he saw the name Abdul several times, on second reading it became obvious that there were the names Abubakar, Abdullah, Abdurrahman, Abdelaziz and Aariz. Nothing to go on there. Ash pictured the beer and ready meal he had in the fridge. He estimated that he would be there in around half an hour. Two minutes to check the addresses on his list, five to type up his note to Gus (his handwriting wasn't good enough to rely on in important matters) and then that left him 23 minutes to get home and slam the food in the microwave. It was a cottage pie and would sit perfectly with the beer that he would have already half-drunk by the time the ping went on the microwave and he would be ready to eat.

Ash looked down the list of addresses, and even wondered if they were real.

26 Valley Parade

24 The Rowans

96 Bull Lane

148 High Street

22 Smith Street

They all felt like the names that a novelist would give to streets. He hadn't the same encyclopaedic knowledge of street names as some in the force, so couldn't immediately tell if they were imaginary, to fool a quick inspection or if they related to actual parts of the city. Ash looked further down the list and saw another flurry of street names that could have been written down on a whim. He was just about to start typing his note to Augustine when something caught his eye. At the bottom of the page, presumably from a driving licence, he saw the address 24 The Rowans again. Then as he scanned back up to find where he saw it last, a third edition of the same address appeared. Ash knocked his coffee on the floor as he shot up in shock at the words on the page. The same address 3 times? Surely that's more than a coincidence, Ash thought to himself. He clicked off the word processor on his page and onto a browser. Ash typed in the street address and waited a few seconds before he looked back up at the screen. It the meantime he threw a couple of paper napkins he had in his top drawer in the general direction of the coffee spill. They turned a shade of teak similar to his desk as they soaked up most of the liquid. He was still standing from the surprise that a routine check gave him something to go on. His back was starting to twinge at the awkward angle he was operating his computer from, but he couldn't sit back down again. He was a ball of nervous energy. The screen revealed what he wanted to see. There was a 24 The Rowans in the city. It was a ten-minute drive away. He looked back through the documents to find the three that matched the address. Ash was so engulfed in the envelope that he failed to notice someone enter the room behind him.

The other occupant of the room walked slowly along the opposite side of the room to Ash. It was as though he hadn't noticed the detective stood at the desk only a few yards away. But he was aware that there was another body in the room. He didn't want to be detected. The second occupant slid his feet along the ground so they wouldn't make any sound when pressed against or removed from the vinyl flooring that covered the office. It was in grey and black squares that might have once been black and white. They had obviously been there for some time and looked as though the grey wasn't uniform across the floor. The second occupant of the room stopped in his tracks directly behind Ash but only a few feet away. It was the point in the room where he was least likely to be seen by the detective.

Ash continued to search through the envelope and found the first item he was looking for. It was a rent book with the name Abdullah Abubaker typed on the front with what appeared to be a typewriter. The days and months were handwritten on the inside but there was no year shown at all. Ash guessed this must be several years old from the condition and the fact that most of this was now done online. He searched the driving licences to see which matched the address and found it at the bottom of the pile. Ash told himself that if he had started at the bottom of the pile, it would have been on the top. It was always the last place he looked. The photograph was faded almost to the point where you couldn't make out if there was someone in the picture or not. It wouldn't help Ash identify the killer if he bumped into him in the street. He hoped that whoever lived in that address now would have some more information on where he had gone to. He was now excited to gather these documents and get across town to check the address out. His cottage pie and beer would have to wait, but The Rowans wasn't much of a detour on his way home, so he could put up with that.

As Ash found the final item that matched the address, an insurance document for the property, the other occupant was approaching from behind. The second occupant of the room raised both his hands as he reached Ash. By now the detective could see a shadow move across his line of sight, but it was too late. He was pushed towards the desk. Ash spun around to get a glimpse of his attacker, He reached to one side for something to use in defence or attack but could only find a hole punch. It would have to do. He looked up and found the person in the room with him had chosen the perfect line. He couldn't make them out against the light. He heard them clear their throat and waited to hear what he suspected were going to be the last words he ever heard.

"Ash. What are you doing here this late?"

Gary had a few things to pick up from the station after the funeral. He had got changed out of his black suit after the funeral and left it behind at the end of the day. He didn't like to leave anything away from home overnight, so decided to pick it up as he made his way back from a restaurant meal to home. He saw the light on in the office, realised it was Ash and decided to play a trick on him. Ash was still panting as Gary stepped back and laughed.

"You're lucky you didn't get this across the face," he spat out between large breaths.

"And what the fuck would that have done to me? Might as well hit me with a pea shooter!" Gary countered in his usual combative style. Even if he could see that his prank hadn't been taken in the way it was intended, he wasn't about to back down.

"What were you trying to achieve? Did you think we would have a laugh about this afterwards? You are a prick, Gary. You always have been and always will be," Ash let out years of frustration with his colleague. He forgot his earlier thoughts that he would step into the catalyst role that Lou was vacating and let rip, "There is something wrong with you. You don't want to be part of this team, so why are you here?"

"Go fuck yourself," were Gary's last words on the subject as he walked out of the office. He picked up his suit and disappeared for the night. Ash felt his skin crawl when Gary got that close. Maybe this case going wrong was supposed to happen. Maybe it was fate that the team was broken up and he didn't have to put up with Gary's shit any more. Ash packed his stuff and put the documents in the top pocket of his shirt. He made his way to the car and set out to the address that had appeared 3 times in his search – 24 The Rowans. Maybe the present resident would know where Alaaldin Hussein had gone to.

77

Al was patient. He knew that there would be an ideal time to strike, and this was going to be a little later in the evening, when the traffic had almost completely disappeared and he could work undetected. There was plenty of time. His prey wouldn't move for some time once they had arrived where he expected them. He had seen the detective he wanted leave the police station and had an idea where they were headed. The case looked to be pointing towards him now, so he decided at that moment to act once that night and then vanish until the following year. It gave him time to plan again and would put them off the scent. By the time he killed again, there would be a focus on a new killer or a new menace on the streets of the city. He will have been forgotten about and could resume his message where it left off, even if his message would live on during that time.

But that night was to be the most important of his mission. This would be the killing that would turn heads across the world. People would read the headlines and see the beginning of the message he was trying to spread. They would look at their own life and decide if they were on the side of right or wrong. This would be the act that would change the ways of the world. This would stop sinners from continuing with a life that they knew deep down was amoral.

Al found a square block of streets that he could walk. This meant he could stave off the chill from the night air, burn off his nervous tension and not cause suspicion by staying in one place. He was sure that these streets wouldn't have CCTV cameras, but kept his hood pulled tight over his face just in case. This was all the kind of research he would have to go through over the next 8 months to be ready for the next summer and the continuation of his work. He tried to walk along the streets as softly as he could. He felt like a tiger on the prowl for his next kill and was aware enough of this emotion to consider that others might see it in him too. In a city that was filled with fear from the killings he had already enacted, all he needed was some do-gooder to call the police because he looked suspicious and undo all of his good work. One kill and then off to safety. That was the only way that Al could reconcile why he was out in the cold looking for a big target without having all the research he would normally have at his disposal. He looked at his watch and it showed a few minutes before half past nine. He could feel the adrenaline surge through his body. It felt like an internal pressure on his face. Al stepped up the pace and tried to walk it off. He would need to have a steady mind and hand to carry out his work.

78

"I didn't think you would come," Christine said to Augustine as he walked through the door. It was a strange place. He had been in some dives during his days at university. The kind of places that might as well have had a sign on the door saying, 'no students.' The kind of places where the noise generated by a hundred people talking would stop in a heartbeat and every pair of eyes would hit the outsiders at the door at the same time. This was something different altogether.

Augustine looked around. He wasn't deliberately ignoring Christine, but wanted to take it all in. It was the opposite of the theatre on the first date. It was as though all the vibrant colour had been erased from the scene, to be replaced with greys, browns and blacks. Augustine felt more at home in this kind of place than the theatre, but wished that he didn't. This was a public house like they used to be. It obviously hadn't been updated like the rest of the bars in town. A mix of charm and disgust washed over Augustine's face. He liked the idea that the place had resisted the makeovers and modern décor that he was used to in a pub, but the reality wasn't a patch on that idea. A single central light shone above the bar, presumably to allow the bar staff the opportunity to see what they were pouring. After that you would return to the darker corners of the pub and drink in darkness it seemed. The pub was busy with what looked like people who wanted a piece of the good times from their youth but were not enjoying it one bit. Augustine counted the faces quickly and got to around 25 before realising that not one of them wore even the faintest hint of a smile. He thought that he must have looked as though he was meant to be there, and tried to make eye contact with another patron to see if they could smile together. All eyes were on their drinks or the floor.

Augustine looked back in the direction that his welcome came from. He had left it too long to reply, so asked Christine if she wanted a drink. She didn't, so he went to the bar for one solitary drink. It felt strange to order just one drink at a time but Augustine had the feeling that the staff there were used to it. The barman looked him up and down as he approached as though he was deciding whether Augustine was worthy of his service. It appeared that he was and Augustine returned to the table with a beer that was still settling in the glass. It was as though the yeast was still doing its work and the beer was very much alive. Augustine took a sip to make it easier to carry without spilling. He looked at the area surrounding Christine. The table she had chosen was one of those high ones with stools around. It was placed in an alcove that appeared even darker than the rest of the bar. The curtains behind her were drawn. It looked as though they had never been opened. They were thinning from years of assault by the sun. Augustine swore he could see people walk past in the street through them and tried to make them out but thought better of it. If someone was going to the trouble of putting up these curtains in a pub when every other pub and bar in town didn't, then they were there for a purpose, he reasoned.

"Hi. I'm sorry about that. I was taken aback by your choice of meeting place. I didn't expect to find you in here," Augustine offered something by way of apology. He didn't know what to say or where to start with Christine after the last date. He wanted to pick up where they left off before heading backstage but knew that wasn't possible. The time after that would always be with them. He didn't know what else he could say or do to make things feel any different.

"Don't worry. I don't make a habit of it. In fact, it took me some time on Trip Advisor to find somewhere so dark," Christine explained. She broke into the slightest smile with the last sentence. They both hoped it would break the ice.

"I have wanted to call you, but didn't know what to say," Augustine went for the elephant in the room as though it had trampled him at some stage in the past and needed to be tamed. Christine sat forward and looked him in the eye. It was meant as a gesture of reconciliation and to show that she was listening, but Augustine took it as a prompt to shut up. The silence took over. Augustine started to count, aware that he had missed the first few seconds. He started at 5. By the time he reached 20 there was a tension in the air, Augustine felt that the rest of the pub were looking at the two of them waiting to see who would break the silence and where the conversation would go. If he had eyes in the back of his head then he would see a pub that resembled the one he saw when he first looked in. Every one of them concentrating on their drink or with eyes trained on something on the floor.

He had to break it, "I am sorry about Betty. I'm sorry I couldn't do any more. He was so close..."

Christine looked into his eyes. She had mixed feelings about the man that was sat over the round tatty table that she had chosen because it was near the door. She felt like this was a place that she might need to escape from in a hurry. This man had made her feel young and wanted again for the few hours on their last date. She hadn't felt like that in a long time. He made her feel cool. She knew parts of town and people that he didn't. he was excited to be there, and she was the one that showed him a night that he had never experienced before. To a point. And he was also the cop that let her friend's killer walk straight past him. She didn't expect that he could have known but it was still the cold hard facts. A man killed her friend and then walked right past this detective that she felt something for.

"There was nothing you could have done. I was sure he was going to tell me something. I will never know what that was. Do you understand how that makes me feel?" Christine decided that the conversation was hers. She would ask the questions and he would answer. That way she wouldn't have to feel uncomfortable with her words. That way she could listen to what he had to say.

"I can only imagine. I don't want to make things any worse. I enjoyed my time with you in the bar and in the audience, but the night ended in so much tragedy I can only feel that I am forever entwined with that in your eyes. This is what I deal with every day. One of the reasons I deal with it is so that the rest of society doesn't have to," Augustine spoke with such clarity that it was Christine's turn to look around the room for an answer. But his honesty turned the conversation to something lighter. They sat and talked. The rest of the bar sat motionless as though they were extras in the scene. Outside the chill of the air was starting to bite. The city was preparing for autumn and the winter that followed.

79

Ash arrived at the street and drove up and down looking for the number 24 on a door, a bin or a gate. It didn't seem to be there. He pulled up in the middle of the road and looked across at the nearest house. Number 17. So, he needed to be on the other side of the road and a little further one way or another. But which way? To the left was the number 15 and to the right the number 19. Across the road and right. Ash looked up and down the road before deciding to walk on the side he was already on. This would give him a better view of the property he was there to study. Ash liked to approach on foot and from a little distance so he had time to check things out. He watched lots of horror films when he was younger and the biggest problem the victims had was that they were caught by surprise. They were too close to the killer and couldn't move when he (it was almost always a 'he' in the movies just like his experience in real life murder investigations) jumped out and attacked. Ash resolved to keep his distance in life as much as he could. He thought of the danger in every situation. He was as cautious as they came. When starting a relationship, Ash would take no details from them. He didn't want to be seen as presumptuous or pushy. He kept his distance and let the woman do all the running. It cost him relationships because he came across as cold or aloof. But he didn't want the danger of being called out for his actions.

It was probably why he was developing into an excellent detective. He didn't jump into any situation. He looked at it on its merits and made a calm decision. He was willing to change that decision if needed. Ash never knew when he was right. He always thought twice about what appeared to be in front of him.

He peered across the street and tried to make out the numbers he was looking for without much more success than he had in the car. Ash didn't see a light on in any of the properties. It was approaching complete darkness and the sun had pretty much disappeared so he felt that any occupant at the front of any of these houses would need a light to do anything except sleep. He told himself that it was safe to cross, safe to get close, before looking along the road to see if there was any movement from cars or people. There was nothing. This big city was home to hundreds of thousands of people, possibly more if you looked at those that were not on official figures, but there were always parts of the city that were silent for hours at a time. Ash crossed and was immediately face on to number 28. He had walked a little too far so checked back and counted two houses down. Number 24 was set back a little further than the others. It was street that hadn't been developed at once. The plots must have been sold one by one and each was built on at a different time. Most were at the same depth, but 24 was maybe a foot further back. Not so far that it looked massively out of place but far enough back to be noticed. Ash walked the few steps to the front door and knocked loudly. It was the first sound he had heard since switching off the engine on his car and closing the door. Ash startled himself with the volume, so was sure if there was anyone inside they would know there was a knock at the door.

Nothing. No answer. No movement. No twitch of the neighbour's curtains. Still nothing on the street. Ash looked to the left of the property and saw a small walkway that led to the back of the house. It was only a few inches wider than his shoulders and ran along the side of the property next door. Ash walked side-on like a crab as not to scuff his leather jacket. He had bought it from a vintage shop in New York on holiday years before and was especially protective of it. Ash was one of those people who bought things to last. The jacket could have been 40 years old for all he knew, but he intended to keep it and use it for many more. All of his shoes were in pristine condition as he wiped off even the slightest mark, on the shoe or the sole, as soon as he could. Nothing would be left dirty in Ash's presence. At least nothing he owned.

Ash slipped down the side of the house and looked across the back of the property. At the front, there was no light and no sign of life. Ash looked left and right and saw a similar view as far as he could see. He put the torch function on his phone and looked for the back door. The back garden was surrounded by trees that blocked out the last vestiges of light the day had to offer so he needed the extra light created by his phone. The handle of the back door drooped in a sad fashion that indicated it was broken. Ash tried a gentle nudge with his knee and the door slowly creaked open to reveal a kitchen. Ash was always more comfortable with a kitchen at the back of the house. He had been to friends' houses where kitchens were along the front aspect and he always felt as though he was being watched. The kitchen was a place to relax and be yourself. He wasn't comfortable doing that at the front of a property where anyone walking past could see.

The kitchen was even darker than the back garden. It had a low ceiling, so low that Ash's head nearly touched it and the dark kitchen cupboards encroached to the middle of the room cutting off space and light. Even in the darkness of the late evening, Ash could feel that the kitchen was dark and stifling. He wasn't comfortable. Ash had gone to the property looking to speak to the current occupant but all signs were that there was nobody there, but something told him that he might find something interesting if he looked around. It wasn't his style to walk into a building without following procedure, but it felt as though he had to act quickly with this one. He took a small risk and would be out of there in a few minutes. The kitchen wasn't going to reveal any secrets. It smelt as though it hadn't been used in some time, like the contents of a refrigerator that had been left for months on end. Not quite rotten, but certainly not fresh. He tried the light switch but nothing happened. He turned his phone upwards and saw a blackened bulb. He had to get out of that room.

The hall was in front of Ash and he chose the second door to the right. It was the living room and a dull bulb lit up when he clicked the switch. Ash looked at his phone to turn it off and blinded himself for a second. As he regained his vision, the right button was found and he could rely on the light. It was an energy-saving bulb so Ash hoped it would warm up and offer better light after a few minutes. The drawers to the left of the room seemed to glow and attract Ash to their contents. He hoped that his intuition was right. He was getting the feeling that nobody else had lived at the address since Alaaldin Hussein appeared to. But he could be wrong. The drawers were filled with newspapers from the a few years ago. There were certain articles marked with a red pen, but nothing seemed to link them. Maybe it was just whatever caught the interest of the reader. Ash's mother used to do the same thing. She would have a set of numbers on the front of the newspaper which denoted the pages of interest. Inside, at these pages, there would be a mark next to the relevant article and maybe a few odd underlined sentences. Ash never knew if she went back to read them or if the articles made any difference to her life, but he was aware that there were people out there that marked articles in newspapers. He looked for more, but the room was almost empty apart from the small drawers. Ash decided that he would take one quick look upstairs before calling it a night.

The stairs had no natural light and, just like the kitchen, the bulb had burned out. Ash propped the living room door open and tried to borrow light from there. It worked well enough for him to get up the stairs and find he light switch in the first room. This felt more 'lived-in.' Ash was sure someone had been there recently. There was a warmth that felt like it came from body heat rather than just the late summer conditions outside. All of the curtains across the front of the house were drawn. The cautious Ash decided he would make this his last room and go. He may have to come back the next day, but that was better than being found in a property without a search warrant. Augustine would kill him.

Ash looked across the room and saw nothing but a small case in the far corner. It looked incriminating. It looked as though it had been placed there deliberately. Ash was immediately reminded of the secretive CCTV recordings that people made of their relatives in care homes. They were set up to catch out whoever was supposed to be giving them care but was mistreating relatives who were not able to stand up for themselves. The case could have easily contained a hidden camera. Ash wondered if he was being watched. He pulled on a pair of latex gloves and approached the case from the side, giving as much room between himself and the potential camera as possible. It only added to the feeling that he ought to get out of there quickly. He tried to hold his head away as he put his hand inside. The light bulb in the bedroom, if you could call a room without a bed that, wasn't an energy saver and by his best estimate was 100 watts. It burned an image of a bulb onto his eyes as he looked away from the case. Nothing inside felt like it was large enough to be a camera so he turned his head back around and let the image of the bulb slowly work away from his eyes. Ash picked our several pieces of paper and noticed straight away that they resembled the ones he had seen at the property where Andy Lane was murdered. The handwriting, the precision of the maps, the disturbed notes and the images all took him right back to that room. He could taste the charred building around him again.

Ash picked up his phone. He needed to speak to Augustine at once. As he dialled, Ash noticed the battery only had a slither left. If he was going to get through to Augustine, then the conversation wouldn't last long. He formulated the best way to deliver news quickly as the call rang.

"Gus, 24 The Rowans. Major development."

That would have to do. Speak slowly and clearly. Ash pushed the phone closer to his ear to listen to the ringing sound and be ready for the shortest conversation he would ever have with his boss, or anyone else for that matter, but after it rang for the tenth time, there was nothing but silence. Ash studied the screen. There was nothing there. He walked down the stairs and into the living room. He had to decide what to do next. The energy-saving bulb had warmed up nicely. From the street, a passer-by was walking past the alley directly opposite number 24. This was the only light as far as the eye could see from the front of a house on The Rowans. The silhouette of Ash was lit up as he paced backwards and forwards. He had a decision to make.

80

Al had walked all he could walk. The streets had slowly emptied of cars like the sweets in a pack in front of a child. First the people disappeared; then the cars followed. He only walked an extra couple of laps after that to calm his rising adrenaline and set his mind to what he had to do. The other killings came easy to him. He had every last detail planned out weeks in advance and only killed when he was totally sure of the circumstances. Even the rushed killing of the entertainer in the theatre was someone that he had tracked for weeks and had detailed charts on. He could have killed that guy at any performance he liked. In the end Al went there the night that he found the newspaper article because he wanted to show the police and the public that he was ruthless and organised. But they still didn't show him the respect he deserved. They still didn't let people know about his message, his mission. But now they would.

Al walked slowly towards a dark alley near the building he knew he had some preparation to do. He took off his rucksack and studied the contents. There were several knives that he had sharpened before leaving his brothers home, some rope cut into small pieces so they were easy to handle, some tourniquets and a hammer. Al was wearing a large jacket with pockets that seemed to never end, so he put the rope, tourniquets and hammer in different pockets so they were all within easy reach. He didn't want to stall when he was in full swing. He had to stay in control. From the alley, he surveyed the situation. The building that he had targeted had the curtains closed and a light on inside. He could see some movement and assumed that it was the person he was looking for. He had watched them leave the station earlier and had seen the direction they were headed in. He knew their movements and was confident that this was a typical night for them. At least it would be until he caught up with them. Then it would be the last night of their life. The final item in the rucksack was a laptop. Al had plans for that, so stuck it back in the bag, put it on his back and continued to watch the movement behind the curtain.

There was definitely someone there, and Al couldn't think that it would be anyone other than his target. He watched the street between the alley where he was hidden. He looked for movement, for a police presence, for something unusual. But nothing happened at all. He stopped, bowed his head and said a few words to himself. It always went like this. He knew that he was protected from on high. Al had faith that others lacked. He believed that his mission was one that was sent to his mind from a higher force. The ability to look at every little detail life threw at him and sort out the important ones was always a trait that he had, even from school. He would listen to teachers talk about ox bow lakes, deforestation, the history of the Roman Empire and cut out all that he would never need during his life outside of school. He paid attention in maths, he loved the clinical nature of science and absorbed enough English to survive on the streets. But the rest of it just washed over him and away down the gutter. He only listened to pieces of information that would serve him in later life.

In the last few years he had spoken to others who felt that the march of capitalism, the invasions of Iraq and Afghanistan and the oppression of the Muslim people in Europe needed to be put high on the international agenda. But even when he met with others, he would filter out a lot of their information. Some talked about the way that the Muslim world was before The Crusades, but he didn't want to go back hundreds of years. Progress for the sake of money was against his beliefs, but Al he had no desire to return to a time when people lived off the land and there were no modern facilities like the internet, motorways or sanitation. The way they told it, you would think that the times when there was no travel, no trade and no technology was a utopia that we should aspire to. Not for Al. He filtered out their ideas on this and formed his own opinions. The morality of people in the modern world concerned Al. Some of the people he spoke to were focused on causing mayhem for the sake of it. For Al, the killing without the message was pointless. It was like taking out an advert in the newspaper and leaving it blank. They had the attention of the world for a short space of time and Al felt that they wasted it. If they were going to pay the ultimate sacrifice of their lives then the least they could do would be to spread the message of why they killed. Terror wouldn't change the way that people thought or lived. The only way to take people away from greed, homosexuality, political misgivings and the other sins Al had identified was to change their ideology. This wouldn't happen by what the media call a 'senseless act' but by an act that was planned, executed well and with the motive expressed clearly. His idea of the letters building up as a message was perfect in his eyes. The police had sat on it and stopped the message from becoming strong and clear. This was what the West did to Muslims. It stopped them from having a voice. It stopped then from having a message.

Al was there to change all of that. His hand was forced. He had to up the stakes. He was going to kill one of the detectives that were working on his murders. He was going to show the world the message that had been supressed by these detectives. He was going to stream it live on Facebook. Then he would disappear until the following year. It would all start again, but the following year would see his message written large across the western world. He was going to make the difference. Al was going to teach the world how to live.

He had worked himself up into a frenzy. But he needed to calm down. Al took long deep breaths and went through the plan in his mind. It was fluid. It could change if he needed it to. He was always adaptable. Al looked one last time at the curtains and the silhouette the target made inside. He stepped out of the alley and across the street. It was time.

81

Al knew that this was his moment. His eyes never moved from the window with the silhouette of his target as he walked over the road and made his way to the front door. He was completely focused and wouldn't let any distractions stop his mission. Al tried the handle on the front door but it wouldn't budge on the first attempt. It looked like an old door that wouldn't stand up to any pressure. But that might alert whoever was inside. Al tried to pick the lock with some tools he bought from the internet a few years before. He had practiced them on the door of his home, the one he torched, with some success. He wasn't going to make a master criminal that got in and out of buildings in no time at all, but he felt proficient enough to work his way through the door in less than a minute. He still wasn't sure whether it was locked or just stiff, but wanted to enter as stealthy as he could. Within 30 seconds, Al was inside. The contrast of the light from the room he was watching with the dark of the night outside disappeared in an instant as the first room he entered was unlit. Not even the creeping light from under a door was evident. He knew that the silhouette he wanted to meet was to the right, so looked low in order to make out a door frame. It didn't take him long to see something on the other side of the stairs. It had to be the only way to get to the room on the right. Al turned the handle and stepped inside, grabbing a knife and the hammer at the same time. Now wasn't the time for subtlety. It was the time for decisive action.

His eyes met those of a man who was much shorter and much older than he had been expecting. Al stopped in his tracks for half a second like a rabbit when full beam headlights are shone, before continuing his march forward. All the time he raised his hands higher, showing the two weapons to the older man who was stepping back as quickly as Al was stepping forward. Al had the benefit of being able to see where his opponent was walking, and knew he was running out of room. He stepped to his left with the next step to corner his prey. He didn't want to use either of the weapons, but would if he had to. This wasn't the detective he had come to kill, but was bound to be connected to him in some way. Al was confident that he had the right address.

Lou stepped back one more time and felt his heel against the skirting board. He knew there was nowhere else to go, so put his hands up. It was a gesture that he had seen from the other side of the equation many times before. He didn't think it would ever be him indicating surrender. Al dropped the hammer, thinking that the knife was more of a deterrent to try anything and pulled a length of rope from his back pocket. Lou turned around instinctively and Al tied his hands together, before moving in front of Lou and pushing him back to the settee. Once seated, he tied the legs together and then one leg of his capture to the leg of the settee. Al was sure that the man was going nowhere.

"Who are you? Where is the detective?" Al asked. He looked Lou in the eye. And at that moment they both realised who each other was. "I know you. You work with the detective. What are you doing here?"

"I know you. And whatever you have in mind, you have lost," Lou tried to rile the killer immediately. He had studied killers and knew that this one was calculating and calm. If he became upset or angry then Lou might stand a better chance. It was a long shot, but Lou had already seen what happened to people when Alaaldin was cool and calm. "You've fucked up now. Killing one police officer was pretty fucking stupid. Walking into the home of the detective who is chasing you is a whole other level of dumb."

"Listen to me. You might sit there and have plenty to say, but remember who is in charge Your only chance to stop me was before you were tied up," Al spoke softly like he didn't need to raise his voice. It was the cool and calm exterior that he wanted to show the world at all times. Those that had seen the other side of Al were no longer alive to tell. Lou took a deep breath as he saw that his first attempt to rile his captor had no visible effect at all. He had to hope that there was a reaction under the surface. He would try again. But first he wanted the man to talk. He could see from the other victims and the meticulous detail in his flat that Alaaldin Hussein was engulfed in his killings. He could see the attention to detail was something that would consume a man like this. Once he opened the floodgates then he could probably keep him talking for enough time maybe even for Augustine to come back.

"What do you want to achieve? You have already killed one police officer. Another won't add anything to you. People are already tired of what you have to say. The news has moved on. Did you see it today? All about politics. Nothing about an inconsequential murderer," Lou mixed his two tactics. Maybe the odd provocation and stringing out the conversation might give him a glimmer of hope. Only a glimmer.

"You are not *another* police officer. You are a detective. Not only that, you are a detective that has been assigned to catch me. Thanks to you guys, my message isn't even out there. Thanks to you guys, people don't know what I have to say. But all of that will change tonight. I will reveal my message and my mission. You will help me make the news all about me for the next few weeks, possibly even years. Don't worry about me. I can handle myself," Al spoke with his eyes half closed. It was a sure sign that he was about to go off on a long ramble about his mission. Lou sat back in silence and let him get on with it.

"I'm the acceptable face of Muslim extremism. The others want terror and death to all nonbelievers. I want to convert. There is nothing uncalculated or random about any of my acts. Everything I do is for a reason. It has been this way all my life. I have no desire to spread terror. I want people to truly take a look at their lives and make a decision on how they wish to live. They can decide to live by the rules of the Quran or they can live with the fear that their sins might be the end of them. Science gets in the way of true progress. AIDS was supposed to wipe off the face of the earth men who chose to lay with men, but science warned of the dangers and worked for a cure. There should be no intervention except that which is righteous. To provide a cure without considering the lifestyle of the individuals is amoral. I am the moral guidance that people have forgotten. Only a few will die, from a worldwide population of billions. They will go down in history as accomplices to my masterful work. I will save the morality of this planet. People will look on what I have done in the future not as murder, but as the beginning of a new world. I will be hailed as a hero; not as a killer," Al opened his eyes, half expecting that his prey would have disappeared somehow. He had tied him tight enough and the doors were closed, but Al lost himself in his own world when talking about the brilliance of his work. He could close his eyes and imagine a future shaped by his hand for hours on end. It would contain nothing that went against his beliefs. And in this imaginary future that existed between his ears he was hailed as a hero. He was seen as a liberator.

"I'm not sure what you are talking about. I've seen the people you killed. I have spoken to their family. I have consoled them when telling how their son, their daughter, their husband, wife or parent has been killed and defiled by an evil act. They don't see you as a hero. They see you for the scum that you are," Lou felt that his words were having an effect. He couldn't quite see the clock on the mantelpiece above the settee where he sat but guessed that maybe fifteen minutes had elapsed since Alaaldin had entered Augustine's flat. He tried to calculate how many monologues from Alaaldin it would take to eat up an hour. The murderer spoke softly and slowly, so Lou guessed that with short silences in between, it might take ten to fifteen speeches like this to fill an hour. He maybe had three hours to fill. He hoped that there was a lot that the killer hadn't already revealed. The more he had to taunt Lou with, the longer Lou might be able to hold out. He had never known discomfort like it. The nights sat up at his wife's bedside when she was in her final days were bad for his aching bones. But he had something to focus on and knew that she was in a much worse situation then he was. He had time to think about what issues she might develop next, his own plans for the future and how much love he could show her before she left the shell of her body.

But sat in front of a killer, he had none of that. He couldn't think of anyone that would swap places with him from any part of the planet. He couldn't make future plans because it looked like his future was only going to be half an hour long at most, all of it spent tied to this sofa. He could only show his emotions to the man stood a few feet away. Instead of the love he showed for his wife, the overriding emotion now was hatred. This was mixed with pity. Not for himself, he had led a long life and had one eye on a reunion with his wife, but for all the other people this man had killed.

"Tell me something. We found a message in your apartment. And we have all the letters in order except one. Is there a body we haven't found?" Lou could see that this question struck a nerve. The message left on the chest of his victims obviously irked Alaaldin. He wanted this to get out to the world, but without it his killings made no sense. He looked like any common or garden serial killer. With it he became what he wanted to be seen as – a messenger from Allah, a bringer of justice, a hero as he wished. Lou listened intently as Al closed his eyes and began to speak. It was even softer and even slower than before. Lou shuffled to the edge of the sofa and tried to block out all other noise.

82

Augustine was smiling again. It was the same smile that he had worn when at the theatre with Christine. Once they had broken the ice, it was like they slipped back into the same groove. He was smitten, he didn't mind admitting that to himself. She saw the man that she first met, not the man that found her friend dead.

Augustine was working his way up to asking Christine if she would like to move on somewhere else. He had nothing particular in mind, nothing special, but he felt as though the venue was chosen for its banality and neutrality. Now they no longer needed the banal or the neutral it had served its purpose. Augustine tried to think about the different places that were nearby. His knowledge of nightlife in the city was almost non-existent and confined to the venues where he had to investigate a crime.

The Vaults? No. he had a suspicion that one of the barmen was involved in drugging women to be raped a few years ago. Nothing that could be proven, but enough to stay in his memory.

The Star Bar? No. A body was discovered in the back alley near to their bins that had been there for months at the best estimate. The staff has been literally walking backwards and forwards past this body for weeks without noticing. It wasn't until the manager realised that the bins hadn't been empty in I-don't-know-how-long that the rotting remains were uncovered. Even then it took 24 hours to call the police. They all wanted to make sure they weren't in any trouble before reporting it.

Bar 76? No. it probably hadn't been cleaned since '76. Augustine had been there only a few weeks before as it was near to the headquarters of Britain Excelsior. It was as grubby as the politicians that hung out there.

How about the 3 Badgers? It was only recently opened and had been named as a tongue-in-cheek tribute to the way that pubs were named in the past. It hadn't been open long enough for any crimes to have been committed there or to get dirty. Augustine was sure it was the right place.

Christine could see Augustine go through the gears. She knew he was thinking about something and was worried that the lighter mood would be broken by it. She grabbed his hand and led him to the door.

"Let's go somewhere else. This place is dragging me down. I'm happy again and I want to see a bit more of the city with you before the night is over. Do you know anywhere suitably gritty? The kind of place a detective might take his girl?" Christine spoke with mischief obvious at every word.

"How about the 3 Badgers? It might not be gritty, but could be worth a look?" Augustine explained. He wasn't sure what she meant by gritty. Maybe The Vaults, Star Bar and Bar 76 were better options.

"I'll give it a go, but if I don't like it then it's one drink and we move on," she explained. Augustine loved the way she took control. He had searched all his life for a woman that would lead him to places that he never dreamed of visiting himself. He stuck to the same restaurants, the same bars and the same people all the time. He could see a life with Christine would be one of a new experience every time he left his front door. Pretty much like his work. It breathed new life into him. Augustine had considered a life like Lou's over the previous few weeks. Not the Lou who had a loving relationship and bond with his wife but the Lou of now. The alone Lou. Augustine had almost resigned himself that this was the way it was going to be. But when he was with Christine it felt different. It felt as though he was already married and the two of them were destined to spend the rest of their lives together. This was after the sum of one and a half dates. One that had ended horrifically and one that hadn't started that well either. He couldn't put his finger on it, but Augustine felt content.

Thinking of Lou sparked something in Augustine's brain. It was a small moment of worry in a sea of excitement. He let the excitement wash over it and instantly the worry was pushed to the furthest reaches of his mind. Augustine walked along the street towards the 3 Badgers with a beaming smile written across his face. He couldn't help it.

But suddenly the smile disappeared as the worry came racing back to the forefront of his mind. The alley opposite his home. There was something not right about it. The alley had overgrown weeds that had cumulated over a number of years. As the alley led nowhere and didn't seem to belong to anyone, they had just been left to grow. At the time, his mind was on his date, his taxi and his colleague. He must have glanced at it but been in no mind to take it in. Now he was relaxed, Augustine vividly remembered that the weeds had been trampled. It looked the same as the woodland near the body Sally and her dog had found. But what if it was significant? What if it was a sign that the killer had been near to his home? He had to run.

"Christine, I have to go. I think that someone is in grave danger. I think it is the killer again," he didn't wait for an answer and ran off along the street looking through the darkness for a taxi. He spotted one around 20 cars away and ran as fast as he could to catch it through the slow-moving traffic of kicking-out time. The lights and pedestrian crossings were slowing traffic to a few miles an hour so Augustine was able to catch up quickly. He didn't want to give anything away to the taxi driver, so decided that a phone call was out of the question. After the publicity of earlier murders, Augustine didn't want to be the person that inadvertently tipped off the press. So, he texted Marie and the rest of the team. He wanted them to know what he was doing.

'Lou at mine. I think the killer is there. I'm on my way. Be there in ten.'

Augustine switched his phone off. He knew that he would forget about it and it could ring and ruin any chance of surprise if his suspicions were true and the killer was at his home. He looked left and right at every junction with the driver. It was as though there were dual controls and Augustine was giving a driving lesson. His eyes were trained on the road but his mind was working overtime. He had no idea how the killer knew where he lived or if the trampled weeds meant something sinister. Augustine started counting the seconds in his head and registering the minutes on his fingers. It served no purpose but made him feel more in control somehow.

"How long do you think?" he asked the taxi driver but didn't listen to the reply. Augustine went back to counting and looking at the streets. It wasn't long before he arrived in his own street.

"Forget it. Just drop me off here," he said, suddenly thinking that the element of surprise might be lost by pulling up right outside the address.

"It's the same price," the taxi driver replied. He could see that his fare would be in no mood to argue. He shoved a note in the driver's hand and jumped out. The taxi driver started to pull away when the strange man he had driven knocked on the window.

"Do you mind turning around and going out that way? It is kind of important to me," Augustine tried to explain without giving away any information. The taxi driver shrugged, muttered 'fuck me' under his breath and turned around. Augustine smiled like he would to someone who held the door open for him. It was not a smile that was returned by the taxi driver who screeched his tyres as he pulled away. Augustine crossed the road and slowly made his way towards the alleyway opposite his home. He spied the trampled weeds and his mind went into overdrive. What had he let his friend and colleague in for? Christine was stood outside the pub that they had been walking to. She got there a few minutes after Augustine left he but didn't want to go in on her own. She asked a stranger for a cigarette and passed a few minutes conversation with them. She decided that the 3 Badgers would be a venue that she would visit with Augustine, not on her own. She looked down the street for a taxi.

83

Augustine looked up and down at his home. It looked and felt different now that he was sure a stranger was in there with one of his colleagues. The place that had been his sanctuary away from all the pain he saw at work had been converted into another crime scene, he was sure. Augustine saw no option but to cross the street as quietly as he could and go inside.

The street felt darker than usual. He didn't study things like this when he came back from a night out or left early for work. These were just everyday journeys – part of his normal life. But with the potential of his home being the scene of a murder, the darkness was evident across the street. It was evident in the alley along the side of his house where he kept his bins. It was evident in the neighbour's habit of going to bed early with no sign of life left while asleep. It was evident in the fact that the house three doors away was empty and had been for months. Augustine looked at the front door. It was locked. He had taken a key. Before he left, Augustine had removed it from a bunch and slipped the single key into his wallet, as he always did on a night out. This saved him taking all of his keys everywhere he went. It also felt safer tucked away in the folds of his wallet, where he usually only kept a photograph of his grandmother and some old ID cards he never needed.

The key slipped silently into the lock and he turned. In all his years as a detective, Augustine had never needed to open a door silently. He had seen acts like this in the movies. Never could he imagine that it would be his front door that needed his attention in this way. He was oblivious to the world around him on a normal day. He couldn't tell you if the hinges on his door creaked. He had no idea if the door would hit the wall behind if he let it run that far. Augustine was embarrassed that of all the places in the world he should know inside out, the one he ought to had him baffled. He pushed slowly on the door with his left hand while the right controlled the movement. At the slightest hint of a creak he could stop the door from moving and return the situation to silent. He pushed.

84

Ash and Marie were stood together at the end of the street. They were the only ones still awake at that hour and had responded immediately to Augustine's text message. When they both got no reply when calling him, they were each other's next port of call. Ash got there a few seconds earlier than Marie and her phone was ringing as she looked up his number. They agreed to meet at the end of the street and go together. It was what they wished Augustine had done. Maybe that was why he had switched his phone off. It wasn't ignoring the advice of a colleague or the instructions of your boss if you didn't hear the instructions. By the time they got to the front door, they could see it was too late. They could see it was all over.

The blood was spattered across the front door and was running down the path into the street. They climbed the stairs to a room that had obviously been the scene of a struggle. There was a single piece of paper on the chest of a body. Marie looked away. Ash looked down to see a letter 'H' on the paper. He held Marie. She looked up to the ceiling. It was a scene she didn't expect.

85

Before his boss and colleague got to the scene, Augustine was working his way over the threshold. The door opened with only the slightest creak. He stopped it in its tracks and waited for a few seconds before starting to push again. It opened and revealed his hallway. But nothing else. There were no obvious sources of light. Augustine could only see light coming from the living room from outside the house. His best bet was to start there. As he approached the door, the light he expected to creep around the bottom of the door wasn't present. Augustine dropped slowly to the floor and saw something laid across the bottom of the door. He had no idea what it was but assumed it had two purposes. Firstly, to block out the light, and secondly to slow anyone trying to enter the room.

Augustine decided that raw power was the best bet. He had watched far too many episodes of Top Gear than was healthy for a grown man and pictured Jeremy Clarkson shouting 'powwweerrr,' as he floored the accelerator. Channelling his inner-Clarkson (not something recommended under any other circumstances) and smashed his shoulder into the door. It opened rather more easily than he expected and within a second he ended up on the floor. Augustine jumped to his feet and looked around the room. Nothing. Then he heard footsteps upstairs. He turned around and made his way to the bottom of the stairs near the front door.

He rushed up the first few steps before looking up. He saw nothing but the faint glow of a computer screen from the back bedroom. He walked the rest of the steps, looking to see what was above him. Augustine tiptoed like the crashing sound of him barging into a door downstairs hadn't just happened. When he reached the top of the stairs he gasped. Sat tied to his computer chair was Lou. He was sat on the right of the room with Augustine's desk pulled over to the left with a laptop sat squarely opposite. Augustine tasted vomit. Not enough to spit out, but enough to coat the inside of his mouth. As he looked back towards Lou it became obvious that there was a man dressed full in black was stood behind the computer chair with a large knife in his hand.

"There's no need to use violence. We can work this out," Augustine said to the figure who was now moving the knife slowly closer to Lou. It wasn't in an attempt to harm him, but to warn the third person in the room that he shouldn't come any closer.

"We both know that's not true, detective. How are you going to work something out with someone who in your eyes is a serial killer? Either I go to prison, I die or you do. There's nothing else to work out from this situation," Al replied. His logic was sound. Not all of them were going to leave the room as free men.

"Don't do anything hasty. I'm more interested in the life of my friend than catching you. If I need to let you go to save him then that's what I'll do," Augustine explained. He wasn't sure whether he meant what he had just said or not, but his concern for Lou was at the front of his mind. He looked at his colleague and friend and wondered what it would take to get him out alive.

"That won't happen," Al replied, "In fact, you have arrived to see the end of events, not the beginning. You might think that you have arrived just in time, detective, but your friend has become somewhat of an internet sensation. He has starred live on Facebook for the last twenty minutes while I have let the people of the world know the message that you have tried to uncover. I came here for you, but this one will do."

Augustine looked around the room for answers. Fucking Facebook. He never liked social media. This was the final blow. If he got out of this alive then he would remove his profile immediately. It was as though he had been hit in the chest with a hammer. He could see the death in Lou's eyes. It was as though he had given up. Augustine looked again at the man stood over his colleague. He had killed before. He would have no qualms about doing to again, Augustine was sure of that.

"It's his first time on Facebook – shame it will also be his last. He has spent the time begging for his life and agreeing that my mission is a righteous one," Al explained with glee in his voice. It was the voice of someone who truly rejoiced in the mayhem they were causing. As he spoke, Augustine edged closer. He wasn't trying to get between Al and Lou, but to look at the screen of the laptop and see if the claims he made were correct. He was spotted.

"Go ahead! Look at the screen. There are thousands of people watching and more tuning in all the time as word spreads. The internet is a marvellous thing. News spreads like wildfire. People may recoil in horror at a killing when the read about it in the news but they can't help watching when given the chance. The mob mentality exists in every human being. Look at how many people go back and watch videos of others being beheaded. I think we should bring back public executions. The public would pay more for that than they do to watch Arsenal. And it's twice as entertaining. It would solve the deficit in no time at all," Al was back in monologue mode. He was enjoying the power that the situation brought him. He enjoyed the power he had in all his killings. It was a power he hadn't experienced in the rest of his life. He didn't mind Augustine looking at the screen and even encouraged him to say 'hi!' to the watching world. He laughed when the detective moved his head away from the screen as not to be live on the internet at the scene of his friend's downfall.

"My work is almost complete for this year. The last killing was supposed to be you, detective. This is your home, right?"

Augustine nodded.

"But you left this other detective here with me. Now he will die, you too and the world will know the message I have begun to deliver. I will complete it next year, but that won't mean anything to you. By then you will have already become fish and chip paper. One police dead makes headline news. Three dead makes people go numb. They stop thinking about this in terms of the police and start to think about their own life. The last policeman was a martyr. You are part of the wider message. You can become heroes like me. You can save the people of the earth," Al spoke as though he was addressing Augustine but every word was put in the direction of the camera and the Facebook live event he had created.

Augustine picked up on this. He knew that this was all about the show.

"I don't think this is still live. The Wi-Fi in here is temperamental. I have all kinds of problems with it," Augustine offered, pointing at the screen. Al was incensed by this news. He dropped the knife and made his way over to the screen, pushing Augustine out of the way. As Al reached over the screen, Augustine picked the printer up from the desk and brought it down hard and fast on Al's head. The back of his head took the blow before the front of his head crashed into the desk. He dropped to the floor, mumbling some words, apparently in a daze. Augustine tried again with the printer, but the force of the first blow meant that it fell into parts on the killer's back rather than landing with the same satisfying thud as the first time. He looked around the room for something else. There was nothing. Fucking minimal living, Augustine thought to himself. He picked at the rope that tied Lou to the chair. That was the only thing left in the room that was sturdy enough to deliver a blow that would render Alaaldin Hussein useless. As soon as Lou was free he ran down the stairs. There was blood coming from his wrists where the rope had been tied so tightly as well as a gash in his leg inflicted by Al in the first few moments of the live stream he had been forced to be a part of. Lou knocked on the next door as hard as he could and shouted with the last volume he has left in his lungs. Lights came on in the upper rooms of a few houses in the street. Some windows opened. He felt safe.

Augustine let the chair crash down on Al's body just as he was starting to climb to his knees again. Augustine added a kick for good measure. The killer stopped moving for a short time before kicking out at Augustine's shins. The blow made Augustine recoil and grab his shin in his hand. The other hand steadied him against the wall. In this position of vulnerability, he could see Al jump to his feet and start swinging punches. The laptop had stayed more or less in the middle of the desk and was relaying the scene to those that were still watching. It was obvious that Al didn't quite know where he was, like a boxer who had been stunned but saw attack as the best form of defence.

The swings were getting wilder and all it would take was for one to land. Augustine sensed it was the time to move forward but was caught flush on the side of the head by one of the blows. He dropped to the floor reaching out with his hands for something to steady his swirling head. But there was nothing to save him. Al made one final blow to the detective before dropping a piece of paper on his chest. He picked up his laptop and ran down the stairs and into the cold of the night. He ran past Lou without glancing at his former prisoner and disappeared into the distance on the left before the flash of blue lights appeared at the opposite end of the street.

86

Christine walked over to the bar and ordered a round of drinks. She had been invited to meet the people Augustine worked with.

"Two lagers, two ciders and two white wines," she said to the barman, who had already served the same round of drinks several times that night and was busy pouring before the words came out of her mouth.

She spent most of the night talking to Lou. As soon as she saw him, she knew they would get along. He was everything Augustine had described. She loved to hear him laugh. Lou thought that he had laughed for the last time. That was the thought that kept entering his head. All the time he was sat in that chair facing the laptop, the overriding thought was that he wanted to laugh again before Alaaldin Hussein killed him. He built up a laugh inside his stomach and tried to add to it. He would think about the television comedies that he used to watch endlessly on repeat or one of those moments with his wife. But he couldn't bring it out of his body onto his face. That was when Lou conceded defeat. When all the laughter had been driven from his body did he resign himself to his fate.

Christine went to meet the team with a mixture of sadness and joy. These were the people who helped Augustine Boyle put the worst criminals in the city behind bars. She wanted to meet them all and hear about how they worked together to keep the streets safe, but missed Augustine so much. She had found happiness and seen it taken away twice in two dates with this man. Christine thought she wouldn't date ever again.

She thought about Augustine sat in intensive care fighting for his life. The doctors were not hopeful that he would pull through. This was the second date they had been on that had ended in some form of tragedy. She would spend as much time as possible by his bedside, but meeting the team he worked with felt like it was a suitable excuse to leave for a few hours. The monitors bleeped and blinked by his bed. Augustine looked nothing like the man she had met on that date. She feared he would never be the same again.

38124233R00174

Printed in Great Britain
by Amazon